MW01602871

Special thanks to my father, Colin Waterford, who has contributed to all my System Series novels, including some I haven't written yet. In particular, he provided the idea of using a Jupiter flare in Mars.

Your support has been the best thing any son could hope for.

Thanks Dad.

MARS

Twin Prophecies

BOOK ONE OF TWO

A System Series novel

KYNAN WATERFORD

FUTURE FANTASY PUBLISHING

Mars - Twin Prophecies

Cover art by: Kynan Waterford

Contributing artists:
Walter Myers - provided beautiful (and accurate)
rendering of Mars' Valles Marineris Canyon.
You can find more of Walter's art at www.arcadiastreet.com

National Library of Australia Cataloguing-in-Publication data:

Waterford, Kynan (Kynan Stewart), 1978- author.

Mars : Twin Prophecies / Kynan Waterford ; Walter Myers (artist)

ISBN 978 0 992 56554 1 (pbk.)

Science fiction.
Prophecies--Fiction.
Mars (Planet)--Fiction.

Other Contributors: Myers, Walter, artist.

Dewey Number: A823.4

www.kynanwaterford.com.au

Email: kynanwaterford@gmail.com

Printed by Lightning Source

For my Dad.

You gave me life, love, and support in so many ways.

As I start my own family, I only hope that I live up to the example of a father, husband, and man you have shown me.

Thanks for everything.

Explore another planet!
For Kathryn.
Welcome to the System Series!
I hope you enjoy Mrs.
All the best

[signature]

17/6/18

IT WAS FINALLY TIME. ISAAC AND HIS IDENTICAL TWIN brother, Jason, were finally ready. Today they would prove the existence of something that had remained scientifically illusive for thousands of years.

Psychic energy.

That was, of course, if everything worked properly. Isaac certainly expected it to, but he could feel the doubt in his brother's mind.

He glanced up at Jason, who was already seated in one of their specially designed chairs, and smiled. His brother's look of fierce concentration was somewhat spoiled by a skull cap that bristled with hundreds of wires and jiggled festively every time he turned his head.

"A little focus, please," Jason said absently. "I know we look stupid, but we're about to attempt some serious cerebral enhancements here. I'd appreciate a little maturity."

"Sorry, bro," Isaac replied, wiping the grin from his face. "I'm trying. Really."

And he was too. Today was the culmination of many years of hard work and he wanted it to succeed more than anything. But there was no way he could stop Jason from sensing his playful optimism, just as Isaac couldn't help but notice his brother's sober caution.

Like most identical twins, Isaac and Jason shared a strong psychic link – the very thing they were attempting to measure. They didn't need proof for themselves, of course. They'd accepted their special abilities a long time ago. But being scientists, they weren't content with merely *knowing* it was real. They wanted to objectively measure it. To *prove* it to the rest of the world.

Isaac could still remember the day they'd agreed to search for evidence of psychic abilities. It was their thirteenth birthday and, rather than make a wish before blowing out their candles, the two of them had made a solemn pact to find out exactly what it was that made them so different to everyone else.

Being different didn't seem to worry Jason, but Isaac found it irritating and sometimes downright unfair. Growing up, they'd learned that children could be rotten to the core when they wanted to be and, in Isaac's opinion, were genetically hard-wired to search for anyone who stood out from the pack just so they could hammer them back down again.

Isaac hated the way they'd been treated, but it was hard to complain when the reason for their vilification was so... well, awesome.

The psychic link he shared with Jason not only allowed them to share thoughts, but to unconsciously absorb what the other was reading or listening to as well. While Isaac focussed on one aspect of a problem, Jason tackled another, and it allowed them to acquire knowledge at an incredible rate.

While their confused and resentful peers plodded along with the help of only one brain apiece, Isaac and Jason accelerated through the educational system in barely a third of the time it took everyone else.

And yet, despite their gifts, it turned out that finding evidence of their abilities wasn't so easy. Very early in their tertiary studies, it became clear that modern science had no answers to offer them. In fact, most of the professional scientists they approached did nothing more than try to discourage them from pursuing the question altogether, saying it was a waste of their potential.

But Isaac and Jason were determined and stubborn in equal measure.

With the enthusiasm of youth, they sought out experts in psychology and then neurology, learning all they could about the human brain and its capacity for thought and emotion. Then, when they felt their understanding couldn't get any better, they turned to the mysterious world of psychics.

At first, most of the so-called 'psychics' they found turned out to be frauds. These people understood human psychology and behaviour well enough to pass themselves off as being psychic, but none of them were capable of proving they had any real abilities.

It frustrated Isaac greatly and he wanted to expose them as publicly as possible, but, as usual, Jason stopped him from going through with it. Where Isaac generally saw things in black and white, his brother viewed the problem in complex shades of grey and he explained to Isaac that there were too many people who desperately wanted to believe. They would be the ones who suffered most if the frauds were exposed. And besides, even if they did manage to get the word out, the believers would simply seek out another to take the fraud's place. It was a classic lesson in economics. Where there is demand, humans will always find a way to supply.

And so Isaac allowed his heart to crystallise with a little cynicism and they continued their search. It took several years of following rumours and talking to dozens of fakes before they found a few people who were genuine psychics. It was immediately clear that they were the real deal, but none of them were as enthusiastic about their abilities as the frauds seemed to be. And whereas the fakes all seemed to share a thirst for money and attention, real psychics seemed to share either a genuine desire to help others, or a desperate need to stay away from them. None of them were scientists like Isaac and Jason, but all were extremely self-aware and, with a bit of coaxing, they provided more than enough anecdotal information for the twins to reach some pivotal conclusions.

It turned out there was a kind of psychic background that permeated the universe, like a unique form of radiation that occurred outside the electromagnetic spectrum. Psychics seemed to have the ability to sense this radiation and, in some cases, control or influence it. Isaac and Jason believed their psychic link was an example of this ability and so they spent nearly ten years creating a prototype that could translate this psychic background into a more conventional form of energy that could be objectively measured by those without psychic gifts.

The result was a machine they named P.A.T.R.I.C. – short for Psychic Amplification Through Resonant Interface Crystals – and if it worked as they hoped, in one spectacular stroke they would prove both the existence of this theoretical psychic background and that their psychic link was real.

Isaac couldn't wait. He was tired of working out of the cramped study in their parent's apartment. Chasing this dream meant they'd passed up several opportunities that could have seen them incredibly wealthy by now. But today was going to change everything. When word of their success got out, this day would be counted amongst the greatest moments in scientific history and Isaac was looking forward to all the fame and fortune that would come with it.

As usual, they'd instinctively split the final preparations between them. While Jason tested the circuits that would feed carefully-phased electricity into the crystalline resonance pads that covered their skull caps, Isaac calibrated their psychoactive connection with the transparent viewing screen that hung between them.

When he was done, Isaac pulled on his own bristling skull cap and stifled a laugh when he caught a reflection of himself in the viewing screen. Jason raised another disapproving eyebrow, but Isaac could tell he wanted to laugh too.

"You ready?" Jason asked in his usual, measured tone.

"You know I am," Isaac replied with a grin.

"Then it's time to get serious."

"Hey, you know me," Isaac said, letting the smile fall from his face. "I'll be ready when you are, bro."

Jason nodded, making the wires above his head jiggle again, but this time Isaac didn't laugh. He could feel his brother's concentration flowing through their psychic link and it calmed him. It was time to go to work.

"Begin phase one," Jason said quietly.

At his prompting, Isaac stroked a finger across the controls on his armrest and a series of measurements appeared on the transparent screen hanging between them. They both watched the indicators that measured the psychic background for a moment – they were randomly fluctuating at their usual level – then Jason spoke again.

"Begin phase two."

This time Isaac tapped the controls with his middle finger and felt an immediate shock at his temples. A new, differently coloured indicator that measured their psychic link spiked above the background for a moment and then returned to the baseline, lost within the ambient psychic noise of the universe.

P.A.T.R.I.C. was now converting electricity into psychic energy via the crystals imbedded in their skull caps. The amount of psychic amplification seemed to depend on how they used the psychic link rather than how much electricity they fed into the skull cap and so all they had to do was share something complicated and their signal should, theoretically, be boosted above the constant psychic background, proving once and for all that what they were experiencing was real.

"Alright, Isaac," Jason said, his expression as intense as his tone. "Let's see if we were right."

"I'm ready," Isaac replied breathlessly.

"Then it's time to play The Game. Begin phase three. "

Isaac grinned in anticipation. The Game was one of his favourite pastimes. It had started life as a juvenile way to occupy themselves when they were much younger, but now it served as the perfect way to gradually increase the psychic energy being shared between them.

The object of The Game was simple. Isaac would create an image in his mind and psychically share it with Jason. Jason would then take the image, add a simple detail, and allow Isaac to take it back. Isaac would then add another detail, pass it back to Jason, and they would continue adding details and passing the image back and forth until one of them couldn't hold it all in his mind.

Whoever held the image when it all fell apart lost The Game. If you added something that was already there, or dropped a detail when it was passed to you, you lost The Game. If you took longer than sixty seconds to add another detail and pass it back, you lost The Game.

Isaac was much better at imagining new details than Jason was, but he usually lost because he lacked the concentration required to hold all the previous details in place. But not today. This time he was going to beat his brother hands down and his victory would be immortalised in the history logs that would very soon document the day that the Taylor twins achieved definitive proof of psychic energy.

Focussing his mind, Isaac started by imagining a small, white dog. A Maltese terrier. Clean and fluffy with glistening black eyes and nose above a bright pink tongue.

As he created the image in his mind, it appeared in a dedicated window on the viewing screen – a perfect copy of what he imagined. He then passed the mental picture to Jason and waited for his brother to take it from him.

At this early stage, the psychic transition was quick and in seconds the little white dog started yapping.

They both paused to look at the psychic indicator displayed beside the yapping dog and saw that their psychic link was now tracking a little closer to the highest peaks within the background noise.

"Looking good," Isaac said with a grin.

"Your turn," Jason added calmly.

Isaac nodded and then took the image from his brother. He was careful to make sure the little dog kept yapping the way Jason had imagined and then changed it so the dog was now jumping in circles.

Again, the two brothers paused to look at the indicator. It had moved a fraction higher.

"All yours, bro," Isaac said, trying to keep his excitement in check.

This time, Jason added a trampoline under the yapping, jumping dog and it bounced higher, just like their psychic indicator.

"It's working," Isaac said with a thrill.

He could almost feel the future that had been driving them forward since their thirteenth birthday rapidly approaching and his confidence grew along with it.

"Keep calm," Jason said quietly, "and keep going."

Isaac looked at his brother. All their protocols stated that progression needed to be slow and steady to ensure clear, easy-to-follow results. But something inside him didn't want clear and easy-to-follow results. He wanted this moment to be spectacular. He wanted to push through to success with a flair that future generations would admire.

And so, rather than adding just one extra detail, he imagined three colourful jugglers, a pair of swinging acrobats, and an elephant balancing on the upturned beak of a penguin.

"Isaac," Jason said, his disapproval clear.

"Come on, bro," Isaac replied, adding a colourful beach ball under the penguin.

"We had a protocol," Jason replied firmly. "I'd like to follow it, please."

Isaac felt a little irritated at his brother's tone, but only because he knew he was right. And so he removed all the extra circus acts apart from the bouncing dog and the balancing elephant.

"You're such a stickler sometimes," he said with a sigh. "Happy now?"

"Right," Jason said with a nod.

The psychic indicator had moved much closer to the highest background spikes when Isaac added the extra detail, but there was no way to know if it would have remained that high.

Trying his best to remain patient, Isaac allowed Jason to direct the experiment as he wanted, slowly adding details one at a time until the image was as complex as the one he'd created on his own.

"Interesting," Jason said quietly.

"The indicator's higher than it was before," Isaac added. "How is that possible?"

"It appears the amount of detail in the image isn't as important as the level of cooperation that went into creating it," Jason answered.

"So... do we take it further?" Isaac asked hopefully.

Jason paused and Isaac knew he was checking the other indicators they were monitoring.

"We're getting close to the maximum amount of safe electrical input," Jason said eventually. "And I'm feeling a bit stretched."

Isaac sighed inwardly, but he couldn't deny the facts. As their psychic connection grew stronger, more electricity was being drawn through P.A.T.R.I.C. and being pumped into their brains. It came with a kind of mental tension that felt a little like physical pain and although Isaac didn't believe it was possible to injure your mind, Jason did, and that was enough to make it important.

"We can handle it," he said carefully.

He wanted to say more, but he knew any aggressive attempt to coax his brother would just give him a reason to pull back. He could also sense curiosity in his brother and knew that it would execute an argument much better than he ever could. If there was one thing that motivated his brother more than anything else, it was curiosity.

"Alright," Jason said after a moment, making Isaac's heart leap with joy, "but if we're going to take this further, we need to be ready. If the psychic tension spikes, I'm purging the image immediately and freeing us both. There's no winner this time, Isaac, just experimental data."

"I get it, bro," Isaac said, trying without much success to keep his excitement in check.

Jason gave him a look that said he knew exactly what Isaac was feeling, but he thankfully didn't change his mind.

"Your turn," he said calmly.

Taking a deep breath, Isaac returned to the psychic image being offered to him and began to take it from Jason. As always, he carefully ticked off every added detail in his mind and then glanced at the psychic indicator. It was close to the highest background spike they'd ever recorded.

"*This is it*," he thought to himself. "*This is the detail that will finally breach the barrier. This is the moment that will go down in history. But what should I add? What's missing?*"

He thought about it for a few seconds, not sure what detail could be worthy of such an important occasion, then the answer hit him.

A crowd. Where was the crowd for this amazing circus performance?

And almost before he knew what he was doing, Isaac's mind carved out an enormous circus tent and began to fill it with people.

The first person he thought of was a mother pointing out the elephant to her son. Then he a pictured a father holding a toddler on his shoulders. Then a fat man pushing an enormous stick of fairy floss into his face. After that, a young couple kissing and fondling each other in the back row.

As he created the people, Isaac kept a careful eye on the tension rising in his mind, but it was barely noticeable. Jason wasn't protesting yet either and so he decided a few more details wouldn't hurt. He could always get rid of them again if he had to.

And so he added an old man with a bowed back leaning against a walking frame that he shared with an even older woman. Then a dozen babies forming a human pyramid in an attempt to reach a large lollypop that dangled from the ropes above them. Then a policeman whistling and waving his truncheon at a man who was stealing the purse from a lady almost completely hidden within the folds of a gargantuan fur coat.

"Isaac..." Jason finally interrupted.

Isaac glanced up at his brother with a pang of irritation and saw an expression of distress he'd never seen before. He quickly moved his focus to the psychic indicator that glowed beside the image and saw that their signal had leapt far above the background noise.

"It's working, bro," he said excitedly, "and I can take it, don't worry. The tension doesn't feel any worse."

"No..." Jason said with fear in his eyes. "I can't... purge."

Isaac frowned. For a moment, he wondered if his brother was playing some kind of trick, but he knew Jason wouldn't joke at a moment like this. He quickly tried to purge the image himself, but couldn't seem to move it from their shared mental landscape.

He felt the creeping cold of panic settle over him and tried harder, but the image remained bright and clear in his mind.

"I... can't purge the image either," he said, frightened as well now. "What do we do?"

"The tension..." Jason replied. "I can't..."

Isaac stared at his brother and realised he was in serious trouble.

"Tell me what to do, bro," he said in desperation. "I can fix it."

"Hit... phase... two," Jason said slowly, the strain clear in his eyes.

"Of course," Isaac said with a flood of relief. "Sever the connection with P.A.T.R.I.C."

He glanced down at the button on his armrest and lifted a hand to press it, but suddenly everything seemed to slow down around him. His finger became impossibly heavy and the mere act of pushing it through the air took all the strength he had. But even stranger, as Isaac forced his hand forward, he got the bizarre impression that his creeping finger was actually moving at an incredible velocity.

"Phase... two..." Jason repeated in a whisper.

Isaac tried to reply, to assure his brother that he was trying, but he couldn't make his lips move any faster than his finger.

After what seemed like an eternity, the button finally lit up under his finger, but when Isaac glanced back up, Jason looked distorted, as if he were sitting behind a warped pane of glass.

At that moment, the psychic tension in Isaac's mind suddenly spiked and real physical pain wrenched at his body.

"Rrrrrrr..." he growled in confusion and pain, unable to even open his mouth and scream.

It felt as if every atom in his body was being ripped away from the ones around them and, inside his mind, the image Isaac had constructed with Jason shattered into a million motes of coloured light. The glittering cloud gradually faded, taking the room along with it, and Isaac was swallowed by darkness.

For a long moment, all he could do was quake in terror, wondering if he was dead. Then the darkness gave way to a series of vivid images that rushed forward and filled the void.

The first was a dark, water-filled cavern, lit by a strange red light. The second was an unfamiliar blue-eyed woman, beautiful, but incredibly sad. The third was an unfamiliar bedroom, empty and dark. Then a star-filled sky with a single red spark at its centre that grew brighter with each second.

After that came an unfamiliar landscape of dense forest, rolling hills, and towering mountains, as if seen from several kilometres up. Boiling clouds covered the unfamiliar landscape and they were stained with a crimson light that grew brighter and brighter until the entire image exploded.

The red light washed over Isaac with a wave of intense emotions – terror, sadness, despair and anger – all hammering at his mind with an insistence he'd never experienced before. He tried to claw through them, to slip past the emotions without feeling their full force, but they kept catching against his mind like barbed fishing hooks and tearing at his psyche.

They seemed to pull him in a direction that Isaac instinctively didn't want to go, but after resisting for one long, drawn out moment, he was jerked into the heart of the raging red storm and flung into the unknown.

It was at this point that he was finally allowed to scream, but Isaac's voice barely registered above the roaring red light.

When he eventually ran out of breath, the last of his strength seemed to leave him and, as if in recognition of his surrender, the red light finally began to fade.

Darkness once more closed in around him and this time Isaac slipped into a cold, exhausted unconsciousness.

THE GLISTENING BLACK ROCK WAS FREEZING THIS FAR beneath the surface of Mars. Every few hundred metres Detective Raiken and her forensic assistant, Lance, were reminded via a head up display in their helmets to stay on the illuminated path, but Det. Raiken didn't need reminding.

She'd never travelled this deep into the Marsian crust before and being surrounded by so much wet, black rock was making her feel claustrophobic. The sooner this was over, the better.

In parts, the black walls were barely discernible from sudden openings that framed impenetrable darkness. The echo of her footsteps suggested large caverns waited beyond them, but it was impossible to tell without the scanning equipment Lance was using to navigate their way ahead.

"Make sure you document everything," she told him, as much to ground herself in the task at hand as for any real need to remind him.

"Yes, ma'am," he replied in his distinct nasal tone, "but you should know, there's not much to document."

"Nevertheless," she said, without bothering to repeat herself.

This was Lance's first live crime scene. He'd scored well at the Marsian Forensic Academy, but Det. Raiken knew how different reality could be. The carefully constructed scenarios they studied at the Academy were great for learning the basics, but real crime was never that neat or tidy. And it certainly didn't come with answers provided at the end of each exercise.

Miana had graduated from the same place more than twenty years earlier and although the forensic equipment had become far more user-friendly, the basic concepts hadn't changed.

So far, they'd found evidence that two other people had been down here before them. One was Dr. Naseem Indari – the man they were here for – the other was unidentified. In fact, the only evidence a second person had been here at all came in the form of microscopic scuff marks left by a survival suit like the ones currently keeping Det. Raiken and Lance supplied with warm, breathable air.

What they knew about Dr. Indari was that he was a geologist, specifically a speleologist, famous for studying the deepest cave formations on Mars. The Red Planet's crust was more than a hundred kilometres thick in places – much thicker than the ten or so kilometres of Earth – and due to the fact that most volcanic activity had ended long ago, there were hundreds of incredibly deep, incredibly complex subselenean tunnels left by ancient lava flows.

The cave system they were in now contained one of five underground fresh water oceans that had been discovered since colonization. It should have been a useful resource, but the cost required to pump it all the way up to the surface was prohibitive and so all commercial attempts to make use of the water had been abandoned long ago.

The surface entrance was also located more than three hundred kilometres from the nearest colonized area and so it was no surprise when Det. Raiken and her rookie partner Lance had been the lucky ones tasked with driving all the way out here.

"*I wonder what I did to deserve this one?*" Det. Raiken thought to herself.

So far, she'd come to understand that Dr. Indari was a classic introvert. Brilliant in his own right and well-respected in the scientific community, but outside of purely academic correspondence he kept to himself. There were only a few people even aware of his current research and fewer still who knew where he could be found.

In fact, Det. Raiken was certain his disappearance would have gone unnoticed if Dr. Indari hadn't owed someone a debt.

That, at least, was quite normal. If there was one constant Miana knew she could always rely on, it was the fact that money was – and always will be – the most dependable human motivator. In this case it was a small personal loan that had drawn attention to Dr. Indari's absence. It wasn't recorded in any official capacity, but, nevertheless, after going unpaid for six months the lender had been motivated to contact the police.

It was sad in a way, because despite the length of time Dr. Indari had been missing no one else had raised the alarm. When Det. Raiken contacted the few relatives she could find, none of them had even noticed his absence and most freely admitted they wouldn't have gone looking for him even if they did.

"His fault, or theirs?" she wondered absently.

"We're here," Lance said ahead of her.

Det. Raiken looked up and saw the illuminated path they were following had opened onto a large, well-lit cavern. The floor was smooth and relatively level, but it dropped away at the far end where the smashed remains of a research station could be seen. There was also a living habitat – seemingly untouched – set against the far left wall.

Det. Raiken paused at the entrance and took a moment to survey the damaged research station. It didn't take a detective to see that someone, or something, had smashed every piece of equipment. Shattered electronics were strewn across the cavern floor and torn cabling was scattered like jungle vines amidst the resulting carnage.

"Lance," she said, motioning toward the crime scene.

"Yes, ma'am," he replied, before lowering his enormous backpack.

The first piece of equipment he extracted was a tall tripod that Det. Raiken knew had hundreds of tiny cameras imbedded in the central shaft. When it was fully extended, a fine grid of light splashed out across the cavern floor and Det. Raiken's helmet began to display all the information it was collecting.

Grid lines that traced the cavern's rocky contours created a more precise and easy-to-interpret map of the area. Spectral signatures identified rock, plastic, metal, glass, and water. Scuff marks and other signs of disturbance lit up in soft magenta tones and anything still intact was quickly identified and labelled.

As the cavern slowly filled with glowing icons and data, Det. Raiken casually surveyed the scene for useful clues. There was nothing new here. The rescue 'bots that attended the scene before them had documented it all thoroughly. In fact, this was nothing more than a formality to give Lance some field experience and ensure the rescue 'bots hadn't missed anything.

Lance was certainly taking his time. Personally, Det. Raiken would have given up much sooner, but she knew it paid to be patient with rookies. Their methodical nature always took longer, but sometimes the extra time they spent on analysis highlighted details that even the most seasoned detectives could miss.

She also knew she'd been assigned a man of Lance's meticulous nature for a reason. It was well known that Det. Raiken relied on instinct more than she did the devil in the detail. And yet, despite an exemplary arrest record, that fact had never sat well with her superiors. Apparently due process was more important to them than results.

"Ready, ma'am," Lance said eventually.

"Right then," Det. Raiken replied, "let's clean up this mess."

Returning to his large backpack, Lance pulled out three evidence-gathering robots the size of his head and placed them on the ground. When each egg-shaped robot was activated, it rose off the floor on eight, insect-like legs while the body unfurled into a large, empty vessel.

As they swept across the cavern floor, Det. Raiken watched another set of triple-segmented limbs collecting everything they could find. Every chip of rock and broken piece of circuitry was sealed in a protective coating and then carefully placed inside the large compartment on the robots' back, for later examination. The pattern of collection followed the glowing grid lines precisely and, as the cavern floor gradually cleared, Det. Raiken moved closer to the smashed research station.

"Shall I set up another imaging staff, ma'am?" Lance asked when the robots began to attack the research station itself.

"Sure," she replied, though it was doubtful it would make any difference.

Returning her attention to the research station, Det. Raiken noted how thorough the destruction was and immediately doubted they would recover anything useful. Then a sudden splash interrupted her thoughts.

"Crap!" Lance swore with feeling.

Det. Raiken turned to find him standing at the edge of a shimmering set of ripples. It was almost impossible to see without the distortion of light, but there was a pool of perfectly clear water that began where the cavern sloped downward.

"The scans clearly showed the waterline, Lance," she said with a disapproving look.

"Sorry, ma'am," he replied, gingerly stepping out of the water. "I turned off my spectral map to focus on the research station. I thought I'd be able to see some kind of difference in the rock, but… the water's so clear. I mean *look* at it. Even when it's rippling you can hardly see the surface."

"Learn the lesson," Det. Raiken told him. "When you're working a live crime scene, it's important to develop a sense of your surroundings from the initial forensic scan. Primarily so you don't put your foot in something and contaminate the evidence, but also to help you reconstruct what happened."

"Yes, ma'am," Lance replied, gingerly shaking water off his boot.

Turning back to the smashed research station, Det. Raiken let her instincts go to work again. It was clear that whoever had done this knew what they were doing. Not a single piece of equipment had been left intact.

As the robots continued cataloguing the various smashed pieces of machinery, she ran a program that would piece them together in the most likely formation.

Holographic representations of the parts gradually lined themselves up in her helmet's head up display and the resulting object began to look like a remote submersible – one of the pieces of equipment Det. Raiken knew Dr. Indari had brought with him. It didn't look big enough to carry a human passenger, but from the bits left over, it appeared to have been carrying some powerful drilling and scanning equipment. Dr. Indari's main purpose must have been exploring the deeper cave systems that were filled with water.

"*What were you searching for, doctor?*" she thought to herself. "*And did you find something that might explain all this?*"

After a few minutes of watching other unrecognizable objects slowly piece themselves together, Det. Raiken turned her attention to the living habitat that waited against the far wall. She moved toward it, as far as the evidence robots had cleared, and then allowed her instincts to assess the scene.

In stark contrast with the violence of the destroyed research station, the living habitat appeared completely untouched. The smooth polymer walls were unblemished and, from what she could see through the slightly ajar doorway, there was no sign of internal damage either.

"*More evidence this wasn't some insane rampage,*" she thought.

When the evidence robots had finished cleaning the area in front of the habitat, one of them opened the doorway all the way and Det. Raiken frowned. The pictures taken by the rescue 'bots didn't do the crime scene justice.

Dr. Indari's body sat in a chair facing the left side of the habitat. His head was slumped forward, but he remained sitting upright with his hands resting casually in his lap, palms up. He was also naked from the waste up and every visible section of skin was smeared with dried blood. The blood was thick and mostly black, but it didn't quite obscure the hundreds of strange symbols that had been carved into his flesh. There were also two lumpy black mounds in the palm of his right hand.

"*His eyes,*" Det. Raiken thought with a grimace.

Based on the information collected by the rescue 'bots, the body had been down here close to six months, but the frigid cavern air had held the decomposition process at bay and so Dr. Indari's corpse was far from skeletal.

"Oh…" Lance gasped behind her.

Det. Raiken felt a wave of sympathy as she turned to find Lance pale and shaking. She remembered the first time she'd seen a dead body outside the strictly controlled environment of the Forensic Academy. It had not been a pleasant experience.

She gave him a moment to regain his composure then spoke firmly into the clinging silence.

"I need you to examine the body, Lance."

"Uh… yes, ma'am," he replied, making a visible effort to pull himself together. "Sorry, ma'am."

With only a hint of the reluctance he must have felt, Lance stepped into the habitat and crouched next to Dr. Indari's body. As he began to take measurements and samples, Det. Raiken moved in behind him and surveyed the rest of the habitat.

There was a small desk next to the body with several neatly placed food cartons beside some writing implements Det. Raiken had never seen outside of a museum. She already knew from her initial investigations that Dr. Indari was known for utilising the archaic practice of writing manually with ink or graphite onto paper, but it was strange seeing it in person.

"*But is it as strange as spending your life studying the most remote regions of a planet?*" she thought to herself.

19

Tapping her suit's wrist computer, Det. Raiken had one of the evidence robots open the desk drawers one by one. They were all empty. She then made them do a quick search for hidden compartments, but wasn't surprised when she didn't find any. Why would Dr. Indari need to hide anything all the way down here?

The rest of the habitat consisted of a small bed pressed against the far wall, a series of empty perspex shelves, and a small shower and toilet in the opposite corner. Nothing seemed out of place or unexpected.

"Ma'am?" Lance interrupted her inspection.

"Tell me," she said, turning around.

"I've finished the preliminary examination," he replied, sending a file to her helmet's head up display. "There are callouses on his hands that match the tools used to smash the equipment outside and clear fingerprints on the tools as well."

Det. Raiken wasn't surprised. It made sense that Dr. Indari was the culprit, even if the act of destroying the equipment still didn't. He would have known better than anyone how to destroy all evidence of what he was doing.

"And the physical trauma?" she said with a frown.

"The angle of every cut is consistent with… with self-mutilation, ma'am," Lance said, looking up as if he expected to be corrected.

"The wounds are self-inflicted?" Det. Raiken said, frowning harder. "Are you sure?"

"Well, technically, ma'am, it may be possible to fake a scenario where Dr. Indari did this to himself, but it wouldn't be easy. And the killer would have had to accomplish this while Dr. Indari was both alive and unrestrained. His tox screen came back negative for all known sedatives and there are no ligature marks that would suggest he was tied down. Not to mention the fact that anyone moving the body after all these cuts would have left an awful mess."

"What about our second party?" Det. Raiken asked. "Have you found any further evidence that could help us identify them?"

"Not beyond the entrance to the cavern, ma'am," Lance answered with a shake of his head. "It will take some time to complete my assessment back at the precinct, but I've found nothing to suggest there was anyone else present at the time of Dr. Indari's death."

"He had no history of mental illness," Det. Raiken said quietly. "Something serious must have happened to trigger this psychotic episode."

"There's something else," Lance said.

"Tell me."

"There are no hesitation marks. Dr. Indari did this to himself purposefully and, by the looks of it, didn't flinch once. His blood work contains all the chemical evidence of nervous trauma, so he must have felt pain. But for some reason, it appears he... didn't react to it."

Det. Raiken was more shocked than surprised this time. What Lance was describing was unheard of. She'd already pondered the possibility of self-hypnosis, which was a well-understood technique that magicians often used to put their bodies in dangerous situations whilst controlling the bodily responses that would otherwise do them harm. But this was something else.

Dr. Indari's blood showed evidence that he'd actually felt the pain he was inflicting and yet he continued anyway. Either his mind really had snapped, or he had an inhuman amount of willpower.

"Good work," she said, calmly factoring the information into what she already knew. "What about the symbols?"

"They don't match anything in our database, ma'am. There's enough repetition to suggest a code, or language of some kind, but I've never seen anything like it. And if the database doesn't recognise it... well..."

"It could be gibberish," Det. Raiken finished for him, "and the first real sign of mental imbalance we've found. What's your final conclusion?"

"Uh... the evidence suggests Dr. Indari acted alone," Lance answered awkwardly, once again acting as if he was about to be rebuked. "Over an extended period he used several tools to smash his research equipment. All stored data was lost in the destruction. Paper records were torn up and passed through the living habitat's sewage reclamation system. When the vandalism was complete, Dr. Indari sat at his desk, carved the unidentified symbols into his stomach, chest and arms, and then cut out his eyes. Blood loss killed him not long after."

Det. Raiken frowned in thought. She didn't like crime scenes that didn't make sense. It usually meant someone had removed or tampered with evidence. But the victim also seemed to be the sole perpetrator in this case, which suggested there was no one living who could have removed evidence. And there was still something missing. She could sense it.

Who was the second party? Why did they come down here in the first place? Had they travelled all the way here, seen what Dr. Indari had done to himself and then simply returned the way they'd come? Could they have been a witness to this bizarre event?

"Good work, Lance," she said after a moment. "I don't think we can do anything more down here. Prep the body for transport and let's wrap this up."

"Yes, ma'am."

Det. Raiken shook her head in frustration. She could feel the case growing cold already. There was no record of what Dr. Indari was actually doing down here and he'd been careful to keep any record of his work out of public forums. His destruction of the research station had also been thorough and, despite the violent nature of his death, the wounds were clearly self-inflicted. As Lance had concluded, all the evidence pointed to a psychotic break that made Dr. Indari destroy his work and then kill himself.

But Det. Raiken's intuition wasn't so easily satisfied. There was something else going on here and she wanted answers.

"*I'll find the truth,*" she promised herself as she stepped out of the habitat. "*I just need to find a few leads.*"

ISAAC WOKE TO THE SOUND OF A WOMAN SCREAMING. He grimaced in confusion and blinked his blurry eyes. For some reason he was lying on the ground and his whole body ached like he'd been pummelled from head-to-toe with a baseball bat.

He still wore P.A.T.R.I.C.'s skull cap, but for some reason the bristling cables had been severed about a foot from his head – he could see them bobbing in and out of view – and beyond them was a living room that Isaac didn't recognise.

Whoever was screaming didn't seem likely to stop anytime soon and so he pushed himself painfully to his feet and looked around.

"Where am I?"

Icy fingers of shock began to press against his spine, but he barely had time to acknowledge them before something slammed into him from behind. He yelped in terror and ducked away instinctively, but another blow caught him on the shoulder. He twisted round with his hands held high and found the screaming woman frantically waving something that looked like a mop.

"What are you- Ow! What are you doing?" he yelled. "Look, I don't know where I am! Stop- Argh! Stop hitting me, please! I'm- Ow! I'm not going to hurt you!"

But the woman just kept hitting him and Isaac could sense there was nothing he could say that would calm her down. She looked more terrified than he was.

He ducked away from another swipe of the mop and suddenly registered a baby crying in the background.

"*Oh crap,*" he thought. "*No wonder she's hysterical. How the hell did I get in here?*"

Looking frantically for an exit, Isaac leapt over a low, lime-green sofa and ran out of the room. The hallway beyond ended in what looked like a front door and so he headed straight for it. He glanced over his shoulder, hoping he'd left the woman behind, but she was charging right at him with her mop held high.

"*What is going on?*" he thought as he stumbled over a stack of shoes next to the front door.

He quickly fumbled with the door lock and sustained several more blows before finally bursting out of the house backwards, still trying to ward off the screaming woman.

As soon as he was outside the woman slammed the door in his face and Isaac heard the lock re-engage with a final *clack!*

"Thank... God," he gasped, breathing heavily.

Then he turned around.

"Jatz'n frickin' cheese balls..." he cursed quietly.

The hall he'd just stepped into only contained apartments on one side. The other was actually a long segmented window and beyond it was a steaming, 3D jigsaw-like collection of towering buildings and twisted, glowing walkways.

"But that looks like... the Valles Dome!" he said in stunned disbelief.

The Valles Dome was an enormous greenhouse city constructed between cliffs at one end of the Valles Marineris Canyon – the largest canyon on Mars, if not the solar system. It was also half a world away from the crowded laboratory Isaac shared with Jason back in Lynt City.

"*What the hell happened to me?*" he thought in a panic.

24

Shaking his head in confusion, Isaac decided his first priority was to get as far away from the screaming woman's apartment as possible. If she hadn't already called the police then she was sure to do it soon. He quickly pulled the skull cap off his head and turned it inside-out so he could stuff the cabling inside, then he turned and ran to the end of the corridor.

There was an elevator waiting next to a door that led to a set of stairs and Isaac quickly pressed the call button. The number displayed above the elevator began counting up through the twenties and Isaac moved his gaze to a sign next to the stairs. He was on the thirty-eighth floor.

"Come on, come on," he murmured, tapping the elevator button again.

As the count approached thirty, Isaac felt a sudden tension in his mind and took an instinctive step back. A second later the elevator opened and a burly security guard stepped out with a serious look on his face. Isaac took another step back, certain he was about to be arrested, and the security guard raised a thick-fingered hand. Then he suddenly vanished, leaving the tightly closed elevator doors in his place.

"Wh... what?" Isaac said, his heart racing.

He looked up at the elevator's glowing indicator and saw that it was still five floors away.

"That... was weird," he muttered with a frown.

Unsure of what had just happened, but unwilling to tempt fate, Isaac quickly moved to the stairwell and ducked inside, just as a tone sounded behind him. He turned to peek through the door's small window and was surprised to find the same burly security guard stepping out of the elevator.

"*What the hell?*" he thought in disbelief. "*How did... how did I do that?*"

But the unanswered question didn't stop him from taking advantage of the situation. As soon as the security guard moved down the corridor, Isaac quietly ducked out of the stairwell, slipped into the elevator, and hit the ground floor button.

"*That was precognition,*" he reasoned as the doors closed behind him. "*But… but I've never been able to see the future before. What the hell happened to me? Was it our experiment? Something must have gone seriously wrong. God, I hope Jason's okay. And who was that woman? How did I even get into her apartment? Did I break in and then pass out… or something? What the hell is going on? I've lost some time, I know that. But how much? And how could I travel to the other side of Mars without remembering it? Damn it, where's Jason when I need him?*"

Isaac leant against the elevator wall in despair. He wasn't used to working through problems on his own and it felt wrong being so far away from his brother. He felt… *lonely* in a way he'd never experienced before.

He glanced up at the elevator's floor counter and saw that he was now only a dozen floors above ground level. He pushed himself off the wall, ready to get the hell out of there, and felt the same mental tension he'd experienced earlier.

Suddenly the elevator doors were opening again, only this time the security guard on the other side looked different and he was pointing a pistol straight at Isaac's face.

"Wait!" Isaac shouted, raising his hands in terror.

But before the guard could fire, he vanished just like the first one had.

"Huh?" Isaac whimpered, his eyes flickering to the floor counter again.

He was still several floors above ground.

"Shit!" he swore, before quickly slapping the floor buttons at the bottom of the panel.

The elevator tone sounded almost immediately and when the doors opened on level two – thankfully without revealing any security guards – Isaac ran into the hallway.

This far down, the view out of the windows was quite different. He could now clearly see the bustling crowds that streamed along the lower, illuminated walkways. The people looked far more eclectic than what Isaac was used to, but that was only to be expected. The Valles Dome was considered the most cosmopolitan city in the solar system.

Hoping there weren't any police officer's in the crowd who might notice him, Isaac began walking further down the corridor.

"How am I going to get out of here?" he thought in desperation.

He hadn't done anything wrong – at least, nothing he could remember – but he certainly didn't like the idea of trying to convince an armed security guard of that.

A scraping noise suddenly caught his attention and Isaac turned to find an old woman coming out an apartment.

"Excuse me, ma'am," he said, walking toward her. "May I talk to you for a moment, please?"

The old woman looked up at him suspiciously and Isaac stopped at a safe distance, not wanting to spook her.

"Good… morning, ma'am," he said, realising he didn't even know if it was the first or second half of the day. "My name's… Cracker… lint… uh, Simon Crackerlint."

He tried not to wince at his fumbling excuse for a name, but the old woman seemed willing to accept it, for now.

"Yes?" she said warily.

"I'm sorry to catch you as you were leaving," Isaac continued quickly. "I'm here on behalf of building maintenance. The manager sent me."

"Yes?" she repeated, looking even more suspicious now.

Isaac hesitated. It was clear the old woman expected the manager's name. He tried to think of a reason he might not know it, but in place of an excuse, a light female voice spoke in his mind.

"Gordon Bramble."

"Ah…" he said, pausing a moment longer before saying the name out loud. "Gordon Bramble?"

"Oh, yes," the old woman said with a nod, her suspicions disappearing in a smile. "Mr. Bramble."

"*Woah, where did that come from?*" Isaac thought in surprise, before continuing. "I was told you've been having some trouble with your..."

Again, he hesitated, and this time the answer appeared in his head almost straight away.

"*My plumbing.*"

"Your plumbing," he finished, trying not to let his amazement show.

Had he really just heard the old woman's thoughts? It was the only explanation, even if the age of the voice didn't match the age of the woman.

"That's right," she said, smiling wider, "are you here to fix it?"

"I'm going to try," Isaac said, smiling back and taking a few steps forward. "May I come in, please?"

"Of course, Simon," the old lady said, obviously glad her complaint had finally been noticed. "Come in, come in."

Breathing a quick sigh of relief, Isaac ducked into the old lady's apartment and felt much better when the door closed behind him.

"It really has been a pain," she continued, leading him further inside. "My water pressure is so weak sometimes that I have to stand at the tap for nearly fifteen minutes, just to fill my watering can. And Jasmine gets so cranky when her water bowl is empty. But I won't let her lick from the tap. Oh no. That would be naughty, wouldn't it Jasmine?"

Isaac felt something brush against his leg and looked down to find a black and white cat peering up at him.

"*Jasmine, I presume,*" he thought, ignoring an urge to kick it away from him.

On their way to the kitchen, Isaac glanced into the lounge room opposite and saw a large virtual window set to a majestic river view.

"*My way out,*" he thought, feeling an unexpected thrill of excitement.

28

"I wouldn't know what to do with myself if I had no water for my plants, or Jasmine, of course," the old woman continued unabated. "It's just in here."

"Oh," Isaac said, an idea occurring to him. "I seem to have forgotten my tools. You don't have any I could borrow, do you, ma'am?"

"None I know how to use," the old woman said with a wink, "but yes, the bottom drawer there, dear."

Isaac turned to where she was pointing and then crouched down to open the bottom drawer. Inside, he found a neat array of tools. He slipped several of the more familiar ones into his pockets and then chose a large wrench that hopefully looked the part.

"Thank you, ma'am," he said, brandishing the wrench with a smile. "That will save me trudging all the way back up to the maintenance level. Now, the quickest way to diagnose a pressure problem is to check the mains connection. I should be able to get to it through your lounge room window. Would you be able to open it for me, ma'am?"

"Of course, Simon," the old woman said, hobbling over to the kitchen drawers, "but please, call me Miriam."

"Thank you, Miriam," Isaac said, smiling at her back.

"It's so nice to have company," she said as she retrieved a key from another drawer. "I used to have regular high teas, you know. Every Tuesday at four. They were always so well attended. A book club too. Thursdays at six. It was amazing how much we could get through in an hour. But I have to say…"

Isaac nodded absently and allowed Miriam's voice to fade into the background as she plodded out to the lounge room and opened the window. Now that they were on a first name basis it appeared she trusted him completely and so he had time to focus on working out what he was going to do next. He still wasn't certain he'd be able to get out of the building this way, but after what had happened in the elevator, there didn't seem to be any other option.

The image of a beautiful river surrounded by giant willow trees and flowery mounds of moss flickered and disappeared when Miriam opened the window and Isaac wasted no time stepping through the gap onto the dingy landing on the other side. There were pipes and electrical conduits running up and down the building on the opposite side of the landing and they interfaced with Miriam's apartment via a large, easy to identify junction box that sat beside the virtual window. In the other direction, the landing terminated in a ladder that led down to an even more crowded space, but this one had a door at the end.

"*That'll do nicely,*" Isaac thought, before turning back to Miriam.

She was still chatting away happily with her cat cradled in her arms and it didn't look like she was going to stop talking any time soon.

"Uh, could you do me a favour, Miriam?" Isaac said when she eventually paused to take a breath.

"Of course, Simon," she replied eagerly.

"Could you please go and turn on the cold water tap in the kitchen? I'll make a few adjustments out here and see if they make a difference. You may have to wait awhile, I'm afraid, but make sure you stay by the tap. Something is guaranteed to happen eventually."

"Certainly," Miriam replied. "Come on, Jasmine. Let's go see if Simon can bring an end to our troubles."

Isaac felt bad leaving Miriam like this, especially with a shonky plumbing system, but he felt worse about being caught. And so as soon as she was gone, he quickly shimmied down the ladder at the end of the landing and headed for the door that would hopefully lead him out of there.

He remembered a Sci-Fact documentary on the building of the Valles Dome that had talked about enormous maintenance tunnels built into the cliff-face behind some of the residential buildings. From the view he'd seen on the thirty-eighth level, he assumed this was one of those buildings and so he hoped the maintenance tunnel would allow him to get a long way away before the security guards started looking outside their own building.

Not surprisingly, the door at the end of the landing was locked, but with the tools he'd taken from Miriam's kitchen, Isaac was easily able to pull it apart so he could try to hack his way through.

For a moment, he wondered how good a thief he would make, especially given his new pre-cog abilities, but an image of the security guard pointing a gun at him quickly stopped that fantasy in its tracks. Isaac just didn't have the stomach for violence, particularly when it was directed at him.

When the door finally swung open, Isaac felt a wave of relief that turned into a smile when he saw the large space beyond.

"*I was right,*" he thought.

The maintenance tunnel was much larger than he expected and seemed to be cut directly from the rocky canyon cliff. There was a long row of bright lights illuminating what would have otherwise been a pitch black space and it allowed him to see several garbage and delivery trucks trundling along the tunnel's impressive length.

One of the garbage trucks was slowly accelerating away from the docking station that serviced Miriam's building and Isaac quickly ran forward and leapt onto its tailgate before it could move out of reach. A sturdy safety rail allowed him to hold on as it carried him down the tunnel and Isaac nervously looked back over his shoulder. He expected to see the security guards appear at the same doorway he'd just come through, but it remained firmly closed.

"*Thank God for that,*" he thought, slowly letting out a deep breath.

He turned away from the doorway and was about to search for another exit when a sudden shout made him almost jump out of his skin.

"Hey! What the fuck you think you're doin'?"

The voice had a strange echoing quality to it and Isaac's shocked mind found it hard to verify the direction it had come from.

He looked around wildly, trying to find the voice's owner, but after a few moments, he realised it hadn't come from anywhere.

31

"Not yet, anyway," he thought incredulously. *"That was precognition again."*

Deciding to trust the unexpected warning, he leapt off the vehicle immediately and watched the garbage truck accelerate away from him with a loud grumble. He then headed for the first steps he could find, scurried through a thankfully unlocked door, and closed it firmly behind him with a grimace.

"This seriously sucks," he mumbled, breathing hard.

The alleyway he'd entered wasn't very long and Isaac could clearly see people streaming past the entrance in both directions. He didn't particularly want to join them, but he did so anyway, intentionally moving away from the apartment building he'd just escaped from.

His body still ached from being hit with a mop, his mind still reeled with the strange pre-cog visions he'd witnessed, and nothing was clear about what had happened to him, but Isaac only cared about one thing now.

"I have to get back to Jason," he thought as he lost himself in the crowd. *"One way or another, he'll help me work this all out."*

THE ALL-TERRAIN VEHICLE THAT HAD TRANSPORTED
Det. Raiken and Lance to the remote crime scene trundled across
Mars' arid landscape on its way back to Lynt City.

The dawn sky was gradually brightening to a brilliant blue before
transitioning to its usual reddish haze and Det. Raiken stared out at
it with a frown. She knew it was pointless feeling frustrated so early
in an investigation, but she couldn't help it. Crime scenes weren't
that hard to read when you understood how the criminal mind
worked. The real trick was linking the most likely explanation to
a person, or persons, so an arrest could be made. But Dr. Indari's
death was just too bizarre to explain with experience alone.

It was clear he was responsible for both the damage that had been
done to his research equipment and the mutilation of his own body,
but what was his motive? What could make a person destroy their
life's work and then unflinchingly carve symbols into their flesh and
remove their own eyes?

All she could think to do next was find someone familiar with
Dr. Indari or his work so she could ask more questions. The number
of cases that were solved by deciphering the lies, misconceptions,
and occasional truths provided by those related to the victim far
outweighed the number solved using forensic evidence alone.

The only problem was that in order to find Dr. Indari, Det. Raiken had already contacted everyone who knew him and she doubted any of them had more to offer.

She turned to Lance in defeat and found him industriously tapping away at his computer console. Having long since logged all the evidence they'd gathered at the crime scene, Det. Raiken had allowed him to spend some time following up leads of his own.

"What are you working on?" she asked.

"I'm trying to find out who, if anyone, Dr. Indari communicated with," he replied.

"His satellite relay logged no communication."

"Yes ma'am, but I found it hard to believe someone would go so long without reaching out to touch someone. Uh... figuratively speaking, of course. I thought it might be possible to find other data that could verify his self-imposed isolation."

"Acting on instinct," Det. Raiken said with a nod. "I like it. Did you find anything?"

"Well... yes, but it's kind of... strange."

"Tell me."

"Well, first I contacted Mars Global Communications to see if they had any transmissions logged with Dr. Indari's satellite relay address. They didn't, which I expected. So I decided to... think outside the box."

Lance paused to look at her and Det. Raiken could tell he was reluctant to continue.

"Go on," she prompted. "When you reach a dead end, every idea is worth exploring, no matter how unorthodox."

"Yes, ma'am," Lance replied dutifully before turning back to his console. "Well, I searched for other transmissions that might originate within the area Dr. Indari was operating in and came across Payco Mining. They're conducting mineral surveys in the Denison Basin, a few hundred kilometres north of here. I did a bit of digging – no pun intended – and found that their exploratory transmissions are powerful enough to reach Dr. Indari's satellite relay. They also measure the signal's feedback with incredible precision. In fact, they're so precise they can measure the disruptive effects caused by any nearby radio transmissions."

"Good thinking, Lance," Det. Raiken said, genuinely impressed. "How were you planning on gaining access to the data?"

"Oh, it's publicly available, ma'am. That's how Payco markets their Prosp-Ants. You know, those A.I. mining robots you hire online? You pay for the energy requirements and maintenance costs of one or more Prosp-Ants then you're allocated a part of their licensed territory. If your Prosp-Ant strikes a viable seam before anyone else's, you win a share of the mining proceeds. It's how Payco manages to operate this far from the cities. The online community treats it like a game and the secondary gambling revenue they provide is almost as much as Payco gets for eventually selling the ore."

"*Well, you learn something new every day,*" Det. Raiken thought, before adding out loud, "fair enough. Did you find the supporting evidence you were looking for?"

"I did," Lance replied, frowning in thought. "I checked data for all surveying periods that coincided with Dr. Indari's presence in the caves and found several interference patterns that suggest nearly a dozen radio transmissions were made over the course of a few days, about six and a half months ago."

"While he may have still been alive," Det. Raiken said thoughtfully.

"Yes, ma'am. Either that, or he was already dead and the second person made the calls," Lance offered.

"Good point," Det. Raiken conceded, "but either way, someone didn't want us to know they'd made any calls at all. Can you pinpoint the exact time of those communications?"

"I can and did, ma'am," Lance replied, "which is where things get a little weird. I contacted Mars Global Communications again and requested a record of any data packages matching the first time signature. It turns out there was a short period of solar interference at that exact time."

35

"That's not so weird," Det. Raiken said. "It happens all the time when I try to contact Earth jurisdictions."

"Yes, ma'am," Lance agreed with a nod, "but then I gave them the second time signature and it turns out there was another solar event then as well. It was the same story for every other time signature. The M.G.C. officer was just as surprised as I was. Every single time signature I gave her corresponded to a period of solar interference."

"So whoever sent those transmissions was constantly getting a busy signal?" Det. Raiken asked.

"That's what the information suggests," Lance replied, "but the duration of each transmission doesn't reflect that at all. It looks more like what you'd expect from one side of a conversation, not someone continuously trying to resend the same transmission."

"Hmmm…" Det. Raiken mused for a moment. "Can a period of solar interference be faked?"

"Well… technically, yes. If you had the right equipment," Lance said, though his tone suggested he didn't believe it was likely.

"Could Dr. Indari have faked them?"

"Definitely not. Creating a fraudulent period of solar interference would require direct access to M.G.C. satellites. The only people with that capability would be their own tech-services team."

"Then it's possible," Det. Raiken said grimly. "Did you record your contact with the M.G.C.?"

"Yes, ma'am. The operative wasn't lying."

"That doesn't mean her answers were accurate. Okay, Lance, let's operate under the assumption that Dr. Indari, or his mysterious visitor, did send several packets of data to someone. I know the contents will probably never be found, but I need to know who they were meant for. Do you think you can you find a way to identify them?"

"Not without access to the databanks at M.G.C."

"Hmmm. That could be tricky. But we'll see what we can do once we're back at the precinct."

Det. Raiken sat back with a frown. This case just got more complicated and more serious. If Lance was right and the transmissions were covered up, Dr. Indari wasn't the only one who wanted his work to remain hidden. And whoever that was either worked for M.G.C., had a personal connection inside M.G.C., or was powerful enough not to need one.

A familiar tone interrupted her musing and Det. Raiken looked up to find they were approaching Lynt City.

"*Home sweet home,*" she thought with a smile.

Lynt City was the largest established colony on Mars and home to the most powerful men and women in both big business and organised crime. It didn't look like much from the outside. The massive dome that held in the precious atmosphere and protected the buildings and inhabitants from Mars' incessant dust storms was filthy around the edges, which made the shadowy skyline of tightly packed skyscrapers barely visible. But inside was another matter entirely.

To the right of the city's main entrance, enormous cranes with complex looking factories at their base relentlessly pushed the border outwards and Det. Raiken shook her head as she watched the colossal machines at work. She didn't envy the people operating them. Spending so much time in the cold, gritty atmosphere of Mars was no way to live.

Turning her gaze back to the city entrance, Det. Raiken noted a modest amount of traffic was waiting to gain access at the looming check point. Most were courier trucks and mining transports, but she could also see a few tourist rovers – probably back from hiking one of Mars' enormous mountains. There were even a few private vehicles about the same size as their own.

If they were to join that line, it would take at least an hour to be processed, but that queue wasn't for them. Their rover slipped into a well-lit side road that headed toward a much smaller gateway plastered with official warnings.

As they approached, their authorisation was scanned automatically from the insignia on their dash and the heavy-looking gates immediately rumbled out of the way. The rover moved into a space just large enough to fit their vehicle then the gates rolled closed behind them. Det. Raiken heard a distinct *hissssss* as the chamber was flooded with warm atmosphere then, when the pressure outside matched their cabin, the second set of gates rolled smoothly aside.

They trundled through into a large hangar lined with dozens of similar vehicles and parked at the end of the line. A uniformed Customs officer greeted them as they got out and Det. Raiken offered her a quick smile before turning to Lance.

"Escort the evidence through Customs and then head back to the precinct. I'm going to see if I can find someone who can shed some light on the symbols we found at the scene. Or at least prove they're gibberish. I'll join you when I'm done."

"Yes, ma'am," Lance replied with a nod.

Leaving him to deal with the Customs officer, Det. Raiken strode down the long line of vehicles and climbed a short flight of stairs to the security station. There was a line of three empty chairs along the wall to her right and a large window on the left where a large security guard with hulking shoulders, a thick neck, and a warm grin waited.

"Hi Trevin," she said, placing her data pad in the evidence slot below the window.

"Hey beautiful," he replied, giving her a wink and resting his enormous forearms on the bench between them. "Haven't seen you in a while. What they got you lookin' at out in the big bad desert?"

"The usual," she said with a smile and a shrug. "Dead body with no reasonable explanation."

"Not too gruesome, I hope," Trevin said, leaning back with an apologetic grimace.

"Don't ask," Det. Raiken said meaningfully.

"That bad, huh? Well if anyone's gonna find out what happened, it's the famous Detective Raiken. Scourge of the Lynt City underworld."

"Ha! Thanks Trevin," Det. Raiken said with a laugh, "but I'm not so sure this time. We'll see, I guess."

With a mischievous grin, Trevin took her data pad from the evidence slot and Det. Raiken waited as he cleared it through. When he was done, he buzzed her through to the other side of the security station.

"So, how's the new partner?" Trevin asked, handing her the data pad.

"How'd you know they assigned me a new partner?" she asked, feigning ignorance. Trevin loved to play detective.

"You're only checking through a data pad," he said, his rosy cheeks glowing with pleasure. "That means you've got some poor sod escorting the rest of the evidence through Customs while you gallivant off to bully someone into giving you answers."

"Very astute," she said, raising an eyebrow. "I don't know why you haven't applied to become a detective."

"Are you kidding?" Trevin replied. "All that studyin' they make you do? No thanks. I'd rather spend my time in the gym. And besides, it's all computers and robots these days. You know what I'm like with hardware."

"Nine thumbs and a toe," Det. Raiken said with a grin. "Stay safe, Trevin."

"You too, beautiful," he replied as she walked through the far door. "An' don't stay away so long next time. I miss that gorgeous smile o' yours."

"Bye Trevin."

Striding down the corridor outside, Det. Raiken let the smile fall from her face and activated her data pad with a touch. She waited a moment as it accessed the Lynt City network and then quickly searched for any nearby linguist or semiotic experts. She could easily contact someone with the right expertise from Earth, but given the recent increase in solar activity, inter-planetary communication just wasn't reliable these days.

It was a short search. Not surprisingly, there wasn't much call for people who studied language and symbols on Mars. In fact, there were only three candidates living in Lynt City.

Det. Raiken selected the first with a touch and a map of her current location appeared with a route traced all the way to the expert's door. It was a simple set of directions, but she studied it closely as she moved through the bustling customs area. She wanted to avoid small talk with the many officers she was familiar with and the only way to do that was to look busy.

When she eventually stepped out the front entrance, Det. Raiken looked up from her data pad and paused to take in the thriving metropolis of Lynt City.

"The best and worst of civilization all rolled into one," she thought to herself.

It looked completely different on this side of the dusty dome. Award-winning skyscrapers of every description stretched all the way to the thermal dome far above, glistening with skins made of flawless smart glass and pristine, white duracrete. Between them, dozens of levels designed for different kinds of traffic were connected by a sinuous web of actively lit escalators and crosswalks, and it made the entire thing look like a giant version of the enormous shopping malls on Earth.

Taking a breath of the fresh, filtered air, Det. Raiken smiled to herself and headed down the steps toward a row of vehicles that waited next to the curb. Unlike the rover they'd used to cross the Marsian landscape, these vehicles were mag-drive and didn't have wheels. They were also striped white and blue in the official Lynt City Police Department's distinctive graphics, signifying that they weren't available to the general public.

As Det. Raiken approached, the nearest one recognised her authorisation badge and opened its windscreen to allow her access. She climbed into the small, two person compartment and placed her data pad on the dashboard, where the map she'd just pulled up instantly linked with the vehicle's computer.

A request for confirmation appeared on the console in front of her and, after strapping herself in, Det. Raiken tapped the green confirm button. In response, the windscreen lowered and the vehicle pulled smoothly away from the curb.

It was good to be home, but even better was the feeling that she was heading toward potential answers.

"*I need to make sense of this,*" she thought with a frown. "*Or Doctor Indari's death is destined to go as unnoticed as his life.*"

STAGE 1: SOLAR FLARE ERUPTS FROM SUN

June 5, 2147 - 6.07 am

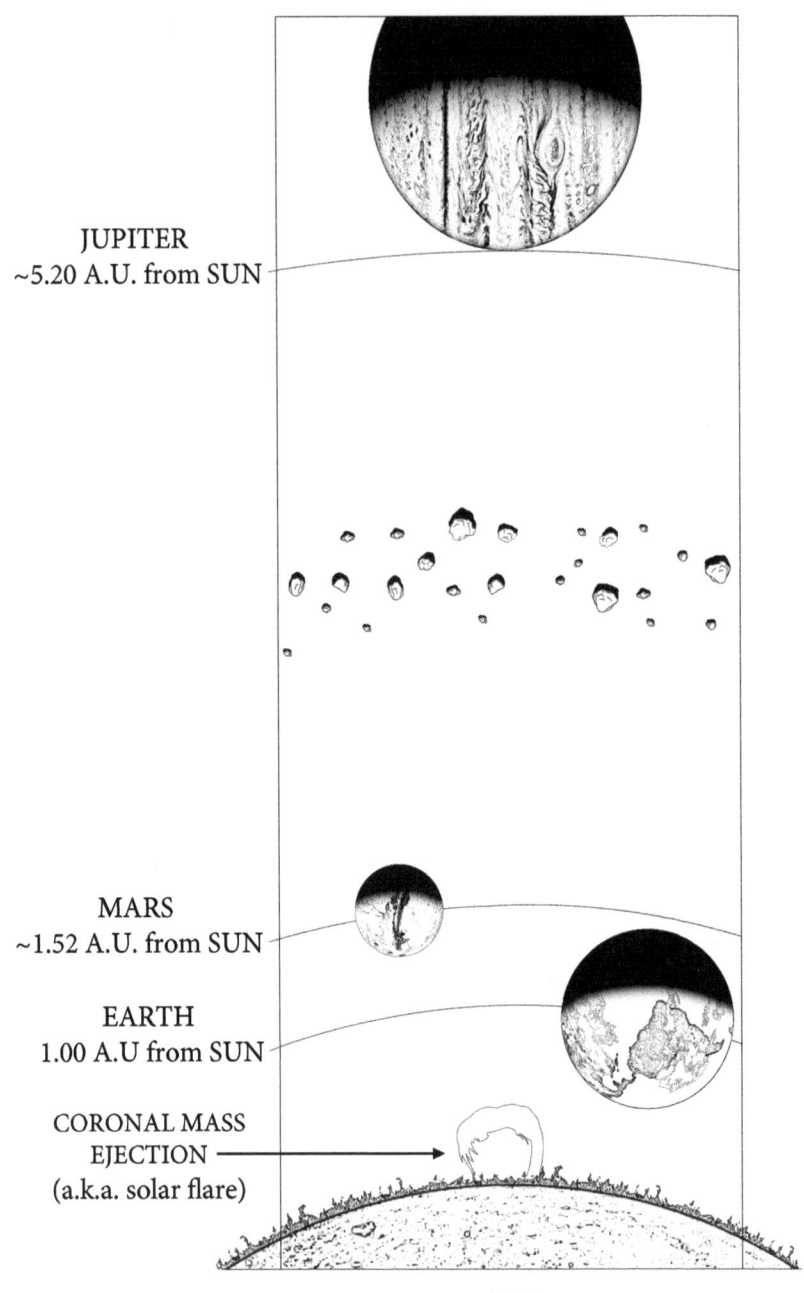

JUPITER
~5.20 A.U. from SUN

MARS
~1.52 A.U. from SUN

EARTH
1.00 A.U from SUN

CORONAL MASS
EJECTION
(a.k.a. solar flare)

SUN

1 Astronomical Unit (A.U.) = ~149.6 x 10⁶ km

FAR ABOVE MARS, IN THE NEAT, CONFINED SPACE OF HIS orbital space station, Sabian Cruz methodically went through the process of cleaning his coffee machine. The gleaming parts didn't need the attention, but he was habitually meticulous in everything he did. Obsessive, any psych evaluation would say.

Sabian also enjoyed the faint smell of lubricant that mixed with the aroma of expensive coffee beans. It combined with the sensation of manipulating cool machine parts in a way that brought his senses alive. And Sabian relied heavily on his senses. Without them, he could never absorb all the information being displayed on the panoramic curve of glass that surrounded him.

As his hands expertly reconstructed the cleaned and polished coffee machine, hundreds of video streams, administrative reports, and live graphs cast a ghostly, ever-changing glow across his gaunt features. There wasn't a piece of information routed through any satellite or stored on any server on Mars that wasn't available to him.

And it was almost time. Sabian could sense it in the flow of information, as if the bustling world below was aware of what was coming and had grown tense with anticipation.

Absently pausing in the reconstruction of his coffee machine, Sabian reached for the ruby-encrusted crucifix that hung at his chest.

"*I am ready, Lord God.*"

As the thought registered, Sabian's eyes flickered almost involuntarily to an image at the far right of his vision. It was a live image of the Sun surrounded by several complex graphs. Or as live as it was possible to get, given that Mars was currently 12.6 light minutes from the Sun.

He winked at it, causing the image to expand and move to the centre of the screen, and felt a rush of elation as the information registered. He already knew that solar activity had recently grown violent and erratic, but it was the end result of this activity that Sabian was interested in.

"The first sign," he whispered with a shiver.

He winked once again and as the image zoomed into a portion of the Sun's surface, Sabian watched in excitement as an enormous wave of fiery plasma was driven out into the solar system at close to three thousand kilometres per second. It was an enormous coronal mass ejection, more commonly known as a solar flare, and based on its current velocity and projected rate of acceleration Sabian calculated the vast cloud of plasma would reach Mars in less than eighteen hours.

"It has begun," he said with an overwhelming sense of resolve.

Keeping his breath carefully measured, he gently grasped his jewel-encrusted crucifix with both hands and bowed his head.

"My Lord and God," he prayed quietly, "the first sign has appeared. Guide me, my Lord. Command me and I shall obey."

In response, a tingling sensation appeared at the base of his neck and a shudder rolled through Sabian's body. It felt as if the entire satellite was shaking, but Sabian knew it was merely an illusion created by his connection with God.

A moment later, the tingling in his neck changed to a sudden, sharp pain and Sabian's eyes rolled back into his head, plunging him into darkness. But the darkness didn't last. Almost immediately, a blazing, white light broke through the gloom and the indistinct form of a tall, winged figure appeared above him.

"Sabian," a deep, echoing voice intoned.

"Blessed messenger," Sabian replied breathlessly. "Command me, Angel of God."

"As it was foreseen, so the End of Days has come. The first sign of the Apocalypse has been revealed and the Messiah is now among us."

"The Messiah," Sabian whispered, the implication sending another shiver of elation through him.

"He has manifested within the Valles Dome," the Angel continued.

"I… I have not detected his presence," Sabian admitted, feeling ashamed.

"You will not before it is time," the Angel assured him, "but you must find him, Sabian. Just as the Messiah has come, so too have the forces of darkness."

Sabian felt a cold hand close over his heart.

"The Antichrist," he whispered.

"Yes," the Angel replied.

"I will do whatever it takes," Sabian said eagerly.

"You will do only what is necessary," the Angel replied firmly. "Go to the Valles Dome. Watch. Wait. The Messiah will reveal himself at the appointed time and you must be ready."

"I will leave at once."

At this, the Angel's wings opened wide and its light grew painfully bright as its beautiful voice echoed through Sabian's mind one more time.

"God loves you, Sabian."

Then the light faded, along with the voice, and the tingling in Sabian's neck was replaced by a searing heat. His eyes rolled forward again, bringing the station back into focus, and he breathed deeply as he waited for the faint shuddering in his muscles to subside.

As always, Sabian felt a pang of regret after leaving the Angel's presence, but it was quickly swamped by a new sense of divine purpose.

He disliked venturing outside his satellite station. The order he was able to impose upon his surroundings here was simply not possible beyond its sterile walls. But this was God's Holy mission and he accepted it without question or doubt.

For Sabian had been blessed. He had been chosen to live above the clumsy, foolish masses that seemed incapable of absorbing and filtering information as he did. And when his God commanded he fight for those wretched fools, he did so with all his strength. Not for their shallow, sinful lives, of course, but for their immortal souls.

And, just as his God had prophesied, the final battle approached. Very soon, the Lord's divine fire would engulf this world and only those who were deemed worthy would ascend to the heavens and be gifted with eternal life.

At the thought, Sabian felt another shudder of ecstasy. The Messiah's coming heralded the end of a wicked, sinful age and it could not have come sooner. This world deserved to be judged and he felt no pity for the millions that would burn within the Lord's divine light.

"The fire shall cleanse us all," he whispered, moving his hand in the sign of the Cross. "Glory be to God."

VALLES DOME STREETS - June 5, 2147 - 7.52am

ISAAC TRUDGED THROUGH THE VALLES DOME'S labyrinthine streets, feeling completely lost. The area he was currently walking through was roofed with vines that hung heavy with all kinds of fruit, but what really made things strange were the multi-coloured rope lights intertwined along with them. At least half the lights blinked constantly, possibly providing Li-Fi signals to the passing crowd, while the rest shone steadily in pink and violet shades, likely providing the solar frequencies they required for photosynthesis and would never receive this far from the actual sun.

The effect should have been pleasant, but instead Isaac found it disconcerting. He wasn't familiar with any of the obvious landmarks he'd come across and the people surrounding him were just as strange.

The Valles Dome he'd heard about was iconic for its multicultural population, but Isaac saw nothing even remotely familiar in the fashions, hairstyles, or extravagant, glowing tattoos that decorated the crowd around him. And there were so many of them. It made getting around the city much harder than it looked. The trick seemed to be moving with whoever was nearest to you and thinking well ahead so if you needed to turn a corner, you could manoeuvre into position before the crowd swept you beyond it.

It wasn't an easy trick to master, especially when your skull felt like it had shrunk a few sizes around your brain.

"What's wrong with me?" Isaac thought, massaging his temple.

The uncomfortable tension he'd felt earlier had only gotten worse with time and it was now itching in a way that made him want to stick a finger up his nose so he could scratch his brain.

Careful not to slow down, Isaac pulled out the retro data pad he'd just stolen from a roadside dealer and switched it on. He felt really bad about taking it, but it wasn't like he had a choice. He'd tried to buy one legitimately, but for some reason his bank didn't recognise him in the Valles Dome. He was sure he'd seen ads saying he could access his account anywhere in the solar system, but apparently that was about as much bullshit as their claim to 'care for their customers' before anything else.

The data pad was cheap and a far cry from the latest models – which had security mods that made them virtually unhackable – but it gave Isaac access to all the free local networks and, better still, showed him where he was inside the Valles Dome.

"I've got to get out of here," he thought with a grimace.

But first things first, he had to call Jason and let his brother know he was okay. Of course, even that wasn't easy when you had no bank account. Without the ability to pay, he would have to piggyback on someone else's personal network connection. The hacking process was simple enough for anyone with a passing knowledge of transmission encryption, but the real trick was staying within a few metres of the registered user so the satellites didn't detect a dual signal and shut them both down.

Looking for a place to stop, Isaac saw an empty alcove nestled within the vines not far ahead and quickly began to manoeuvre toward it. Sensing his intention, the crowd reluctantly gave way and Isaac was eventually allowed to step out of the main flow.

Now that he was free of the human maelstrom, Isaac turned his full attention on the data pad and quickly wrote a program that would give him administrative access to the list of local network users. He then ran the application and the crowd streaming past him began to appear on his data pad as identity photos.

He glanced up and down quickly, trying to recognise the faces that flashed onto his screen, but it wasn't easy with so many to choose from. The people moving slower were the easiest to identify and so Isaac eventually chose a large man who waddled toward him with a large white packet in his chubby fist. He seemed totally engrossed in consuming whatever the packet held and so Isaac didn't think he'd be accessing his network connection anytime soon.

Quickly selecting the fat man's profile, Isaac set up a hijacking signal and then re-entered the flow of people a few steps behind his target. The hijacked network signal soon blinked to life and Isaac used it to switch all the fat man's notification tones to silent, just in case he received a call. Then, with a deep, hopeful breath, he opened a video phone app and dialled Jason's number.

"The number you have dialled is not in service. Please check the number before-"

"Shit," Isaac swore quietly, before hanging up in frustration. "I didn't screw it up, did I?"

He dialled the number again, slower this time.

"The number you have dialled-"

"Shit balls!" Isaac swore again, loud enough to earn a disapproving glance from a middle-aged woman wearing a black, ribbed jumpsuit and enormous blue sunglasses.

He didn't know what was going on. There was no reason their phone would have been disconnected. Unless…

"*Oh crap, was it my month to pay the bills?*" he thought with a sinking feeling.

Isaac usually relied on Jason to remind him about things like that, but it wasn't always the best method. On occasion, his brother felt it necessary to 'teach him a lesson' in personal management and would sometimes let this kind of thing happen just so Isaac would suffer the consequences.

"*What do I do now?*" he thought wretchedly.

49

He slowed to a halt, allowing the fat man to waddle round a corner, and the crowd around him immediately began to make disapproving sounds. Several people roughly pushed into him as they skirted the unexpected blockage, but Isaac barely noticed them. His head hurt too much and he didn't know what else to do.

With dirty looks and aggressive efficiency, the crowd gradually shunted Isaac into another empty alcove and he slumped into the seat within, feeling defeated and alone.

"*Damn it, why is everything suddenly so difficult?*" he thought, rubbing his eyes.

He just wanted to hop the first Mag-lev back to Lynt City, but even that required money he didn't have access to. And to make matters worse, the more he thought about it, the more his head hurt.

"*Maybe I need a doctor?*" he thought, moving his hand back to his temple.

He wasn't sure if he'd been injured during his… relocation, but he certainly didn't feel healthy. Had he been drugged? Is that how he'd travelled halfway across the planet without remembering it? But why would anyone do that? And why him? Could Jason be trying to teach him the biggest lesson yet?

"*No,*" Isaac thought, sure of that at least. "*Jase would never do something like this.*"

Which meant someone else was responsible. Could it be someone trying to steal their research? To snatch their fame and glory away just when they were about to achieve their goal? At least that would make some kind of sense. But why would they go to all this trouble? And why the Valles Dome?

Shaking his head in frustration, Isaac decided that whatever the truth was, he would be foolish not to stay under the radar for a while. Even if there wasn't some conspiracy to steal P.A.T.R.I.C. and the intellectual property that came with it, he didn't like the idea of explaining his accidental break-and-enter or the petty theft of an old lady's tools and a second-hand data pad to the police.

At this point, the tension in Isaac's head spiked and he hissed in agony.

"*Well that settles it,*" he thought with a grimace. "*I've really gotta find myself a doctor.*"

But he knew it wasn't going to be that simple. Public hospitals required registration and all the attention that might come with it. No. What he needed was someone with medical training who would allow him to remain anonymous.

The first option that occurred to him was a sexual health clinic, but Isaac quickly decided he wasn't that desperate. The second was a religious chapel, who he seemed to remember had to keep confessions confidential.

"*What am I thinking?*" he thought to himself. "*No 'Holy person' will have the qualifications I need.*"

Growling in frustration, Isaac was about give up and go to a public hospital when another thought occurred to him. Psychiatrists. They had a legal obligation to keep any contact with clients confidential, didn't they? And surely he could find one with medical training in the Valles Dome.

With a slight feeling of desperation, Isaac used his data pad to access the public network again, this time pulling up a list of local businesses. Not surprisingly, a place like the Valles Dome seemed to create a lot of demand for psychiatrists and so Isaac was soon skimming through a long list of them. He noted several that had the qualifications he needed, some even operating as part-time medical practitioners, but one in particular caught his eye.

"Anya Polovski," he said, reading her name slowly.

Along with several medical qualifications, Ms. Polovski had more university degrees listed than the other four psychiatrists within walking distance combined.

"*She must have spent most of her life studying,*" Isaac thought with a frown.

But what surprised him even more was the fact Anya claimed to hold a PhD in parapsychology – the study of psychic abilities.

He hadn't thought about it before now, but it made sense that his mental condition might be related to the psychic experiment.

His opened Ms. Polovski's profile further and felt a shiver of recognition when he saw her picture. It was the same sad, beautiful woman from his vision.

"No way," Isaac muttered under his breath.

For the first time since waking in the Valles Dome, he wondered if his visions were actually a collection of premonitions, like the ones he'd experienced whilst escaping the screaming mother's apartment building.

"*God, I hope not,*" he thought, remembering the burning red sky.

But should he go to her? Should he make it a premonition and maybe ensure the rest of them would come true as well? He really didn't want to think about that final vision becoming real, but something inside him needed to know why he'd seen this woman, Anya Polovski.

Shaking his head, Isaac checked the local map and saw that she was operating out of an apartment on the twenty-second floor of a residential building only a few blocks away.

"*I guess I'd better get moving,*" he thought with a sigh.

As he built up the courage to re-join the human traffic streaming by him, Isaac expected another stressful journey through the Valles Dome, but what he experienced was actually quite different. The map quickly guided him off the main streets he'd been wandering and so the crowd actually thinned a little, allowing him to take more notice of the actual city. And being the first permanent colony to be established on Mars, the Valles Dome had more charismatic charm than he expected.

The original city was built in a simple grid-like pattern that extended all the way to the enormous dome that stretched across the canyon, but over the decades it had grown in an unorganised way that made each new area distinct. While some purposefully maintained the regular architecture of the original plans, others seemed to flaunt their quirky designs like a rare bird's plumage.

Dozens of brightly painted habitats hung precariously from the higher levels or simply jutted from the side of larger buildings, and nearly every time Isaac turned a corner, he was confronted with a new type of building façade. Some were painted with display microbes that streamed endless colourful advertisements while others seemed to want to show off the building's water reclamation and aquaponics set up, as if the entire side of the building was a giant, maze-like fish tank. Some were simply mirrored and highly polished, making Isaac wonder who might be looking at him from the other side, while several looked as if a bunch of school children had glued thousands of different coloured polymer sheets in a random pattern across the walls.

Staircases, both moving and static, seemed to appear out of nowhere and Isaac was consistently dumped on levels that had no similarity to the one he was just on. Vibrant plants and trees kept turning up in places that should not have been able to sustain them. like the corner of a ceiling, or a small gap between two sets of stairs, but every one of them looked lush and healthy, with some even bearing fruit that loud street vendors sold to the passing crowds.

When he finally reached his destination, Isaac found Ms. Polovski's building literally dripping with thick layers of moss and wondered for a moment if it was meant to regulate the temperature inside or simply scrub carbon dioxide from the air. But his throbbing brain quickly reminded him of why he was really here.

"*Get moving*," he thought with a frown.

Trudging up another well-lit staircase, he was surprised when he found the front door of Ms. Polovski's apartment wide open. He tentatively peered through it, wondering if she was about to go somewhere, and heard a voice call out from the back of the apartment.

"Come in, come in. And close the door behind you, please."

Isaac hesitated for a moment, wondering if he'd been mistaken for someone else, then a woman who looked just like Ms. Polovski's photo appeared in the main corridor and gestured him inside.

"I'm free," she said cheerily. "Well, not financially free, of course. Hah! So if you're here to see me professionally, please come in. If not, come in anyway and we'll have a cup of tea while you introduce yourself."

She was wearing a white, knitted cardigan over a long blue dress, and her straight, light blonde hair hung free, ending just past her shoulders.

"Ah," Isaac said uncertainly. "I've... come professionally."

"Yes, yes, very good," she said with a warm smile, "which, as I just mentioned, means you should come in and close the door."

Isaac realised he was still standing in the doorway and so he quickly stepped inside and shut the door behind him.

"Sorry," he said, feeling a little stupid.

"No need for apologies," she said, holding up a hand. "Not yet, anyway."

"Are you... Anya Polovski, the psychiatrist?"

"I am," she replied, "and you, young man, would like to remain anonymous."

"I, uh..." Isaac spluttered, taken completely by surprise.

"And I shall ensure you do," she continued with a knowing smile, "but I shall still require your name, for politeness sake, if nothing else."

"I'm... Isaac. Isaac Taylor."

"Very good," she said with a nod. "And you already know my name. Very pleased to meet you. Now, before we begin, let's talk about the contract for my services. I can either offer you a fixed rate of five thousand dollars-"

"Five thousand?" Isaac gasped.

"Or," she continued with a raised finger, "an hourly rate of two-hundred and fifty. In both contracts, my services will continue until you verbally end the session. In your case, I would highly recommend the fixed rate."

Isaac had to choke back a snort of indignation. Of course she would recommend the fixed rate. But even two-fifty an hour was steeper than he expected and he wasn't even sure she could help him yet.

"I think…" he said slowly, "I'll go with the hourly rate, thanks."

"Certainly," Anya replied, holding out a data pad she'd just pulled from a pocket, "please verify here, here, and here."

As she indicated the places she wanted Isaac to touch the screen, he took a moment to read through the contract. It was as simple as she'd already mentioned. He was procuring Ms. Polovski's services at an hourly rate of two-hundred and fifty dollars. The contract would remain binding until he verbally ended the session.

Certain he had no other choice, Isaac touched his index finger, middle finger, and thumb to the data pad, leaving a series of fingerprint, nerve, and capillary maps. Ms. Polovski then took it back and gestured toward the next room.

"Please, come through into the lounge and make yourself at home. Choose any seat you'd like. I'll be in the kitchen making some tea."

Isaac watched her stride back down the corridor and then tentatively stepped through the archway. The room beyond was large and contained five chairs, each completely different from the others. The floor beneath each of them was unique as well. Two were covered with different coloured carpet, one was tiled, another wood-panelled, and the last looked like polished concrete. Some of the spaces were smaller than the others and seemed a little cramped to Isaac's mind, so he chose a bench-like recliner that sat on a thick, grey carpet in the hopes it would be easier for Ms. Polovski to examine him.

As he walked toward it, he pulled the skull cap out of his pocket so it wouldn't dig into him when he sat down and placed it on a small table beside the recliner. He then probed the recliner's cushioning for a moment and turned to sit down.

"What the…?" he said in surprise.

The entire room had changed behind him. Now, rather than being segregated into six different areas, the entire room was decorated in the same distinctive style that he'd chosen.

"Ah," Ms. Polovski said, entering the newly furnished room with a tray full of different sized cups. "You've chosen, I see. Very good. Would you like some tea? I have pure green, strawberry, Chinese herbal, white, and traditional English breakfast."

"Uh… no tea, thanks," Isaac replied, confused at all the choices he was being given.

"Very well," Ms. Polovski said with a nod, placing the tray down on another side table. "Please lie down."

"Lie down?"

"If you'd like me to examine you, I need you to lie down."

Isaac stared at her with his mouth open. How did she know all this? Was she psychic as well?

"We're on your time, remember?" she reminded him with a smile.

"Oh," Isaac said, coming back to himself. "Yes. Okay."

As he lay down awkwardly, the change in elevation made his head throb again, and Isaac winced in pain.

"Hmmm…" Ms. Polovski said quietly, moving in close enough to lay a hand on his shoulder.

While Isaac tried to relax, she gently probed his neck and shoulder muscles before grasping one arm and moving it in a wide circle. She then did the same with his other arm, shone a small pen light in his eyes, and then looked into his ears and nose with a small tool. After that, she laid a hand on his forehead.

"Close your eyes, please," she said quietly.

Isaac did as she asked and, moments later, felt a calming sensation wash through him. The tension in his head immediately began to fade and the itching in his skull disappeared along with it. He noticed that beneath his pain, he'd been holding several muscles tense, but the calming sensation relaxed them just as quickly.

For a long moment, Isaac wallowed in silent contentment.

"Feeling better?" Ms. Polovski asked eventually.

"What… did you do?" he asked slowly.

"I cleansed your aura."

"My aura?"

"That's right. Your mind was panicking and you were feeling incredibly lonely."

"I..." Isaac began, but he stopped mid-sentence.

It was the perfect word to describe the strange feeling in his chest.

"Yes... I am feeling lonely," he said. "How did you know?"

"Aura's are quite sensitive to such things," Ms. Polovski replied with a knowing smile. "You'd be surprised what you can read in one. Tell me, Isaac, who is Jason?"

"He's... my brother," he said slowly, feeling suspicious again. "My twin brother. How did you know that?"

"Your twin?" Ms. Polovski said, raising her eyebrows. "Well, that explains a lot. May I ask how long it's been since he passed away?"

"Passed away?" Isaac said, abruptly sitting up. "Oh no, Jason isn't dead. He's just not here. He's back in Lynt City. I think I forgot to pay this month's network account and so I haven't been able to call him."

For a moment, Ms. Polovski gave him a sad look then her face firmed, her back straightened and her eyes sparkled in a menacing way.

"Denying the truth is unhealthy," she said in a hard, disapproving tone. "Your twin brother is gone, Isaac. You have to let him go."

"I'm... I'm not denying anything," Isaac protested, feeling intimidated in a way he'd never felt before. "My brother isn't dead, he's just... he just isn't here."

Ms Polovski's startling eyes glared at him a moment longer then they abruptly softened and her face returned to the friendly expression from earlier.

"I believe you, Isaac," she said with a smile. "Now please, tell me how you were separated."

Isaac stared at her for a moment, wondering if he'd imagined the sudden change in Ms. Polovski or if this was the one psychiatrist in the area more mentally disturbed than her patients.

"Uh... well, I'm not exactly sure what happened," he said slowly. "I think I've lost some memories."

"Go on," she prompted, sitting back.

"Well, my brother and I are..." Isaac paused, not sure he should be admitting this so soon.

"You're psychic," Anya finished for him, "as are most twins, to some degree."

"Well... yeah," Isaac agreed with a frown. "How did you-?"

"All twins share a psychic bond," she replied, as if it were obvious.

"Right," Isaac said uncertainly. He wasn't used to people believing it so readily "And so," he continued, "for the last twelve years we've been trying to engineer a device that can measure psychic energy."

"Hmmm..." Ms. Polovski mused.

"We thought we finally had it," Isaac added. "We theorized that psychic energy exists within a spectrum all of its own, like electromagnetic energy."

Isaac wasn't sure why he felt compelled to explain this to Ms. Polovski, but there was something about the look of genuine interest in her eyes that drew the words out of him.

"We believe all humans experience this energy in a similar way to the electromagnetic spectrum," he continued. "Just like the follicles in our eyes are sensitive to visible light, which allows us to see the world around us, we believe our minds are sensitive to the psychic spectrum. This allows us to both feel emotion and project it as well. Each emotion – love, hate, anger, fear, happiness – all exist at a specific level of energy along the psychic bandwidth, just like colours exist along the electromagnetic spectrum. Most humans can sense energies outside the emotional part of the spectrum, but very few understand it and even fewer have the ability to manipulate it. The ones who can are what we consider to be psychic."

"Very interesting," Ms. Polovski said. "And did you find a way to measure this psychic spectrum?"

"We did," Isaac replied. "At least... I think we did. Transforming psychic energy into a different medium that can be measured with traditional technology proved simple enough once we discovered a suitable mechanism. The real problem was causing a change in the psychic spectrum large enough to be measured. You see, just like we're constantly surrounded by a background of electromagnetic noise, so too is there a background of psychic energy. We're not sure where it comes from, but it makes resolving any change in the spectrum difficult. It's like trying to construct a hearing aid that can distinguish between the sounds you want to hear and everything else."

"So what did you do?"

"We did exactly what someone with a hearing aid would do," Isaac replied. "We asked the person talking to speak up."

"You found a way to boost your psychic signal?"

"That's right."

"How?"

"Ever heard of psychic crystals?" Isaac asked.

Ms. Polovski frowned slightly.

"I have," she said, clearly not a believer.

"Well they're not all just pretty rocks," Isaac assured her with a smile. "In fact, psychic crystals were the secret to both measuring the psychic spectrum and boosting our psychic signal. It took us a long time to work out how to use crystals to convert psychic energy into an electrical signal that could be measured, but after that, it was a simple matter of using the same mechanism in the opposite direction."

"You fed electricity back into the psychic link," Ms. Polovski said.

"That's right," Isaac confirmed. "The electrical energy was converted into psychic energy via psychically resonant crystals and then fed into our psychic link, boosting its energy above the background noise and allowing us to definitively measure it. It worked perfectly. Well... right up to the point that something went wrong."

"Tell me what happened," Ms. Polovski said with a serious expression.

And so Isaac explained The Game and how it had taken a bizarre turn, giving him strange visions and ending with him waking within the Valles Dome. He left out the part where he'd seen Ms.

Polovski's face, of course, but it felt good to finally get the whole episode out of his head. Without Jason around to talk it through with, the experience hadn't felt entirely real, until now.

"I don't even know if they were images of real events or places," he finished with a shrug, "or if they just came from my own imagination."

"Please," Ms. Polovski said slowly, "explain the visions you saw to me again."

"Actually, I can do better than that," Isaac said, turning to pick up the skull cap he'd placed on the side table. "Do you have a virtual window?"

"Of course," she replied with a nod.

"Well, if you don't mind me temporarily re-configuring it, I can show you what I saw."

"Hmmm," Ms. Polovski said with a nod. "Please do."

"Great," Isaac said, popping the skull cap inside out again. "This won't take long."

As he contemplated the task, Isaac found that he was looking forward to it. He never felt more in control than when he was fiddling with something mechanical and it was good to have a clear sense of direction again. He still had no idea what had happened to him, but Ms. Polovski was making him think it would all work itself out, eventually.

"*I'll find a way home, Jason*," he promised as she led him to her virtual window. "*Just you wait.*"

LOC BREEDEN STARED AT HIMSELF IN THE FLAWLESS executive washroom mirror.

It was an impressive sight. His dark, Gildon pinstripe suit shined as if it had just rolled off the production line and his silver shirt gleamed subtly behind a jet black tie. His perfectly tanned skin was as smooth as the spider silk of his shirt and, beneath his immaculate blonde hair, his beautiful facial structure exuded only confidence.

Loc always enjoyed this moment, just before public speaking, when his nerves flooded him with adrenalin. He already knew his presentation would be a resounding success. He was Cosmotech Defence's top business representative and his reputation as a diplomatic liaison was nothing short of legendary. But even his lofty role within Cosmotech Defence could not compare to the real power he commanded. Admittedly, this time he was announcing a project that would echo into the future with the momentum of trillions of dollars, but when you chose who lived and died on a daily basis and occasionally held the fate of entire nations in your hand, it just didn't stack up.

Allowing the sick chill of adrenalin to wash through him one more time, Loc flashed his warm, patented smile, kissed the chunky

61

red-stoned ring on the middle finger of his right hand, and then turned to the washroom door.

The adjoining boardroom was enormous. It was dominated by a curved walnut-brown table and behind it, through flawless, curved windows two stories high, lay the main street of Lynt City – Loc's current base of operations.

Seated around the table were carefully chosen representatives from Lynt City's most powerful organisations. These women and men were collectively responsible for managing its political, economic, and technological progress, and they would ultimately be the ones responsible for wringing as much profit out of today's announcement as possible.

Loc felt a sudden urge to laugh.

Every one of these fools believed it was their considerable influence that had ensured their presence in this room. But despite these illusions of grandeur, they were little more than pieces on a chessboard that spanned half the solar system and stretched back thousands of years.

"Ladies and gentlemen," Loc began, striding to the centre of the room. "Good morning and welcome. First, I'd like to begin by assuring you all that I am not here to sell you an idea. If you are present here today then you already understand that Mars will one day resemble Earth."

With a gesture, Loc activated his holographic slides and a large globe – its diameter almost as wide as he was tall – blinked into existence beside him. Through the sinuous white patterns of a dense cloud system, the globe shimmered with deep blue oceans that surrounded vast tracks of unfamiliar continents coloured green, yellow, and brown.

"Mars will, one day, have a viable atmosphere," Loc continued. "Its own weather systems. Vast swathes of prime agricultural lands and, of course, more cities. Cities that will rival even the largest and greatest of those on Earth. This future is inevitable, ladies and gentlemen. In fact, the only variable that matters is time."

With another gesture, Loc activated his slides and the shimmering globe suddenly lost its lustre and became the dull, rusty brown of a pre-colonised Mars. On his other side, a series of animated graphs appeared, displaying complex financial data. Then, with a final wave of his hand, Loc set a simulated time line in motion.

Gradually, the globe beside him began to change, showing signs of colonisation as the financial graphs rose and fell in turn, displaying associated resource costs, revenues, and share market prices.

"Piece by hard-won piece," he continued as terraformed areas were magnified and highlighted in green, "the human race has reclaimed the Martian airspace and flooded it with heat and life-giving oxygen. Progress, at first, was gradual to ensure reclamation remained both sustainable and profitable, but the Mars we know today was already being planned for. Innovation and industry leant their shoulder to the wheel and progress accelerated to a pace even the most clairvoyant of forecasters could not have predicted.

"And yet, despite the incredible achievements that have made our modern Mars possible, it is still the single most valuable resource we have that dictates the rate of future progress. Time."

Loc paused to look around the boardroom before continuing.

"Given current levels of technology, along with the most optimistic projections of future innovation, the dream of an Earth-like Mars is still centuries away. Beyond the lifetime of even the most well-preserved of us."

A murmur of amusement rolled through the room at this and Loc waited for it to subside before continuing.

"That, ladies and gentlemen, is what Cosmotech Defence has decided to change. Today you will learn how this future will be realised sooner. In *your* lifetime."

The murmur was much louder this time, a mixture of reactions that Loc glanced around quickly to gauge. He immediately recognised the calculated enthusiasm in some, the stubborn prudence in others, even the aggressive refusal to give anything away in a few, but all those present were now listening intently.

"Cosmotech Defence," he said loudly, the name activating a well-known logo that swept the financial data aside and took its place in sparkling high-definition. "As you all know, Cosmotech Defence has literally saved the human race on two scientifically proven and publicly accepted occasions. By redirecting the orbital paths of asteroids Calcius-four and D.Y. Seven-Eighty, Cosmotech averted global catastrophes that would have destroyed Earth's fragile atmosphere and – in all but the most optimistic of projections – led to the extinction of the human race.

"These incidents occurred more than sixty years ago, but I can assure you, ladies and gentlemen, Cosmotech has not been idle since. They have utilised the resources gifted to them by Earth's most grateful nations to perfect the technologies needed to find and efficiently deal with future threats. Because of this, our accumulated experience in manipulating the solar orbits of asteroids has increased substantially and the likelihood of a catastrophic impact is now all but impossible."

Again, Loc gave them a moment to let his words sink in.

"Ladies and gentlemen, the human race has never been in a better position to monitor and safeguard our homes on a system-wide scale."

With another gesture, the Cosmotech logo receded into the top right corner of Loc's presentation and a new set of financial tables and graphs appeared in its place. But rather than Mars, these were focussed on Cosmotech's impressive market history.

"Although publicly-funded at its core," he continued, "which helps to maintain transparency and keep all scientific discoveries within the public domain, Cosmotech Defence also has the authority to run commercially-funded projects. This has allowed many private contributors to drive innovation and, in many cases, capitalise on significant intellectual properties before they become public property."

There was another murmur at this point, just as Loc expected. During the colonisation of Mars, the issue of Intellectual Property rights had sparked heated international debate. Enforcing copyright laws across borders on Earth was hard enough, but doing so on another planet was thought to be near impossible. Many organisations operating on Mars had suffered financially due to the wide release of patent information that occurred during the first half-century of colonisation and Loc was well aware that Cosmotech's reputation around its handling of intellectual property would be seen as a significant advantage.

"With the demand for increasingly rare metals growing at astronomical rates, Cosmotech has helped mining conglomerates turn the once fictional process of asteroid mining into a lucrative business. We have assisted the International Space Agency in constructing wide-array telescopes in synchronous solar orbit, allowing us to see further into our universe than ever before. We have assisted universities in seventy-four separate Nations pioneer technologies that have led to remote exploration of Venus and Mercury, as well as more than half the moons around Jupiter and Saturn. We have even helped the I.S.A. anchor a research platform near the surface of the sun."

Loc didn't want to labour this point. He knew everyone in the room was aware of these achievements. He just wanted to make it clear that if anyone could achieve what he was about to reveal, it was Cosmotech Defence.

"But that is not why you're here today," he finished with a smile. "Whether you're familiar with these collaborations or not, it is Cosmotech's most recent actions that will define the future of Mars."

With another gesture, Loc made the financial data disappear and replaced it with something that no one outside of Cosmotech Defence had yet seen, something that resembled an enormous, glowing mass of light with a tail of gas that trailed out behind it in a web of intricate arcs.

"This, ladies and gentlemen, is the Vita Nova," he said after a suitable pause, "a hyperbolic comet that will pass through our solar system once, and once only. What you are looking at is actual footage of the Vita Nova captured by Cosmotech probes that have been orbiting the comet since it first entered the outer reaches of our solar system.

"The Vita Nova is the largest comet on record. Its core is roughly five-hundred-and-forty kilometres in diameter and it is made primarily of ammonia and water ice, with some traces of carbon dioxide. But that is not what you are seeing here. The icy core is tiny in relation to this image. What you are seeing is the comet's coma – a vast atmosphere of evaporated gases – and its tail – an immense body of gas that is evaporating off the icy core and being ionised by solar radiation so that it glows."

Loc gestured again and the glowing image began to shrink, bringing a representation of the solar system and its planets into view. The orbiting path of the Vita Nova was highlighted as a bright white curve and the planet Mars glowed red as the simulation moved forward in time.

"Given its initial trajectory, it was calculated many months ago that the Vita Nova would pass dangerously close to Mars, creating a thirteen percent chance of a collision. It was therefore decided that under the United Nations Impact Intervention act, 2089, that Cosmotech Defence would take measures to ensure such a collision would never take place. It was also decided that the Vita Nova's existence would be concealed from the general public."

Another murmur rose to fill the room and Loc had to lift his hands for silence.

"Please, ladies and gentlemen, I know you are wondering how Cosmotech Defence could possibly keep something like this a secret, both legally and logistically, but I can assure you all, the same legislation that gives us authority to prevent such a disaster also allows us to do so in the best interests of the human race, without consultation. And, as you will see, understanding the logistics of keeping this information secure is irrelevant when placed against the opportunity it has afforded you all."

The room quickly grew quiet at this and Loc smiled. As expected, there was not a person in this room who would not look past the moral ambiguity of Cosmotech's decision so they could focus on the advantage it provided them.

"While investigating solutions," Loc continued, "Cosmotech scientists realised that with a subtle change in the asteroid's solar orbit they could not only avoid a collision, but also create a situation where Mars would encounter a substantial amount of the frozen material left in the Vita Nova's wake."

The images floating next to Loc altered to show the comet's new orbit, and the animation ran through again, showing the alternative scenario he'd described.

"These frozen gases are the perfect ingredient for terraforming an atmosphere and by setting off a series of detonations on the comet's surface, Cosmotech Defence has ensured a much denser tail of frozen water, ammonia and carbon dioxide will soon intersect with Mars, saturating the atmosphere with billions upon billions of tonnes of the precious, terraforming material."

The simulation once more returned to Mars and a complex model of its atmosphere began to show the effects of the gaseous bombardment.

"Not only will this drastically alter the composition of Mars' atmosphere," Loc said as the scenario played out beside him, "it will also cause a rapid heating effect, which will speed up the terraforming process even further. All relevant data will be made available to you at the close of this presentation, but in short, in a projected thirty to seventy years, more than fifty-seven percent of Mars' unusable surface will be completely terraformed."

Gasps of disbelief followed the statement and, with a gesture, Loc caused the areas that would benefit most from the terraforming process to be highlighted. The eyes of those present immediately lit up in turn. This was where the true profit resided. In land rights, development contracts, and foreknowledge of which parts of Mars would eventually become the most valuable.

"The terraforming process will not require any evacuation of already established cities," Loc continued smoothly, "and the projected impact on the mining sector is negligible. Growth will be the only hard-to-predict side effect. It is this privileged information, ladies and gentlemen, that you have purchased here today. The news of Cosmotech's third successful mission to save a human planet will not be released for several months, leaving you all a generous window to determine in what way, and how rapidly, you will allow your planet to grow and prosper. Thank you for your attention."

To finish, Loc smiled his winning smile and bowed, allowing a sudden, warm applause to wash over him. As expected, his audience had been well and truly won over, which was not at all surprising given he'd just outlined a future in which they would likely gain power and wealth beyond anything they'd dared to imagine.

When he eventually rose from his bow, Loc took a moment to enjoy the new, calculated expressions among his audience. Many of them had played their best hand to win the opportunity to be part of this new game and were just starting to realise that the only players that now mattered were the others in this room. He could already see them sizing each other up, assessing potential alliances and rivals. Whilst they were still in this boardroom, there was no opportunity to communicate with anyone outside, but Loc was sure that once the meeting was done, the bloodletting would begin. His smile widened. He looked forward to witnessing the next stage of play.

He lifted his hands for silence, ready to fire the starting pistol, but was interrupted by a warning pain in the back of his neck.

"*Damn it,*" he thought in irritation. "*What can they want now?*"

It was the worst timing, but there was nothing he could do about it. This was one disruption he could not ignore.

"As promised, you will all be issued with secure data files containing Cosmotech's best projections," he said quickly over the last of the dying applause. "If you have any questions, please follow the security protocols provided with the files and submit them directly to Cosmotech's Lynt City offices. I look forward to assisting you in any way I can. Thank you for your attention."

Loc could see there were delegates who were hoping to speak to him immediately and he noted them in his mind. But for now, he had other, far more important matters to attend to and so he gave them only a cursory nod before striding out of the room.

He kept his smile firmly in place until he was out of sight then he let it disappear as he crossed the corridor to an unassuming door. At his approach, it slid open silently and then sealed behind him with a series of heavy, whirring noises that suggested it was well and truly secure.

Inside was a large desk that Loc immediately sat behind and placed his hands on to steady himself. The red stone in his ring seemed to glint with an inner light then the pain in his neck spiked and the room was momentarily obscured by a flash of white.

The light persisted for a moment and then faded to reveal three distinct figures standing on the opposite side of the desk, all staring at Loc with frighteningly serious expressions.

To those few who were even aware they existed, they were known as the *Triumvirate* and they were the real power behind Cosmotech Defence, along with an unknown number of other organisations. Although they rarely controlled things directly, the Triumvirate were so well connected that they appeared almost clairvoyant when it came to financial and political situations. They also used their incredible predictive powers to great effect, manipulating the markets as easily as they did their enemies to ensure that their interests were always satisfied first.

For his expert, loyal and devoted service, Loc had been promised an eventual place among them, but his impatience sometimes got the better of him. To be fair, he already commanded a position of considerable power, but it was nothing compared to what he would wield once he ascended to the ranks of the Triumvirate.

At the moment, the three figures appeared to be standing only a few metres away, but Loc knew their real location could be anywhere in the solar system. The high-tech implant that had just caused him so much pain used a kind of quantum entanglement to allow for instantaneous communication and it was hooked directly into his brain, which meant he would see the Triumvirate whenever they wished an audience. Thankfully, that was not a common occurrence.

"Triumvirate," he said, taking a deep breath. "I've just finished my presentation. The negotiations are proceeding as planned."

"We are aware," said the tallest of the three, known only as the Second. He was a hulking figure dressed in a suit similar to Loc's and he had long, jet black hair, piercing brown eyes, and a square, closely shaved jaw. "Your work, as always, has been exemplary."

"Thank you," Loc replied with a small bow of his head.

"There is something else that requires your attention," the man to his left added. He was known as the Third – a slender figure dressed in some kind of advanced survival suit that revealed a head with spiked red hair and a goatee as sharp as his green-eyed gaze.

Loc disliked the Third immensely and was sure the feeling was mutual. He never let his feelings show, of course, but he'd always found the man to be overly suspicious. Perhaps it was Loc's imminent ascension to the Triumvirate – he could only hope – but the Third never had any words of praise for him.

"Of course," Loc replied with a nod.

"Doctor Rashid Indari has been found," the Second said.

Loc looked at him in surprise.

"How is that possible?" he asked with a frown.

"Is that not a question we should be asking you?" the Third said with narrowed eyes.

"Enough," the woman standing next to him barked in a disapproving tone.

The Third turned to offer her an ingratiating smile and then returned his accusing stare to Loc.

The woman who'd shut him down was the First – the highest ranking of the three and, in Loc's experience, the one with the least patience. She was more than a head shorter than the other two and her graceful features were framed by a black, traditional burka.

Her light brown eyes bore into him with more fire than the other two combined and she rarely spoke, which Loc found quite agreeable. But when she did, it was always to say something important that usually had undesirable implications attached.

"What would you have me do?" he asked.

"Take steps to ensure any investigation ends quickly," the Second replied firmly.

"Immediately," Loc agreed.

"There is also a woman," the Third added, his sneer and pointed goatee making him look slightly demonic. "She must not be allowed to find the truth. Any truth."

"A woman?" Loc said, a little confused.

"Forensic detective Miana Raiken," the First added, her piercing eyes boring into him.

A forensic detective. That certainly added some clarification to their anger. From what he already knew of the situation, Loc was confident the details of Dr. Indari's death were no threat to the Triumvirate. But if they were worried about this detective then it was clear he wasn't privy to all the relevant facts.

"What truth does she seek?" he asked carefully.

"None you need to be aware of," the Third replied smugly.

"She works with the Lynt City Police Department," the Second added. "Do whatever is necessary to close down her investigation and ensure no progress is made. This is a delicate time. We cannot afford any surprises."

"I... understand," Loc said with a nod.

"I suggest you do more than understand," the Third added.

"The detective will be dealt with immediately," Loc replied, holding back his irritation.

"Very well," the Second replied. "We will be watching."

And with that, the three figures flickered once and were gone.

71

The pain at the base of Loc's neck immediately eased and he blinked several times before sitting back.

The Triumvirate were never the most pleasant of conversationalists, but this time it was clear they were concerned about this forensic detective.

"Miana Raiken," he said, locking the name in his memory. "Well, detective, let's see if you've made any progress and hope, for both our sakes, that you haven't."

DET. RAIKEN EXITED ANOTHER GLEAMING OFFICE building and climbed into the police vehicle that waited for her. Her investigation into the symbols was not going well. All the experts she'd visited so far had found them extremely interesting, but none had any idea what they might mean.

Frowning in exasperation, Det. Raiken turned to the last address on her list and saw that it was several levels up and five blocks away. She activated the route with a touch of her finger and then sat back and closed her eyes as the vehicle pulled away from the curb.

Since she was authorised to travel in emergency lanes, it didn't take her vehicle long to zip past the slower moving traffic, curve up a few smooth ramps and then coast to a stop outside a large residential building.

According to Det. Raiken's data pad, this final linguist was an expert in some of the more obscure languages used by minority populations on Mars. He'd also published dozens of papers on the artistic depictions left behind by ancient cultures.

"I just hope he can shed some light on this," she thought as she climbed out of the vehicle.

As with all single proprietor businesses that didn't require access to special infrastructure, the linguist's office was also his residence. The small community he lived in wasn't exactly bustling, but there were several signs of life. Some children played in a padded gaming area beside the community's local aquaponics garden. A few parents chatted as they harvested fruits and vegetables, but there wasn't much pedestrian traffic, not that Det. Raiken expected any at this time of day.

Weaving through the communal area, she eventually stopped in front of the linguist's door and touched the clean white surface. A viewing screen immediately blinked to life at its centre and, not long after, a respectable looking bearded man in his fifties appeared.

"Yes, may I help you?" he said, squinting at her.

"Good afternoon, Professor Meiket. My name is Miana Raiken, forensic detective with the Lynt City Police Department. May I have a moment of your time, please?"

"Yes, of course, come in," he said with a wave of his hand.

He moved off screen for a moment and the door opened with a faint *whirrrr*.

Det. Raiken stepped through into a small foyer that was typical of Lynt City. It had been years since there'd been a dome breach, but all new residences were still required to install a basic airlock at the entrance, just in case.

When the first door shut behind her, a second door opened on the other side and the first thing Det. Raiken noticed was the smell. It registered as dust, slightly organic, and took her a few seconds to recognise.

"*Paper,*" she thought to herself. "*Old paper.*"

Like Dr. Indari, the linguist seemed to either make use of the old method of writing, or perhaps he owned a lot of written material. When she moved into the inner office, Det. Raiken saw that both assumptions were probably true. The walls were covered in sheets of paper that were in turn covered with symbols written in a myriad of inks and styles, including many that looked like they'd been carved into stone or wood. There were also several charts that looked like alphabets of some kind, but the letters were completely unfamiliar.

"Welcome detective," the Professor said, standing with a smile and gesturing to a chair on the other side of his desk, "what can I do for you?"

"I'm hoping you can help me identify some symbols found at a crime scene," Det. Raiken explained as she sat.

"Of course," Meiket agreed, looking interested. "I'll do my best."

Det. Raiken handed him her data pad and Meiket looked over the symbols Lance had catalogued for several minutes without speaking. They were only black and white approximations, rather than images of the Dr. Indari's carved flesh, but even without the blood Det. Raiken thought they looked sinister.

"May I ask where these symbols were found?" Meiket said, looking up at her.

"I'm sorry, but that information is classified," Det. Raiken replied.

"I understand," Meiket said with a calculating look, "carved into someone's flesh, were they?"

Det. Raiken frowned. He was the first linguist she'd interviewed to reach that conclusion.

"Why do you say that?" she asked carefully.

"The strokes clearly indicate carved symbols, not brushed or scrawled," he replied, looking a little smug, "and given the varying width of each stroke, I merely guessed that flesh was the carving medium."

Det. Raiken stared at him, at a complete loss for words.

Meiket chuckled lightly. "I can see that I'm correct, but I should confess to having an unfair advantage. You see, I've seen this type of ritual mutilation before."

"Ritual mutilation?"

"Yes. Messy business, I'm afraid. Several ancient human cultures believed that carving the words spoken by their pagan gods into the flesh of sacrificial victims gave the inscriptions power. The ceremonies were usually undertaken to appease a god's wrath, give their priests special powers, ensure productive crops, that sort of thing."

"Do you recognise these symbols?"

"I'm afraid not," Meiket replied, turning back to the data pad. "Not from memory at least. But there are familiarities in the text that I can't quite put my finger on. May I run this through my personal database?"

"Of course," Det. Raiken said, retrieving her data pad for a moment so she could authorise the transfer.

When Meiket took the data pad back, he placed it beside him and then swept a hand across his desk. The movement initiated the download and a thin, transparent screen the length of his desk rose between them. As the download continued, Meiket tapped his fingers across a glowing keyboard that appeared in front of him and squinted at the screen.

"There's certainly no modern text that fits the patterns seen here," he said, studying information that Det. Raiken couldn't see from her side of the screen. "But there may be some ancient languages that…"

At this point, his voice abruptly trailed into silence and Det. Raiken's instincts flare.

"*He's found something,*" she thought, before saying out loud, "you found a match?"

"Please," Meiket said, holding up a hand.

Det. Raiken noticed some of the colour had drained from his face, but she allowed him to continue without comment. Something had certainly unnerved the linguist and he was now tapping furiously against his keyboard. He continued this way for several minutes then the screen between them suddenly slid back into the desk.

He sighed, shook his head, and pushed Det. Raiken's data pad across the desk.

"I'm afraid the symbols mean nothing," he said, looking more in control than he had a moment earlier. "There are some superficial similarities to ancient Egyptian and Mayan – I've referenced them in my analysis – but I don't believe they warrant further investigation.

Although at first glance these symbols appear to be part of a single language, it is my professional opinion that they're a fabrication with no link to any legitimate human culture."

"*He's lying,*" Det. Raiken thought immediately.

"I'm lacking some context due to the classified nature of your crime scene," Meiket continued, clasping his hands before him, "but I'd wager whoever created these symbols was either not in their right mind, or deliberately trying to confuse you. Is there anything else you'd like me to look at?"

"No," Det. Raiken replied.

"Then if you'll excuse me, I have work to attend to," Meiket finished, standing up.

"I do have one more question," Det. Raiken replied, staying in her seat.

"Yes?" Meiket replied with a frown.

"Why are you lying to me?"

At this, Meiket eyes narrowed and his face paled again, but he returned her stare without flinching.

"I'm not lying."

"Yes, you are," Det. Raiken replied calmly, "and I'd like to know why."

"I've given you my professional opinion, detective," Meiket continued coldly, "as you requested. Now I'm afraid I must ask you to leave."

"Afraid," Det. Raiken repeated, nodding. "You're a hard man to read, Professor Meiket, but I believe that's exactly what you are. What are you afraid of?"

Meiket leaned forward, placing his fists on the desk.

"I asked you to leave," he said with a glare.

Det. Raiken matched his gaze firmly. She'd stared down dozens of sociopaths before and even a psychopath once. Meiket was good – given her assumption that he was neither – but she was better.

After a long, awkward silence, he eventually leaned backward again and looked away. For a moment Det. Raiken hoped he'd find an excuse to tell her the truth, but instead he snatched her data pad off the desk and thrust it toward her.

"The only thing I'm afraid of, detective, is you wasting my time," he said firmly. "Now please, do I need to ask you again?"

Det. Raiken stared at him a moment longer then she calmly took the data pad and rose to her feet.

"Very well, Professor Meiket, but if you should change your mind-"

"I know where to find you," Meiket finished for her.

Allowing him to usher her to the door, Det. Raiken wondered what could instil such fear in a clearly strong-willed man.

"*Something serious,*" she concluded silently.

As soon as she was through the airlock foyer, Meiket closed the door without another word and Det. Raiken turned to stare at the white surface. Before leaving, she paused to read through Meiket's report, but it appeared to be little more than a carefully fabricated lie.

"Useless," she growled beneath her breath.

She returned her gaze to Meiket's door and contemplated pushing him further, but soon thought better of it. She still had to get back to the precinct station and, besides, it would do Meiket good to sit and stew on whatever had frightened him.

"*I'll be back, Professor Meiket,*" she promised before turning to leave. "*And I'll find out what's got you so scared.*"

MARS ORBIT - June 5, 2147 - 9.09am

SABIAN GLANCED AT THE VIEW THROUGH THE COCKPIT window of his re-entry vehicle. It was a beautiful. Mars was stretched out beneath him in a great ochre curve and it contrasted sharply with the grey-blue corona of sky that traced the edge of space.

He enjoyed seeing the world at this altitude, where the curvature of the planet reinforced the divine perfection that occurred at such cosmic scales. And yet, it also made him lament his place in the order of things.

The same divine perfection seen here was duplicated on the microscopic scale, in the flawless design of insects or the crystalline structure of a rock. But so much of the natural world as seen from the perspective of a human was clumsy, dirty, and chaotic. The same insects, so beautiful when seen through a microscope, were little more than buzzing, biting carriers of disease. The same incredible crystalline structures in rock were nothing but dirt, mud, and sand that clogged, abraded, and choked.

It had always puzzled him. God's plan was sacrosanct, of course, but Sabian was certain that if humans could witness the order and beauty of his creations with their own woefully inadequate eyes, the endless millennia of struggle and sin that had brought them to this end could have been avoided.

As his re-entry vehicle reached the edge of Mars' thin, gaseous troposphere, the view began to glow a distinct orange and Sabian prepared himself. Like the social disorder he so often witnessed in news reports, he despised the violence of re-entry. It was only by studying the data his ship was collecting that he managed to endure it. He assessed approach vectors, checked hull integrity, and scrutinised fuel reserves, filling his mind with the ordered calm of information and ignoring the turbulence that shook the cabin.

Eventually, when his speed had been sufficiently drained, the view cleared once more and Sabian looked up to see the Valles Dome gleaming in the distance. The terrain surrounding the enormous canyon city was chaotic and untamed, but the Dome itself was a shining symbol of God's order as realised through the mind of man. It was a modern marvel of engineering and a triumph of science over nature.

"*If only those within could emulate such order,*" he thought with a scowl.

Focussing once more on the data displayed on his console, Sabian angled his descent so the vehicle would glide toward the runway perched on one side of the canyon. The spaceport towers made contact with his guidance computers and it took only a moment to verify his identity before he was allocated a landing zone.

He purposefully maintained control of his descent until the landing wheels touched down with barely a screech of friction then he allowed the spaceport computers to take over and taxi him toward a hanger.

Sabian unbuckled himself and moved to the back of the cockpit. The small suitcase of equipment he'd brought with him waited at the exit, secured neatly to the wall and he unclasped it with a deft movement. He then ran a finger across the front, making the case transparent so he could confirm the contents.

Most of it was communications equipment that would allow him to maintain a connection with the satellite he'd just left, but there was also a small array of engineering tools and his coffee machine. Everything else he needed was already in his head.

Satisfied that everything was in order, Sabian returned the suitcase to the wall and grasped the transparent head gear secured next to it. It fit neatly over his ears and nose like a custom pair of sunglasses and when he touched the side of the lens a head up display, or HUD, blinked instantly to life. Tiny cameras in the casing began to track his eyes, calculating his focal point, while a small sensor array measured his surroundings and sent the data directly to his HUD.

In moments, measurements of temperature, distance, composition and more were arrayed neatly over anything Sabian looked at and he quickly glanced around the cockpit to make sure it was calibrated correctly. He then turned back to the exit and grasped the cross at his throat, waiting for the short tone that would indicate he'd arrived.

"Dear Lord," he prayed silently, *"walk with me in this time of need. Give me the strength to endure the failings of the sinful and grant me the courage to see Your will done. Amen."*

As his silent prayer was concluded, the tone he was waiting for sounded and the pressurized doors opened with a *hiss*. Sabian paused to tuck the cross carefully beneath his jacket then he retrieved his suitcase and walked through the short connecting corridor.

The small waiting room on the other side contained little more than a large tray beside another door and when Sabian placed his suitcase on it, a small conveyer belt carried it through the wall. The door beside the tray opened onto another short corridor and this one hummed and flashed several times as Sabian walked through it, scanning him for harmful biological agents and inorganic contraband.

The door at the far end of the corridor opened smoothly as he approached and Sabian was greeted by a security detail, five strong. He already knew their names and was familiar with the service records for each man. He'd skimmed their psych evaluations, physical attributes, educational history, even their political affiliations and hobbies on his way down to the planet. But despite an impressive list of credentials, he still didn't feel comfortable trusting them with the mission he'd been given.

Their leader, security Chief Hadrian Levine, was a tall, impassive man. His service record was close to flawless and the few failures he'd presided over would have been much worse if it weren't for his professional conduct. He was a sinner, of course – someone with such symmetrical features would no doubt have given into carnal temptation long ago – but Sabian didn't require men with a gift for abstinence. He needed men who would carry out his orders without question.

"Link your data feed with my personal node," he said sharply.

"Yes, sir," the security Chief replied.

As the data feed coming from the head gear of each officer linked with Sabian's, a small icon in his HUD blinked brighter. He was now able to remotely view what the officers were seeing and make use of any data they collected. It was the most productive way of communicating without having to actually speak to anyone, and Sabian wished he could do this with everyone he came into contact with.

"You will wear light armour and dynamic jumpsuits at all times," he told the Chief. "I will determine the uniforms we are seen in."

"Yes, sir," the Chief replied smartly.

"*Very good,*" Sabian thought to himself.

He disliked discussing the reason behind orders, or anything else for that matter. These men were simply tools to be used and any other kind of conversation always made Sabian feel anxious.

"Have you prepared my communications hub?"

"Yes, sir. The hub has been constructed and calibrated to your exact specifications. The vehicle for transport is waiting as planned."

"Very good," Sabian said, out loud this time, before turning toward the customs officer that had appeared behind him.

"Your luggage, sir," she said, wheeling his suitcase forward on a trolley.

Sabian took it without comment. As expected, his entry had gone smoothly and the illegal contents of his suitcase had not raised any alarms. He nevertheless checked to make sure nothing had been touched.

While he was ticking off items in his mind, Sabian placed the customs officer carefully within the intricate network of spies and corrupted officials that allowed him to move freely through Mars' cities. She didn't know who he was, or what his purpose might be, but she'd been chosen carefully and paid well. She was but a tiny cog in a much larger machine that didn't place much reliance on her, but it was gratifying to see she was nevertheless turning with precision.

As soon as he was satisfied that everything was in order, Sabian gave her a stiff nod and turned to the security Chief.

"I'm ready," he said simply.

In reply, the security Chief turned smartly to his team and barked an order.

"Departure formation!"

The officers immediately broke the line and formed up around Sabian in a tight square.

"Move out!" the security Chief ordered.

As they officers moved forward, Sabian allowed his stride to mimic the four men surrounding him and let the illusion that they were moving as one calm his hungry mind.

"While I'm working you will be ready to move out at a moment's notice," he told the security Chief.

"Yes, sir," he replied, before turning to lead them down another empty corridor.

"I will not be sleeping until I've found what we are looking for. Neither will you."

"Yes, sir."

"There will be no room for error. Disobedience will incur a forty percent drop in commission. Failure will incur immediate dismissal and a loss of your security licence."

"I… understand, sir."

The slight hesitation in the security Chief's reply grated against Sabian's thoughts, but he let it pass without comment. He was going to have to get used to the lack of precision inherent in the communication and behaviour of others.

Their route took them through several more deserted corridors that had been cleared specifically for Sabian's arrival and ended at a freight elevator that would ferry them past the crowds that filled the spaceport.

Sabian took in a deep, calming breath before moving inside. He didn't like being in such a confined space with other people and his anxiety was slowly rising.

Thankfully, the trip was short and the security officers remained silent and almost perfectly still – one of the requirements of their contract. From there, the small group only had to traverse a few more corridors before they emerged into the Valles Dome from a secluded exit that was nowhere near the main entrance.

Sabian paused as he entered the alleyway and turned to scowl at the mass of humans that churned past the far end. The smell out here was quite different to what he was used to. No longer was he in a controlled, sterile environment. Here he was sharing air with the sinful and breathing in skin cells cast off by the unworthy.

Resisting an urge to cover his nose and mouth with his hand, Sabian simply held his breath and looked away from those he was here to save. He couldn't block out the inane chatter that echoed down the alley, but it helped to focus on the fluctuating decibel level and E.Q. meter that translated the sound in his HUD.

As the security Chief had assured him, a vehicle waited just beyond the exit and Sabian quickly ducked through its side door. Then, when the door closed behind him and the decibel meter was flat once again, he took in a deep, measured breath.

No light from outside was allowed to penetrate the windows and Sabian revelled in the clean, filtered air and blessed silence of the darkness. The last of his anxiety soon faded along with the noise and so he opened his suitcase, took out a small signal router and placed it in a socket beside his chair. With the router in place, the vehicle's internal communications array was activated and a virtual screen stretching the width of the vehicle lit up before him. Two keyboard panels blinked into life on the armrests either side of him and Sabian looked them over with a critical eye before sitting back to calibrate the data now flowing across the screen.

It was already set out just as he'd requested, but his brief encounter with humanity had reminded Sabian just how unaccustomed to change his time alone had made him. If he was going to succeed – and there was no alternative – then he would have to prepare himself in every way possible.

"I will not fail You, Lord," he promised as he felt the gentle pull of acceleration. "I will find the Messiah and Your ultimate will shall finally be done."

PRIVATE RESIDENCE, VALLES DOME - June 5, 2147 - 10.08am

ISAAC FOUND THAT DISMANTLING MS. POLOVSKI'S virtual window was almost as good as meditation. Getting his hands dirty had always been what he did best and, even better, this kind of work never required input from Jason. His twin brother was more of an organised thinker, better at making decisions and remembering important details Isaac forgot. But when it came to pulling things apart and putting them back together again, Isaac was king.

When he eventually managed to reconfigure the virtual window and connect it to P.A.T.R.I.C.'s skull cap, Ms. Polovski was waiting patiently with another tray of tea, this time with a selection of cookies as well.

"Thanks," Isaac said, taking a large chocolate-chip cookie and biting into it hungrily. He was famished. "Uh..." he said carefully, trying not to spray crumbs, "how long have I been at this?"

"Three-hundred-and-twenty dollars," Ms. Polovski said firmly.

"Oh, right. No worries," Isaac said, recognising her serious face again. "Well, we'd better get started then."

After hastily tipping some herbal tea down his throat, Isaac put down the cup, wiped his hands on his shirt, and pulled the skull cap over his head. The virtual window flickered for a moment as the connection was made then a blue wave shimmered across its surface, saturating the screen.

"Okay," he said slowly. "I'm going to show you what I saw based on my memories."

"Memories are easily altered," Ms. Polovski warned.

"Sure," Isaac agreed, "but I'm no beginner at this. They'll be accurate, trust me."

Ms. Polovski nodded, though she still looked unconvinced, and Isaac began the process of projecting his memories onto the screen.

At first, the screen's surface simply rippled like a pond in the rain, then shapes began to appear and his first vision swam into focus.

A dark, water-filled cavern, lit by a strange red light.

Given this was the first time he'd seen the image outside his own head, Isaac was surprised when he realised the red glow was coming from the cavern walls themselves. He reached further into his memories to try and focus the image and saw that the light was coming from some kind of writing etched into the rocky surface.

"Do you recognise this place?" Ms. Polovski asked him.

"No, I don't think so," Isaac replied. "I remember visiting the Wombeyan caves near Lynt City when I was, like, seven, but it didn't look anything like this."

"What does the writing on the wall say?"

Isaac focussed on the strange writing and tried to resolve the image further, but the letters remained stubbornly blurred.

"I don't know," he said with a frown. "But this place feels... well, *real*. It doesn't feel like something I made up."

"Interesting," Ms. Polovski replied. "What came next?"

Isaac took a moment to capture an image of the cave then he thought back to the next vision he'd seen.

"Oh," he said, realising it was the image of Ms. Polovski, looking sad, but beautiful.

"What is it?" she asked.

"Nothing," Isaac lied, "this next one is just kind of... boring."

Quickly moving on to the next vision, Isaac pictured the unfamiliar bedroom that had flashed through his mind and took a moment to study it along with Ms. Polovski.

"A woman's bedroom," she said after a moment.

"Really?" Isaac said. "How can you tell?"

"Those clothes draped on the edge of the bed," she replied, "stockings and a skirt, if I'm not mistaken."

Isaac focussed on the clothes and saw that she was right.

"You don't know this place either?" Ms. Polovski guessed.

"Not at all," Isaac replied.

"Hmmm," Ms. Polovski mused. "Well, the architecture doesn't look like anything built in the Valles Dome. It's too clean. If I had to guess, I'd say it was somewhere in Lynt City."

"Really?" Isaac said, not sure what that might mean.

"Possibly," Ms. Polovski replied non-committedly. "What did you see after that?"

Feeling a little let down, Isaac once again saved a copy of the unfamiliar bedroom and then delved into his memories once more to pull out the next, and arguably most bizarre, vision.

A starry sky, with a single, red streak pulsing at the centre.

"Well," Ms. Polovski said, sounding impressed. "That will be useful."

"What do you mean?" Isaac asked.

"We have the stars to guide us," she replied, gesturing toward the image. "They can tell you a lot if you know how to read them."

Isaac hoped she wasn't talking about Astrology, but decided not to say anything. He didn't want to offend her if he could help it.

"We can come back to that," she added. "What did you see next?"

"Right," Isaac agreed, before taking another screen capture and moving on the next vision.

This one was the vast green landscape seen from far above, as if he were floating several kilometres above the Earth. But even now, with the whole thing displayed before him on the virtual window, Isaac couldn't work out where on Earth this could be.

"I've never seen terrain like that before," Ms. Polovski said after a moment.

"Neither have I," Isaac admitted. "I guess this one can't be real."

"Not necessarily," Ms. Polovski said thoughtfully, "but it may require further analysis by someone with the necessary skills. Did you see anything else?"

At the question, Isaac felt an ominous shiver run through him.

"There's… one more vision," he said reluctantly.

"Show me," Ms. Polovski prompted.

But Isaac didn't want to see it again. He could still remember the terrible pain and emotion that had bombarded him the last time. And, if he were being honest, he wasn't sure he wanted a better view of what was in it.

"The more it upsets you, the more important it's likely to be," Ms. Polovski said gently.

Isaac looked up at her, realising she was probably reading him like a book, and found himself resenting her for it. He didn't like this feeling of weakness and fear, but it was far worse knowing that a complete stranger was aware of it before he'd even had a chance to share it with Jason.

"*Don't be an idiot,*" he admonished himself, pushing the resentment away. "*She's only trying to help. Just get it over with already.*"

And so, with a deep breath, Isaac reluctantly reached into his memories and tried his best to recreate the searing red light that had consumed him.

As it appeared on the virtual window, an echo of the violent emotions that had swept him away last time washed through Isaac's mind. Thankfully, the emotions weren't as potent this time, but when he tried to save an image of the red light from his memories, it shifted on the screen as if it was alive.

"I… can't seem to resolve it," he said with a frown. "There's something interacting with the sig-"

But before he could finish, the screen suddenly flashed white and Isaac squinted in alarm. He held a hand up to block out some of the glare and then gasped when the last thing he expected appeared in the centre of the virtual window.

"Jason?" he said, staring at the unmistakable face of his brother.

"Isaac... can you hear me?"

"Jason! What the hell, bro? I can hear you! I can-"

"Isaac? Something... wrong. You... where..."

For some reason, Jason's words were cutting in and out, as if he were calling through a bad radio connection.

"Jason!" Isaac said, moving closer to the screen. "I'm in the Valles Dome! I don't know how I got here and... I tried to call you, but the number's out of service!"

Instead of answering, Jason's image faded in and out of focus, but Isaac could tell his brother hadn't heard him. Desperation took hold and he tried to communicate telepathically instead, but there was only a cold emptiness where he would usually sense his brother.

"Move your lips, you idiot!" he shouted, slamming his fist against the screen. "Then at least I can play this back and work out what you're saying!"

"Don't... do..." Jason's crackling voice stuttered.

The image on the screen kept flickering out of focus, as if the signal were losing strength, then Isaac saw his brother turn away a moment before he disappeared altogether.

"No!" he barked, slamming his fist into the screen again.

He knew he was missing Jason, but it wasn't until he saw his brother like this that he realised just how much. All he could think about now was what would happen if he never saw Jason again and it made him hammer the screen again and again, his eyes welling with tears.

After a moment, he felt hands pulling him away from the virtual window and didn't have the strength to fight them. He barely noticed the arms that folded around him as he cried, but he heard soft soothing noises above him and eventually realised it was Ms. Polovski.

He looked up at her, his cheeks burning with embarrassment, and felt a shiver of recognition when he saw her expression. It was an exact copy of the sad, beautiful face he'd seen in his vision.

"*The first vision to come true,*" he thought in horror.

The shock of it seemed to pull the grief out from under him and Isaac quickly wiped the tears from his burning cheeks.

"I'm... sorry," he said, gently shrugging her off and getting to his feet.

"Don't be," she assured him in a soft voice. "You just had an extremely distressing experience, Isaac. Crying is a very healthy reaction."

But whether she was right or not, Isaac still felt like an idiot and he couldn't help but imagine her judging him with a cold psychiatrist's mind.

"I don't know what's going on," he said, sitting down in a chair and pulling the skull cap from his head. "I don't know how Jason could have contacted me from Lynt City. Not this way."

"You're assuming it was real," Ms. Polovski said quietly.

Isaac looked up at her, wondering if she was joking.

"Of course it was real... wasn't it?"

"Please correct me if I'm wrong," she began calmly, "but you were creating these images from your memories, were you not?"

"Well, yeah," Isaac replied, seeing where she was going, "but I didn't make that part up. It just... came out of nowhere. I mean, why would I create an image of Jason anyway?"

"The conscious and subconscious minds are often misaligned," Ms. Polovski offered with a shrug, "and we're far more proficient at lying to ourselves than we are to others. You have no memory of what happened after the experiment, which suggests that something quite traumatic may have occurred."

Isaac could see where she was headed and didn't like it at all.

"My brother isn't dead," he snapped angrily.

"He's just not here," Ms. Polovski added, repeating what Isaac had said earlier.

Hearing the words coming from someone else made Isaac realise just how pathetic they sounded.

"*Could I be wrong?*" he thought wretchedly.

He truly didn't want to believe his brother could have died, but given the strange things he'd experienced recently – waking in a stranger's house on the other side of Mars; precognitive visions; seeing Jason appear in a virtual window – how could he know anything for sure?

"I don't want to talk about this," he said out loud. "I just... can't, okay?"

"Okay," Ms. Polovski agreed calmly. "Let's focus on your visions then. Thankfully, I have a friend who can help us with that."

"Oh really?" Isaac said in a sarcastic tone. "And how much do they charge?"

Ms Polovski laughed lightly at this and laid a hand on his shoulder.

"Would you like to end our session?" she asked. "All you have to do is say the words, Isaac."

As he looked into her eyes Isaac was sorely tempted to, but he didn't want to try solving this on his own. And, as quirky as Ms. Polovski might be, she was a lot better than no help at all.

"I'm sorry," he apologised with a sigh, "I didn't mean to-"

"Oh, you did," she assured him with a smile, "but I'm made of tougher stuff than that, Isaac. And it's just another normal, human reaction, if not quite so healthy this time."

"Alright," he said, resigned to the fact he was stuck with her for at least a little while longer. "How far is this friend of yours, Ms. Polovski?"

"Now, there's no need for that," she replied with a smile. "Please, call me Anya."

"O...kay," Isaac said slowly. "So, how far is it, Anya?"

"Not far," Anya replied with a sparkle in her eye, "especially if we drive."

LYNT CITY PRECINCT STATION - June 5, 2147 - 11.23am

DET. RAIKEN CLIMBED THE STEPS OF THE LYNT CITY precinct station. The enormous sign on the building was designed to make it look more important than it really was, but Det. Raiken knew better. The only people with the power to stop crime in Lynt City were those 'authorised' to perpetrate it. Not surprisingly, the threat of having your leg cut off and cauterised at the knee was a far more effective deterrent than a jail term in prisons more comfortable than many hotels.

But playing security guard wasn't her concern, investigation was. No matter how corrupt the system may have become, her job was to make sure as much truth as possible made it into the courtroom and onto the public record.

Walking through the precinct's front doors, Det. Raiken ignored the line of citizens waiting for justice or about to have it meted out to them and paused at the inner security gates. She waited a moment as the officer on duty checked her credentials and then stepped into the authorisation chamber so it could take a quick, full-body scan.

When she was finally allowed onto the operational floor, she found the large space bustling with activity. The ceilings inside were at least two stories high and it looked like an enormous hanger had been divided into sections by a maze of glass walls. Via a network of overhead cables, the walls could easily be moved to create different configurations, even single cubicles if necessary, but when large cases were being investigated, the smaller areas were generally amalgamated to allow officers to work in larger teams.

At the moment, other than the corrupt Customs team who continually failed to prevent contraband being shuttled to and from Earth, there was only one other large section set up – a high-profile murder investigation.

Not Det. Raiken's case, however. Her tiny area was tucked away in the far corner between complaints and one of the resident psychiatrists.

Despite her impressive arrest record, Det. Raiken had, for a long time, been a victim of her own moral character and competence. It made her superiors uncomfortable and wouldn't have been such an issue if she played a bit of office politics now and then, but Det. Raiken just didn't have the ambition for that and refused to humour those that did.

And so, she was relegated to a tiny office that barely provided enough room for her, Lance, and a small evidence-viewing alcove.

"Afternoon, ma'am," Lance said as she entered, offering her a smile.

"Afternoon, Lance," Det. Raiken replied, returning his smile briefly. "Have you found the identity of our second person yet?"

"Not yet," he said, clearly disappointed, "but I have leads."

"Leads are all I will ever ask for," Det. Raiken replied, sitting at her desk and swivelling to face him. "Tell me."

"Well, from the material I collected in the tunnels, I've been able to isolate the make and model of the second person's survival-suit. It's a Mylinric."

"A Mylinric life-suit? They're not commercially available."

"That's right, ma'am. They're top of the line prototypes used by only a handful of mining and mineral research companies. I made a list."

"Good work. And what do you propose we do with this information?"

"Um… contact the resource managers working in each corporation and request access to their equipment logs?"

"Hah!" Det. Raiken laughed. "In a perfect world, maybe. No, if we want access to those logs, we'll need to be trickier than that. For one thing, every company on this list has paid substantial bribes to operate within the Lynt City jurisdiction. It's a give and take relationship, Lance. The politicians give the mining companies permits and government grants to dig up whatever they can from Mars, while the mining companies give the politicians a generous amount of any profits they make and allow the politicians to take all the credit for any progress that's been made between elections."

"But this is a murder investigation," Lance said with a frown. "They're required to assist us by law… aren't they?"

"There are laws and then there are laws," Det. Raiken said, wondering if she'd ever been this naïve, "and murder investigation or not, these companies aren't used to co-operating with the police. Certainly not for free. If we want that information, we need to be both careful and clever."

"What do we do, ma'am?" Lance asked, clearly lost.

"Alright, first-" Det. Raiken began, ready to outline their next move, but she was interrupted by a sharp tone that came from her desk.

The sound immediately made her neck and chest muscles tighten in frustration. It was the direct line to her Captain, Kevin Faraday.

Holding an apologetic hand up to Lance, she swivelled back to her desk and reluctantly activated the call. The glass wall behind her desk lit up with an image of her Captain and she could see straight away that he wasn't happy.

"I hope it's not because of me," she thought instinctively.

The holographic screens behind him were filled with summaries from every operation currently being run, but try as she always did, Det. Raiken couldn't make out any of it.

"Captain Faraday," she began smartly.

"I thought I told you to wrap your case up quickly," he replied bluntly.

"I'm attempting to, sir."

"And I know what that really means, detective," he countered with a thunderous look. "This is no time to satisfy your curiosity. I've just read through your findings and this is a clear cut suicide, however bizarre the details may be. Any information you hope to obtain by identifying the second person is irrelevant. No punishable crime has occurred. Case closed."

"With respect, sir, I can't report that no punishable crime has occurred until I've uncovered all the facts. Doctor Indari's death may appear to be a suicide, but there could be other crimes involved. Serious crimes."

"You're talking about allegations of fraudulent activity at Mars Global Communications," Capt. Faraday said, his expression grim.

"Yes, sir," Det. Raiken replied with a nod.

"I assume you understand the seriousness of such a claim? If you're wrong – and the likelihood is quite high that you are, detective – this could result in a considerable amount of negative media attention."

"I understand that, sir."

"Of course, you do," Capt. Faraday said, closing his eyes and pinching the bridge of his nose, "but that doesn't mean you care. I'd like to trust you have our best interests at heart here, detective, but we both know there's nothing you've done in the past that would support such an assumption."

"I have always operated within LCPD guidelines, sir."

"Of course you have," Capt. Faraday snapped. "Otherwise you would have been dismissed a long time ago. Don't get me wrong, detective, I value your particular… skill set, more than most Captains would. But my job isn't simply catching criminals. While you're out there investigating, I'm managing relationships. Keeping lines of communications open so enquiries at all levels can occur without the road blocks caused by mistrust or affront. You have not made that easy in the past, detective, and I can't help wondering how much harder you're about to make it."

Det. Raiken kept her face carefully neutral. She'd heard this many times before and was sick of hearing it.

"No one should be afraid of the truth, sir," she said.

"The truths you uncover aren't frightening, detective," Captain Faraday growled. "They're embarrassing. The kind that should never see the light of day."

Again, she kept her expression neutral.

"Discomfort is never intended, sir."

"No," Captain Faraday said, glaring at her. "Of course it isn't."

"I honestly believe that spending more time on this could lead to real results, sir."

"I'm sorry, detective," Capt. Faraday said, shaking his head, "but I'm not risking this one. You are to stay away from Mars Global Communications. Do you understand me?"

Det. Raiken felt a surge of frustration and knew her expression would give it away this time, but she nodded nonetheless. She didn't want her Captain thinking she was going to disobey him, even if she eventually decided to. He was already watching her progress too closely.

"Yes, sir," she said.

"You can follow up on the owner of this Mylinric suit you've found," her Captain added, "but I strongly advise you to be cautious in your approach. If I see even one complaint on my desk in relation to that line of investigation, detective, I will shut you down faster than you can explain any moral justification."

"Understood, sir," Det. Raiken replied smartly.

"Good," Captain Faraday replied. "Then barring any new actionable evidence relating to the death of Doctor Indari, I expect you to wrap this up by the end of today. If not, I'll be expecting some serious answers of my own. Dismissed."

"Sir," she said with a nod.

As soon as the Captain was gone, Det. Raiken slapped her palm hard on the desk. The pain it caused her was sharp and somewhat satisfying in the heat of the moment, but her frustration went nowhere.

"Ma'am?" Lance asked.

"Sorry, Lance," she sighed. "As you probably heard, the M.G.C. is off limits. And to be honest, I don't like our chances of finding the owner of that Mylinric life-suit, either."

"Understood, ma'am," he replied calmly.

Det. Raiken turned to him and wondered if she'd ever been so agreeable. If she'd been told as a graduate that two of her own leads, and good ones at that, couldn't be followed up, she would have made trouble for someone. Herself, most likely. But the detectives they were spitting out these days seemed much better behaved and apparently came pre-installed with pragmatism. Either that or the Captain had spent a lot more time selecting her new graduate than she thought.

"Don't worry," she assured him, "there'll be other opportunities to follow one of your leads through to the end. This one just seems to have hit one of the Captain's many political nerves."

She was a little disappointed when Lance didn't ask any further questions, but decided to leave it at that for now. Turning her attention to the data pad on her desk, she wondered why the connection light hadn't flicked on yet.

"Damn it, not now," she growled. "I can't afford any glitches with this new time line."

"What is it, ma'am?" Lance asked.

"My data pad," she replied. "It's not docking with my desk."

"May I?" he asked, holding out a hand.

"Be my guest," Det. Raiken said, before handing it over. She knew Lance was more qualified to find the problem than she was.

Turning back to his own desk, Lance placed the data pad next to his and began tapping away at it. In moments, he had the two wirelessly connected and was searching through files Det. Raiken didn't recognise.

"I'm afraid I can't recover anything on the hard drive," Lance told her, looking up apologetically, "but I can tell you this was no glitch, ma'am. It was deliberate."

"Deliberate?" Det. Raiken said, not sure if she should be more or less angry. "Deliberate how?"

"It looks like a memory chip failure, but there's nothing wrong with the hardware itself. Which can only mean a virus, ma'am. One engineered to remove all traces of itself along with your files."

Det. Raiken frowned. How had her data pad contracted a virus? Trevin had checked it out at the customs office and it had worked fine after that. The only other person she'd given access to was…

"*Professor Meiket,*" she thought. "*Of course!*"

Suddenly it all made sense; the fear in his eyes; the way he'd wanted her out of there as quickly as possible. He *was* hiding something and if he was willing to deliberately infect a forensic detective's data pad, he was more afraid than she thought.

"Ma'am?" Lance asked politely.

"The last symbologist I visited found something and tried to hide it with this virus," she told him. "It's the only explanation that fits. But why trash my data pad? He wouldn't have left anything on it, would he?"

"It's possible he did, ma'am. It's not common knowledge, but after two data pads have been connected, it's possible to hack the information registry and pull up everything that was shared between them. This doesn't include anything below a set security level, but once a file had been shared it can't be erased. The only way to get rid of it is to infect the data pad with a virus like this one and destroy everything."

"Right," Det. Raiken said firmly. "I'm going to pay Professor Meiket another visit. Do I need to get another data pad?"

"No, ma'am. This one should do fine. As I said, the hardware is undamaged. It's just the operating system that was affected.

I'll re-sync it with your desk computer and it should be as good as new, although any data you collected after we split up earlier is unfortunately gone for good."

"Okay," she said. "You do that and then you can come with me. We'll see what our symbologist has to say for himself."

"Yes, ma'am."

Det. Raiken clasped her hands in front of her and sat back with a determined expression. She didn't care if this investigation ended up a black mark on her record anymore. She just wanted some answers and Professor Meiket better be ready to give them to her, because if he didn't, he was going to find himself very quickly dumped out of the frying pan and into the fire.

PRIVATE RESIDENCE, LYNT CITY - June 5, 2147 - 11.37am

PROFESSOR MEIKET SPLASHED COLD WATER OVER HIS face and steadied himself against the sink. The fear and paranoia that had gripped him since that damned forensic detective had visited was making him feel sick. He knew she'd be back at some point, asking about the computer virus he'd uploaded to her data pad, but that didn't worry him. He could easily claim he'd inadvertently shared a virus that had affected his own pad as well. What he was really scared of was dying horribly.

He shouldn't have agreed to look at the symbols she'd found at her crime scene. He should have known what he was looking at when he realised they'd been carved into a body. But he couldn't resist an opportunity to show off, could he?

"*You arrogant fool,*" he thought, glaring at himself in the mirror.

If only he'd recognised them sooner, he could have written his fictional report without accessing his own data banks. But now there was a chance, no matter how small, that a twenty year old nightmare would finally catch up with him.

The symbols certainly weren't the creation of an unbalanced mind. They were part of an ancient language that had been burned from the collective human consciousness long ago.

Well, nearly all of it. Somewhere, there still existed a murderous cult hell-bent on keeping it secret. They were called the One True Path and that was what they believed. There was no free will, no choices beyond the insignificant compulsions our animal biology allowed us. Destiny was already set. There was only One True Path.

The only reason Professor Meiket had any knowledge of its existence was because he'd stolen some data from a university colleague, decades earlier. Back then, he'd been completing a doctorate in ancient languages on Earth and was a hard, disciplined worker. His work ethic had led to overwhelming academic success, but it also came with a fierce competitive streak that made him occasionally take other, more morally dubious, pathways to the top.

Although language studies were his passion, Meiket was just as skilled in computer programming, which allowed him to keep tabs on his fellow students. And so, when one of his self-proclaimed rivals – Phillip Droder – began to boast that he'd found an ancient lost language, Meiket quickly decided to investigate just how strong his competition was.

It had been exciting at first, planning an elaborate break and enter and programming a Trojan virus that would allow him to extract information from Phillip's computer whilst leaving no trace of the digital intrusion. Meiket never found out how the information had been acquired in the first place, but it was a remarkable find nonetheless. The language was truly ancient – older than anything he'd considered – and the evidence clearly suggested it had been used in spectacularly brutal religious rites and ceremonies.

In its own dialect, it was known as Divsek, literally translated as 'the forbidden language' and Phillip explained its omission from contemporary history with a rich mythology of curses that rendered all those who stumbled across the language dead in countless inventive and horrifying ways.

It was a compelling story, but while studying the evidence in the safety of his campus bedroom, Meiket began to suspect Phillip had made the entire thing up.

There was no evidence of the Divsek in any other scholarly archive and yet the report was so well written that their professor would more than likely accept it as real. Which meant Phillip Droder would achieve top honours at the end of the year.

The depression that came with the knowledge was worse than anything Meiket had felt before. This was the pinnacle of his academic career and after systematically winning every significant intellectual race up to that point he couldn't afford to come in second place now. But his pitiful fears were nothing compared to the terror that was to come.

Ready to endure another gloating lecture from his rival the next day, Meiket was puzzled when their class was abruptly cancelled. He enquired about the cancellation and was told that Phillip Droder was dead, burned to death in his dorm room.

The tragedy left Meiket conflicted with shock and shameful relief. For a short time, he even contemplated passing off the stolen information as his own because the fire had apparently erased all evidence of what Phillip had been working on. But then he'd heard the circumstances surrounding the fire.

The coroner ruled that Phillip had set fire to his own dorm room, using accelerants that burned so hot that none of his personal effects had survived. The media speculated about a possible suicide, but Meiket had seen no signs of depression and refused to believe someone could intentionally burn themselves to death when they were on the cusp of such an academic achievement.

But the evidence was clear. For whatever reason, Phillip had done this to himself.

As the campus got back into the swing of things, the whole affair was soon forgotten, but Meiket remained unsettled. He didn't want to believe the Divsek curse was responsible for Phillip's death, but he certainly wasn't brave enough to use the stolen information himself. Whether the curse was real or not, he didn't want to openly admit he knew anything about the forbidden language.

It took him a long time to accept that death wasn't stalking him and it was these concerns that ultimately led him to settle on Mars. He kept the information he'd stolen on the Divsek language because something inside him refused to erase what could be the only evidence left of an ancient human culture, but he made sure it was locked away so no one would ever find out he had it.

After so many years, the fear that made him quarantine the information dissipated enough to make the entire thing seem paranoid and ludicrous. But now, he realised it had only made him careless. When the detective's data pad had requested an interrogation of his confidential files, Meiket had agreed without thinking, caught up in the challenge of identifying the symbols. And when the symbols had found a match with his own files, it felt like the floor had disappeared from beneath him.

There was no reason to suspect the detective would actively try to recover the information – there were also strict laws that would render any evidence pulled off the detective's data pad inadmissible in court – but he couldn't risk it. Not after what had happened to Phillip Droder.

Lost in his anxiety, Professor Meiket jumped at the sound of his doorbell. He turned to glare at the screen on his desk and was only a little relieved when he saw that it wasn't the detective. The man waiting patiently at his intercom also didn't look like a member of a dangerous cult, but how would he know? How could anyone know?

For a moment, Professor Meiket entertained the idea of pretending he wasn't home, but something inside him rebelled. It scoffed at his fear and refused to believe he was in any real danger. Twenty years ago, perhaps, but he'd done what was necessary to keep himself safe. Turning away potential business now would just be plain foolish.

Walking back to his desk, Professor Meiket sat down and reached for the glowing answer button.

"Yes?" he said cautiously, allowing the man to see him.

"Professor Meiket?" the man replied, smiling into the camera. "My name is Peter Stilton. I was hoping to hire you as an interpreter."

"Ah," Professor Meiket said, relaxing at the mundane request. "Of course. Please, come in."

Sliding a finger across the access tab, Prof. Meiket let the man in and tried to pull himself together. His decision to infect the detective's data pad might have been rash, but dealing with the consequences still seemed less intimidating than risking the Divsek curse.

He rose to welcome his new client and paused when he met the man's eyes. In an instant, everything went silent, as if he'd been smothered in a thick blanket. At the same time, all the details around the man's eyes began to blur and his face was blanked out along with the rest of the room.

Professor Meiket's heart rate spiked, along with his anxiety. He tried to turn away, but couldn't move. He tried to scream, tried to simply blink his eyes, but he no longer seemed in control of his body. He felt his hands fall limply to his side and the seat pressed against his buttocks as he involuntarily sat down.

For a moment the man's eyes seemed to grow larger, then a commanding voice spoke to him.

"What did detective Raiken ask of you?"

Professor Meiket was so terrified now that he felt like vomiting, but instead, his mouth moved as if he were talking. He could feel the exchange of breath as his lungs pulled the air in and sent it back over his vocal chords. He could feel the tingling vibration as his vocal chords framed the sounds coming out of his mouth. But he couldn't hear what he was saying. All he could do was focus on the man's eyes. Those terrible, piercing eyes.

"What information did you offer her?"

Again, Professor Meiket felt his mouth moving but heard nothing. There was only complete, crushing silence. And the man's eyes.

"Did you recognise the symbols?"

Professor Meiket's mouth moved once more and he tried in vain to scream again.

"Tell me what you know about the Divsek."

107

Now, the fear that had gripped Professor Meiket rose to choke him, but his mouth continued shaping words that he couldn't hear. He couldn't even shed the tears that would have otherwise been streaming down his methodically flexing cheeks.

"Pick up a pen from your desk."

Finally, and with a rush of hope, Prof. Meiket's gaze moved away from the man's eyes and focussed on his desk. He felt and saw his hand reaching for his favourite fountain pen.

"Press the tip of the pen to your left eye."

Mentally clawing against whatever was making him calmly do what the voice told him, Professor Meiket felt himself lift the pen and saw its gleaming tip catch the light just as it came level with his eye. Then his vision blurred as the tip pressed lightly against his cornea.

"Push harder," the voice commanded.

Professor Meiket screamed in the silence of his mind, but felt only the sickly jerking movement as his eyeball popped and a sharp pain as the pen scraped the back of his eye socket.

"Remove the pen and put it back on your desk."

The pain grew sharper as Professor Meiket pulled the pen out, assuring him that he'd just sustained a serious injury, but he couldn't respond. All he could do was watch helplessly with his undamaged eye as his hand placed the fountain pen, now dripping with blood and the white flesh of his sclera, back on the desk.

"Professor Klaus Meiket, you are unworthy of this knowledge. All records you have on the Divsek will be removed from your computers and your life will be given in sacrifice."

Professor Meiket struggled in vain against the forces that held him in check, but it was no use. He knew he was going to die. The ancient curse of the Divsek had finally caught up with him and all he could do was scream helplessly in his mind as his life was claimed in brutal, ritual sacrifice.

ISAAC STARED OUT ACROSS ONE OF THE VALLES DOME'S vast traffic levels in disbelief. There certainly weren't any pedestrians here. Only vehicles were allowed on this level and they weaved around each other with a speed and accuracy that could only be explained by anti-collision tech.

Isaac had never seen anything like it. Lynt City had banned wheeled vehicles along with manual driving a long time ago. Its streets were imbedded with the same kind of superconductor technology used in mag-lev trains and the vehicles were all publicly owned and automatic, so the traffic was always smooth and controlled.

But not here. In the Valles Dome, if residents could afford the registration they were actually allowed to own their vehicles and, even worse, drive them.

Isaac shuddered. To him, and probably anyone who lived in Lynt City, the concept was as archaic as it was dangerous.

"Come on," Anya said, gesturing him toward the sleek two-seater motorcycle she'd wheeled out of a small garage space.

The seats were thankfully enclosed in a cabin-like shell painted metallic pink where it wasn't transparent and a glowing white tattoo traced an intricate pattern down the side.

"Why would a psychiatrist buy something like this?" he thought in confusion.

"Time's wasting," Anya said with a raised eyebrow.

Frowning in trepidation, Isaac gingerly climbed onto the back seat and tried not to stare when Anya slid onto the seat in front of him. He knew it was inappropriate, but ever since they'd left her apartment he'd become acutely aware of Anya's body.

It possibly had to do with the way she'd put her hair up and changed into some far more stylish clothes – long boots, shiny black pants, and a tight white t-shirt – but there was no denying that Anya also had an impressive figure. Her muscles were trim and there were curves in all the right places to make Isaac's hormones sit up and take notice. She also moved with a distinctly feminine sway that was making him feel flustered.

"If only she didn't smell so good," he thought to himself. *"I guess I should be glad there's a seat between us."*

Isaac would have been the first to admit that he and Jason didn't have much experience when it came to women. Given the intense nature of their work, it had been a long time since he'd been in any situation that even resembled flirting, let alone dating. But something about Anya was making him wonder why he hadn't given romance more of a chance.

As he breathed in the soft scent of moisturiser and flowers that wafted over him, his gaze idly traced the soft curve of a thigh that protruded on one side of Anya's seat. It felt a little wrong after the motherly way she'd held him in the apartment, but at the same time it felt... great.

At this point the windscreen closed around them and Anya flicked on the motorcycle's engine before glancing over her shoulder.

"You'd better hold on," she said with a wink.

"Wh-" was all Isaac managed to say before he was pushed roughly back into his seat.

The motorcycle's power was terrifying, but even worse was the obvious fact that Anya clearly didn't like sitting with the rest of the traffic. Their heart-stopping journey consisted of constant proximity alarms and fierce engine revs as they weaved in and out of gaps Isaac would have never seen. And yet somehow, Anya always seemed to pick the right line so the anti-collision tech that should have slowed them down kept letting her through with just enough buffer to spare.

Reminding himself to breathe, Isaac held on tight as they screamed up several levels and moved closer to the Valles Marineris canyon's edge. They eventually came into sight of the original buildings built into the cliffs and Isaac wondered if that was where they were headed.

As they got closer, Anya's reckless pace finally began to slow and a large, official looking building loomed ahead of them. They pulled into a parking space alongside the front entrance and Isaac carefully let go of the seat's safety handles and stretched his fingers to massage some life back into them.

"My... friend is inside," Anya said, pulling a long white garment from beside her seat as the windscreen tipped forward to let them out.

"Cool," Isaac said breathlessly.

The building they'd arrived at had been built at the very edge of the canyon and it reached up so far that it seemed to punch through the dome above.

"What is this place?" Isaac asked, craning his neck so he could trace the dome with his eyes.

"You'll see," Anya said, giving him a smouldering look over her shoulder.

Ignoring a sudden rush of blood to his groin, Isaac followed her to the front entrance and tried not to think about her naked. But the way Anya walked kept dragging his gaze down to her waist and smooth, swaying buttocks, which made it almost impossible.

When they eventually stepped through the front entrance, Anya stopped a short way inside and Isaac quickly caught up, wondering what she was waiting for. Then he witnessed one of the strangest and most disturbing things he'd ever seen.

Anya shrugged on the long white coat she'd been carrying and took in a deep breath, as if tasting the air around them. Then she let it out in a long, drawn out sigh.

The sigh itself wasn't that strange, but as the breath left her, Anya's shoulders drooped, ruining her perfect posture, and the strong, sensual body Isaac had just been admiring seemed to wither away into a frail old one. Even the skin on Anya's face seemed to lose its luminescence, causing wrinkles to appear around her eyes and leaving her expression grim and tired.

She then turned toward Isaac and he flinched in surprise. Her vivid blue eyes had somehow darkened to a light brown.

"Hello there," she said in a deep, gravelly voice. "Welcome to the Valles University labs."

"Uh… what?" Isaac said uncertainly.

"Laboratories, son," Anya replied with a rumbling laugh. "Come in, come in. Anya tells me you have something interesting to show me."

Blinking in confusion, Isaac watched as the frail, old version of Anya wandered away from him.

"*What just happened?*" he thought in confusion.

But Anya didn't seem ready to give him an explanation and he couldn't think of anything to do but follow her.

As they made their way deeper into the building, several employees greeted Anya with a smile and an unfamiliar name that only added to Isaac's confusion.

"Afternoon, Professor Haig."

"Hello dear."

"Hi, Professor Haig."

"Hello there."

Some of them seemed to recognise the bewilderment in Isaac's face, but they didn't say anything. They just winked at him and offered an encouraging smile.

"What on Mars have I gotten myself into?" he thought in dismay. They eventually reached a small lift that carried them up several levels – a few people in the lift calling Anya 'Professor Haig' again – then they stopped in front of some large double doors and Anya punched a code into the activation panel.

"Wow," Isaac thought as the large doors slid aside.

It was a planetarium, a huge planetarium, with a control booth at its centre and hundreds of comfortable looking chairs arrayed around it in concentric circles.

While Isaac stared up at the enormous domed ceiling, Anya shuffled down the central isle and stepped into the operator's booth.

"Come in, come in," she said with a good-natured smile, "we'll need to close the doors if you want to see it properly."

Isaac gingerly stepped through the doorway and walked down the aisle toward Anya, feeling a little awkward being alone in such a daunting space with someone who clearly wasn't sane.

"Now," Anya said in her old woman's voice, "what was it you wanted to show me?"

"Um... okay," Isaac said uncertainly. "Well... I, uh, I'm not sure how much Anya told you... er...?"

"Just call me Professor."

"Sure, sure," Isaac replied quickly, "Professor. I'm... not sure how much Anya told you."

"You saw a vision that included a night sky," Anya said, squinting up at him, "and you wanted to know if it was a fabrication of your mind, or perhaps a premonition."

"Yes," Isaac said, feeling foolish that he too was now pretending Anya had somehow changed into a different person. "I've got the images here."

He handed Anya the data pad he'd stolen earlier and waited as she linked it with the control desk and downloaded the images. She then hunched over a smaller display panel for several minutes, fiddling with a glowing set of parameters, and eventually grunted with satisfaction.

113

"Please, take a seat," she said, gesturing toward one of the reclining chairs that filled the planetarium.

Isaac did so quickly and then waited as Anya underwent the process of sitting beside him. In her 'old lady' persona, she let out a series of gasps and moans as she eased herself down, as if her joints were stiff, then she took a moment to steady her breathing.

When she eventually activated something with a small remote, the planetarium's domed ceiling flickered with light. Suddenly, it was covered with a twinkling representation of the night sky from Isaac's vision.

"Wow," he said in honest appreciation.

Using the planetarium's computers, Anya had transformed his vision into a representation of the night sky, just as it would look if they were actually inside the image.

"Very interesting," Anya said in her perplexing new voice. "I don't believe your mind created this image after all."

"What do you mean?"

"There's a large amount of extra material depicted in this image that doesn't currently exist in the Marsian night sky. Do you see all the sparkling reflections? They aren't stars, Isaac. The stars we can see, however, are perfectly aligned with known constellations. Do you see? You can also clearly make out Venus."

Isaac wasn't sure where to look – he'd never been very interested in astronomy – but a blinking yellow circle guided his eyes to one of the brightest 'stars' he could see.

"In fact, the only thing that seems to be missing is Jupiter," Anya added.

Once again, Isaac was guided by a blinking yellow circle that surrounded the red spark at the very centre of the image. Only this, much larger depiction, looked more like a twisted line of blurry red light with a jagged, asymmetrical shape, like a poorly written lower case 'a' or an 'e'.

"What is it?" Isaac asked with a frown.

"I don't know," Anya said slowly, her voice sounding distant, "but it's obscuring the light from Jupiter. And it's moving. Your vision lasted several seconds, it seems. As you can see, the line of light is growing at an appreciable rate. Whatever it is, like all the other 'noise' we're seeing, it's occurring somewhere between Mars and Jupiter. Without knowing where exactly, I can't estimate how fast it's moving, or how large it is. But both variables appear to be quite significant."

Isaac's frown deepened. He'd hoped this trip would give him something he could use, but it had only led him to more questions. Questions that seemed harder to answer than the ones he'd walked in with.

"So… this could be some kind of premonition?" he asked.

"I believe it is," Anya replied.

"But for when?"

"June the seventh, 2147"

Isaac turned to Anya in disbelief.

"You can work out the exact date?"

"From the position of the stars, yes," Anya replied with a smile.

Isaac frowned again.

"But… that's only a few days away."

"Fifty nine hours and twelve minutes, to be exact," Anya told him.

"Well, that's something, I guess," Isaac said, looking back up at the stars. "But knowing what the night sky is going to look like in a few days' time isn't much use to me."

"Knowledge is knowledge, son," Anya said firmly. "Take my advice and make an effort to remember it. Useful understanding rarely comes from one piece of information alone. It is more often an amalgam of pieces – some directly related to a central idea, others coming from unpredictable sources – that eventually leads us to epiphany. Don't let a little confusion dishearten you. It is but a necessary step along the road to enlightenment."

Isaac knew she was right. His best breakthroughs always came after a lot of thinking, extensive research, and sometimes bizarre associations. Like Isaac Newton, his name sake, who studied mathematics and the world around him for decades before coming up with an elegant theory to explain gravity after he saw an apple fall from a tree.

"Do you have any idea what all that extra material is?" he asked.

"Perhaps," Anya replied, "but we can't run any spectrographic analysis because this is only an approximation of the light we might actually measure in three days' time. However, given the way the star light is being distorted, I'd say we're looking at a large body of particulate matter, probably ice, in a degrading orbit around Mars. The evidence can be seen here, and here, showing clear examples of refraction and the trails of several larger chunks burning up in Mars' atmosphere."

"Ice," Isaac said, staring up at the glittering motes of light.

"There's also some indication of depth," Anya continued, "suggesting the ice cloud extends beyond Marsian orbit. How far, I'm reluctant to guess with this limited amount of data."

"So…" Isaac said, still feeling lost. "Where to from here?"

"We ask for help," Anya said, as if it were obvious.

Isaac turned to her, not sure if he was about to witness another bizarre change of persona, but Anya just smiled back at him as her seat returned upright.

"I have several colleagues who would greatly enjoy the challenge of gleaning more information from this image," she said as she got up and shuffled back to the control booth. "I'd like to send it to them, with your permission, of course."

"Ah… I guess so," Isaac replied, a little reluctantly, "but where are you going to tell them it came from?"

"I was going to tell them the truth," Anya said, squinting at him again. "I wouldn't include your name, of course, but I'd certainly need to explain it has come from a person's memory of a vision."

Isaac could see all sorts of uncomfortable questions arising from that simple admission alone. Was he taking some kind of drug when he saw this vision? Did he really believe he was psychic? How had he captured the image so clearly? But he could also see the value in outsourcing the problem. He was by no means an expert in what might help them decipher his visions, and he certainly didn't have any other ideas.

"Alright, fine," he said after a moment. "Just make sure any discussion sticks to deciphering the image, not how we created it in the first place."

"I'll try," Anya said, though her tone suggested it wasn't going to be easy. "Don't worry, Isaac. We'll get to the bottom of this."

"I hope so," Isaac replied honestly. "I really do."

BLACK SITE ALPHA, VALLES DOME - June 5, 2147 - 12.45pm

SECURITY CHIEF HADRIAN LEVINE TOOK ANOTHER SIP of the best coffee he'd ever tasted and wondered what their mission would entail. He'd worked as a high-end security consultant for nearly a decade now and had been paid to do every legal and illegal thing imaginable, but he'd never worked with this Sabian character before.

In a way, the man was refreshing. He was clinical, precise, and provided all relevant information before expecting any work to be done. It was the way Hadrian liked to work and perhaps why he'd been chosen for this mission. But at the same time, something about the man left him feeling unsettled. It wasn't his arrogance, which Hadrian was well accustomed to, it was the fanatical gleam in his eye – an assurance of purpose that he'd only ever seen in the eyes of religious extremists.

It was a dangerous dichotomy. In Hadrian's experience, such a look usually meant the owner was dangerously unpredictable, but there was nothing unpredictable about Sabian. He was cool, calm, and calculated in everything he did.

"*Even making coffee,*" he thought, taking another sip of the rich, delicious brew.

Putting the mystery aside for the moment, Hadrian looked over at his team. Not surprisingly, they hadn't warmed to their new boss. They were soldiers, trained for action and strategic thinking. When they spoke to one another it was with an almost deliberate casualness that made light of the seriousness of their jobs. But Sabian was the complete opposite. He never said anything that wasn't necessary and certainly never said it casually. It was the kind of attitude soldiers found hard to respect. They wouldn't dare disobey the man, of course. At this level of the game, there was far more than money at stake if you were stupid enough to disobey an order. But that didn't mean they had to respect someone they obviously didn't.

Chen and Harris were currently playing a violent video game that was being beamed into their head sets. Their replica weapons shuddered with simulated recoil as they tore into whatever enemies the game offered up, but there wasn't any sound. Like the virtual world they were fighting in, the audible part of the simulation was thankfully confined to the soldiers' headsets.

Greer and Baines were also playing a war game, but this one looked more strategic than visceral. They sat either side of a small table with glowing terrain laid out between them. The map was built up with mining operations, factories and training installations built to construct their armies and, of course, the armies themselves. Between the two players, a screen blocked the view of their opponent's gaming surface and displayed all the information they were allowed to know about the enemy.

Hadrian smiled. He didn't mind his team playing games while they waited for orders. Sabian had made it abundantly clear they were expected to be ready at a moment's notice, and so they were. All equipment had been checked, rechecked, and stored for easy selection. They were all well-fed and their muscles warmed and stretched. There was nothing to do now but wait and so it was logical to allow them something to occupy their minds.

Hadrian himself was about to go through their inventory of equipment once more when his HUD suddenly flashed to life.

A list of equipment scrolled into view and when Hadrian glanced at his team, he saw that they'd already abandoned their games and were collecting the relevant items from the inventory.

As he joined them, he saw a location flash in his HUD – a research institute specialising in astrological science. Then came a map of their route and an entrance strategy with details on who they would pretend to be, including how close they would be able to get to the target before their pretence could be dropped.

And last but not least, the target – a male, aged in his mid-twenties. No distinguishing features. Threat level minimum.

It was all standard information apart from one additional order. Under no circumstances was the target to be harmed. They were not to take any lethal weapons with them and any injuries incurred by the target would result in significant financial penalties. Apart from that they had authorisation to use whatever force was necessary. Collateral damage was noted as undesirable, but not forbidden.

"*Whoever this guy is,*" Hadrian thought to himself, "*Sabian wants him bad.*"

It was a nearly text book snatch and grab, but the detail in the planning was incredible, especially given the time stamp on the internet log that had apparently led Sabian to the target's location.

"*This guy is scary good,*" Hadrian thought with a respectful shake of his head.

When he glanced at the door leading to Sabian's computer station, he saw the man emerge and quickly turned to his team. Thankfully, they were already waiting in a line, kitted out with the equipment detailed in the list and dressed in full uniform.

If Sabian appreciated or even noticed the efficiency with which they'd assembled, he didn't give any indication. He simply walked up to Hadrian and, not quite looking at him, spoke in his usual, brisk manner.

"This target is of the highest priority."

"I understand, sir," Hadrian replied. "Your instructions have been received and we're ready to execute."

"You will see that all force is authorised," Sabian continued, his eyes flickering on and off Hadrian, "but I cannot emphasise enough how important it is to keep this man alive and unharmed."

"Understood, sir," Hadrian replied.

For a moment, Sabian paused as if he was going to say more and Hadrian noticed a trembling hand was grasping the jewel-encrusted cross at his neck. He waited patiently, expecting something more, but Sabian eventually just nodded.

"Very good. You may leave."

At this, Hadrian motioned to his team and they sprang into action.

Whatever they might think about Sabian, everything they'd seen so far led Hadrian to believe the man's strange personality would only help them complete this mission sooner. And he was glad. He wanted this over as soon as possible so he could get paid and get out from under the command of this unsettling man.

"*Time to get this done,*" he thought determinedly.

DETECTIVE RAIKEN LED LANCE OUT OF THE STATION and down the front steps. She was still bristling at Professor Meiket's sabotage and looked forward to confronting him about it. He wasn't going to get away with lying to her twice.

When they reached the curb, she stopped in front of a police vehicle and allowed Lance to take the back seat before stepping in herself. She then linked her repaired data pad with its computer and pulled up Professor Meiket's home address. The map responded by zooming-in to a flashing emergency icon.

"Oh no," she said, a chill washing through her. "Lance, there's a fire at Professor Meiket's apartment. Hold on."

"Yes, ma'am."

Quickly strapping herself in, Det. Raiken activated the vehicle's sirens and authorised the vehicle to travel in the emergency lanes at maximum speed. The vehicle responded immediately by accelerating away from the curb and the hum of the engine changed tone sharply as they entered the clear, tube-like emergency lane.

Det. Raiken disliked moving this fast and tried to avoid it whenever possible, but she wasn't going to let a bit of motion sickness delay her now.

She firmly ignored the multi-coloured blur of pedestrians that whipped past them and closed her eyes each time the vehicle turned a corner or curved upward to reach another level.

When they finally approached Professor Meiket's apartment and began to slow down, their vehicle was diverted to a secondary exit to avoid the fire response units already at the residence.

Fires were managed with almost perfect efficiency in Lynt City. Apart from a distinct lack of flammable building materials, there were so many cheap, fool-proof firefighting systems in residential apartments that it was nearly impossible for one to keep burning without deliberate intervention. The fact there were so many units in attendance here was not a good sign.

One of the attending officers guided them into a nearby parking space and Det. Raiken thanked him as she exited the vehicle. Beyond the flashing blue police cordon, an atmospheric containment team had already set up a collection pod at the apartment's entrance to capture all the smoke still pouring out of it. The site coordinator sat at a temporary control booth beside it and he looked up when Det. Raiken's badge activated a notification on his screen.

"Detective," he began, looking puzzled but cooperative. "What can I do for you?"

"I'm here to talk with the occupant," she told him.

"Klaus Meiket?"

"Right," she said with a nod.

"He's dead, I'm afraid. Incinerated in the fire," the officer replied, glancing back at his screen. "There were barely enough remains left for a DNA profile."

"What happened? Why didn't the fire suppression systems stop this sooner?"

"We think they were sabotaged. In fact, it looks like the occupant deliberately shut them off. Which isn't easy, I can tell you. This guy must have been a skilled programmer. He not only disabled his apartment's fire systems, but also made sure the atmospheric scrubbers kept feeding the fire concentrated oxygen. I don't know why, but this guy really wanted to burn."

Det. Raiken frowned. What could possibly motivate Professor Meiket to burn himself alive?

"I need to know if you recovered any data storage devices," she told the site coordinator.

"We haven't gotten that far yet, detective," he replied, "but I'll be happy to pass on whatever we find once we're done."

"That will be fine," Det. Raiken said with a nod. "Thanks for taking a moment."

"You got it," he replied, returning her nod.

Det. Raiken turned to Lance.

"Set up next to the site coordinator, but stay out of his way. I want every scrap of information captured by the apartment computers. Start with visual feeds and work your way down to the appliance activation logs. I want to know everything that happened between the time of my visit and now. I want to know who else visited him, whether or not he left the apartment, if he made or received any calls, anything that might help explain what happened here."

"Yes, ma'am," Lance said with an eager expression.

Leaving him to it, Det. Raiken turned to the gathering crowd. There were a lot of people watching the clean-up, which wasn't much of a surprise. Fires were an extremely rare occurrence in Lynt City and so they made for quite a spectacle.

"Human curiosity at its best," she thought. *"Just the thing I need to get some answers."*

Striding toward the perimeter cordon, Det. Raiken scanned the crowd carefully. Most of the onlookers were clearly just passing through the area and wanted to see what was happening, but it wasn't hard to pick out the local residents. They looked more concerned than excited and were actively spreading the gossip as they watched the proceedings.

After a moment, Det. Raiken noticed a mature-looking woman standing away from the bulk of the crowd. She was nodding slowly as a more animated, much younger woman yapped away beside her.

"*That's the one I need to talk to,*" she thought to herself.

As she moved through the cordon, the woman noticed her and Det. Raiken saw a look in her eyes that spoke directly to her intuition. This woman had something to share.

"Good afternoon," she began with a nod, activating the badge on her uniform so her credentials appeared in a large, easy to read patch across her chest. "My name is Miana Raiken, I'm a forensic detective with the Lynt City Police Department. May I ask you a few questions?"

The younger woman glanced at the older, who nodded in agreement, then she returned her gaze to Det. Raiken.

"Of course."

"Do you mind if I ask for your names?" Det. Raiken began.

"Laura Short," the younger woman replied quickly.

"Julia Wensing," the older woman added.

"Thank you, Julia, thank you, Laura," Det. Raiken said with a smile, before turning her attention to the older of the two. "Did you know Klaus Meiket?"

"I did," Julia replied, her expression calm but concerned. "Is he alright?"

"No, I'm afraid not," Det. Raiken said in a solemn tone. "He was killed in the fire."

Laura, the younger woman, gasped and put a hand over her mouth, but Julia just nodded slowly.

"Such a shame. He was a nice man."

Det. Raiken usually wouldn't disclose that kind of information to a civilian, but she knew this type of woman well. Julia was clearly a matriarch within the local community and would only offer up information if she received some in return.

"Did you know Professor Meiket well?" she asked.

"Not particularly," Julia replied. "He was a little... eccentric at times and generally kept to himself. But if anyone had a problem with their computer, he was always willing to help. He saved us all a lot of time and money over the years."

"He was good with computers?"

"Excellent," she replied with a nod. "And if he wasn't able to fix it on the spot, he always knew what was wrong and who we needed to call."

Det. Raiken wasn't surprised. If he'd been able to trash her data pad and rig the fire systems in his apartment, he had to be good.

"Did you see anyone entering Professor Meiket's apartment today?"

"He doesn't get many visitors," Julia said thoughtfully.

"You didn't see anyone?" Det. Raiken persisted.

Julia looked at Laura, as if to confirm there wasn't any information she hadn't been given.

"No," Laura said with a disappointed look. Then her eyes lit up again. "But if anyone did come past, the children might have noticed."

"Could you ask them for me, please?" Det. Raiken asked her.

This time Laura didn't bother to wait for permission. She simply glanced at a thick bracelet on her wrist, swiped at it to pull up a map Det. Raiken assumed showed the location of the local children, and then ducked away into the crowd, calling out names.

"She won't be long," Julia assured her.

"Thank you," Det. Raiken replied. "I appreciate your help."

They waited in silence for a few moments then Julia spoke again.

"He wouldn't kill himself."

Det. Raiken looked at her closely.

"Why do you say that?"

"I can see you're thinking the same thing."

Det. Raiken was impressed. She should have known a woman like Julia would be able to read her as easily as she was being read.

"I have my doubts," she offered in reply.

127

"Well, I just wanted to agree with them," Julia added. "Klaus had no reason to kill himself. He was successful and, in my experience at least, a genuinely happy man. His only failing was a competitive streak that occasionally had him bumping heads with some of the local alpha males."

"Alpha males?" Det. Raiken asked.

"I could give you names if you like, but the altercations were never aggressive. In fact, I believe they brought Klaus and his competitors closer together. They certainly wouldn't have led to something like this."

Det. Raiken decided to go with Julia on this one. In her experience, local disputes didn't play out with this kind of violence, and certainly not with any finesse. She severely doubted any alpha males in the community would have gone to the trouble of faking Professor Meiket's suicide in retaliation for some ego-bashing they'd received. Of course, it didn't mean she couldn't check back later if something changed her mind.

"Was he generally liked, or disliked?" she asked.

Julia thought about it for a moment.

"I… wouldn't be comfortable choosing either," she said thoughtfully. "What I can say is as long as we acknowledged him as an expert and gave him a not unreasonable amount of respect, he was always polite and kind. I've known Klaus for over ten years, detective, and I can honestly say that I've never seen any indication he would be capable of doing something like this."

"That's very helpful," Det. Raiken said with a nod. "Thank you for your assessment, Julia."

Before she could discuss anything further, Laura returned with five excited children in tow. None of them looked older than ten. Two were whispering to each other and giggling as they tapped away on bracelets similar to Laura's, while the other three stared up at her with a mix of fear and awe in their eyes.

"Swizzy," Laura said, smiling at Det. Raiken before turning to the oldest of the staring children. "Please tell the detective what you told me."

"Yes, Mum," the boy said, nodding vigorously. "We, um, saw someone come out of the Hackman's apartment."

"Professor Meiket," Laura corrected him, giving the child a disapproving look.

"Yeah, Hackman," the boy said, nodding again. "He was, um, dressed in a Gildon suit. With Trinium cuff-links and everything!"

Det. Raiken felt a spark of hope. This was the first piece of information that didn't suggest suicide.

"Did you see where the man went?" she asked.

"Yeah," the boy answered, scratching his arm. "He went round the block and got into one o' them govermen' cars with the blue sides. You know, um, the ones that drive in the emergency lane?"

"I know them," Det. Raiken said, before turning to Laura. "May I have permission to view your son's visual log? I'll only need the last hour of footage."

Laura once again looked at Julia and when she didn't offer any objections, she turned back to her son.

"You haven't been doing anything naughty, have you?"

"No, Mum," he said reproachfully. "Just playing Seg-races with Hapster and Keef."

"I guess we'll see then, won't we?" Laura said before returning her gaze to Det. Raiken. "You have my permission."

"Thank you, Laura," she replied with a smile.

Det. Raiken brought up a consent form with the relevant time signatures on her data pad and handed it to Laura, who glanced at it for a moment before touching three fingers to the screen. When the consent was formalized, Det. Raiken waited a moment as her data pad made a connection with Swizzy's retinal camera.

In Lynt City, like many cities on Earth, it was mandatory to have children below the age of thirteen fitted with retinal cameras. Parents could then keep track of their children with the touch of a screen and, in special circumstances, see what they'd been up to. Law enforcement authorities could also access the footage, with the proper consent, but it was a contentious issue.

Entire new branches of the legal system had been created to deal with questions that arose from their use. And yet, even with all its flaws, a majority of parents still agreed it was worth the complications.

As Det. Raiken watched the video footage from Swizzy's retinal camera play back on her screen at four times normal speed, she waited for some sign of the man in the Gildon suit. As Swizzy had said, he was playing a virtual racing game with several of his friends, but after one particular race ended, he turned toward Professor Meiket's apartment.

"*This is it,*" Det. Raiken thought to herself.

But just as she was expecting to finally see the face of her one and only suspect, the screen suddenly went blank and an error message appeared.

| SIGNAL FAILURE. RECORDING HALTED. |

Det. Raiken frowned and accepted the message with a touch before moving on to the next piece of viable footage. The video blinked to a view of Swizzy's friends and it was clear from the footage that he was running back to them. When his viewpoint turned toward Professor Meiket's apartment, smoke was billowing out the front entrance.

Det. Raiken's jaw muscles tightened.

"What is it?" Julia asked, noticing her reaction.

"Part of the recording was corrupted," she replied, looking up at her.

"The part you were interested in?" Julia predicted.

Det. Raiken nodded.

"I didn't do anything," Swizzy said, sounding scared.

"It's okay, Swizzy," Det. Raiken told him with a smile. "I know you didn't do anything wrong. I think your retinal camera may have malfunctioned, that's all. Did anyone else see the man you told me about?"

"Don't think so."

Det. Raiken turned to Laura.

"I'd like to access the retinal feeds from the other children," she said. "Do you think you could locate their parents?"

"I'll help you," Julia said, removing the need for Laura to agree, and the two of them quickly headed into the crowd.

It didn't take them long to round them up and, soon enough, Det. Raiken was surrounded by a group of concerned looking parents. She took a moment to explain the situation and, probably because she had Julia Wensing's approval, it wasn't long before she'd obtained the permissions she needed.

One by one, she checked the retinal videos from each child and wasn't at all surprised when every one of them went blank at the same time as Swizzy's.

"*Once could be a malfunction,*" she thought to herself. "*Five times is deliberate.*"

When she was done, she turned to the small gathering of parents and mentally debated the value of keeping the footage against the further worry it might cause them.

"Rest assured, your children saw nothing inappropriate," she said to them. "I won't be retaining any of the footage. Thank you very much for your assistance."

As the parents exchanged relieved looks, Swizzy tugged on his mother's dress.

"Can we go now?" he asked in a clearly frustrated voice.

Laura quickly looked at Det. Raiken for permission and then shooed the children away.

"Alright, off you go then. And don't go near the cordon. If we hear any alarms you'll be in big trouble."

"Yes, Mum," Swizzy replied, rolling his eyes as he turned away.

When the children were gone, Det. Raiken addressed the waiting parents again.

"Did any of you notice the man Swizzy described?"

She received a few shaking heads and a "No," from Laura, but Julia only frowned.

"Okay, thank you all very much for your cooperation," she said. "I'll be in touch if I need anything further."

As the other parents slowly drifted away in concerned conversation, Det. Raiken waited until they were gone and then turned to Julia.

"You didn't see anything?" she asked again.

"No, I didn't," Julia added, glancing at the departing parents with a frown, "but someone should have."

"What do you mean?" Det. Raiken asked.

"A man in a Gildon suit doesn't just walk in and out of our block without being noticed. And I can assure you, if any of the adults had seen him, I would know."

"I believe you," Det. Raiken replied. She knew this woman would have social networks that could rival even the best surveillance systems.

"I don't like it," Julia said, her expression grim.

For a moment, the two of them shared a look and Det. Raiken knew Julia was feeling the same unease that she did.

"Well, thank you for your help," she said with a sincerity she knew Julia would appreciate. "When I find out what really happened, I'll make sure I take the time to share what I can."

"Please do," Julia said with a nod.

At this, Det. Raiken turned to offer Laura a quick smile and then headed back to the cordon with a sour feeling in her gut. Lance was waiting patiently for her, but she didn't say anything to him until they were both well away from the crowd.

"What did you find out?" she asked.

"He wiped everything from his computer's memory before starting the fire. I couldn't find any stored data and, honestly, I don't think I will. Not even after a lengthy reconstruction."

"Just like Dr. Indari," Det. Raiken said quietly.

"Yes, ma'am. They did find some data pads near his body, but they were smashed even before the fire melted them. A large quantity of paper documents were also destroyed in the fire along with most of the flammable items in the apartment. The rest didn't have time to burn before the fire crew got here."

"Any sign of a struggle? Forced entry?"

"None, ma'am," Lance replied.

"Another dead end," she said.

"Another suicide," Lance added.

Det. Raiken thought about it for a moment. Even without Julia's opinion, she found it hard to believe two otherwise unrelated men would kill themselves in such horrific fashion while at the same time destroying any evidence that might point to a motive.

"Did you find anything, ma'am?" Lance asked politely.

"A description," she replied, "but no tangible evidence. One of the local kids saw a man in a Gildon suit leave Professor Meiket's apartment and get into a government vehicle with blue sides. But his retinal camera was somehow tampered with along with all the other children that were with him. The very moment he would have recorded the suspect and his vehicle, something corrupted the signal."

"That sounds suspicious," Lance said.

"Do you know of anything that can do that?" Det. Raiken asked him.

"Did the recording resume afterwards?"

"It did."

"Then sure," Lance replied, "but if the retinal camera was merely stopped from recording and not actually damaged in the process, and it was deliberate, then the device would have to be high-level military spec. Black ops hardware or something similar. I've heard of that kind of technology being developed, but I had no idea it was already in use."

"So, all we have to go on is an expensive suit, military spec hardware, and a high-end survival suit."

"And a diplomatic vehicle," Lance added.

"Why do you say that?" Det. Raiken asked.

"The kid's description. Government vehicles with blue markings have electrostatic suspension set for extra weight. That usually means armour plating."

"And government vehicles aren't usually armour plated," Det. Raiken finished for him.

"Yes, ma'am. As far as I know, armour plated government vehicles are exclusively loaned to visiting dignitaries."

Det. Raiken felt a spark of hope, but it came with a warning. Captain Faraday would never let her interrogate a diplomat. And as her data pad regularly synced with LCPD servers, he would have this information in the next ten minutes if she didn't do something quickly.

"Okay," she said, thinking fast, "use my data pad to get me a list of all visiting dignitaries."

"I'm... not meant to use another detective's data pad," Lance said, looking confused.

"I know. I'll explain why I need you to do this in a moment," she continued. "I want you to prioritise any dignitaries that have been given, or negotiated for, diplomatic immunity."

"Yes, ma'am," Lance replied before going to work with a troubled expression.

Det. Raiken knew she was going to face some heat if she talked to a diplomat without first clearing it with Captain Faraday, but her intuition was telling her this was the last lead she was going to get.

"Ma'am?" Lance said, handing her the data pad.

The list of diplomatic visitors was short and there was only one not engaged in important meetings over the last few hours.

"Loc Breeden," she said, locking the name in her memory.

He was a high-ranking business representative for Cosmotech Defence – a colossal, publicly funded corporation with dozens of privately owned labs that worked in all areas of technological development.

"Damn," she swore quietly.

This man didn't need to negotiate diplomatic immunity, he already had it in spades. Even if he was somehow responsible for the fire, there was nothing she could do about it.

"Alright," she said, handing the data pad back to Lance, "search for any information that might provide his whereabouts over the last year."

"Yes, ma'am," Lance replied, not hesitating this time.

When he was done, Det. Raiken saw that Loc Breeden had returned to Earth several times. She focussed on the time he'd spent in Lynt city and saw that he'd been instrumental in negotiating several large-scale mining contracts for Cosmotech Defence, with the same mining companies that had appeared on the list Lance had pulled together earlier.

"*He has access to a Mylinric life suit,*" she thought to herself.

It was circumstantial evidence at best, but Det. Raiken's instincts were quivering. She still had no motive, of course, but Loc Breeden was now her last and best lead. If Captain Faraday learned of it before she could capitalise, she may as well close the case now.

"Okay," she said, resolved despite the risks, "Lance, I'm going to ask you to do something else for me now. But before you agree, I need you to really think about what I'm asking you to do. I won't be upset if you decline my request."

"Yes, ma'am," Lance replied with an intent expression.

"I have reason to believe this Loc Breeden has information that could help with our case. But if Captain Faraday receives the information we've just downloaded, he'll terminate our investigation immediately. And so I'd like you to re-infect my data pad with the virus Professor Meiket used."

As she finished, Lance looked at her with wide eyes and then looked away as he contemplated the request. He knew the virus would wipe all the information from her data pad and prevent Captain Faraday from being updated. At least temporarily.

"I'll make sure the blame for re-infection isn't placed on your shoulders," she added after a moment. "Whatever the consequences, and there will be some, I'll face them all."

Lance looked at her again and Det. Raiken knew straight away he was going to agree. She'd tried her best not to influence him unfairly, but she knew that was impossible. Despite their relatively short time working together, he trusted and looked up to her.

"I'll do it, ma'am," he said, holding out a hand.

"Thank you, Lance," she replied, feeling a little rotten as she gave him her data pad.

It took Lance a surprisingly short time to do what she asked and, when he was finished, Det. Raiken could sense a change in him.

"*Your first real lesson,*" she thought, before adding firmly, "Right. We're going to the offices of Cosmotech Defence. It's time to roll the dice one last time."

"Yes, ma'am," Lance said with a grim expression.

PLANETARIUM, VALLES UNIVERSITY - June 5, 2147 - 1.25pm

ISAAC PACED THE FLOOR OF THE PLANETARIUM, NOT sure what else to do. Anya had been chatting with her online colleagues for some time now – none of whom seemed to have any problem with her 'old woman' act – and he'd given up trying to keep up with their conversation. The discussion was interesting enough and he was no stranger to mathematics, but when they started to apply it on a cosmological scale, he quickly lost interest.

"*I bet Jason would have loved it,*" he thought glumly.

He'd been trying to keep his mind off his brother since leaving Anya's apartment, but it wasn't getting easier. Everything he saw, did, even thought, seemed to remind him of Jason and the emptiness it created inside him was hard to cope with. It felt like an essential part of him was missing. More than a limb. Even more than his sight. It was as if half his senses had suddenly shut down and he was being forced to view the world through a keyhole.

"*I hate it,*" Isaac thought with a grimace.

"Isaac," Anya said, interrupting his sulk.

"Yes?" he replied quickly, glad for the distraction.

"I believe we may have a few interesting possibilities."

"Like…?"

"Well, first of all, some of my colleagues believe the red light may be something known as a Jupiter flare."

"A Jupiter flare?" Isaac said with a frown.

"Yes," Anya replied, nodding slowly. "Somewhat like a solar flare, but instead of coming from the surface of the sun, the transmission of plasma originates from Jupiter. This has been known to occur when asteroids impact with – and are vaporised by – Jupiter's upper atmosphere. Gases locked in the asteroid are released and, in the presence of a solar flare, are ionised to form a construct the plasma can travel along. After that, the Jupiter flare occurs very much like the propagation of lightning."

"A lightning bolt of plasma," Isaac said slowly, imagining what it might look like.

"But the consensus is it can't be a Jupiter flare," Anya added.

"Really?" Isaac said, looking back at her. "Why?"

"If it was, your vision would suggest a plasma bolt of such immense proportions that it would require conditions that have never been seen in our solar system."

"Oh," Isaac said, a little disappointed.

"There is, however, an argument for-" Anya continued, but before she could finish, a loud *BANG* cut her off and Isaac was blinded by an intense, white light.

"Argh!" he yelled, shielding his burning eyes and turning away from the source of the glare.

He heard shouts and the sound of heavy footsteps, but couldn't open his eyes to see who it was. A wave of panic washed through him and he staggered to one side, his balance completely gone. He rubbed his eyes in desperation, trying to see something beyond the glaring after-image, and yelped again when he felt someone take hold of his arm.

"Isaac?" Anya said in her old woman voice. "What is it?"

Isaac blinked. His eyes were fine. He looked around himself, searching for some sign of the shouting, running people, but the planetarium was empty.

"What happened?" Anya asked. "What did you see?"

"I... don't know," Isaac said, squinting as he remembered the intense light that had blinded him. "I just... I heard a loud bang and then a light blinded me. There was shouting and someone grabbed my arm."

"There was no bang," Anya said, shuffling toward him, "and no light either. You had another precognitive vision."

"What?" Isaac said with a frown. Then the implication hit him. "Oh no! We have to get out of here."

"This way," Anya said, guiding him toward the planetarium's projector.

"I don't know how long we have before time catches up," Isaac said quickly, his mind reeling, "but it won't be long."

"Then move faster, young man," Anya scolded him.

When they reached the projector, Anya grasped a handle on its side and pushed down. The switch caused a panel in the projector's curved base to slide aside and a small section of floor opened to reveal a narrow staircase.

"It leads down to the data servers," Anya said, before ushering him inside. "There's another way out at the west end of the room, just turn left at the bottom and watch out for the-"

But before she could finish, the flash-bang Isaac had seen moments earlier happened for real.

BANG!

Isaac expected it to be better with a bit of forewarning, but the shock sent him tumbling down the stairs, away from the light. His ears rang and he had to squint to see anything, but once he'd caught his balance, the light in the stairway was enough to guide him the rest of the way.

He heard Anya's voice urging him to "Go, go, go!" and so he rushed downward without looking back. He heard the distant sound of shouting, which urged him on faster, and almost slammed into the wall at the bottom of the stairs.

"*Go left*," he thought quickly, before pushing himself in that direction. "*And watch out for the... um...*"

He turned to ask Anya what to watch out for, but she was nowhere to be seen.

"Anya?" he called out hesitantly.

For a long moment, there was nothing but silence. Even the shouting had stopped. Then another deafening BANG split the air and Isaac barely had time to wince before a shock wave lifted him off his feet and slammed him into the blinking wall of lights behind him.

"Shizz," he swore breathlessly as he crumpled to the floor.

He didn't know what had happened to Anya, but it was clear that whoever had set off the explosion was still after him and Isaac felt a kind of primal panic take over. He scrambled to his feet and dashed away from the stairway without thinking, not sure if he was even going in the right direction, and noticed a low, transparent crossbeam just before he slammed into it.

"Shizz, shizz, shizz!" he swore again, hissing and rubbing his forehead.

At least he knew what Anya had tried to warn him about.

Stumbling on, Isaac headed for what he hoped was the west side of the server room and heard a third *BANG* split the air just as a flash of light burned his shadow onto the servers in front of him.

"*They're right behind me,*" he thought in a panic.

He ducked through a gap in the blinking servers, hoping they hadn't seen him, and finally saw an exit sign ahead. With a flush of relief, he pushed the door open with unexpected ease, but came to a sudden halt when something sharp stung his neck. He slapped at the pain and felt something small and hard against his fingers. He tore whatever it was from his neck and looked down to see a tiny needle with a soft, sprouting tail. Then his fingers went numb and a rush of warmth flowed through him.

"*What's... going on?*" he thought slowly.

He managed to blink, his eyes still burning from the earlier flash, then he saw a swinging door that towered over him at a strange angle.

"*I've... fallen over,*" he realised in surprise.

Something told him he should be fighting the numbing sensation with everything he had, but Isaac wasn't sure why. It felt good. And as a shadow stepped into view above him, he smiled gently.

"*Night, night,*" he thought as he drifted into a warm, comforting sleep.

Security Chief Hadrian Levine stared down at the target he'd just anaesthetised. Sabian's detailed planning had paid off. He wasn't sure how the target had anticipated their attack, but by ensuring all likely and unlikely avenues of escape were covered, the target was now safely secured.

All they had to do now was get him out of there.

"Chen, Harris," he said, "cradle the package."

At his command, Chen and Harris – who'd just appeared from the server room – went to work quickly. In moments they had fitted the target with a supporting harness that allowed them to fold him into a foetal position and pack his body into a medium sized equipment cabinet. It was the kind that resident lab assistants used to transport equipment between laboratories, so it was unlikely to arouse unwanted attention.

As they finished loading the target, Hadrian heard Greer and Baines enter the far end of the corridor.

"What did you do with the old woman?" he asked.

"She's sedated and sleeping it off in the planetarium," Greer replied. "She won't remember a thing."

"Good. I don't want her alerting security. The sooner we get out of here, the better."

Turning back to Chen and Harris, Hadrian saw that they were now ready to go.

"Right," he said. "Chen, you take point. Harris, you're on the package. Greer and Baines, you stalk the perimeter with me. Head off anyone who looks like they going to intercept Harris. The package has to get out in one piece so if there's any trouble, I don't want things to escalate. If you can't resolve the situation peacefully, simply delay them long enough for Harris to get out."

"Understood," his team replied quietly.

"Move out," Hadrian said.

At his command, the group moved to the end of the corridor and then exited one-by-one, making sure they weren't being observed. Hadrian was the last to join them and they were soon moving through the university in a loose formation that would avoid any suggestion they were associated with each other.

As they headed for the pre-arranged exit, the small group didn't attract any undue attention and Hadrian wasn't surprised. The planetarium where they'd made their initial assault was sturdy and soundproof. No one would have heard their incursion. And the computer server junction where they'd caught up with the target was even more deserted.

Hadrian noticed that Harris and the equipment cabinet received a few looks, but the witnesses must have constructed a believable explanation in their own minds, because none of them moved to intercept him and ask for one.

True to form, their fastidious employer, Sabian, had provided them with a route to the safest exit. Although moving the cabinet through the university was a simple matter, taking it out the front entrance would have been far too suspicious. So instead, they were headed for one of the remotely monitored delivery docks. By cloning the data transmissions being sent to security – which included video along with several temperature and chemical measurements – they could easily exit the building without being noticed.

When they reached the correct level, Chen took a moment to open the docking bay's large doors and Hadrian was pleased to see the vehicles they'd arrive in, just where they'd left them.

Harris moved to the closest one and was about to load the equipment cabinet into the rear compartment when Greer suddenly spoke up behind them.

"We have incoming."

Hadrian's eyes flickered to the security feeds Greer had been monitoring.

"Security?" he asked.

"No, I don't think so. It... it looks like the old lady we sedated, only... she's too young. Could be her daughter? She's closing fast."

"Delay her," Hadrian ordered. "Chen, Harris, get the package to the drop off point. Baines, you're in the support vehicle with me. Greer, once you've dealt with the threat, meet us at the drop off point."

"Understood," his team replied as one.

By now, Chen and Harris had finished loading the package and Hadrian watched them pull away with the whine of a powerful electric motor. He then joined Baines in the second vehicle and as they accelerated away themselves, quickly switched the vehicle's console display to the security feed they'd hijacked from the university.

Greer was right. The assailant was approaching fast and looked incredibly angry. As she closed on Greer, he raised his arms in a non-threatening way, but she simply lowered her shoulder, barrelled into him and tackled him to the ground.

Hadrian heard Greer grunt in surprise and saw him move his hips so he could throw the woman off, but she was too quick. As soon as he tried to get out from under her, the now snarling woman began pummelling him with several hard, accurate blows.

Hadrian knew Greer was tough, but he was still impressed when he saw the soldier scramble out from under the onslaught and get back to his feet.

In response, the woman leapt up and hit him a few more times in the midsection before she leapt back suddenly and threw a wild kick at his head. Greer dodged it, barely, and managed to throw a few well-placed punches of his own, but the woman absorbed the blows without seeming to feel them and was soon throwing another wild series of punches, elbows, and knees of her own.

"*Who is she?*" Hadrian thought in confusion.

He had the security feed take an image of her snarling face and ran some facial recognition software which quickly identified her.

"*Anya Polovski,*" he thought with a frown. "*A registered psychiatrist.*"

Turning his attention back to the battle being played out on the vehicle's console, Hadrian could tell Greer was in trouble. Rather than fighting back, he was now focussed solely on defending himself and, in a last ditch effort, he exploded away from the wall and tackled the woman to the floor. She landed hard with a grunt Hadrian knew meant she was winded and Greer didn't hesitate to take the advantage and sprint away with a limp.

Glancing at the map on their vehicle's dash, Hadrian shook his head. He would have liked to have been further away than this, but this woman was clearly more than one soldier could handle.

Turning back to the security feed, Hadrian watched as Greer reached the docking bay and leapt into the last vehicle. The woman wasn't far behind him, but even as fast as she was running, she couldn't reach Greer before he pulled out of the docking bay.

Letting out a quiet breath, Hadrian frowned deeper and wondered if he should be worried about this Anya Polovski.

"I'm away," Greer said, sounding breathless.

"The assailant?" Hadrian asked.

"I think I lost her," Greer replied.

"Lost her?" Baines scoffed. "You mean, you couldn't finish her off?"

"Fuck you, Baines," Greer swore at him. "You didn't see her! She's some kind of... martial arts expert, or something."

"She fucked you up?" Chen laughed.

"Skive off, Chen. She would have wiped the floor with you. It was all I could do to get away."

"Alright, Greer," Hadrian stepped in. "What's the level of threat here?"

"Low, sir. She's well behind…"

But before he finished the sentence, Greer trailed off and Hadrian felt a warning sensation at the back of his neck.

"What is it?" he asked quickly.

"Shit! She got to a vehicle and… holy fuck, she's driving like a maniac! She's coming up on me, fast!"

"Change your route," Hadrian said quickly. "Lead her away from the package."

"Understood," Greer growled, clearly as frustrated as he was angry.

Hadrian waited a moment for confirmation the threat was following the bait.

"Shit!" Greer swore again. "She's gone past me! I don't know how, but she must have identified the lead vehicle back at the university. She knows you have the package."

Hadrian paused. Whoever this Anya Polovski was, she was good. Professionally good, perhaps. Sabian hadn't said anything about the package being guarded, but it was hard to believe a man like him could miss such an important detail.

"Catch up to her and take her out if you can," he told Greer quickly. "I'm calling the boss."

Hadrian didn't like the idea of involving Sabian and knew his superior wouldn't appreciate the call, but this was rapidly getting out of control and he didn't want to make the mistake of forgetting who was really in charge.

"Yes?" Sabian asked, his gaunt, disapproving face appearing on the vehicle's console.

"Sir," Hadrian said quickly, "we are inbound, twelve minutes from the rendezvous point, but we're being followed. Request permission to leave the package and deal with the threat personally."

Sabian remained quiet for a moment then he spoke in a calculating tone.

"Will you reach the rendezvous before your pursuer?"

"Yes, sir."

"Then your request is denied," Sabian added abruptly. "Do not abandon the target. Bring him directly to me."

Hadrian paused in confusion. This didn't sound like the order of someone as meticulous as Sabian.

"Sir, if we don't take strategic action, it is highly likely the threat will follow us all the way to the rendezvous point. May I at least have permission to change our route so we can undertake an ambush?"

"Negative," Sabian answered firmly. "Whoever is following you, once the target is in my presence they will no longer pose a threat. Just get the target to me as quickly as possible."

Hadrian didn't like Sabian's response any more than he knew his team would. This wasn't how you protected your objective, your team, or yourself. But what any of them thought didn't matter. When you operated at this level, the rules were simple. Orders were orders.

"Understood, sir," he finished promptly.

Sabian ended the communication without another word and Hadrian was left shaking his head in frustration.

"Sir?" Baines spoke in his ear piece.

"We keep moving," Hadrian said firmly.

"But that woman's an obvious threat," Baines began in a disapproving tone. "We could easily take her out if we just-"

"We have our orders," Hadrian interrupted him harshly. "We get the target to our employer as quickly as possible."

"With respect, sir, but what kind of bullshit order is that? We're leading a potential threat straight to home fucking base! If this package is as important as that twitchy shut-in says it is, we can't afford to let her get that close. She overwhelmed Greer for fucks sake!"

"I'm well aware of the situation, Baines," Hadrian replied smartly, "but we're getting paid to follow orders. We do what Sabian says and handle the threat back at the base. Is that clear?"

Baines paused as if he was about to say more, but he just grunted something unintelligible and thankfully didn't push any further.

Hadrian didn't blame the man for his concern, but on missions like this you couldn't always control how things played out. If Sabian thought he had things under control then they would play along like good soldiers. And if things went to shit then they would do their jobs and clean up the mess like they always did.

Hadrian's real concern was that he didn't have all the pertinent facts. Sabian clearly had a reason for being so confident and while Hadrian didn't know that reason, there was a risk he might make a bad tactical decision.

"*I just hope he knows what he's doing,*" he thought with a frown. "*One way or another, we're bringing this party straight to him.*"

LOC BREEDEN PRIDED HIMSELF ON KNOWING ABOUT important events before they occurred. It was an important precursor to his position with the Triumvirate and it allowed him to very effectively manipulate the world around him. And so it was a decidedly unpleasant surprise when he was informed detective Miana Raiken and her young protégé were requesting to meet with him.

"*What is she doing here?*" he thought, spinning the red-stoned ring around his middle finger in irritation.

Since the Triumvirate had commanded him to watch her, Loc had gained access to all the information she'd collected in her investigation. It was a thorough accounting of what little evidence had been left at the scene of Dr. Indari's death, but there was nothing in it that could explain her presence now.

"*It appears I should have taken this detective more seriously,*" he thought, releasing the ring and sitting back in his chair.

It would have been a simple matter to have her followed, but with the information he'd analysed and the ongoing updates he was receiving from his agents in the LCPD, it didn't seem necessary.

Of course, his current predicament suggested an unacceptably weak link in the LCPD's information chain.

"Something I'll have to deal with later," he noted coldly.

The other surprise was that Det. Raiken was willing to confront him at all. Any normal detective would surely understand the dangers of approaching someone with diplomatic immunity. He could very easily create political trouble for Det. Raiken and with the career history he'd read through, she would be unlikely to survive another serious infraction.

As the thoughts sifted through his mind, Loc watched her on the security screen that hovered above his desk. She was a handsome woman, clearly confident in her social and professional abilities. He could see by her body language that she would not be easily manipulated – at least, not in the conventional sense – but he wasn't overly concerned. There were always other, more drastic measures to fall back on.

The detective's assistant, Lance Hendrickson, was another matter entirely. He appeared calm on the surface, but Loc could tell he wasn't comfortable being here. He may have been assured that any political backlash would fall squarely on Det. Raiken's shoulders, but his body language told a different story. His sense of self-preservation was clearly more evolved than his superior's.

"But what does she know?" Loc wondered.

He already knew from his conversation with the unfortunate symbologist that the detective wasn't even close to understanding the truth. And yet, despite her ignorance, she had somehow found him. It was an intriguing situation. Either Det. Raiken had information that Loc wasn't aware of, or he'd made a mistake. Both explanations implied fallibility on his part and so both were equally unacceptable.

"But what to do?" he thought to himself.

Normally, he would never allow someone like this an audience, particularly given the Triumvirate's warning. But he wanted to know what had led her to him, if only so he could avoid making the same mistake in the future.

"*There's no threat here,*" he decided, "*and this could be the perfect opportunity to end this pointless investigation once and for all.*"

Leaning forward so he could touch a glowing icon at the edge of his desk, Loc called Security.

"Yes, sir?" a voice answered immediately.

"There's a forensic detective at the front desk," he said, watching her on the screen. "Bring her and her assistant directly to my office."

"Right away, sir," the voice replied.

Sitting back again, Loc absently kissed his red-stoned ring and then clasped his hands as he watched the detective being informed she would be allowed an immediate audience. She looked suitably surprised and even glanced up at the camera that was filming her.

"That's right," Loc said with a smile. "It's your lucky day, detective."

As directed, the security staff escorted Det. Raiken and her assistant directly to Loc's office. A short tone announced their arrival and Loc touched another icon on his desk before standing politely to greet them.

"Detectives Raiken and Hendrickson," he said with a smile and a welcoming gesture. "Welcome to Cosmotech Defence. Please, have a seat."

Det. Raiken returned his smile, but betrayed nothing as she moved around to sit in the seat he'd just offered them.

"Thank you, Mr. Breeden," she acknowledged in a formal tone.

Lance, however, responded to the welcoming behaviour by relaxing noticeably and Loc could see he'd already descended several levels of anxiety.

"I believe you have some questions for me," Loc began, taking his own seat and sitting forward in a relaxed, helpful position. "Please, ask away."

Det. Raiken paused for a moment and Loc felt a small thrill as he pondered what she would lead with.

"I'd like to confirm your whereabouts this morning at eleven-forty-five," she said, clearly not pulling any punches.

"Of course," Loc said with an accommodating smile. "I was taking in the sights of your wonderful city. I'm not sure exactly where I was at eleven-forty-five, but my movement logs will confirm a location for you. I'll have my people send you the information directly."

The detective didn't react to this, but Loc knew she wouldn't expect to receive the information. Despite his words, she would know that as soon as she walked out of his office there were a dozen ways Loc could quite easily, and legally, avoid honouring his promise.

"Thank you," she replied after a moment, "that will be quite useful. Did you visit anyone in particular in your travels?"

"Hmmm…" Loc said, stroking his chin theatrically. "I don't believe so, but I could be wrong. Again, I will have my people look into it."

The detective stared at him for a moment, but no frustration showed. She was better at this game than Loc expected.

"Have you ever met a man named Klaus Meiket?" she asked after a moment.

"*Ah,*" Loc thought, smiling inside. "*Now she goads me directly to gauge my reaction. The battle is truly joined.*"

"Klaus Meiket," he said out loud, staring directly into her eyes. "The name seems familiar, but I meet many people in my line of work. Some are very important and some are barely worthy of notice."

The last he said with a tone that suggested the detective and her side-kick were placed firmly in the second category.

"He was killed this afternoon," Det. Raiken added bluntly.

Loc carefully held his expression neutral, but was surprised to find that he was actually annoyed at her indirect accusation. Despite enjoying this battle of wits, he wasn't used to such bold confrontation and didn't like the way it was now making him feel.

"Killed, you say?" he said, prepared to see how far she would take this.

152

"Someone burned him to death," she added.

"That's terrible," Loc replied, sitting back and baiting her with a shocked expression. "Someone deliberately burned him?"

"His apartment's computers were hacked so the fire would be fed with oxygen. Almost everything he owned was destroyed in the fire."

"But, I don't understand," Loc said, "why are you telling me this? You don't honestly believe I could have been involved?"

Det. Raiken remained silent for a long moment and Loc could almost hear her mentally debating the merits of pushing him further. It must have taken a considerable amount of courage to come here in the first place, but there was a very large difference between making enquiries about Loc's whereabouts and insinuating he was involved in another man's death.

After a moment the detective seemed to decide to change her approach and Loc watched with interest as she pulled something from her pocket, unfolded it, and placed it on the desk in front of her. He glanced down at it, eager to see what evidence she was trying to shock him with, and immediately felt a tension in his chest. It was a piece of paper covered in the symbols Dr. Indari had carved into his flesh.

"What's this?" he asked, consciously relaxing his chest muscles and putting on a confused expression.

He should have known this was coming and yet by using this barbaric paper technology, she'd managed to ambush him. It was annoying. Loc knew very little about these symbols other than what the symbologist had told him – some nonsense about an ancient language linked to a religion known as the 'One True Path' – but he knew they had significance to the Triumvirate. They wouldn't have made Dr. Indari carve them so deeply into his own flesh for nothing.

And yet, despite being present when Dr. Indari had cut out his own eyes, Loc still didn't know any more about the incident than the detective did. It was one of the few occasions he'd allowed the Triumvirate to 'use' him like a psychic puppet and so he retained no memory of it. All he knew for certain was that whatever Dr.

Indari had been doing in those caves, it had made the Triumvirate angrier than Loc had ever seen them. He certainly didn't know why they'd chosen to leave such damning evidence behind, but it wasn't his place to question them. Nor was it the place of this petulant, if strong-willed, detective.

"Have you seen these symbols before?" she asked, her tone cold.

"No," Loc lied as he searched for any hint of understanding in her eyes. "What do you think they are?"

"Professor Klaus Meiket knew," she replied, ignoring his question.

"Did he tell you that?" Loc asked, knowing he hadn't.

"He didn't need to," the detective answered pointedly.

Again, Loc felt a surge of irritation. This woman's arrogance was beginning to get on his nerves. She had no idea what he was capable of and yet here she sat, challenging him with her eyes and with her snide, impolite questions.

"I'm struggling to see the point of this, detective," he said, wearing an inquisitive expression as his temper ran out.

"I was hoping you'd share what you know about these symbols," she said, pulling the page toward her, "but it's obvious you know less than I do."

At this, Loc's jaw muscles tightened.

"I didn't say that," he said slowly.

"Not out loud," she replied, offering him a smile that was almost as good as his own.

Loc frowned, which was an appropriate response given the detective's behaviour, but he knew it was more because his anger was very close to boiling over.

"You think you can read me, detective?" he asked.

"I apologise for this intrusion," she continued, ignoring him in a way that made Loc's fist tighten. "I'm certain now that you know nothing of any worth."

Loc very rarely indulged in violent action, but he suddenly felt an urge to stand up and strike this woman.

"What are you implying, detective?" he asked, carefully keeping his expression neutral.

"Implying?" she said, locking gazes with him suddenly. "Just that you're not as important to this case as I'd imagined. Clearly there are higher powers at play."

Loc knew she was baiting him now, but he didn't care. It had been so long since he'd been tested like this that he'd almost forgotten what it was like. She may have beaten him at his own manipulative game, but he was going to teach this pretentious bitch a lesson she would never forget.

Staring into her eyes, he almost laughed at the arrogance she offered him in return. The detective was making it so easy for him. She may know that everyone experienced some level of psychic connection when they met another's gaze, but she clearly didn't realise that for Loc, it was also a conduit straight into her mind.

With a practiced thought, he drew on the psychic power the Triumvirate had gifted him with and slammed into Det. Raiken's closely guarded mind with everything he had. His psychic attack scoured through her subconscious defences like rice paper and he could tell immediately that her will was strong and her intuition sharply honed. But she had no defences against a direct psychic attack. Her resistance lasted less than a second and as Loc took control of her body, the detective's momentarily terrified expression fell slack.

She was now unable to look away, talk, or move in any way.

"I think it would be a good idea if we talked alone," Loc said calmly. "Would you ask your assistant to wait outside, please, detective?"

Det. Raiken turned to Lance.

"Wait outside," she said in the characteristic monotone of an enthralled mind.

Lance gave her a confused look.

"Uh, yes, ma'am," he said uncertainly.

Loc offered him a smile as he rose to leave and only returned his gaze to Det. Raiken when the door had closed behind him.

"And now," he said, "tell me, detective, what led you to me?"

"A young boy named Swizzy saw you leave Professor Meiket's apartment," she continued in monotone. "He followed you to your diplomatic vehicle and saw you pull away from the curb."

"Of course," Loc said, "a child."

One of his psychic gifts included the ability to cloud the minds of those in general proximity so they either failed to notice him, or simply didn't remember they had. But the minds of children were much harder to influence than adults. They had less social conditioning and so were not as vulnerable to the psychic tricks that worked so well on their parents. He hadn't noticed the boy and coldly noted that he would have to be more careful in the future.

"What did you plan to achieve by coming here?" he asked after a moment.

"I wanted answers," the detective replied simply.

"Answers," Loc said with a raised eyebrow. "What makes you think you deserve answers?"

"I'm a forensic detective," she answered simply, "and I'm smarter than you."

Loc felt a sudden chill of outrage and glared at her for several seconds before breaking into laughter.

"Smarter than me?" he said. "Oh, detective, you're more ignorant than I thought. Surely you're aware I have diplomatic immunity within Lynt City limits. And even if that weren't true, did you really believe you could manipulate me into confessing?"

"If I could speak to you, yes."

Loc shook his head in amazement.

"Such arrogance," he said, but at the same time, he realised she had managed to coax at least some reaction from him.

And with that, his anger returned, swamping his short-lived amusement.

"Let me tell you why I granted you this audience, detective," he said in a spiteful tone. "I wanted you to know just how insignificant and ineffective you really are. You neither have the law to back you up, or the ability to stop me from doing whatever I want. And yet… even now, fully aware of what I'm capable of… I can still feel you fighting me."

Loc frowned again. This detective's subconscious was surprisingly strong. He had hoped to leave a suggestion in her mind that would cause her to close the investigation and then kill herself, but after seeing how strong her psyche was, he couldn't be sure such a suggestion would hold long enough to be carried out.

"What shall I do with you?" he said thoughtfully.

Killing her would no doubt be satisfying, but a forensic detective's death, even if it was clearly a suicide, would raise too many questions. And besides, he felt compelled to make this woman suffer for her impertinence. Not only had she shown him contempt in a way Loc hadn't experienced in years, but she honestly believed she was better than him. That, in itself, deserved a lesson.

"I'm not an unreasonable man, detective," he said after a short pause, "and I think you deserve to know a few things before I let you go. First, let me assure you that I made both Doctor Indari and professor Meiket kill themselves. I could do the same to you, right here and now, in fact. But I've decided not to. Do you know why, detective?"

"No," she answered dutifully.

Loc smiled.

"Because I don't need to," he replied simply. "Despite the knowledge you now possess, you can do nothing about it. There is no evidence to convict me of these crimes and, even if there were, I'm protected in ways you can't possibly imagine. I could destroy you in so many ways, detective. So many *interesting* ways. But why should I bother? You've already done the job for me. Your actions today were reckless, detective, even for someone of your dubious history. And yet, quite fortuitously, they have ensured your pointless investigation will end prematurely, just as I would like it to."

Loc paused for a moment to allow the facts to sink in. He wanted this woman to know just how foolish and stupid she really was.

"But fear not," he continued after a moment. "You will leave here of your own free will. You will remain free to suffer the consequences of your arrogance and live on knowing just how helpless you really are. Perhaps you will despair and commit suicide without needing any prompting on my part? Well, we can only wait and see. But before I let you go, I have a small test for you."

At this, Loc stood up, walked around the table and stared into the detective's eyes a moment longer before withdrawing from her mind. As soon as his influence was gone, the detective leapt to her feet, sending the chair she'd been sitting on clattering to the floor.

"What will you do with your free will, detective?" he asked, holding out his hands. "Do you truly believe your actions can make a difference? You don't know how I do it, but you're now fully aware of what I'm capable of and can easily surmise my guilt. So there's only one unanswered question that remains. Will you dare to arrest me?"

Det. Raiken stood in shocked silence, staring at the monster before her. She'd never felt so afraid in her life. Afraid and *angry*. This man, this *murderer*, was guilty of forcing both Dr. Indari and Professor Meiket to kill themselves, and could easily do the same to her or anyone else that might get in his way. And yet there was nothing she could do about it.

Det. Raiken's eyes moved from Loc's mocking smile to his hands. She knew he wanted her to try and arrest him. She knew he wanted her to see what would happen. She knew he wanted her to experience just how powerless she really was. But despite knowing all this, the urge to put cuffs on him was stronger than ever.

Her principles demanded she lock his hands together, no matter how severe the repercussions, but her sense of self-preservation screamed that someone with this much power, even without his terrifying psychic abilities, could end her career with a single phone call. There was no choice here. She had to back down.

"Damn it, no!" she thought savagely. *"I will not submit to this man!"*

Perhaps it was an instinctual urge to deny the first truly evil human she'd ever met, perhaps it was a self-destructive streak, or even simple pig-headedness, but Det. Raiken couldn't seem to stop herself from clasping the cuffs that hung at her waist and deliberately placing them over the waiting hands of Loc Breeden, Cosmotech Defence's business liaison to Lynt City.

He didn't resist, he simply smiled wider and the second she placed the cuffs on him, the doors to his office burst open and half a dozen Cosmotech security officers rushed in. They surrounded Det. Raiken and Loc in seconds, levelling their weapons aggressively, and close behind them were men and women who looked suspiciously like lawyers. They planted themselves on either side of Loc with expressions that shouted indignation and malicious, intellectual portent and yet, despite the seriousness of the situation, none of them spoke.

For a long moment the bizarre scene was frozen in its overwhelming absurdity. Then Loc spoke in a casual tone.

"Remove the cuffs."

Det. Raiken stared into his smiling, dangerous eyes, refusing to let her fear show.

"No," she replied defiantly.

"I admire your bravery, detective, I really do," Loc said, still smiling, "but you're on Cosmotech property. This is effectively sovereign territory. Not only do I have the authority to arrest and detain you at my pleasure, but I could quite legally have my security shoot you. Now, I don't think either response is appropriate here. We're both reasonable people, detective, and I have very generously offered you a way out. All you have to do is what I have commanded. Remove... the... cuffs."

Det. Raiken clenched her jaw and felt a wave of anxiety sour her stomach. She refused to break Loc's insidious gaze, but her good sense finally managed to burst free of her stubborn nature and so she very slowly removed the cuffs from his wrists.

"Well done," he said, before lowering his hands and clasping them behind his back. "It appears you can be compliant all on your own, detective. Another lesson well learned, I hope."

Det. Raiken wanted to say something to unsettle him, to defy the fact he'd just dominated her so brazenly, but fear kept her silent.

"Isn't the human spirit a wonderful thing?" Loc asked with a smile. Then he took in a deep breath and shooed her away with an arrogant wave of his hand. "Now you may go."

Det. Raiken turned from his goading eyes without a word and tried to ignore the weapons still trained on her as she exited.

When she was outside the room, Lance rushed up to her with a concerned expression.

"Ma'am? What happened in there? When I came out there were security officers waiting and… when they stormed the office, I… are you alright?"

"No, I don't think so," she said, struggling to hold back tears. "Let's get out of here. I'll debrief you when we get back to the precinct."

Lance seemed to realise she was in no mood to talk and so he remained thankfully silent as they left Cosmotech offices. Det. Raiken noticed that security was much more conspicuous on the way out than it had been on the way in, but the large men with their deadly weapons didn't seem quite so frightening after what she'd just experienced.

She led Lance back to the vehicle they'd arrived in and not thirty seconds after they'd pulled away from the curb, Det. Raiken's console lit up with an incoming call.

"Here we go," she sighed, activating the call.

An image of Captain Faraday appeared on the console, looking just as angry as she expected.

"What do you think you're doing?" he roared. "I've just had the unfortunate pleasure of being contacted by the most expensive fucking lawyer on Mars. He informed me that for reasons you'd better be able to explain, you've been making serious accusations in relation to the suicide cases you're investigating, against a man with diplomatic immunity no less!"

"Loc Breeden is connected to the deaths, Captain," she said firmly. "I just wanted to-"

"Suicides, detective! They were suicides! Which means it doesn't matter what connection Loc Breeden may or may not have had with them. Do you know what your suspect was doing earlier today, detective? He was meeting with the corporations that *own* Lynt City. Do you have *any* idea what kind of trouble you've caused with your little interview?"

"These suicides are part of something much bigger, Captain," Det. Raiken said firmly. "I was merely trying to gather enough information to convince you of that. You gave me till the end of today and I did what I believed was necessary to stop this case from ending up a small packet of unused data in an abandoned case file."

"I trust your instincts, Raiken, truly I do," Captain Faraday said, his voice losing its edge, "but this is well out of my hands now. You don't know how powerful Loc Breeden is."

"Why should that matter?" she snapped.

"Don't give me that, detective, you know it matters," Captain Faraday shot back. "It always matters."

"Well that's not good enough," Det. Raiken almost shouted. "That man is clearly connected to one of two horrendous, unexplainable deaths, suicides or not. I refuse to accept that his station means I can't even talk to him without repercussions. Why don't you just admit it, Captain? The real reason you won't back me up is that you're scared of losing your job."

The Captain sat back with a grim expression.

"Yes, Raiken. As usual, you're exactly right."

Det. Raiken saw the sudden fatigue in her Captain's eyes and felt a chill run down her spine.

"I tried to warn you," he continued, shaking his head, "so many times. But now? Well, now it's too late. As of this moment, you're relieved of duty. You are no longer a forensic detective with the Lynt City precinct."

Det. Raiken – now simply Miana Raiken – opened her mouth, stunned despite being ready for something like this.

"You will retain your access privileges temporarily so you can remove any personal items from your office," Captain Faraday continued, not meeting her shocked gaze. "You will be accompanied by a Corporate Section officer whilst inside the precinct and your access will be revoked as soon as you leave the station. I'm… sorry about this, Miana, I truly am. You were a valuable asset. But… you just don't know when to back off."

Miana tried to think of something to say. She knew Loc Breeden was sadistic and capable of forcing her dismissal, but not this quickly. This was her Captain's decision alone and it hurt that the one person who might have backed her up, who *should* have backed her up, was giving up on her.

"Loc Breeden is-" she began to say.

"I don't want to hear anything more about it," Captain Faraday interrupted her firmly. "That is no longer your case. I advise you not to mention it again, to anyone, or you might find yourself losing more than your job."

Miana didn't miss the threat in his words, or his tone.

"*He thinks he's doing me a favour,*" she thought to herself.

The knowledge that her Captain was at least trying to look out for her was heartening, but it didn't make much of a difference after what had just happened.

"I understand," she said after a moment.

"Very well," Captain Faraday said, before pausing awkwardly.

"What about Lance?" Miana asked.

"He's already been reassigned. He'll be studying under detective Boulton."

"Boulton is an idiot," Miana protested, glad she had something else to focus on. "He wouldn't know the first thing about developing Lance's talents. I know what I'm talking about Captain. You've seen my on-going assessments. If you want the best from Lance, give him to Hamdii, not Boulton."

"I'll... take it under advisement."

"You'd better," she told him firmly. "Lance is a highly capable officer and if you invest in him, I promise you'll be glad you did."

"Alright, Miana," Captain Faraday said, raising his hands in supplication. "You don't have to convince me, I'll give him to Hamdii."

"Good," she said after a moment. "Thank you, Captain."

Captain Faraday gave her a final, sad look.

"I'm not your Captain anymore," he said with a cold finality. "Goodbye, Miana, and whatever you choose to do... good luck."

"Goodbye," Miana replied with a hollow feeling in her chest.

Her Captain's image disappeared a moment later and she sat back, feeling numb.

"Ma'am?" Lance said quietly.

Miana turned her head a little, but couldn't bring herself to meet Lance's eyes.

"I'm... sorry," she said automatically.

"No, you've got nothing to apologise for, ma'am. They're wrong. You've done nothing to warrant dismissal. Nothing. I'll explain to Captain Faraday-"

"Don't," she said sharply, finally looking him in the eyes. "I'm finished Lance and there's nothing you can do or say that will change that. If you try to defend me you'll only harm your career. I can handle what they're doing to me, but not if it means taking you down as well. Do you understand that, Lance? Do you realise how important it is that you forget this and do the best you can under Hamdii?"

"I... yes, ma'am," Lance said reluctantly. "This is just... it's just wrong."

"You're right, Lance," Miana said softly. "But that's life in Lynt City. I obviously didn't learn that lesson well enough, but you can."

"Just tell me one thing," Lance told her.

"What is it?"

"What happened after you asked me to leave Loc Breeden's office?"

For a moment, Miana thought about telling Lance everything and was ashamed to find that she was honestly tempted. But she knew it would only put him in danger. If he believed her, there was no way he would leave it alone and Loc would eventually find out. For whatever reason, he'd decided to let her live, but there was no guarantee he would do the same for Lance.

"You saw me show him the symbols," she said, deciding that some truth was better than none, "and based on his reaction, I goaded him into an angry response, hoping he would slip up and give us something we could use. He didn't give me anything in the end, but when you left the room he... insulted me and I... I tried to arrest him."

"Arrest him?" Lance said, "but why? You told me he had diplomatic immunity."

"I was angry that his office meant he didn't have to answer my questions," she replied, the lie bitter on her tongue, "and it made me reckless. It was a stupid thing to do and... well, look what it got me. Don't make the same mistake, Lance. Never let your emotions get in the way of an investigation."

She wanted to explain herself better, say the words out loud so she could analyse them in a context outside her own thoughts, but she knew Lance wasn't the one to do it with.

"Yes, ma'am," he said quietly.

She could tell by the tone of his voice that he wouldn't ask any more questions. He was too embarrassed for her. Accusing a man with diplomatic immunity was bad enough, but trying to arrest him? It was a rookie mistake at best and at worst…

"*I've lost my mind,*" she thought bitterly.

And as they headed back to the LCPD precinct station, Miana felt a tear finally break free of her control, spill from her eyelid, and roll down her cheek.

THE VEHICLE CARRYING HADRIAN AND BAINES screeched into the alleyway next to the building they were using as a base of operations. Chen and Harris had already unloaded the package and were ready to move it inside.

As soon as they were parked, Hadrian jumped out of the vehicle and joined them.

"Chen, get that up to Sabian right away," he snapped. "Harris, you're with me. Baines, go with Chen and get some real weapons. After what that woman did to Greer, I don't want to engage her without the right tools."

"Sir!" Baines barked.

Hadrian turned to Harris.

"You and I are hanging back to engage the threat once she's inside the building," he said quickly "I'm not giving her an opportunity to use that vehicle against us. It's the deadliest and possibly only weapon she's got."

"Understood, sir," Harris replied quickly.

Hadrian activated his comlink.

"Greer, do you have the threat in sight?"

"Only just," Greer replied, his voice tense. "She's coming in hot. You have about ten seconds!"

"Then ease off," Hadrian replied quickly. "Let her pull up and exit the vehicle, then take her out with yours."

"My pleasure," Greer growled, before adding, "six seconds."

"Right," Hadrian said, before running to the entrance Chen and Baines had just disappeared through.

As he counted down in his mind, Hadrian took up position beneath the stairwell just inside the doorway so he could see the end of the alley. Then, just as Greer predicted, the woman who'd chased them through the Valles Dome screeched into view and zoomed down the alley toward them.

Her glistening pink vehicle screamed to a precise halt right next to the entrance and the windshield rose almost instantly. Hadrian saw the occupant – Anya Polovski – and was immediately struck by how beautiful and non-threatening she appeared. How had this young, soft looking woman taken out Greer, one of his best hand-to-hand fighters?

Then something happened that took him completely by surprise. Just as the windshield reached its full height, the woman's expression changed. What began as something close to excitement and pleasure was twisted into the most intense grimace of anger Hadrian had ever seen. And as the bizarre change came over her face, the woman's body seemed to change as well. Her muscles tensed and her relaxed, curvaceous figure was replaced by a trembling apparition that leapt out of the vehicle with the same speed she'd used to take on Greer.

As soon as she was out of the vehicle, Anya whirled toward the end of the alley and stood ready.

"*She knows what's coming,*" Hadrian thought, just as Greer's vehicle screamed into view.

A plan to try and sedate the target while she was distracted flashed into Hadrian's mind, but Greer was already accelerating toward her and in the next instant he crashed into the pink motorcycle with a mighty *CRUNCH!*

The impact should have taken Anya along with it, but she somehow managed to leap onto the side of her vehicle just before it was hit and spring into a perfectly timed summersault that carried her safely out of harm's way.

"*Incredible,*" Hadrian thought in amazement.

He was sure Greer would be okay, but realised it was now up to him and Harris to stop her from getting any further.

As Anya sprinted toward the building's entrance, Hadrian carefully aimed his dart gun at the place her neck was about to pass through and fired just as she barrelled through.

The *sssft* of the gas propelling the dart reached his ears and Hadrian focussed on the spot he'd just aimed at, hoping it would soon contain the soft flesh of his target's neck, but the body moving through the doorway was too low.

"*She's sliding through,*" Hadrian thought, a moment before Harris stepped in to intercept her.

As the two fighters clashed, Hadrian took a step back and witnessed one of the most violent and rapid exchanges he'd ever seen. Harris wasn't quite the fighter Greer was, but he knew how to handle himself, and yet it was immediately obvious he was outclassed. Anya seemed to anticipate his attacks with an instinctual bobbing movement that left her completely unscathed whilst countering with powerful punches and kicks that looked like they should have come from a much heavier person.

As the one-sided battle progressed, Hadrian reloaded and raised his dart gun again, but Anya saw what he was doing and managed to pull Harris into a Muay Thai grapple that put him squarely in the way.

"Get clear!" Hadrian yelled, hoping Harris would understand and give him the opening he needed.

But as soon as Harris tried to duck out of the way, Anya used the movement to twist him round and force an arm up behind his back. Her grimace showed the effort she was putting into the hold and Hadrian wasn't surprised when a sickening *CRACK* split the air.

Harris screamed in pain, his arm clearly broken, and Hadrian clenched his teeth in frustration, searching for something to aim at. But before he could fire, Anya pushed Harris at him and forced him back. He avoided the stumbling Harris and quickly looked for a target, but something hard smacked into his hand and the dart gun was ripped from his grip.

Ignoring the weapon as it clattered loudly to the floor, Hadrian instinctively moved into a defensive stance and barely managed to fend off another blow that would have knocked him out cold.

"*God, she's fast,*" he thought to himself, "*and angry.*"

He took several quick steps back as she advanced on him, trying to find the right distance so he could retaliate in a meaningful way, but just as they were about to engage, Greer sprinted in through the entrance and crash-tackled Anya to the ground.

With cat-like reflexes, she spun in mid-fall so she could gain a better position on Greer and Hadrian knew he had to do something if they were going to have any chance of putting her down.

"We're taking this fight upstairs," he shouted, before turning to sprint upwards.

He knew Greer would be able to extract himself and wasn't worried about Harris. He would be fine as long as he kept out of the fight. The priority now was getting to Baines and some real weapons so they could finish this once and for all.

"Baines?" Hadrian hissed as he bounded up the stairs. "Have you reached the inventory yet?"

"The boss ordered me to tie up the target with Chen," Baines replied in his earpiece. "I don't know what the fuck he's doing, but-"

"I don't care what he's doing," Hadrian snapped. "Just get to the weapons cache and meet me outside the door with the standard kit. We're taking this bitch out permanently."

"Yes, sir," Baines replied quickly.

Hadrian ignored his eagerness and pumped his legs harder.

"*This is going to end soon,*" he promised himself grimly, "*one way or another.*"

170

ISAAC TAYLOR'S MIND - June 5, 2147 - 2.13pm

ISAAC'S EYES FLICKERED OPEN. HE COULDN'T REMEMBER waking, but somehow he was sitting cross-legged in the middle of a tiled courtyard.

The tiles were made of white marble, polished, and shot through with brilliant streaks of blue and grey. The courtyard was surrounded by ornately carved arches made of the same white marble, and they dripped with flowering vines and lush, grape-like fruits. Beyond the arches, a carpet of fluffy clouds stretched to the horizon beneath a brilliant blue sky and it looked as if the courtyard were perched on the apex of a mountain.

"*I'm dreaming,*" Isaac thought, confused but not alarmed.

"You're not dreaming," someone said nearby.

Isaac looked toward the voice and saw a figure standing in one of the archways. He was of medium height with brown hair and a gaunt, plain face, and he wore a robe that glowed as if it was literally made of light. There was also a cross hanging at his neck and its red jewels glistened brightly within the ethereal light of his robes.

Isaac tried to speak, but for some reason his mouth wouldn't cooperate and the words were thought instead of spoken.

"*Who are you?*"

"My name is Sabian," the man answered as he stepped down into the courtyard and slowly walked toward Isaac. "But I am unimportant. The question you should be asking is who are you?"

"*Me?*" Isaac thought, confused now. "*I'm Isaac. I know who I am.*"

"Yes and no, Isaac Taylor. You are who you believe you are, and yet so much more."

"*I don't understand.*"

At this point the man smiled wide and lifted his arms like a preacher in mid-praise.

"You are the Messiah!" he said joyfully.

At the words, Isaac felt an uneasy feeling wash through him and tried to get up so he could keep his distance from this strange man. But again, his body wouldn't respond.

"*The Messiah?*" he thought, watching Sabian warily. "*What are you talking about?*"

"Tell me, Isaac," Sabian said, lowering his arms and sitting down in front of him, "does the world seem strange to you? Is it different to the one you know?"

"*I… don't know what you're talking about,*" Isaac replied, feeling more uncomfortable with each passing second.

"Yes, you do," Sabian countered. "You simply find it hard to accept."

Isaac frowned deeper, wondering what he meant.

"*Can you… help me understand?*" he asked slowly.

"I know what you've seen, Isaac," Sabian said, his eyes flashing dangerously. "I've seen it too."

Again, Isaac paused, unsure what the man was referring to.

"*Then tell me what I've seen,*" he challenged.

"The divine light," Sabian replied, his eyes boring into Isaac with a chilling intensity. "The end of days. The Holy Apocalypse."

At this, Isaac's mind instinctively flashed to the visions he'd seen when his experiment with Jason had gone wrong.

"Yes," Sabian said, as if acknowledging his thoughts. "It is the reason you've been brought here, Isaac. You are the Messiah. You are here to save us all."

Isaac stared at him with an entirely new confusion now. He didn't like what he was hearing, but the dream-like quality of his surroundings was making him more curious than afraid.

"*I... still don't understand,*" he thought after a moment. "*Please, explain it to me.*"

"This world has been corrupted, Isaac. God's Holy laws have been cast aside and the sinful have risen to power uncontested."

Isaac could see the passion in Sabian's eyes and knew he believed everything he was saying.

"But now the Messiah has come! To spare those who have remained true to God," Sabian continued. "To protect them from His Holy retribution and transport them to paradise. You will raise them all up, Isaac, and we will be granted everlasting life in heaven."

Isaac noticed that the man used 'we' in his last sentence – including himself in the chosen few to be saved – and somehow wasn't surprised. But he didn't know what to say. It all sounded so unreal and he didn't want to say anything that might upset this person of uncertain mental state.

"*I don't know what you want me to do,*" he thought warily.

"You must accept your divinity, Isaac," Sabian replied, a hint of desperation in his eyes now. "You must play your role in the coming Apocalypse and save us before-"

But the dire warning was interrupted by a familiar voice that echoed across the courtyard.

"Isaac!"

"*Jason?*" Isaac thought in surprise.

"Isaac, I can hear you," Jason's voice spoke again, echoing across the sky.

"*I can hear you too, bro!*"

"Wait," Sabian said, raising a hand with a shocked expression. "You are not ready!"

173

"*What are you talking about?*" Isaac thought, feeling angry now. "*Jason, where are you?*"

"Isaac? I don't know what you're-"

But before Jason could say any more, the floor beneath Isaac suddenly began to crumble and he could feel himself sinking into it.

"*Jason,*" he thought quickly. "*I can't-*"

Then the courtyard floor gave way completely and Isaac fell into a thick, clinging darkness. His frozen limbs finally broke free of whatever held them, but all he could do was flail helplessly as the sky disappeared above him.

"*Jason!*" he thought desperately. "*Jason! Help!*"

But his brother's voice was gone now and as the light above him dwindled to a glistening point, Isaac noticed a red glow coming from the darkness around him. He lowered his gaze in trepidation and saw rock walls zipping past him. They were imbedded with strange, glowing red symbols that looked as if they'd been carved from precious stones.

"*Just like my vision,*" he thought in confusion.

A sudden urge to understand them washed through him, but he was falling too fast and the symbols were soon nothing more than a sparkling red blur.

It created a kind of flaring red light that reminded Isaac of the roaring red energy from his vision and, as if triggered by the memory, the symbols ignited. Red flames leapt toward his falling body in claw-like waves and as the fire poured in around him, Isaac felt a pain like nothing he'd never experienced.

"Argh!" Isaac yelped, waking for real this time.

His heart beat loud in his chest and his muscles were pulled taught, but he still couldn't move properly. He looked around in a panic and realised he was tied to a chair with the man from his dream – Sabian – standing only a few steps away.

His flowing white robes had been replaced by a clean, unfamiliar uniform, but the same gleaming, ruby-encrusted cross hung from his neck. His calm smile was also gone and he wore a look of disappointed confusion.

"How did you-?" Sabian began, but before he could finish a blood curdling scream came from outside the room.

Isaac cringed at the sound. It wasn't a scream of pain, or fear, but one of outrage. A scream he could imagine had last been heard on a primitive battlefield long ago where the edge of a blade or the weight of a club had been the weapon of choice.

Sabian whipped his head toward the door and Isaac blinked in confusion when it opened and a scared looking soldier barged into the room.

"What is going on?" Sabian demanded, his voice filled with contempt. "Report!"

"We're under attack," the soldier barked, turning to make sure the door slid shut behind him. "Chen's down and Harris is... he's down too. That bitch is-"

A sudden burst of gunfire drowned out the end of his sentence and the soldier took a quick step back.

"I told you we were *not* to be disturbed," Sabian hissed. "Baines? Baines! Get back out there! Now!"

But in place of a reply, something heavy slammed into the door and the two men took an involuntary step back.

"Who the fuck *is* she?" the soldier called Baines growled. "You said he wouldn't be guarded!"

Without waiting for an answer, the soldier turned to Isaac.

"Who is that?" he barked, pointing at the door.

"I... I don't know," Isaac replied honestly, watching the door in trepidation.

"You fucking tell us who that is," the soldier shouted, aiming his rifle at Isaac.

"Lower your weapon," Sabian ordered.

"I don't know!" Isaac cried, cringing away from the rifle's barrel. "Seriously, I don't!"

He was about to add more, but was cut off by the slowly ascending *woop-woop-woop* of an alarm.

"Please, evacuate the building," a calm, official-sounding voice spoke over the alarm. "Please, evacuate the building."

"I said lower your weapon," Sabian repeated firmly.

"Fuck you," the soldier replied, not looking at him. "I'm done taking orders from you or anyone else."

Something hit the door again, making Sabian clutch the cross at his throat with a troubled expression.

"This was… not foreseen," he said, shaking his head.

"Well, fuck this," the soldier swore, striding toward Isaac.

Isaac tried to say that he didn't know what was going on, but the soldier cut him off by slamming the butt of his rifle into his face. White hot pain exploded in Isaac's nose and he screwed his eyes shut with a gasp. He felt his chair being dragged roughly along the ground and when he opened his watering eyes, he was facing the doorway with a rifle resting on his shoulder.

"Come and get him, bitch!" the soldier roared from behind him.

"Stand down," Sabian said firmly.

"Didn't you hear me before?" the soldier told him harshly. "I said *fuck* you! I'm not dying for you, for this little shit, or for anybody!"

"Incorrect," Sabian replied in an ominous tone.

Isaac squinted at him through tears of pain and saw Sabian's eyes flash red for an instant. He blinked, not sure he'd actually seen what he thought he'd seen, then the weight of the rifle lifted from his shoulder. He didn't know what could have changed, but suddenly the soldier standing behind him wasn't breathing so loud.

"Put the end of your rifle's barrel into your mouth," Sabian said calmly.

Isaac didn't know how he could expect the soldier to do as he asked, but he heard the clink of gun metal against teeth and his eyes went wide.

"Pull the trigger."

Panic flushed through Isaac's body at the words and he flinched violently when a loud *BLAM* sounded behind him. He cried out as something wet splattered across the back of his neck and his mind cringed away from an image of what must have happened.

He noticed Sabian moving toward him and tried not to flinch again as the man knelt next to him and began to undo the restraints that held him to the chair.

"What are you doing?" Isaac asked, feeling numb with shock.

"Your life was never in danger," Sabian said, holding Isaac's gaze for a moment before moving to the door and standing beside the activation panel.

"Who are you?" Isaac asked him.

"Your humble servant, Messiah," he replied.

Isaac didn't know how to respond, but before he could think of something to say, the man activated the door and then abruptly fell to the floor, as if he'd suddenly fallen unconscious.

Isaac sprung to his feet, confused, riddled with chills, and terrified of what was about to enter the room. Then a dishevelled figure leapt into view.

"Anya?" he said incredulously.

The figure crouched, as if ready to attack, but when its darting eyes took in the unconscious man and the bloody mess behind Isaac, it simply strode forward and grasped him by the arm.

"We have to move," she said in a voice Isaac didn't recognise. "There could be more of them."

Not strong enough to stop her, Isaac was dragged behind Anya into the adjoining room where he found two other soldiers strewn across the floor. There was thankfully no blood in here, but the leg on one of the men was twisted in an unnatural direction.

"They're not dead," he heard himself saying.

"Of course not," Anya growled, before pulling him through another doorway. "Keep moving."

Isaac felt a little better knowing that Anya hadn't killed anyone, but he was still confused and more than a little scared. Luckily, the only thing Anya seemed to be interested in right now was getting out of there as quickly as possible and Isaac was in happy agreement. He certainly didn't want to be at odds with a woman who'd just single-handedly taken out a team of heavily armed soldiers.

"*Jason,*" he thought in silent prayer, "*how I wish you were here, bro.*"

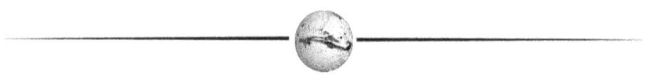

Anya could feel Fayina's strength flowing through her like a shot of adrenalin and she wrenched on Isaac's arm again. It was always difficult controlling Fayina. She was perpetually angry. Powerful, yes, but constantly enraged. And she didn't like wasting time.

"Where are we going?" Isaac asked as they ducked into a stairwell.

"Follow the crowd," Fayina told him firmly.

There were a lot of people moving down the wide staircase on the opposite side of the building to where Anya had first arrived. She knew that exit was too dangerous now and could still feel Celia – one of her other personalities – mourning the loss of her fancy, pink motorbike.

No one in the crowd seemed particularly concerned about the evacuation. They clearly thought it was a drill, which was good, because Fayina had only tripped the alarm to provide cover for their escape.

The crowd backed up a little as they reached the bottom of the staircase, but Fayina simply pushed her way through and scowled at anyone who protested. Isaac remained thankfully silent, but behind the personality that now controlled Anya's body, she could tell he had plenty of questions.

Outside, the crowd was slowly making its way to the designated gathering point, ready to wait for an announcement that would allow them to re-enter the building, and when Fayina began to push her way through them, Anya decided it was time to retake control of her body.

As usual, it wasn't as easy as it should have been. Of all her personalities, Fayina was the most stubborn and always wanted to stay longer than Anya would allow – one of many reasons she rarely allowed her to manifest.

When Fayina grudgingly slipped back into her subconscious, Anya felt her aggression drain away and loosened her hold on Isaac. He pulled away from her as soon as he was able.

"Who are you?" he demanded, standing his ground in the middle of the crowd. "I mean now. Who are you now?"

"Anya," she replied. "I'm Anya, Isaac."

"Then who were you back there?" he demanded, pointing to the building they'd just left. "And how the hell did you... do what you just did?"

"That was Fayina," Anya told him, feeling embarrassed. "She's... look, it's a long story, Isaac. Please, we need to keep moving. I'll explain everything when we're back at my apartment."

Now that she was in control again, Anya could see the fear and confusion streaking through Isaac's aura and knew he was going to argue further.

"I promise you'll get answers," she said, offering him her hand. "Perhaps not all of them, but some. Please, Isaac, you have to trust me."

He stared at her hand for a moment, as if debating whether or not to take it, then he looked around at the milling crowd, many of whom had paused to watch their argument with interest.

"Alright," he said at last, reluctantly taking her hand.

Anya smiled her thanks and then quickly turned to lead him on. As soon as they were beyond the crowd's ragged edge, she changed direction and lead them down two adjacent streets before joining the pedestrian traffic that would take them home.

She didn't like the idea of using an automated taxi at the moment. Those men Fayina had severely beaten were professional and their equipment expensive. Whoever wanted Isaac would no doubt be able to find them again if she paid for anything with her personal I.D.

Luckily, the place they'd taken Isaac was within walking distance to her apartment and so it wouldn't take them long to get back there and regroup before working out what to do next.

As they allowed the afternoon crowd to herd them in the right direction, Anya tried to ignore the auras of all the people they passed. To her, they were as distinctive as faces and it always reminded her that no matter what might be going on in a person's mind, it was the state of their spirit that really mattered.

It was why she loved the Valles Dome so much. Despite her... unique nature, its eclectic population made her feel right at home. And they certainly provided more than enough business to keep her gainfully employed.

When they eventually reached the moss-covered building she called home, Anya reluctantly led Isaac up to her apartment and let them inside. Isaac paused in the foyer, just as he had on his first visit, and Anya couldn't help noticing that the fear and confusion in his aura had only grown worse in the absence of any reassurance.

"Would you like me to cleanse your aura again?" she offered, reaching out to touch his shoulder.

"No," Isaac said, pulling away from her. "I want those answers you promised, Anya. Why do you act like other people?"

"It's... complicated," she replied, turning toward the kitchen. "And I need some tea. Would you like some tea?"

"Complicated?" Isaac said, following her down the hall. "That's got to be the understatement of the century. Just tell me what's wrong with you."

Anya felt Ianka – her older, no-nonsense personality – push forward to respond and couldn't muster enough strength to stop her.

"There's nothing wrong with us," she replied in Ianka's stern voice. "We have merely made the best of a historically misunderstood and grossly misrepresented psychological condition. Multiple personalities are not a disorder. They can, in fact, be quite valuable in the right circumstances, as you should now know."

"Multiple personalities," Isaac repeated. "So... you pretend you're more than one person?"

Anya opened a cabinet and pulled out some tea cups as Ianka answered for her.

"We *are* more than one person," she said firmly.

Isaac looked aghast at this and Anya took back control so she could continue in a gentler voice.

"I have several personalities living inside me, Isaac. Most people do, to some extent, but they usually only manifest as thoughts. I... experienced something when I was younger. Something terrible. To cope with the trauma my mind split into several personalities and I... allowed them more control than they would normally be given."

"What happened?" Isaac asked, as Anya knew he would.

"That's... not important," she said slowly, turning to the hot water tap and filling her cup. "I went to see a professional about it..."

At this point, Ianka wanted to cut in with a more accurate description for the professional she'd gone to for help, but this time Anya stopped her.

"...but she was no help to me," she finished firmly. "And so I decided to work things out for myself. I went to the Valles University to study medicine and psychiatry. My goal was to gather the knowledge I needed to help myself, but after I graduated, I decided to go against the traditional treatment protocols and... experiment a little."

"Experiment?" Isaac said with a frown.

"My technique for dealing with my alternate personalities is unprecedented," Anya clarified quickly. "I found that by accepting them – rather than using medication to limit their influence and trying to convince myself they didn't exist – I was able to exercise control over them. I can't always stop them from manifesting, certainly not in emotional situations, but I no longer lose myself in the process. My primary self, what I like to call my 'parent' personality, is always here, aware of what my other personalities are doing and able to take back control when their behaviour occasionally becomes… inappropriate. It is certainly easier to regain control than it is to avoid losing it in the first place."

"Okay, that… makes sense," Isaac said, frowning, "kind of."

Anya could see the streak of distrust was gone from his aura, but was embarrassed when a blue tinge of sadness took its place.

"I'm sorry I didn't tell you sooner," she said, turning back to her tea, "but you came to me, Isaac. We were focussing on your problems, not mine. I've never had to use so many personalities in such a short time and there just never seemed to be an opportunity to explain. And… well, then those men took you."

Isaac watched her preparing the tea for a moment.

"So how many personalities do you have?"

"Five, including my parent self," Anya replied. "Ianka you met first. She's the most dominant personality and generally the most critical."

"I think I remember her," Isaac said slowly.

"Then there's Celia, my more… feminine personality. I usually defer to her when it comes to fashion, hairstyle, and makeup, but you also witnessed her love of driving."

"She was… hard to miss," Isaac said after a moment. "So, what about Professor Haig? Is she the third?"

"The third, yes," Anya agreed, "but not a she."

"One of your personalities is male?" Isaac said incredulously.

"That's right," Anya confirmed with a nod. "I like to think of him as the wisest part of me. A heavy thinker and intelligent in a very specialised way. You saw the world he lives in."

"I guess I did," Isaac said slowly. "So, what about the last one?"

Anya remained quiet for a moment, ready to stop Fayina if she tried to retake control, but she thankfully stayed quiet.

"Her name is Fayina," she replied simply. "You saw what she's capable of."

"How did she do that?" Isaac asked.

"She trains," Anya said, focussing on pouring the tea. "Constantly. I have her to thank for my figure."

"She was very… angry," Isaac said hesitantly.

"Yes, she usually is," Anya replied carefully.

Isaac remained silent as he watched her pour tea, then he turned and collapsed onto a stool at the edge of the kitchen.

"This is too much," he said, rubbing his eyes.

Anya finished pouring and then placed one of the cups next to Isaac.

"Do you remember anything after they took you?" she asked, hoping he wouldn't resist the change of subject. She didn't like talking about her personalities as if they weren't right there in her head, listening to every word.

"I… remember dreaming," Isaac said, his eyes focussed beyond the walls of the kitchen. "I mean, it didn't feel like a dream, but it had to be. I was on a mountain top. In a courtyard, or something. One of the men that took me was there. Sabian, he said his name was. He glowed like he was wearing a robe made of Fluoro-cloth and there was a red cross around his neck."

"Did he say anything about your kidnapping?"

Isaac glanced at her with a reluctant look in his eyes.

"Kind of," he said after a moment.

"What did he say?"

"Well… he said that… he said I was the Messiah."

Anya carefully held her expression neutral, but Isaac took her silence the same way he would have taken a look of disbelief.

"I know," he said, throwing his hands in the air. "It's crazy, right? I mean, what the hell? Why would I dream something like that?"

Ianka rose to offer several suggestions, but Anya firmly kept her quiet. Isaac was already doubting his sanity and didn't need any more help with that.

"Did he say anything else?" she prompted.

"Plenty," Isaac replied, "but none of it made any sense. I mean, he said something about this world seeming strange to me."

"This world," Anya repeated thoughtfully. "And does it seem strange to you, Isaac?"

"Well... yeah, it does," Isaac replied with a frown. "Kind of, anyway. But I don't know why. Things just look a bit... weird. As if they're not made right. But I've never been to the Valles Dome before so how do I know what it's meant to look like."

"But you feel something is wrong?"

"Of course I feel something's wrong," Isaac snapped angrily. "I told you, I woke up in a strange woman's apartment! I've been experiencing psychic abilities I've never had before today and I was kidnapped, for jatz sake! Not to mention the fact that the person helping me keeps changing personalities. What's right about any of it?"

"Okay, Isaac," Anya said in a gentle voice. "I know things seem a bit crazy at the moment. Just take a deep breath and try to calm down. I promise it will help."

Isaac's frown changed to a look of despair, but he eventually closed his eyes and did as she asked.

"The tea will help," Anya added after a moment and Isaac turned to look at it.

He stared at it without moving, as if contemplating whether he should drink it, then he reached out and lifted it briefly to his lips.

"What else did Sabian tell you?" Anya asked when he'd calmed down.

"He mentioned a... divine light, or something."

"Do you think he meant-"

"My vision," Isaac interrupted her. "Yeah. But it was just a dream. It had to be."

"Why?" Anya asked.

"Well, he said... he said he'd seen it too," Isaac replied, "which is stupid."

"Did he tell you anything else about the vision?"

Isaac looked away again, clearly reluctant to answer.

"This could be important," Anya coaxed him.

She knew that whether this was a dream or something else entirely, Isaac's interpretation of the mysterious figure, Sabian, was directly related to his own understanding of events.

"Okay, look," he said, his frown returning. "This is going to sound crazy. Well... crazier at least."

"Tell me, Isaac," Anya replied calmly.

Isaac looked at her for a long moment then he spoke in a quiet voice.

"He said it was the Holy Apocalypse. The end of days. Those were his exact words. And then he said I'm meant to save all the non-sinners and take them to heaven... or something."

Anya could see the effect those words had on Isaac. He was as terrified as he was confused. She felt Ianka pushing forward to say something and decided that this time it was probably best to let her speak.

"The idea of the Apocalypse has been around for thousands of years," Ianka explained. "Many people have claimed to know when it will occur and every one of them has been wrong. Whatever this man might believe, the Apocalypse isn't real."

Isaac remained silent following her explanation, his expression more forlorn than ever. Anya could see him struggling to believe her, wanting to believe her, and knew he would seek out something familiar and comforting.

"*He's going to bring up his brother again,*" Ianka predicted.

"I have to go to Lynt City," Isaac said after a moment.

"What's in Lynt City?" Anya asked him.

"I made contact with Jason again," he replied, looking up at her with a defiant gleam in his eye.

"When?" Anya asked, ignoring the smug feeling that came from Ianka.

185

"In my dream, or whatever it was. I think he might have been the one who pulled me out of it."

"What did he say?"

Isaac looked away again.

"There wasn't enough time to say much, but it doesn't matter. I have to get back to him. I can't do this alone anymore."

Anya could feel Ianka pushing forward again, but Isaac didn't need to hear what she had to say.

"Okay," she said quietly, deciding not to push for any more details. "We'll find a way to get you to Lynt City, Isaac."

"Really?" he asked, looking at her again.

"Really," she replied. "It might take a bit of organising, but you're still on the clock. You haven't formally ended out agreement."

"Hmmm," Isaac mused. "Thanks for reminding me."

"There's no need for that," Anya said with a smile. "Things will look different when you're somewhere familiar, Isaac. You'll see."

"I hope so," he replied with that same haunted expression. "I really do."

SABIAN WOKE WITH A START. HE QUICKLY LOOKED around himself and saw that he was in the same courtyard he'd constructed in the Messiah's mind.

"*No,*" he thought with a shudder.

If he was here then he had failed his God.

A desperate, wretched howl rose within him and Sabian clutched the cross at his chest as it ripped from his throat. He was a failure. Worthless. He deserved to be punished.

But as the breath ran out of him, a brilliant flash of light appeared in the sky and Sabian cowered in shame. The Lord's angel was here, gleaming with God's Holy light.

"I have failed you, blessed Messenger," he sobbed. "I could not save the Messiah."

"Do not be afraid, Sabian," the angel replied, his voice calm and soothing. "All that has transpired was as it must be. You have served your God well."

As the words registered in his mind, Sabian looked up, feeling wretchedly grateful.

"I... have?" he asked slowly.

"Yes," the angel replied. "You have told the Messiah what he needed to hear and set him upon the One True Path, as it was written. Do not fear for His safety, Sabian. He will not be harmed."

"May I..." Sabian began, hesitating for a moment, "may I ask a question, Holy Messenger?"

"You wish to know more about the woman who took the Messiah from you," the angel predicted.

"Yes," Sabian replied, remembering the bizarre profile he'd studied after Chief Levine had identified her. "Anya Polovski. Please, forgive my arrogance."

"There is no need for forgiveness, Sabian. Anya Polovski is more than she seems. She was with the Messiah when you found him."

"The old woman?" Sabian replied, confused. "But... how did she manage to overcome my team?"

"Appearances can be deceiving, son of Adam," the angel replied. "And this one appears in many forms."

"Is she... one of the chosen?" Sabian asked slowly.

"God's grace is infinite, Sabian," the angel replied. "Do not feel threatened by this daughter of Eve."

"Forgive my jealousy," Sabian said, bowing low. "My soul is laid bare in your presence, Holy messenger."

"Have faith in the Path, son of Adam," the angel replied. "The sins that plague you and all your kin will be forfeit when the Messiah's destiny is fulfilled."

"Tell me what I must do," Sabian said solemnly.

"Follow the Messiah," the angel commanded, its voice becoming stronger. "Watch over him and be ready to act when the second sign appears."

"I will do as you command, Holy messenger," Sabian vowed with all the conviction he could muster.

"You will do as God wills," the angel countered, spreading its arms wide.

Sabian flinched as a bolt of lightning cracked down and a sudden *BOOM* of thunder rolled across the sky.

When he looked up, the angel was gone and he stared into the heavens for a long moment, filled with elation at the knowledge that he had not, as he'd feared, failed his God. Then he felt a tingling sensation at the back of his neck and knew he was about to wake once more, this time into the real world.

"*I am ready,*" he thought, determination filling him. "*God's will be done.*"

Sabian woke with a start.

"What happened to Baines?" a voice demanded from somewhere above him.

Sabian squinted in confusion at the voice's owner and immediately realised he wasn't wearing his glasses. A wave of anxiety washed away his religious fervour and the voice above him spoke again.

"What the fuck happened to Baines, you bastard?" it demanded.

The owner shook his shoulder roughly and Sabian blinked. It was Greer, one of the soldiers from his security team. And the man was touching him.

A sudden revulsion rolled through Sabian and his anxiety spiked. He tried to turn away, to get as far away from this sinful filth as he could manage, but the man simply snarled in anger and dragged him to his feet.

"Get the fuck up!"

Sabian fought the panic that threatened to overwhelm him and tried to pull away, but Greer was too strong. He could do nothing to stop himself being dragged over to the bloody remains of Baines and his face forced right next to the sickening mess.

"No," he protested, almost gagging on the smell.

"Look at it!" Greer snarled at him.

Sabian stared at the torn flesh, the bloody destruction and disorder, and dry-wretched in revulsion. He couldn't breathe. He didn't want to suck the fetid odour into his lungs. His chest muscles convulsed, forcing him to take another breath, then Greer pulled him away and roughly slammed him against the wall.

"You tell me what happened right now you skiving little *fuck* or I'm gonna make you look exactly like Baines!"

Sabian felt Greer's spittle spray across his mouth and couldn't take it anymore. With every ounce of strength he had left, he pushed beyond his anxiety and managed to look the slavering beast square in the eye.

"Stop!" he screamed, drawing upon the divine power of God.

At his command, Greer suddenly froze in place and his hateful, violent expression slid into one of empty compliance.

"Let go of me and step back!" Sabian commanded.

Greer's grip immediately went slack and Sabian stumbled to the side, swiping at the spit that covered his face.

"What in the name of…?" someone said from the doorway.

Sabian spun toward the voice and saw Hadrian, the security Chief, standing just inside the room. This time he didn't hesitate. He immediately met the man's bewildered gaze and drew on God's power once again.

"Close the door," he said firmly.

In an instant the security Chief was also under his control, and Sabian gasped in relief as the man did as he was told.

"*I'm a fool,*" he thought harshly. "*I've barely finished regretting my last mistake and I almost failed my God again.*"

After a quick search of the room, he found his glasses lying against the wall. The security officer must have flung them aside before dragging him to his feet. He took a moment to inspect them for damage and then initiated a quick re-calibration. Soon enough, the familiar layers of information appeared over everything he could see and Sabian silently thanked God.

"Where are the rest of your team?" he asked, turning to the security Chief.

"Harris is outside, applying medical aid to Chen," the man said in a monotone.

"How are they injured?" Sabian asked.

"Harris has a broken humerus," the security Chief replied. "Chen has a broken tibia, fibula, and three dislocated fingers."

Sabian scowled. This wouldn't do at all.

"Kill them both," he commanded briskly. "Then return to me."

The security Chief turned without comment, lifting his rifle, and opened the door once more.

Sabian listened carefully as his orders were carried out.

"Chief? What are you-" one of the officers said, but the voice was interrupted by the brief *hiss-hiss* of two silenced rifle shots.

There was a grunt of surprise then another, much weaker voice, spoke into the silence.

"No, please-" it said, just before the sound of two more shots *hiss*ed through the doorway.

A moment later, the security Chief walked back into the room with no expression on his face, waiting for more commands.

"Good," Sabian said, taking another deep, calming breath. "Your mind is suitably compliant, just what I'm going to need."

He turned to Greer, the man who'd touched him, who'd *spat* on him, and his anxiety gave way to anger. He'd killed many in the name of God and would have gladly added one more to that tally if there were any other reason than sinful retribution.

For a long moment, he let the compulsion roll through his mind, tasting it and studying it from every angle. It seethed inside him, making him want to strike out at this man. To smash the butt of a rifle into his face. To hurt him badly. To *kill* him.

"No," Sabian said coldly, pulling himself back from the roiling emotion. "I will not allow your sins to infect me. There is work to be done and you are nothing when compared to God's divine purpose."

Tearing his gaze from the soldier, Sabian turned to his computers and grimaced at the now blood-spattered equipment. There was much to be done if he was to bring about God's will.

"The Messiah needs me," he said quietly, before adding a small prayer. "God's will be done."

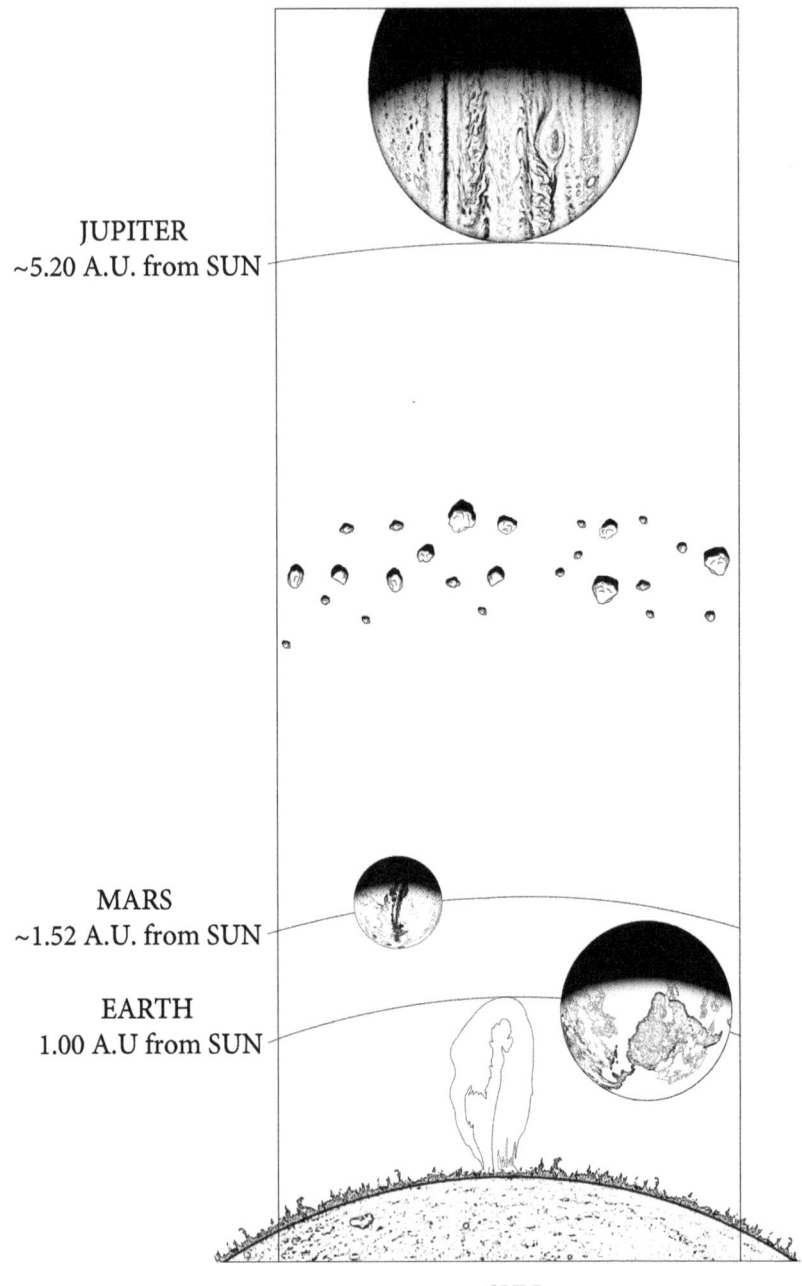

JUPITER
~5.20 A.U. from SUN

MARS
~1.52 A.U. from SUN

EARTH
1.00 A.U from SUN

SUN

1 Astronomical Unit (A.U.) = ~149.6 x 10^6 km

LYNT CITY STREETS - June 5, 2147 - 6.47pm

MIANA RAIKEN, NOW EX-FORENSIC DETECTIVE, WALKED aimlessly through Lynt City's immaculate streets. After leaving the local precinct, she'd started with a vague idea of heading back to her apartment, but had ended up wandering in a completely different direction.

Where she slept had never felt like much of a sanctuary. The precinct station had always been her real home.

"*No,*" she thought to herself bitterly. "*My work was what made it home.*"

Collecting her personal possessions had been a drawn out process that was both awkward and painful. News of her dismissal had spread fast and every pair of eyes she'd met contained some kind of judgement. A few contained pity, as did their promises of help if she ever needed anything, but most were vindictive and unpleasant.

Although Miana was well liked amongst those she had no direct professional relationship with, she'd made several enemies by refusing to play office politics with those that she did. She was well aware of the motivations behind most interactions that occurred within the precinct, but she never used that knowledge for her own ends.

Her target had always been the criminals, not her co-workers, and yet refusing to play the game was sometimes worse than playing it poorly.

She'd expected some gloating, but was surprised at how hurtful it actually was to witness the sadistic pleasure in some of her colleagues. She'd never done anything except what she believed was right and justified under the principles they all worked for. To see some of her co-workers clearly rejoicing in her misfortune was a depressing reminder of what people were capable of.

At least Lance had been respectful. He was still disappointed with her explanation and several times Miana had to ignore the urge to tell him the truth, but losing his trust was a price she was willing to pay if it kept him safe. Loc Breeden may have decided she wasn't a threat, but if Lance made a nuisance of himself on her behalf, he might not restrain himself twice.

Miana shuddered at the thought of Loc's goading smile and evil eyes. She could still remember the horrible feeling of being under his control. It was an obscene power to have over anyone and she couldn't help wondering how many people he'd used it on before her. Or what other horrors he might be capable of. Could there be more people out there with these terrifying abilities? Or was Loc simply a freak of nature?

"No," she answered in her mind. "*If one person can do it, there has to be more.*"

She shuddered again and absently fingered the police-issue tazer in her pocket. There was no guarantee it would work against monsters like Loc, but it still made her feel better. During past investigations, the tazer had been one of her most essential, non-lethal, forensic tools and she trusted it as much as she did her intuition.

"*But what do I do now?*" she thought helplessly.

She knew the first step was always the hardest when it came to change, but this was more than just change. Her work as a forensic detective had defined Miana for so long that it was hard to imagine doing anything else.

"*What other skills do I even have?*" she wondered wretchedly.

Shaking her head, Miana tried to think of something she could do for a living, but an image of Loc kept invading her mind and spoke in his insidious voice.

Perhaps you will despair and commit suicide without needing any prompting on my part?

"No," Miana snapped, startling a young man who was walking just ahead of her.

He offered her an offended expression, but Miana ignored it. She had far more serious things to worry about.

"*This isn't over,*" she thought in determination. "*I'm going to fight you, Loc. Somehow. And I'm not going to stop until my very last breath.*"

It was a bold and perhaps reckless thing to say, but Miana knew that despite hating the idea of suicide now, after a prolonged period of rejection and depression, her attitude might just move in another direction.

"*No. I'll never give that bastard what he wants,*" she thought defiantly. "*But if I'm going to do this, I need to be more careful than I've ever been before.*"

She had no doubt Loc would be keeping a close eye on her and, based on his comments during her 'interview', was likely to have access to any information he wanted.

"*I need to decipher the symbols Doctor Indari carved into himself,*" Miana thought with a frown. "*As powerful as he might be, Loc didn't know what they meant. If I can find their origin and meaning, it might reveal a weakness I can use against him.*"

But even as she thought it, Miana realised that line of investigation was effectively closed to her. She couldn't visit another symbologist without Loc finding out and she definitely didn't want to be responsible for him killing anyone else. And the only other lead she had – the calls Dr. Indari made prior to his death – were just as much a dead end. Miana had to assume Loc knew about Lance's theory – that someone at Mars Global Communications had created fraudulent periods of solar interference – and if there was any chance it might lead back to him, he would have already destroyed the evidence or killed anyone who knew about the crime.

Miana felt a surge of frustration. No matter how she turned the puzzle over in her mind, there didn't seem a way to move forward without alerting Loc or getting herself arrested. For the first time in her life, she had to accept that her investigative skills weren't going to be enough.

At the thought, another wave of despair rose up to wash away her frustration and the drive that had momentarily lifted her spirits disappeared along with it. Her determined stride faltered and she eventually came to a halt, unable to find the energy to take another step.

"Hey, pretty lady," a warm male voice said to her left. "You look like you're in serious need of a vacation."

Miana looked up, ready to politely tell the owner to go away, and paused when she saw an attractive older man grinning at her from a doorway. He had wavy blonde hair that didn't look quite right, given his age, and a brown, neatly trimmed beard that contrasted nicely with his tanned skin and sparkling blue eyes.

Beside him, a large window displayed a video of someone – possibly him – driving an all-terrain vehicle that jolted across the Marsian landscape with several laughing passengers.

"My name's Kurt," he said, holding out a hand. "What's yours?"

"Uh… Miana," she replied, shaking his hand briefly and looking around.

Without realising it, she'd wandered into the tourism district. This street was dominated by adventurists and there were advertisements for extreme sports on almost every doorway. There were even several replica vehicles attached to the walls above them, as if gravity had somehow been turned sideways.

"So, are you looking for adventure?" Kurt asked with a cheeky grin, "or are you really as lost as you look?"

Miana opened her mouth to stop his sales pitch in its tracks, but paused when a thought suddenly occurred to her.

"Of course," she breathed, feeling like an idiot.

She'd contemplated every investigative technique she knew to find information on what Dr. Indari might have found beneath the surface of Mars, but at no point had she considered the most obvious solution – to go and look for herself.

"Of course, what?" Kurt asked, grabbing her attention again.

"Oh," Miana said, looking back at him. "Uh, of course I'm not lost. And I don't know about adventure, but I could certainly do with some equipment."

"Well, whatever you need, I've got it, or I can get it for you at the best price, within the hour," Kurt said with a smile. "And if you need a guide, I happen to be the most qualified person on this big red rock. My safety record is flawless and my Net-rating is as high as they come."

"The equipment will be fine, for now," Miana said quickly.

She didn't want to drag anyone else into this, not after what had happened to Professor Meiket. Nor did she want to risk her plans being shared with anyone else. If she was going to do this, Loc had to be kept in the dark for as long as possible.

"Sure thing, gorgeous," Kurt said, sweeping a hand across the window beside him and bringing up an array of images. "I've got equipment for every kind of adventure sport. Off road driving, gliding, caving–"

"Caving," Miana said, stopping him mid-sentence. "What kind of caving equipment do you have?"

"Ha! I knew you were an explorer as soon as I saw you," Kurt replied with a wink. "You've got that hungry expression all explorers get. And if you ask me, caving is the ultimate in exploration. Do you already have a survival suit?"

"No," Miana replied, realising she no longer had the resources of the Lynt City Police Department at her command.

"Well, let me introduce you to the first and last survival suit you'll ever need to own…"

As Kurt continued his sales pitch, Miana found herself watching his face. He was a handsome man to start with, but the enthusiasm with which he spoke was mesmerising. And he was one hell of a talker. He also appeared to actually know what he was talking about, which was both refreshing and heartening. Miana was certain she would need all the advice she could get if she was going to get this thing done.

"…your muscles. The compression grid tailors itself to your unique musculature and will keep you moving far longer than the other clamp-sacks on the market. The boots have inbuilt massaging nodes that communicate with the on board computers and…"

As the litany of product advice washed over her, Miana took a moment to interrogate her new, civilian data pad. She nodded at Kurt occasionally, making sure he knew she was still with him, but her focus was on the banking app she had open. She held three fingers against the pad until her identification popped up and then quickly checked her bank details.

After what had happened with Loc, she half-expected her accounts to be frozen, or even empty, but her money was still present and available, including her final pay check from the LCPD. It wasn't a lot by any stretch of the imagination, but it was more than enough to afford the equipment Kurt was recommending. And she certainly didn't have anything better to spend it on.

It wasn't going to be easy getting to the caverns as a civilian, but already, Miana could feel the fire of purpose filling her again. Getting there was simply a puzzle that needed solving and although it was different to the ones she usually tackled, it was no less important.

"*I'll find a way*," she promised grimly, before looking back at Kurt.

He'd moved on from the survival suit and was now showing her one of the latest pieces of automatic luggage, which would be perfect for transporting all the equipment she had to take with her.

Miana paused to look into Kurt's warm, helpful eyes, and felt a strange urge to thank him. Without realising it, this man had appeared at just the right time.

"...and, of course," he continued with an emphatic gesture, "it's engineered specifically to deal with Marsian conditions. In fact, I'd go as far as saying that freezing temperatures and driving sand storms are two of its fondest friends."

Miana smiled at this and nodded dutifully once again.

"That sounds perfect," she added. "Now, let's talk about price."

LOC STARED AT THE IMAGE OF MIANA CONVERSING with the adventurist and ran his eyes over the list of items she was about to purchase.

"*What are you up to, Miss Raiken?*" he thought with a frown.

He'd been looking forward to seeing how she would react to being fired, but the signs of terminal depression she'd exhibited since her dismissal had disappeared as soon as she'd met this adventurist, Mr. Kurt Jones.

Loc didn't like it. He'd manufactured many suicides in his time, but all of them had been forced through psychic control. For once he wanted the death to be voluntary. He wanted psychological manipulation to be the sole cause of the suicide and Miana had seemed like the perfect candidate. She was a dedicated forensic detective with no life outside her work and clearly disliked the politics of authority. She relied upon her own intuition to solve cases and used that success to fulfil her pathetic need for purpose.

By showing her the truth and simultaneously ensuring she could never reveal it, Loc knew he'd dealt her sense of justice – and thus her very identity – a significant psychological blow. In combination with her termination from the LCPD, it should have been enough to tip her over the edge, but it now appeared she was contemplating something very dangerous indeed.

"You're going to revisit the crime scene, aren't you Miana?" Loc thought with a frown.

It was disappointing. Loc had hoped she would be the first of many psychologically manipulated suicides, but now it seemed Miana wasn't going to oblige. And, even worse, the Triumvirate wanted him focussing on the deal Cosmotech Defence had just made with their Lynt City pawns and so he didn't have time to deal with this himself. He could easily have her eliminated, of course, but the thought of someone else ending Miana's life left a bad taste in his mouth.

"There has to be another option."

What he really wanted was to force Miana to give in to despair. But to do that, he first had to remove the thing that was fuelling her new-found resolve.

Slowly, Loc's frown turned into a smile.

"Perhaps the game isn't finished after all."

Quickly searching his personal reference files, Loc set up a secure communications link and dialled a man he'd used many times before. A few seconds later, a familiar face appeared above his desk.

"Mister Drevit," he said with a small nod. "It's good to see you."

"And you, Mister Breeden," the man replied, nodding as well. "What can I do for you?"

"Two things," Loc said as he activated a data transfer. "First, there's a woman I need followed. You should be receiving her profile and current location as we speak."

Mr. Drevit looked away for a moment and turned back with a nod.

"She's intending to leave Lynt City," Loc continued, sitting back in his chair and clasping his hands. "I don't know when, but I'm sure it will be soon. I also believe I know her destination – a natural cave system at the following coordinates."

Loc reached forward again and entered the co-ordinates into the glowing keyboard at the edge of his desk. Again, Mr. Drevit looked away while he viewed the data being sent to him.

"The destruction of that location," Loc said, "*before* the target arrives, is my second request."

"I understand," Mr. Drevit said simply.

"Do not, under any circumstances, let her see you," Loc added, "but monitor her activities closely. I want to know everything she does."

"Should I be ready to terminate the target?"

"No," Loc replied firmly.

The thought of someone other than himself claiming that pleasure made Loc's temper flare.

"I want her to remain alive, Mister Drevit," he added, "unless, of course, she attempts to kill herself when she reaches her destination and finds it destroyed. If that is the case, make sure you document the event in as much detail as possible."

"As you wish, Mister Breeden."

"If she dies by her own hands that will conclude our contract and you will receive a considerable bonus. Otherwise, I simply need you to stay with her until I contact you again. You may... assist in her demoralisation in any way you see fit, but if she dies in the process, your payment will be considered forfeit."

"I understand, Mister Breeden," the man said.

"Excellent, Mister Drevit," Loc replied. "Thank you for your time. I wish you the best of luck in your endeavours."

He nodded before terminating the call and then mused once more on Miana's motives. It was clear she was making a final, desperate run at discovering the cause of her current situation. Or was this a detective's version of a warrior's death?

"How would I choose to die?" Loc said thoughtfully.

It was a question he'd never really considered. His concern had always been about making a suicide plausible and appropriately painful when necessary. He assumed someone who actually wanted to end their life would make it as quick and painless as possible, but there was something… *boring* about such an idea.

Still, despite his curiosity, Loc knew there was no time for idle contemplation. While he enjoyed the thought of finding out what Miana was doing, he had other business to attend to.

"*There's more than one game in play,*" he thought to himself. "*I'll see you soon enough, Miss Raiken. Soon enough.*"

MARSIAN WILDERNESS - June 5, 2147 - 7.32pm

ISAAC STARED OUT AT THE ROCKY LANDSCAPE WHIPPING past the mag-rail's exoskeleton. It was a strange feeling travelling back to somewhere you couldn't remember leaving in the first place, but that wasn't the only strange thing about this trip.

When Anya had tried to purchase mag-rail passage to Lynt city, the booking system didn't recognise him. Apparently they had no record of an 'Isaac Taylor' from Lynt City.

Luckily – and a little suspiciously – one of Anya's personalities knew how to lease a travel identity on the black market. It had worked, so far, but it didn't change the fact that someone had erased Isaac from Lynt City's residential database. It worried him more than anything that had happened up until now. If the people who'd kidnapped him could do that, what else were they capable of?

"*And why erase me so completely?*" he thought with a frown. "*How am I meant to be their 'Messiah' if I don't officially exist?*"

None of it made any sense and Isaac wasn't used to things not making sense. It was making him irritable and only reminded him of what he was missing.

"*I need you, bro,*" he thought to himself.

"Isaac?" Anya said from the seat opposite. "It might help to say it out loud."

He turned to look at her. Despite being crazy, she was a truly beautiful woman. She'd changed into open-toed platform shoes, soft white pants and a light-blue silky blouse that didn't quite cover her breasts. Her hair fell naturally in a casual blonde wave and it made her look almost glamorous.

It was a bizarre feeling, being attracted to someone who also mildly repulsed you. And it had certainly brought up a whole range of disturbing questions in Isaac's mind. Like, if he ever kissed her, how could he be sure he was kissing Anya and not one of her other personalities? And the topic of sex was even worse. What if Professor Haig decided to manifest while they were... intimately engaged? Sex was awkward enough without having to deal with that horrifying possibility.

"Why are you helping me, Anya?" he asked, eager to move away from the subject. "As far as I can tell, none of my bank accounts even exist anymore. I can't pay you."

"We have a contract," Anya told him with a shrug. "Unless you verbally end it, I consider myself gainfully employed. You might not have any money now, but who knows what the future holds? And besides, when all this is over I'm sure you'll find a way to pay the bill... eventually."

Isaac gave her a wry look. Was she being serious, or trying to be kind in some twisted, schizophrenic way?

A musical series of notes sounded above them and he was spared any further awkwardness when a pleasant female voice informed them they were approaching Lynt City. The message was repeated in several different languages and Isaac felt the mag-rail beginning to slow.

"*We're home,*" he thought with a fresh kick of nerves.

He was partly excited and partly worried that the people who'd abducted him might have tried something similar with Jason.

They were twins, after all, and if there was a violent group of people who believed he was a Messiah then what did that make Jason?

Not wanting to think about it, Isaac turned his attention to the platform that slid into view outside his window. To minimise the chance his fake credentials would be discovered, they'd decided not to bring any luggage with them, which wasn't a problem for Isaac. All he had were the clothes on his back and the skull cap that had somehow travelled all the way across the planet with him.

Anya had suggested he leave it behind, but Isaac didn't want to part with it. He knew it was silly, but with Jason being so far away, it felt good to have a piece of home so close at hand.

When the train eventually pulled to a stop, Isaac's heart began to hammer. The passengers around him stood up and began filing toward the exits and so he took in a deep breath and joined them. The identity he'd assumed at the beginning of the trip was supposed to work just as well now, but for some reason Isaac's confidence was low.

"*Don't think, just move,*" he thought to himself.

As they stepped out onto the arrival platform, most of the crowd was funnelled toward the luggage retrieval zone and Isaac soon found himself standing in a quick-moving queue that ended at a customs security station. He tried not to meet anyone's gaze as he moved up the line and hoped his nerves weren't showing.

"*Do they scan for that kind of thing?*" he thought to himself. "*Will they stop me if they can tell I'm nervous? Surely innocent people get nervous too?*"

The questions continued cruelly in his mind until it was his turn to be scanned and Isaac was almost glad to get it over with. He pulled out his skull cap along with the few carefully selected items that would verify his identity and placed them in the small security bin next to the scanner. He then stepped forward and tried to keep his face blank as he entered the small scanning chamber.

The door behind him closed as soon as he was inside and a flashing unit moved up the wall from the base of the chamber.

Isaac held his breath as he was scanned and couldn't help picturing his heart racing on a security screen somewhere. His imagination added the grim face of a customs officer as he pointed to Isaac's out-of-control vital signs and gestured to a nearby security guard. But the grim fantasy never came to pass. As soon as the scanner returned to the floor, the opposite door slid aside and a large, blinking green arrow ushered Isaac through.

Releasing the breath he'd been holding in a quiet sigh, Isaac stepped out of the booth and retrieved his personal items with clammy hands. From there, it was a short walk to the mag-rail's extravagant foyer, where he paused in amazement.

"*Wow*," he thought, looking around himself. "*I didn't know they'd re-modelled.*"

It had been at least a year since he'd used the mag-rail system and it was nothing like he remembered. The ceilings were higher, the ugly sculptures scattered around the edges were bigger and even uglier, and the large business lounge that seemed to float in the enormous ceiling space was completely new.

As Isaac stared around the foyer in awe, the crowd began to herd him toward the one-way barriers that led into the city and so he quickly moved aside to wait for Anya. When he turned to try and find her, he saw her striding through the crowd with a stern expression that he assumed meant Ianka was in control.

"*I wonder what it feels like to switch personalities like that?*" he thought, trying not to stare.

When she eventually caught up with him, Isaac gave her a weak smile and, after a moment, Anya returned it.

"Welcome home, Isaac," she said.

"You have no idea how relieved I'm feeling right now," he replied.

"I can see it in your aura," she replied, before touching him gently on the shoulder.

Ignoring an urge to put his hand on hers, Isaac turned to join the crowd moving through the one-way barriers and unconsciously held his breath as they stepped out into Lynt City.

"*It's good to be ho...*" he began to think, but paused in confusion when he saw the cityscape.

"What's wrong?" Anya said from beside him.

Isaac frowned and quickly walked to the edge of a large white staircase that fed people out into the city. He took in the view for a long moment, searching for something, anything, that looked familiar, but it was all different.

"Isaac?" Anya said sternly. "Talk to me."

"Something's.... really, really wrong," he said slowly.

"What is it?" she asked. "Be specific."

"I don't remember any of this," Isaac replied, his eyes darting around the streets and buildings in desperation. "It all looks... different."

"You don't recognise anything?"

Isaac closed his eyes for a moment and thought back to what he remembered Lynt City looking like. Then he opened them again and looked harder, certain there would be something that jogged his memory. But the longer he looked, the more his certainty was twisted in the opposite direction.

"I don't know this place," he said, shaking his head.

"You didn't remember how you got to the Valles Dome either," Anya reminded him.

"Well, yeah," Isaac agreed hesitantly. "But... I remember my address. And I remember how this *should* look."

"You don't know how long you've been away," Anya offered, "and Lynt City changes as fast as it grows."

"Sure, but this still feels wrong."

"The brain has many coping mechanisms," Anya continued in a voice that was surely Ianka's. "And the memory is notorious for piecing together what is real and what is not, in order to create narratives that make sense. What you're feeling could simply be the after effects of whatever drug they used to capture you back at the planetarium."

Isaac turned to look at her.

"You really think that's possible?" he said, wanting to believe it.

"My abductor did ask me if the world seemed strange."

"Evidence that he knew about this impending neurological effect," Anya added.

"Maybe," Isaac said noncommittally.

"Why don't we check out your home address and see if things get more familiar on the way?" Anya suggested.

"Yeah, okay," Isaac replied, reluctantly turning from the unfamiliar view.

Anya led him down to the tightly parked line of public vehicles that hovered a reassuring distance above the street – at least that detail was consistent with his memories – and they got into the nearest one.

"What's your address?" Anya asked when Isaac was settled next to her.

"Seven-eight-seven, Thadeus Lane, Greenwall," he replied.

His voice triggered a location search on the vehicle's console, but its computer didn't return a location for several seconds.

"Don't tell me," Isaac said wearily. "My address doesn't exist either."

"It appears so," Anya replied thoughtfully. "Well, this at least confirms that the problem is more likely to be linked to your memories."

"Oh, that's great news," Isaac grunted sarcastically.

"No, it actually is," Anya said with raised eyebrows. "There may be another way to get you home."

"Like what?" Isaac asked, trying not to snap at her.

"I could hypnotise you," Anya replied.

"Hypnotise?" Isaac said with a frown. "You mean, like, put me in a trance or something?"

"Exactly that," Anya said with a nod. "You see, our senses provide our brains with a lot more information than we consciously perceive. Your waking memory of this place may have been erased, but your subconscious should still remember. By using hypnosis, I can communicate with your subconscious and have it guide us to where you believe your home should be."

Isaac thought about it for a moment.

"That actually sounds like a good idea," he replied after a moment. "What do you need me to do?"

"Just sit back and relax, close your eyes, and listen to my voice."

Taking in a deep, hopeful breath, Isaac did as she asked and Anya began to guide him through a muscle relaxing process. It started with curling his feet as hard as he could to contract the muscles firmly and then relaxing them. She then moved to his calves, his upper legs, buttocks, and so on until he was contracting the muscles of his face. Her soft, soothing voice then asked him to imagine himself walking down a set of stairs and, about three stairs down, Isaac didn't remember anything else.

The next thing he knew, he was looking out the car window and they were gliding silently through the city. He saw unfamiliar people and buildings zip past them while Anya's voice spoke softly in the background. There was also a distinct pull that seemed to tug his body in one direction or another, and Anya kept asking him about it.

It was the strangest sensation, like being in a lucid dream, and although Isaac knew exactly what was going on it didn't seem to change anything. He distantly expected to recognise more of the city the closer they got to his home, but the opposite was true. Apart from the basic layout of the city and the construction of roads, walkways and apartments, almost everything looked different to what he remembered. There were flashes of familiarity, like the colours used on signs, or the façade on a building, but they felt more like déjà vu than memory and were followed with such an opposing sense of confusion that Isaac began to feel sick.

When his 'subconscious' eventually led them to a particular street, he felt the vehicle pull to the curb and Anya asked him to close his eyes again. Darkness surrounded him for a long moment then he opened his eyes and found Anya smiling at him.

"That worked better than I expected," she said. "How are you feeling?"

"A bit sick, actually," Isaac replied, sitting forward. "But… optimistic."

"Very good," Anya said, as if she'd planned it that way. "Now, let's go see where you've taken us."

Swallowing his nausea, Isaac climbed out of the vehicle and watched for a moment as it slid back into traffic. Then he turned to stare down the walkway that should have led to his home.

He could still feel the strange sensation that had led them there, pulling him forward with surprising strength, but he didn't recognise anything in front of him. The lack of recognition came with a sickly, ominous feeling that seemed to take root in his stomach and it sent tendrils of tension out through his chest.

"Breathe, Isaac," Anya said, laying a hand on his arm. "I know something isn't right, but we'll work it out together. Don't let your emotions control you."

Isaac felt a surge of embarrassment at how easily Anya had read him, but it was closely followed by anger. She might be here to help, but her occasional condescending comment – probably coming from Ianka – was really starting to get under his skin. But instead of acting on his frustration, Isaac took Anya's advice and pulled in a deep breath. The air hurt as it moved past his constricted throat, but after several lungfuls, his chest muscles finally began to relax and he felt ready to continue.

"I'm good," he said resolutely. "Let's go."

Following the strange sensation that had pulled them to this location in the first place, Isaac headed toward an unfamiliar apartment block and found himself drawn toward one in particular.

"This… isn't my home," he said, turning to look at the apartments either side of it.

"Are you sure?" Anya asked him. "Don't trust your memories, Isaac. Trust your feelings."

"Well…" Isaac began, but he couldn't finish.

It was a fair question. The address from his memories clearly wasn't right and, of all the possible explanations for this madness, someone tampering with his memories made the most sense. The explanation also came with the promise of eventual relief, which was at least some consolation, but Isaac was still reluctant to accept it.

"Perhaps we should see who actually lives here?" Anya suggested. "It may not look like home, but it still could be."

"Yeah, okay," Isaac said, nodding slowly.

He took a few steps toward the entrance and then tentatively reached out to activate the doorbell. They waited a few moments for the occupant to reply and, soon enough, a woman's face appeared on the door's comm panel.

"Hello?" she said, clearly not recognising Isaac. "Can I help you?"

"Uh… hi," Isaac said. "My name's Isaac and I… think I used to live here. I was just wondering if I could ask you a question or two?"

"Okay, sure," the woman said, looking puzzled.

"How long have you lived here?"

"About seventeen years," the woman replied.

"Seventeen years?" Isaac spluttered.

"Yes," the woman replied, looking affronted.

"I'm sorry," Isaac apologised quickly, "I just… I'm a little confused. I grew up around here and I was sure I used to live in this apartment. You don't happen to know David and Evina Taylor do you? They're my parents."

"No, sorry," the woman replied, shaking her head. "You must have the wrong address."

"How about Mr. and Mrs. Magnusson? Do they live around here somewhere?"

"No, I don't think so," the woman replied. "But at least four new families have moved into the block this year. Maybe it's one of them."

"No, they've been here longer than I've been alive," Isaac said. "What about the Glynn family? They've got three kids. Two boys and a girl."

"There's no families of that size in this neighbourhood. Look, I don't mean to be rude, but I think you're in the wrong area entirely and I'm a little busy, I really have to go."

"Oh… well, thanks," Isaac said. "I'm sorry for disturbing you."

"That's okay. I hope you find the right address."

And with that, the woman disappeared from view.

Isaac turned to Anya with a frown.

"What's going on?" he asked angrily. "Why did my subconscious lead me here?"

"I don't know," Anya offered. "But there could be several explanations. Unfortunately hypnosis isn't an exact science, Isaac. I asked you to take us to your home, but your subconscious might be trying to tell you something else. Can you think of any other reason you might have a connection with this location?"

Isaac looked around the neighbourhood again, but it only cemented the feeling that he didn't know this place.

"No," he replied. "I've never been here before, I'm sure of it. But…"

"What is it, Isaac?" Anya prompted.

"I just…" he said slowly. "I can still feel whatever it is that brought us here. It feels like… I have to get in there."

"Get in where? The house we just firmly established was not your home?"

Isaac glared at Anya for a moment.

"Yes," he replied firmly. "I know it sounds stupid, but I have to get in there."

"She won't let you in," Anya warned.

"You think I don't know that?" Isaac growled. "She just thinks I'm lost and won't believe any story we might come up with. We'll just… we'll just have to break in."

"That's not a good idea, Isaac," Anya said with a frown.

"It's not rational, I get that," Isaac replied, "and I know it might even get me into trouble. But I'm telling you, Anya, I have to get in there."

Anya looked at him for a long moment and Isaac wondered if she was having a silent argument with her other 'personalities', but whoever it was that eventually made up her mind, the decision was thankfully in his favour.

"Alright," she said, "if you're adamant about this. Sometimes trusting your feelings is the best course of action, no matter how irrational they might seem. How do you plan to get in?"

Isaac smiled. The relief that came with the knowledge Anya wasn't going to try and stop him was palpable.

"Easy," he said. "I know dozens of ways to get past residential security systems. When we were young, Jason and I were almost impossible to keep inside. We drove our parents insane getting past all the latest locks they'd install. I just need to find a few tools."

"Alright," Anya said with a nod, "I can help you with that. But after we do this, we need to have a long talk, Isaac. There are other ways to find out what's going on here."

"Okay, okay," Isaac agreed. "Anything you say. Just let me do this first."

Anya gave him a final nod and Isaac felt much better. Now that he had a challenge he was familiar with he felt like he was on much firmer ground. He had no idea what was inside that apartment, but he was willing to do almost anything to find out.

"I'll work this out," he promised himself, *"one way or another."*

SABIAN CLOSED HIS EYES AND RAN HIS HANDS OVER the smooth, clean desk in front of him. It was good to be alone again. His journey to Lynt City had gone quickly and without mishap, but it didn't make up for the disaster that had occurred at the Valles Dome.

He should have handled things like this from the very beginning. Allowing the men under his command to act of their own free will might have been acceptable under normal circumstances, but this was the end of times. The stakes were too high to rely on those who didn't fully understand the role they were playing.

"They will not fail You again," Sabian silently promised his God.

He could still feel the security Chief – Hadrian Levine – and the more psychically pliable soldier – Greer – as a faint pull at the back of his mind. Despite being half a city away, the two men remained firmly under Sabian's control and would remain so until he decided otherwise.

After cleaning up the mess they'd caused in the Valles Dome, he'd ordered the two soldiers to follow the Messiah and they'd been doing so ever since Isaac had boarded the mag-rail bound for Lynt

City. Sabian's own journey had gone without incident, although he'd been forced to endure more exposure to the local populace than he would have liked.

Sabian shuddered as he thought of the social interactions he'd experienced. It had not been easy, but any sacrifice was worth the success of his Holy mission.

Pulling in a deep, calming breath, Sabian brought his hand to the ruby-encrusted cross at his throat and opened his eyes.

"I am ready, Lord God," he whispered.

The screens in front of him were filled with the usual mass of information, including two video feeds sent directly from Levine and Greer. They were currently shadowing the Messiah and Anya Polovski as they walked through Lynt City's much cleaner streets.

Sabian watched the Messiah for a moment, still unsure as to what he was trying to accomplish. It had certainly been a surprise to hear him claiming to have lived at the residence of Laura Gideon. The Holy Messenger had not said anything about that. The insufferable woman Anya, on the other hand – who Sabian still couldn't acknowledge without a grimace – had proved herself to be quite resourceful. Not only had she managed to get Isaac into Lynt City without a legitimate passport, but she'd also done so without attracting any unwanted attention.

Sabian glared at her with a hatred he knew was sinful. He couldn't understand why this mentally unstable woman was worthy of spending so much time in the presence of the Messiah. Anya Polovski knew nothing of his true importance and, even worse, her interference in the Valles Dome had cut his own interaction with the Messiah short. He should be the one helping Isaac, not this deranged harlot.

Turning away from the video feed in disgust, Sabian checked on the other important event that was currently unfolding.

"The second sign is approaching," he said quietly.

The coronal mass ejection that had heralded the Messiah's coming was now travelling through the solar system at close to three-thousand-five-hundred kilometres per second. It was scheduled to reach Mars within the next few hours and, by the look of the data that scrolled across Sabian's screen, would be the largest solar event ever recorded.

Some local news reports warned of possible satellite interference while others talked of blackouts, damage to electricity grids, and even life-support disruption within orbital stations. But they knew nothing of its true portent.

"No one will escape the consequences of their sins," Sabian thought with a smile.

Returning his attention to the Messiah, he tapped into the psychic connection at the back of his mind and simultaneously opened a communications channel to the men under his control.

"Security Chief Levine," he said calmly. "Report."

"The target has visited several local retailers to purchase food and the tools he requires to enter Laura Gideon's apartment," the Chief replied in a monotone.

Again, Sabian wondered what the Messiah was trying to accomplish. There was nothing here that could help him realise his destiny.

"Hold your position," he told Levine. "Monitor the Messiah from a safe distance and do not allow yourself to be seen."

"Yes, sir."

After breaking contact, Sabian brought up the schematics for Laura Gideon's residence and looked through them again. He'd already gathered a significant amount of intelligence on the structural makeup of the building and could see no obvious link to the Messiah – beyond his claim to have lived in her residence at one time. Laura Gideon, the occupant, also had no obvious connection to Isaac and Sabian doubted she would prove to be of any importance in the coming Apocalypse.

"We shall see," he said quietly, returning his focus to the solar flare.

It wouldn't be long before it interrupted his connection to the satellites that relayed most of the information on his screens and possibly even some of the ground-based networks as well. Sabian felt a chill of anxiety at the thought of losing access to so much information and was glad he could at least rely on his psychic connection with Levine and Greer.

"*Whatever may come, I am ready, Lord God,*" he prayed, clutching the cross at his neck. "*Your will be done.*"

MIANA CREPT ALONG THE GLOOMY MAINTENANCE tunnel, occasionally glancing over her shoulder. She was sure someone was following her, but since her encounter with Loc Breeden her paranoia had been wound so tight she knew it could just be her imagination.

After purchasing the caving equipment and fending off Kurt's many offers for cheap professional guidance, she'd gone past her apartment to pick up a few personal items and then headed for Lynt City's seldom travelled lower levels. She took a winding route that should have made tailing her difficult, if not impossible, but although her instincts were firing on all cylinders she still wasn't confident she was alone.

She'd already donned the survival suit Kurt had sold her and was surprised at how comfortable it was. The fabric was thick, containing several layers that supported her muscles, provided heat and cooling when necessary, and held all the electronics that fed vital statistics to her helmet's head up display. Kurt insisted she customise every part of it and Miana was glad he'd persuaded her. It really did fit like a glove.

The oxygen scrubbers in her helmet would apparently allow her to breathe the Marsian atmosphere indefinitely, but the cold would sap her suit's energy cells in two days. She could top the cells up easily enough, but Kurt had warned her not to forget. Apparently more Marsian adventurers died of hypothermia than any other cause.

Miana had to admit, he was quite the salesman. Although she'd been committed to buying the equipment anyway, she was sure his persuasive manner would have convinced her to buy more than she needed. She glanced over her shoulder again to check on the automatic luggage he'd recommended. It whirred along quietly behind her, packed neatly with all the food, water, and other caving tools she'd purchased. She wasn't sure exactly how its wheel and tread system worked, but Kurt had assured her it would follow her across any kind of terrain without needing to be carried.

In terms of equipment, Miana was certainly ready for anything, but getting to the caves where Dr. Indari had been murdered was another matter entirely. She'd thought long and hard about how to get out of Lynt City undetected and even longer about how to reach Dr. Indari's research station. It would have been easier with the help of friends within the LCPD, but Miana knew that would only put them in danger. She had to do this alone, or not at all.

With a sigh, Miana leaned against the corridor wall for a moment and closed her eyes. It was clear the life she'd known for the past few decades was over, but she knew wallowing in self-pity wasn't the answer. Action was the only true antidote to despair and, given her current situation, Miana needed as large a dose of it as she could afford.

Opening her eyes again, Miana looked toward the end of the corridor. It was here that Lynt City's lowest levels were linked to an extensive network of subterranean tunnels that had been created when the city was first constructed. Most were still used for transporting equipment to mining sites close to the city, but many had been abandoned and it was one of these that Miana was hoping to break into now.

With another quick glance behind her, Miana started moving again and eventually stopped at the corridor's terminating T-junction. She took a moment to study the locking mechanism on a shadowy doorway and frowned in disappointment.

It wasn't the older model she'd expected. Years of analysing the methods used by thieves and killers had taught her plenty about how to get in and out of areas without being detected, but security technology was always advancing. And despite her years of experience, Miana was no field technician. She was good with people, not machines.

"*Giving up already?*" she asked herself mockingly. "*Well, that didn't last long.*"

Shaking her head in frustration, Miana ignored the nagging voice that told her she was now trapped and began to search through her memories. She'd seen this kind of door before and there had to be a way around the locking mechanism.

"*Just follow the logic,*" she thought with a deep, calming breath.

Turning to her luggage, Miana opened the tool box on its side and selected something that would at least give her a look at the lock's internal mechanism. She used it to open the lock's housing and was soon staring at a solid bolt design backed by a fairly simple electronic control system. As expected, it was a design Miana hadn't seen before, but she was confident she recognised enough to get it open. Eventually.

With a quiet sigh of relief, she turned to get another tool from her luggage and froze when a scraping sound echoed down the corridor.

She looked for the cause, scanning as far down the corridor as she could see, but there was nothing there. She touched the computer built into her survival suit's forearm and the thermal imaging camera in her helmet blinked on. A line of red light moved from the top of her visor to the bottom and as it passed the corridor was overlaid with a multi-coloured map of different temperatures.

In the distance, she saw a red shape that could have been a figure, but it disappeared behind a corner almost as soon as she saw it.

Cursing in her mind, Miana quickly rewound the last few seconds of captured footage and watched it again. This time the figure was clear.

"*I was followed,*" she thought with a cold certainty.

Spinning back to the door, Miana glared at the open locking mechanism. She had to make a decision, and fast. Either attempt to finish hacking the lock before her stalker decided to act, or get out of there now.

It was an agonising choice. She was sure she could open the lock now, but could she do it in the next sixty seconds?

"*Get out of here,*" she thought, gritting her teeth in resignation.

She quickly turned to replace the tools in her luggage and then grabbed the EM-tazer from a pocket and started running down the T-junction's right hand tunnel.

"Hey! Wait!" a voice echoed down the tunnel.

The tone didn't sound hostile, but given the powers Loc had at his command, tone of voice was no measure of hostile intent.

Miana ran faster.

After a few hundred metres, she looked over her shoulder and saw a shadowy figure appear where she'd been trying to hack the locked door. Based on the distance her assailant had just covered compared to her own, Miana knew she was in trouble.

"*I can't outrun him,*" she thought quickly. "*I have to deal with this now.*"

Facing forward again, Miana sprinted to the next junction, ducked around the corner and quickly pressed herself up against the wall. She heard an insistent whirring sound growing rapidly louder and jumped when her luggage zipped into view.

"Hey! Where'd you go? Miana!"

Again, the echoing voice didn't sound hostile, but Miana knew she couldn't take any chances. She aimed her EM-tazer at the place her stalker would soon appear and waited as his footsteps grew steadily louder.

With the cold calm she always felt in dangerous situations, Miana visualised her target approaching and, when a figure dashed into view, immediately squeezed the trigger.

The *zZZAT* of the electromagnetic pulse made her ears tingle and the stalker hit the ground with a fleshy thump before sliding a few metres and coming to a halt.

Another quiet whirring noise caught her attention and Miana spun toward another dark shape that appeared behind the unconscious body. It was an automated luggage, just like hers.

"What is going on?" she mumbled, more than a little confused now.

Turning back to her stalker's body, Miana knelt down and carefully rolled it over.

"Kurt?" she gasped when she saw her pursuer's face.

It was the adventurist who'd sold her the survival suit. His neatly trimmed beard and wavy blond hair were unmistakable.

"But why is he following me?" she thought with a frown.

Taking a moment to think, Miana's paranoia immediately suggested that Kurt could be in the employ of Loc Breeden, but her logical side reminded her that she'd come across his business purely by accident and surely even Loc couldn't corrupt someone so quickly.

"Or could he?" she thought with a sinking feeling. *"He's got psychic powers, after all."*

Certain she wouldn't get any answers without first asking some questions, Miana turned to her luggage and took out some of the rope she'd purchased from Kurt earlier so she could tie his hands firmly behind his back. She then propped him up against the wall and aimed her EM-tazer at his forehead.

A second blast of electromagnetic radiation reactivated Kurt's cerebral cortex and he came awake with a snort.

"Shitzniggle!" he sneezed, shaking his head and snorting a few times. "What the frag just happened?"

Miana gave him a moment to realise his hands were tied behind him then he looked up at her with a shocked expression that very quickly melted into a smile.

"Miana," he said warmly. "Thank goodness I caught up with you."

"Why are you following me?" she asked, ignoring his words.

"I just wanna help," he said, eyes wide. "I know you didn't want to tell me what you were planning, but whatever it is, I know I can help. I *want* to help."

"You can't," Miana replied quickly, but couldn't deny that something inside her wanted to take Kurt's offer.

"Sure I can," he disagreed, flashing another handsome smile. "I've been guiding people like you for more than twenty-five years, Miana. Wherever you need to go, I can get you there. Whatever cave system you're planning to explore, I can show you how to get there fast and do it safely. Do you even know how to use all that equipment you bought from me?"

"I'm a quick learner," Miana replied coldly.

"I bet you are," Kurt agreed quickly, "but imagine how much faster you'll learn with the help of an expert?"

Miana could imagine it easily, but the thought only made what she had to do worse.

"I don't need an expert," she said reluctantly.

"I don't want money, if that's what you're worried about," Kurt continued enthusiastically. "The profits on your purchases were enough to support me for months. Even with the discounts I gave you. And when I'm ahead of the game, I always look to go adventuring. I just thought it was only fair that I offer my help to the lady who provided that opportunity."

Miana frowned. Her intuition was telling her Kurt wasn't lying, but she still couldn't bring herself to accept his offer.

"What I'm doing," she said slowly, "it isn't safe."

"Or legal I'd say," Kurt replied with a raised eyebrow. "Were you having trouble hacking that lock back there?"

"I'm serious, Kurt," Miana snapped in irritation. "I'm doing this alone because I don't want to put anyone else in danger."

"Danger?" Kurt said with a laugh. "I love danger. I live for danger."

"I'm not talking about calculated risk. I'm talking about powerful people with even more powerful friends that may try to kill me. You don't want to get involved."

"Woah," Kurt said, his expression finally losing some of its boyish excitement. "That's... gotta be tough, Miana. Is it really that bad?"

"It really is," Miana said, surprised to find no trace of fear in his face – only concern.

"Well I'm sorry, Miana, but I can't accept no for an answer now."

"What?" she said, taken aback. "What are you talking about?"

"You tell me someone could be trying to kill you and honestly expect me to just walk away? That's not who I am, Miana."

"Well..." Miana began, but she couldn't think of anything to say.

"Look, I can help, I know I can," Kurt continued. "So just let me, Miana, please. Whatever this is, you don't have to do it alone."

Miana stared at him, her thoughts conflicted. She knew her decision to fight Loc was dangerous and she had an ominous feeling that even success may cost her life. How could she involve Kurt in that? The thought of sharing that burden was immensely attractive and she liked Kurt, who was nothing like the men she'd known most of her life, but even that only gave her all the more reason to keep him out of it.

"I'm not going home, Miana," Kurt said, adding an unwanted complication to her dilemma. "You can zap me again and go off on your own, but when I wake up I'm telling you now that I'm going to come after you. And I'm as good a tracker as I am a caver. You can't stop me from finding you."

Miana frowned again. She didn't know why Kurt's stubborn refusal to see sense was making her like him even more, but it was.

And she believed him too. He probably would try to come after her if she left him here.

"Look," Kurt said after a moment, "I understand your reluctance to put me in the line of fire, Miana. I totally respect that. But I've already made my decision. I want in and there's nothing you can say that will change my mind. So you may as well make the best of things and just let me help you."

Miana slowly lifted the EM-tazer.

"Alright, if that's how it has to be," Kurt said with a shrug. "I guess I've said my piece. You do what you've gotta do and I'll see you when I see you."

Miana stared into his smiling eyes.

"*Pull the trigger,*" she told herself. "*Do it. Just pull the trigger and keep moving. Get as far away from him as possible and you might still be able to save his life.*"

But she just couldn't shoot that stupid, handsome face.

"Fine," she said with a sigh, lowering the EM-tazer.

"Sweet," Kurt said, bringing his hands out from behind his back with Miana's rope neatly coiled around his palm.

"What…? How did you…?" Miana said in complete surprise.

"Rope is, and always will be, my friend," Kurt said with a laugh. "And besides, you're knots were flimsy at best. You've never tied someone up before, have you?"

"Well, no," Miana replied, feeling a little embarrassed. "I always had cuffs for that kind of thing."

"Oh, really?" Kurt said with raised eyebrows.

"I'm a… I *was* a forensic detective," she said, giving him a disapproving look.

"Hey, I didn't say anything," Kurt replied, raising his hands.

"Look, I've never had to tie someone up, or pick a lock," Miana said, trying to steer the conversation to something more useful. "You wouldn't… happen to know how to do that too, would you?"

"Are you kidding?" Kurt said, bounding to his feet. "There isn't a rope I can't tame or a lock that can keep me from where I wanna go."

And with that, he set off down the corridor at a brisk jog. Miana had to run to catch up with him and was once more thankful for her survival suit. All this exercise would have had her huffing and puffing otherwise.

When they arrived back at the door she'd been trying to open, Kurt took a quick look at the exposed mechanism and then turned to take a tool out of his own automatic luggage. He then used it to remove an electronic component Miana didn't recognise and, after working on it with another tool, slotted it back into place.

"Watch this," he said wiggling his eyebrows and twisting his tool in the mechanism.

A spark of electricity snapped from the panel into Kurt's gloved hand and he barked a laugh, shaking his fingers. At the same time a clunk came from the door and the latch unlocked, allowing the door to swing open a little.

"A bit painful, I'll admit," he said, pulling the door open with his other hand, "but it's the fastest way through."

Beyond the doorway was a roughly hewn cavern, no more than thirty metres wide and twenty long. The walls were made of a light-coloured stone and three dust-covered vehicles were lined up against the side wall. Opposite them was the entrance to another tunnel, the one Miana had hoped would take her to the surface, but it was completely sealed off by a large barrier that was plastered with warning signs.

"No way out," Kurt commented as he strode toward the vehicles. "So, what was your plan, exactly?"

"I've got navigation data for the tunnels… on the other side of that barrier," Miana told him. "There was meant to be a door to the other side."

"Right," Kurt said as he kicked one of the vehicles' tires. "And what are you going to do now there isn't one?"

"Well, I'm not sure," she replied, watching as Kurt methodically inspected each vehicle. "I mean, I didn't think this far ahead. We should probably go back and find another access tunnel."

"No way," Kurt said, looking up from his inspection. "We've hit the jackpot here. I'll have to check under the hood to be sure, but one of these babies is destined to join our little expedition. Don't worry about getting into the access tunnels, I'll look after that."

Miana was a little reluctant to trust Kurt so quickly, but her instincts assured her he was a good man and she didn't like the idea of doubling back to find another entrance.

"*I guess I'll give him the benefit of the doubt,*" she thought. "*At least until he gives me a reason to do otherwise.*"

And so she waited patiently as he disappeared under the bonnet of one of the vehicles and eventually heard him whistle before ducking back out again.

"I've definitely found our wheels," he said, springing to his feet. "All we need is a priming charge to get the fuel cell running."

Miana watched as he reached into his patiently waiting luggage and pulled out a small battery primer that he slapped into place somewhere under the hood. When he was done, Kurt activated the luggage's self-packing program and it moved around to the rear of the vehicle and secured itself to the back.

"Come on," he said with a wave. "Let's get moving."

Miana instructed her own luggage to secure itself beside Kurt's and then tentatively climbed into the passenger seat. Kurt was already in the driver's seat, wearing a mischievous grin, and as soon as she was inside he activated the engines.

A throaty *hummm* filled the cabin.

"We have ignition," he said in a thick, American drawl.

A moment later, the lights on the dashboard stuttered to life.

"Good ol' twenty-first century tech," he said with a smile. "They made it to last back then. Wanna plug in the nav-data?"

"Sure," Miana said, taking out her data pad.

The vehicle's computers appeared on her screen immediately and she accepted the connection before bringing up the relevant files. She then fed the updated tunnel information into the vehicle's navigation pad and a large map appeared on the windscreen.

"You sure you didn't plan to find these work horses?" Kurt asked with a raised eyebrow.

"Of course not, why?"

"Well, this old tech doesn't require a link to the local navigation network so we won't need remote permission to move through the tunnels."

"Huh," Miana said, appreciating the first bit of good luck she'd had in a while.

Using her data pad, she highlighted the path she'd chosen to take through the tunnel system and it appeared on the truck's windscreen.

"Looks simple enough," Kurt said, studying the map. "And we can make any corrections that might be needed on the fly."

Miana was about to agree, but was surprised when Kurt leaned forward, pulled a large section of the dash board away and began fiddling with the electronics beneath.

"What are you doing?" she asked.

"Just checking to see if there's... ah ha! I knew there'd be something."

"What?"

"Crash avoidance," Kurt said as he pulled something out of the mess of cables and electronic circuits. "Stops you from running into things. We can't have that."

"Why not?" Miana asked suspiciously, thinking it was actually quite a useful piece of technology.

"You'd better buckle up," Kurt said with a wink, before flicking on the truck's powerful headlights.

Miana frowned in confusion and then looked from Kurt to the now well-illuminated barrier in front of them.

"Oh no. You're not going to–"

"Yep," he said, grinning as he strapped himself in.

Miana wanted to protest, wanted to tell him not to be an idiot, but Kurt probably knew the risks better than she ever would. If he thought it was possible to smash their way through then she might as well give him the benefit of the doubt... again.

"Have you ever driven one of these before?" she asked, strapping herself in quickly.

"Nope," Kurt replied, grinning again as he gunned the engine, "but really, how hard can it be?"

Miana clenched her jaws to stop herself from swearing, but couldn't hold back a small yelp as Kurt hit the accelerator. The powerful electric motors forced the vehicle forward with incredible speed and she had to resist an urge to cover her eyes as the wall raced toward them.

Her panicked mind picked up a detail from one of the warning signs – that unauthorised access could result in a prison sentence – then they smashed into the seal with a resounding *BOOM!*

The collision slammed Miana hard against her restraints, but Kurt must have kept his foot flat to the floor because the momentum lost in the crash returned almost immediately. She couldn't see much in the dust-filled darkness beyond the barrier, but the virtual map displayed on the windscreen was clear. There was a wall only a few dozen metres ahead.

Miana opened her mouth to scream a warning, but Kurt was already pulling the steering wheel hard to the left and the vehicle responded instantly, pressing her sideways against the restraints. Her heart skipped with panic as she watched the far wall scream by within a few centimetres of their truck's side mirrors, then suddenly they were accelerating down the glowing representation of another tunnel.

As the dust cleared from their powerful headlights, Miana realised that Kurt was laughing and turned to find him slapping the steering wheel. She wasn't used to this kind of behaviour and had to hold back an urge to yell at him. Whether she approved of his methods or not, they were now well and truly on their way out of Lynt City.

"Please don't let Kurt be a mistake," she thought as they rocketed down the tunnel. *"I really don't think I'll survive many more."*

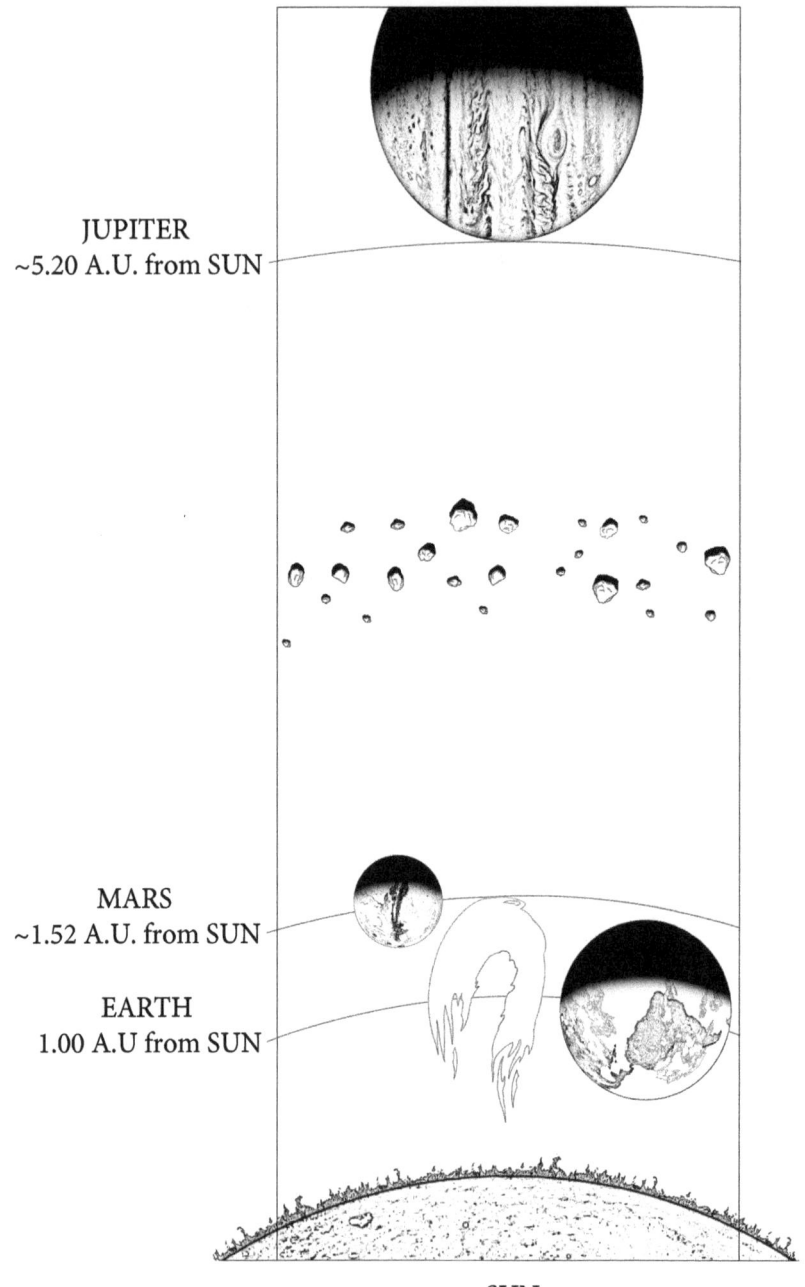

JUPITER
~5.20 A.U. from SUN

MARS
~1.52 A.U. from SUN

EARTH
1.00 A.U from SUN

SUN

1 Astronomical Unit (A.U.) = ~149.6 x 10^6 km

ISAAC STOOD AT THE CORNER OF THE STREET THAT wasn't his and took a deep breath to steady his hand.

It hadn't been easy finding what they needed. Most local retailers didn't trade this late in the evening and those that did weren't the kind that stocked electrician's tools. Nevertheless, with Anya's help he'd managed to scrounge up everything he needed and was now trying to drum up the courage to go through with his plan.

If only it wasn't so late. Isaac was worried that Ms. Gideon may have already gone to bed and, if his vision did turn out to be a premonition, the bedroom he'd seen could be hers. Whatever it was that compelled him to get inside her apartment, Isaac really didn't want to traumatise the woman by showing up in her bedroom in the middle of the night. He didn't even know what he was actually going to do once he got inside, but he had to get in there, one way or another.

At least the lock on her door looked simple enough. Isaac certainly didn't want this to take any longer than it had to. Partly because of his burning desire to get inside and partly because he got the strange feeling he was being watched.

"*Just feeling guilty,*" he thought to himself. "*That's all.*"

Taking another deep breath that didn't help, Isaac turned to Anya. "I don't know what to expect once we get inside, but I don't think I can… well, if Ms. Gideon hears us, can you try to keep her busy while I look for… whatever it is I'm looking for?"

"I'll try," Anya said with a nod, "but I suspect the first thing she'll do is call the police. Whether you find what you need to or not, we may have to get out of there quickly."

"Okay," Isaac replied. "I'll go as fast as I can."

Feeling sick with trepidation, Isaac did his best to look nonchalant as he walked up to Ms. Gideon's apartment. When he was close, he took out one of the tools Anya had bought for him and carefully lined it up with the lock on the front door before pressing a button on its side. In response, a flash of light briefly illuminated the lock and a sizzling *Zzat!* split the air.

"*Done,*" Isaac thought as he felt the tool push through to the lock's internal mechanism.

Pulling it out, he quickly swapped it for a circuit overloader – used for testing safety switches – and pressed it through until he felt it make contact with the circuit board. A tiny camera on the overloader sent an image to the receiver in Isaac's other hand and he used it to line up several vital components before activating the device.

Another flash outlined the small hole he'd cut in the panel then a dull *thunk* indicated that the lock had disengaged.

"We're in," he said to Anya, before slipping the overloader back into his pocket and pushing the door open.

The two of them moved quietly inside the foyer and Isaac immediately felt the strange mental pull growing stronger. The inner door was thankfully unlocked, but when Isaac stepped through, he saw lights in the living area.

"*Okay,*" he thought, trying to stay calm. "*This could be good, this could be bad.*"

He crept forward, the compulsion to rush growing stronger with each step, and then very slowly peeked around the corner.

Ms. Gideon was sitting on a plush recliner with her legs curled beneath her. She was reading a data pad and didn't seem to have noticed their entrance, but she was facing the doorway Isaac would have to cross.

"*Shit,*" he thought, pulling his head back.

He looked at the far side of the doorway and tried to think of a safe way across, but the urge to simply rush deeper into the apartment was overwhelming him. He felt Anya's hand on his arm and looked at her in desperation, but even her sober presence wasn't enough to drown it out.

"*I can't resist it,*" he thought in sudden realisation. "*I have to go, and I have to go now!*"

With a desperation that made his heart hammer inside his chest, Isaac pulled away from Anya and ducked across the doorway as quickly and quietly as he could. He felt the light from the living room splash across his face and, for a moment, thought he might have made it without being noticed. Then he heard her gasp.

"*She's seen me,*" he thought in horror.

Certain that his time was now finite, Isaac ignored the shouts of alarm that fell in his wake and gave in to the compulsion that had brought him here. It carried him deeper into the unfamiliar apartment until he reached a room that should have been the study where he and Jason had set up the experiment.

"*Jason,*" he thought, somehow sure his brother was close.

He burst through the door and found himself in an empty bedroom that looked exactly like the one from his vision. There was even a pair of stockings and a skirt draped on the bed. Isaac had hoped the powerful sensation that had drawn him here would disappear as soon as he arrived, but instead it grew so strong it was painful.

He looked around himself, picturing where P.A.T.R.I.C. and his brother should have been, and felt despair wash over him.

"No..." he mumbled, the room spinning. "This place isn't real... it's all wrong. I don't believe it."

He tried to resist the desperation that had taken hold of him, but soon fell to his knees and clutched at his head.

"No!" he shouted. "Jason! Where are you, bro?"

"*Isaac!*"

The voice broke through the hammering in Isaac's ears and his despair was swept away in an instant.

"Jason?" he gasped in recognition. "Is it really you?"

"*It's me bro,*" Jason's voice answered. "*I can't believe this worked!*"

"Where are you?" Isaac asked, looking around the unfamiliar bedroom in confusion.

"*I'm here, Isaac, right where you left me.*"

"But… what are you talking about? I tried to come home, but… it isn't home anymore."

"*I don't know where you are,*" Jason's voice replied, "*but I've been trying to reach you for weeks.*"

"Weeks?" Isaac said, scrambling back to his feet, "but… I've been awake less than a day."

Jason didn't answer for a moment then he spoke in a serious tone that Isaac remembered well.

"*What's the last thing you remember before waking?*"

"The experiment," Isaac replied. "I added too many details in The Game, P.A.T.R.I.C. overloaded, and I… must have blacked out."

"*You didn't black out, Isaac, you disappeared.*"

"Disappeared?" Isaac said incredulously. "What do you mean?"

"*You vanished along with your head gear and about twenty centimetres of attached cable. Our equipment sucked a few hundred Gigawatts out of the electrical grid and set off a city-wide black out! I thought you'd been vaporised. But I could still feel you, bro. I knew you were alive and I've been trying to contact you ever since. With the help of P.A.T.R.I.C., I've managed to break through a few times, but never like this.*"

Isaac's mind reeled in confusion.

"Broken through to where?" he asked with a frown.

"*I... don't know,*" Jason replied, sounding perplexed in a way Isaac had never heard before.

"Come on, bro. You've got to have a theory," Isaac pushed him. "You always do."

"*Well...*"

"Spit it out, bro," Isaac urged him. "We don't have much time."

"*Do you remember when we studied under François Lemieux?*"

"The particle physics guy? Wasn't he obsessed with... oh no, you can't be serious."

"*It's the only thing that fits.*"

"You think I'm in a parallel universe?" Isaac said incredulously.

"*I told you, I don't know.*"

"But that's your best guess?"

"*It helped me make this connection we're using now,*" Jason replied, "*but there are so many theories out there, Isaac. It's hard to work out what's plausible and what's bogus when you're not here. I really need your help, bro. I can't fix this without you.*"

Isaac was shocked. He'd always thought it was him who needed Jason, not the other way round. Their relationship had always involved Jason guiding his actions, focussing his energies, and reining in his reckless behaviour. It was truly strange to hear that Jason needed him just as badly.

"Don't worry, bro," he said determinedly. "We'll fix this. We can do anything when we're together. What did you do to P.A.T.R.I.C. to try and contact me?"

"*You're obviously not hooked in, so I had to find a way to amplify my side of the psychic link. It took me a while because I didn't have you to put it together for me, and... well, I don't know if it's working at peak efficiency.*"

"Hey, you got me here, didn't you?" Isaac reassured him. "It works well enough, Jason."

"*But not for long,*" Jason said in a grim voice. "*I'm sucking so much power from the grid right now, bro... I don't think the city will let us get away with it twice.*"

"Then we have to work fast," Isaac said. "Tell me which part of your theory made this connection work."

"Okay, I believe it was-"

But before Jason could continue, a sudden *WHUMP* pressed Isaac's ear drums and a wall of searing heat slammed into his side. The next thing he knew, he was crashing into the far wall and crumpling to the floor with the wind knocked out of him.

The room spun as Isaac feebly tried to push himself off the floor then his roaming eyes found the smoking doorway and the bloody, staring form of Anya.

"Anya!" he wheezed, his voice muffled for some reason.

"Isaac! What's happening?"

Isaac blinked at the sound of Jason's voice and suddenly the pain, fire, smoke, and Anya, were all gone. He was standing in the middle of the room again, looking around himself in alarm, and there was no sign of any explosion.

"Oh shit!" he swore loudly.

"Isaac?" Jason called.

But there was no time to explain. It was another premonition, Isaac was sure of it, and if he wanted to save Anya's life, he had to move fast.

"Anya!" he yelled, sprinting for the doorway.

LYNT CITY STREETS - June 5, 2147 - 11.59pm

SECURITY CHIEF HADRIAN LEVINE WATCHED LAURA
Gideon's apartment through the scope of his rifle. Its T-ray emitter
allowed him to see straight through the walls and he could see Anya
Polovski – the secondary target – trying to placate the apartment's
wildly gesticulating owner while Isaac seemed to be talking to
himself in one of the bedrooms.

Hadrian took it all in calmly, despite the terrifying nature of
his predicament. He wasn't in full control of his body, but it didn't
mean he had none. As long as he followed Sabian's orders, he was
able to move as freely as he always had. It was only when he tried
to do something contrary to those orders that he found himself
completely powerless.

Being psychically enslaved was terrifying beyond words, but
much of Hadrian's early training had been specifically designed to
help him overcome fear. It was what allowed him to stay alert and
in control during periods of intense mental stress and this was no
different. If Sabian wanted him dead, then he was dead. The only
chance of getting out of this alive was to accept his situation and
successfully finish the mission. Trying to do anything else was just
wasted energy.

Greer, on the other hand, didn't seem to have reached the same logical conclusion. From what little Hadrian had seen of the soldier since they'd been ordered to follow Isaac Taylor, Greer was pale and constantly tense, as if he were still trying to fight for control.

Hadrian knew exactly how much of a hothead Greer was and, despite the iron mental control he'd drilled into the man over the years, he was worried Sabian's actions would tip him over the edge. Of course, he couldn't guarantee he would get through this with his own wits intact. He very much doubted he would ever forget the final expressions on Harris and Chen as he shot them between the eyes.

"*No*," he thought, mentally pushing the thought away. "*That wasn't me. That was all Sabian.*"

Focussing again on the image in his rifle's scope, Hadrian noted that it was almost time for Sabian to call for another update. He might be a sociopath with psychic powers, but the man remained ever punctual.

He waited patiently for the call, ready to report everything he'd seen since the last point of contact, but when it came, he heard only the hiss of static and a few broken words.

"...atus ...ence ..."

He easily recognised Sabian's voice, but knew the crackling signal could mean only one thing – intense solar interference. He'd been expecting it after hearing about the coronal mass ejection reported earlier that morning, which had been described as one of the largest solar events in centuries. What he didn't expect was the strange physical sensation that came with it.

It was like pins and needles rolling through his body and when it eventually calmed down, something felt different.

"I can move," he heard Greer say in a thick voice.

Hadrian turned toward the soldier and realised that he could move out of position himself as well.

"*Sabian's psychic hold is gone,*" he thought quickly.

"I can fucking move!" Greer repeated as he scrambled to his feet.

Hadrian felt a sudden urge to do the same, to stand up and stretch his newly freed muscles, but his tactical instincts quickly outlined his options and all their likely consequences.

"Get back in position," he told Greer firmly.

"What are you talking about?" Greer said, giving him an incredulous look. "We can move, sir. Whatever else that solar interference is doing to the satellites and relay stations, it's fucking set us free. This could be our only chance to get away from that... that *freak*."

"And you think he won't find us again?" Hadrian said with a frown. "Get back in position, Greer."

"Are you fucking kidding me?" Greer said with a dumbfounded expression.

"No," Hadrian answered firmly. "I'm not fucking kidding you. Get back in position, now!"

"With respect, sir, but *fuck* you!" Greer snarled. "Do you really expect me to keep following that freaks orders after what he did to Baines? After what he made you do to Harris and Chen!"

"We would've been following his orders anyway," Hadrian reasoned, trying to stay calm. "Harris and Chen are casualties of war, period."

"Casualties of war?" Greer snapped. "You can't be fucking serious!"

"I am," Hadrian snapped back. "And if you don't want to join them, I suggest you get with the program and get back in position, *now!*"

"Can you even hear yourself?" Greer asked with an incredulous grimace. "Or is he still controlling you? Is that it?"

"Listen up, soldier," Hadrian hissed, "I get why you want to kill Sabian, I really do, but we have no idea what he's capable of. What we *do* know is that he has connections that extend far higher up the food chain than we'll ever see. Even if he doesn't track us down and use his psychic powers on us, we're dead if we walk away from this mission. Dead! If you want to live through this, our only option is to provide the service we were hired for and hope he decides not to make us kill each other when we're done. Understand?"

Greer stared at him for a long moment, his face twisting through expressions of rage, disbelief and terror, then his face suddenly relaxed and somehow the blank expression was worse.

"You know what, sir?" he said, shucking a round into the chamber of his rifle. "I think you're right. But even if we finish the mission, there's no way they'll let us live through this. Not Sabian and not whatever fucking clandestine employer is pulling the strings above him. But you know what? After what we've been through, I'm not sure I *want* to live through this. And if I'm going to die then I'm taking that fuck's precious Messiah along with me."

"No!" Hadrian barked in desperate realisation.

But it was already too late. Greer turned in one smooth movement, sighted along his rifle, and fired an explosive round straight through the front of Laura Gideon's apartment.

Knowing he couldn't stop it, Hadrian quickly looked through his own scope and was surprised to find Isaac pulling Anya Polovski back into the bedroom, as if he knew the shot was coming. Then the explosive round went off in the foyer with a heavy *WHUMP!*

A searing white light blinded Hadrian's scope for a moment and he instinctively closed his eyes. When he opened them a moment later the apartment was in flames. The front entrance was literally gone and where the front lounge room, kitchen, and corridor had been there was nothing but a huge, smoking hole. He quickly searched for signs of life and found Isaac and Anya sprawled in a heap on the other side of the bedroom, still alive.

"Fuck!" Greer swore, obviously seeing the same thing.

This time Hadrian didn't hesitate. He leapt up immediately and launched himself at Greer. Greer saw him coming and tried to swing his rifle around, but there wasn't enough time to fire. All he managed to do was smash the side of the barrel into Hadrian's face.

An explosion of pain came with bright sparks that obscured Hadrian's vision and he tasted blood in his mouth, but he could now feel Greer in his arms and that was enough for his training to take over. He grappled blind for a moment, feeling for an advantage, and knew he wasn't going to end this quickly. Greer was strong and just as well-trained, but he had nothing on Hadrian's experience. Greer fought aggressively, but didn't conserve any strength, and after wasting all that energy trying to break free of Sabian's control, he was bound to tire quickly.

And so, Hadrian kept the fight a grappling match until he felt the strength in Greer's arms fading. Then he blasted an elbow into Greer's face and as the soldier reeled backward, snaked under one of his arms and managed to manoeuvre behind him and lock-in a rear naked choke.

"Fucking traitor," Greer hissed at him, still fighting with all his strength. "Kill you!"

But Hadrian simply gritted his teeth and squeezed harder, hating himself more than anything he would get from the soldier writhing in his arms.

Greer growled and spat as he was choked, but Hadrian knew it would be over in seconds. He maintained his grip, making sure it would be soon, and noticed Greer reaching for something at his belt. He didn't know what the soldier was reaching for, but felt a moment of panic when he heard the sound of pistol being cocked.

"Don't do it!" he snarled in Greer's ear. "Don't make me kill you!"

But Greer simply grunted and brought the weapon up.

"Fugh you," he growled.

Hadrian's instincts flared and he felt the neck and skull cradled in his arms keenly. He knew exactly how much pressure he had to exert and where to exert it. He didn't want to, would have given anything not to have to, but his life was in imminent danger and there was no other way to save himself.

And so, with a snarl of anger, he flexed his muscles and snapped the bones closest to Greer's skull.

The soldier immediately went limp and Hadrian knew he'd done more than broken a few vertebrae.

With a new sense of urgency, he quickly laid the soldier on the ground and grabbed a medical scanner from the pocket on his vest. When he pressed it gently against Greer's neck and turned it on, a slowly blinking icon appeared in his HUD. The device took a moment to register what it was scanning then the icon turned red and the code **Critical 5** appeared next to it.

The rage Hadrian had felt a moment before returned in an instant and he threw the scanner away from him with a snarl.

Critical 5 meant Greer's spinal cord had been severed and he would die in minutes if we wasn't put on life support. But Hadrian knew there was no way that could happen, not if he wanted any chance to save his own life.

"You stupid fucking jarhead," he muttered, gently closing Greer's staring eyes. "If only you'd followed orders."

This was the third person he'd been forced to kill because of this mission. Because of *Sabian*. But Hadrian knew he couldn't lose his cool now. If he wanted any chance at revenge, any chance at *life*, he had to see this mission through.

Certain there was nothing more he could do for Greer, Hadrian moved back to his own rifle and used its scope to look down on Laura Gideon's apartment. It was still on fire, but the flames weren't spreading. He moved his gaze to the bedroom and saw that Isaac was still lying on the ground where he'd landed. Anya Polovski wasn't far away, but she was already beginning to stir.

"Sir," Hadrian said, trying to make contact with Sabian, "requesting orders, sir."

But the interference still crackled in his ear-piece and Hadrian knew it would be a while before the solar storm ended and his connection with Sabian would be re-established. All he could do now was watch the two targets as they slowly woke up and hope Sabian wouldn't blame him for Greer's violent act of desperation.

"*Stupid fucking jarhead,*" he repeated in his mind. "*He's probably just killed us both.*"

246

PRIVATE RESIDENCE, LYNT CITY - June 6, 2147 - 12.03am

ISAAC WOKE TO A HIGH-PITCHED WHINE AND A spinning room. The last thing he remembered was grabbing Anya's shirt and hauling her back through the doorway, then a searing white light had blinded him and something smacked against his exposed skin with enough sting to steal his breath away.

"Isaac, I can't hold this channel open... they're going to cut me off..."

Jason's voice sounded like it was coming from a great distance and Isaac wasn't sure if it was real or if he was creating it in his mind. He opened his mouth to answer, but his chest was still struggling to pull air back into his lungs.

He felt something tug against his arm and turned to see Anya already on her feet. He let her drag him up and then feebly called out to his brother.

"Jason..."

His voice barely registered above the ringing in his ears and when there was no immediate answer, Isaac felt a stab of panic. Anya began pulling him out through the jagged hole that used to be the bedroom's doorway and although Isaac tried to pull back, she was too strong to resist.

"*Fayina must be back,*" he thought with a grimace before screaming as loud as he could. "Anya! Fayina! Whoever you are right now, you have to let me go. I need to stay just a little longer!"

But her ears must have been ringing as bad as his were because she didn't seem to hear a word.

Screaming in frustration, Isaac again tried to pull himself free, but Anya simply dragged him over the twisted remains of the entrance and into the presence of something that abruptly made his struggles cease.

Ms. Gideon. She was lying crumpled against the wall with blood streaming from her eyes, mouth and ears.

"*I could have saved her,*" Isaac thought, guilt stealing the blood from his face. "*Why didn't I see her die too?*"

But there was no time to wallow in self-pity. Anya seemed determined to get him out of there and she quickly pulled him past the corpse and away from its accusing stare.

"*I have to get free,*" Isaac thought desperately, remembering his brother.

He knew Anya was only trying to protect him, but his link with Jason seemed locked to this physical location somehow and based on his brother's last words the lines of communication wouldn't stay open for long.

He pulled and clawed desperately at the hand holding him, but Anya, or more likely Fayina, was just too strong for him. He wailed and protested the entire way, but she didn't stop until she'd pulled him out of the apartment, dragged him through the gathering crowd and round a corner so they were out of sight of the apartment.

At this point, Isaac dug his heels in and finally managed to pull them to a halt.

"Fayina, stop!"

This time she responded to his voice and when she turned, Isaac saw a distinct change in her expression as Anya retook control of her body.

"We should keep moving," she said quickly. "That was a deliberate attack, Isaac. And the police will be here any minute."

"I found him, Anya," Isaac told her, trying to contain his temper. "I was talking to Jason when the apartment exploded."

"Jason is dead, Isaac," Anya said in Ianka's no-nonsense voice.

"What?" Isaac said, taken by surprise. "Look, I wasn't wrong about the address, Anya. There's something wrong with the whole city. This isn't my home at all."

"We can discuss this later," Anya said, her expression firming as she began to pull on him again. "Come on."

"No!" Isaac told her firmly. "I have to go back."

"You'll be arrested," Anya said, her expression looking suddenly scared and concerned.

"I don't care!" Isaac shouted. "I have to finish talking to Jason. Together we can work out what happened to me."

"This is no time to humour your delusions-" Anya said in Ianka's voice, but Isaac cut her off.

"He's not dead!" he yelled. "And you don't know *anything!*"

Anya looked shocked for a moment then her expression hardened into Ianka's now familiar frown.

"I know you're a twin, Isaac, and that's enough."

"How can that be enough?" Isaac countered, his anger flaring brighter than he expected. "Tell me Anya. Or am I addressing Ianka? Are your imaginary friends like twins? Is that what you're saying?"

"No, Isaac, it's nothing like being a twin," she replied firmly.

"Then how the hell would you know how I feel?" Isaac demanded.

"You need to calm down, Isaac."

"No, I don't," Isaac spat, conscious there were people staring at them. "Being calm hasn't helped me through any of this… this shit! Being calm is *not* a rational response to this situation!"

"I can't help you if you're upset, Isaac. Please, try to step back from your emotions."

"Help me?" Isaac said, the words sounding almost perverse. "You mean like insisting my twin brother is dead? Like dragging me away from a figment of my damaged psyche? The one person who can help me figure all this out? I don't want that kind of help, Anya. I don't need it!"

"You're not thinking clearly," Anya said, her eyes pleading. "I know you believe you were speaking to Jason, but-"

"No!" Isaac shouted, his temper finally breaking the banks of his control.

He knew his brother was alive and he didn't know why Anya kept insisting otherwise. But he wasn't going to let her talk about his brother like that anymore.

"You shut the fuck up!" he yelled, pushing her away from him. "You're just a sad, middle aged schizophrenic! What would you know about sharing the same life as someone else? The same thoughts! How could you possibly understand what it feels like to have lost the very thing that anchored me to reality? I wish I'd never met you!"

Isaac watched Anya flinch with each accusation and waited for her to speak, ready to bite back with another barbed comment, but an expression he'd never seen before crossed her face and, without warning, she suddenly turned and ran.

Isaac watched her go, completely stunned. He hadn't thought for one second that Anya wouldn't be able to handle his anger.

"Anya? Wait!" he called out, starting after her. "I didn't mean-"

But by the time he'd taken a few steps, she was already round another corner. He sped up and quickly reached the corner himself, but Anya was nowhere to be seen. He scanned the crowd desperately, searching for any sign of where she might have gone, but there was nothing.

"*Isaac, you idiot,*" he scolded himself with a grimace. "*Now look what you've done.*"

He didn't want to give up on her, certainly not like this, but time was running out and so he reluctantly turned away from the corner and ran back the way he'd come. His desperation to hear Jason's voice returned, urging him on faster, but when the apartment came into view, it was already cordoned off and surrounded by emergency vehicles.

"Shit," he swore, skidding to a stop.

He didn't know what to do. He certainly wasn't getting back inside the apartment now and that realisation came with a despair that was heavily laced with guilt. He put his hands on his head in helpless frustration and noticed someone in the crowd was pointing him out to one of the attending police officers.

"There he is!"

Isaac's eyes went wide and he stood stunned for a moment, then his fight-or-flight response kicked in with both feet and he spun around so he could run away. But before he could take a single step something hit him in the side and his legs gave out. He fell to the ground awkwardly with pulsing waves of pins and needles coursing out from the impact point and, although they didn't hurt, he suddenly couldn't move or even speak.

He lay like that for what seemed like an eternity, staring at the level walkways above him, then a serious-looking police officer appeared in his field of vision. He felt himself being physically rolled over and cuffs put on his wrists, then the pins and needles finally stopped.

"You are being placed under arrest on suspicion of murder," the officer said in a calm voice. "This arrest is being recorded and anything you say or do will be logged as evidence. You have the right to remain silent. You will be assigned an attorney."

Isaac felt a new kind of despair as the officer continued his speech and had to fight to hold back tears. He knew he was in serious trouble now and the only person who might have been able to help him was probably already on her way back to the Valles Dome.

"*I'm sorry, bro,*" he thought helplessly. "*I've really screwed things up this time.*"

LYNT CITY STREETS - June 6, 2147 - 12.41am

ANYA PUSHED THROUGH THE CROWDED NIGHT-entertainment district, unable to stop. There was a turmoil boiling inside her that she didn't want to face and running made it easier to hold at bay.

She should have been able to weather Isaac's abuse. She understood how fear and confusion could make a person lash out. But his words had triggered something deep inside her and the delicate mental balance that held her multiple personalities in check had been thrown off kilter. Her certainty had been swept away like so much dust and it felt as if something buried in her subconscious was now fighting to be known.

But it wasn't being allowed to rise to the surface without conflict. Another part of Anya's subconscious clearly didn't want this to happen and she could feel the struggle as she ran from the inevitable. Her personalities could feel it too and, while she ran, they did their best to distract her.

"Why does he insist his brother is still alive?" Dr. Haig asked thoughtfully.

"He's paranoid and delusional," Ianka replied firmly. *"The symptoms are clear."*

"*He said he talked to Jason,*" Celia offered.

"*Precisely,*" Ianka sniffed. "*He's created a subconscious persona to replace the loss of his twin brother. He's simply hearing voices in his head.*"

"*Sounds familiar,*" Fayina grunted.

"*We are entirely different,*" Ianka insisted. "*Isaac's mind is unstable. His behaviour was appalling.*"

"*He was frightened,*" Anya reasoned, deciding to join the conversation.

"*He was angry,*" Ianka corrected her, "*and he was wrong.*"

"*He was kidnapped in the Valles Dome and now he's been attacked openly here,*" Anya added. "*His temper is simply fragile.*"

"*His body is fragile,*" Fayina snarled. "*I was close to breaking his face when he called us a sad, middle-aged schizophrenic.*"

"*He didn't mean it,*" Anya said in Isaac's defence. "*He was in great pain.*"

"*He doesn't know what real pain is,*" Fayina growled.

"*Something he said caused me great pain,*" Dr. Haig added.

"*His insults were hasty and laced with desperation,*" Anya reasoned. "*He didn't mean them.*"

"*I wasn't talking about his insults,*" Dr. Haig replied.

"*He insulted my intelligence,*" Ianka cut in indignantly. "*I know more about the psychology of twin relationships than he ever will.*"

"*We haven't experienced it,*" Anya said. "*That's all he was saying.*"

"*Haven't we?*" Dr. Haig asked.

"What?" Anya said out loud.

"*He's a fool,*" Ianka continued over the top of her.

"*Well, I like him,*" Celia added in a pouting tone.

"*You would,*" Ianka replied disapprovingly.

"*Well, he has passion,*" Celia said defensively, "*and he's quite smart, Ianka. Maybe not as smart as you, but he managed to create a machine that amplifies and measures psychic energy, remember?*"

"*It tore them apart,*" Dr. Haig said.

"*What are you talking about?*" Anya asked him.

"*It probably doesn't even exist,*" Ianka said with a sniff of disapproval.

"*Why are we even discussing this?*" Fayina demanded. "*He verbally ended the contract. Our responsibility now only extends to making him pay up.*"

"*Five-thousand, sixty-two dollars and fifty five cents,*" Ianka provided promptly.

"*Will you let Professor Haig speak, please?*" Anya said.

"*I'll make him pay,*" Fayina offered, ignoring her.

"*Oooh, I can afford that new outfit with the Hipsan boots,*" Celia added.

"*I wonder,*" Dr. Haig said in the background, "*what it was that tore us apart?*"

"*What did you say?*" Anya asked, not quite hearing him.

"*I don't remember,*" Dr. Haig said.

"*We have to get back to the Valles Dome,*" Ianka spoke over him again.

"*Please, Ianka,*" Anya said, "*I'm trying to hear Professor Haig.*"

"*We're not leaving until I collect on our contract,*" Fayina added firmly.

"*We should apply interest,*" Ianka said, "*or he can take out a loan to cover his debt and pay interest to someone else.*"

"Stop!" Anya shouted, causing several people around her to jump and then glare at her in shock.

At least the voices in her head had gone silent, but it didn't quite make up for the glares.

"Sorry," she said quickly, "just talking to myself."

One by one, the people she'd startled shook their heads and continued on their way and Anya quickly moved off the street to an empty bench seat. She sat down, put her head in her hands and closed her eyes.

"I don't... remember," she said after a moment. "I don't know what made me accept you all. It was a choice, that much I know, but... I can't remember why."

"We're smarter this way," Ianka replied promptly, using her voice to speak out loud this time.

"Stronger," Fayina added with a hint of contempt.

"Happier," Celia chimed in.

"Protected from the truth," Dr. Haig said last.

"What... truth?" Anya asked slowly.

"None worth pursuing," Ianka replied firmly.

"No," Anya disagreed, "it was in something Isaac said."

"Don't be stupid," Fayina snarled. "He doesn't know anything about us."

"His words triggered something," Anya continued determinedly, "something from my memories."

She tried to remember, to pull forward whatever it was that lurked beyond her reach, but it resisted with surprising strength.

"It hurts," Celia whined. "I don't want to know."

And it was then that Anya realised she didn't want to know either. Something inside of her was trying to keep it hidden. And if it weren't for the questions Dr. Haig had been asking, she knew she would have let it drop already.

"What was it?" Anya asked, forcing the question past her better judgement.

"How many are we, really?" Dr. Haig said slowly.

The question caused a flash of light to appear in the swirling darkness behind Anya's eyelids and she flinched in surprise.

"Five," Ianka answered firmly. "A perfectly balanced personality."

"No..." Anya said slowly, trying to focus on the light.

"Don't do this," Fayina growled.

"I don't want to look," Celia said with a sob.

The sense of unease grew stronger as Anya struggled toward the light and she could feel her personalities resisting.

"I have to see," she told them, pushing harder.

"This isn't going to help," Ianka warned, her voice uncharacteristically frightened.

"It's important," Anya replied.

"Bullshit!" Fayina snarled, wrenching her hard in the other direction. "We all know this isn't going to end well."

"I don't care," Anya pleaded. "I have to know."

"Don't be a fool, girl!" Ianka snapped, her voice becoming shrill.

"I have to know," Anya repeated, reaching toward the light.

As her mental fingers pushed through the last of her resistance, the light seemed to rush forward and everything was suddenly washed in brilliant white.

"The answers are where they've always been..." Dr. Haig said finally, his voice fading into the distance.

All other sounds disappeared along with his voice and Anya was left floating within a silent, brilliant white void. Around her, the light gradually resolved into colours and shapes, and she eventually recognised what looked like a bedroom. There were images plastered all over the walls and ceiling, some of them dancing in time to fast-paced rock music that now filled the air. There was also a bed not far from her and someone was sitting on it – a smiling young woman with long flowing hair who looked just like Anya when she was younger.

"You told a lie," the vision said with a lopsided grin.

"I did not," an almost identical voice replied. "I just left out the bit about Kevin and Dozer."

"Which just happens to be the bit Mum and Dad would most like to know," the vision said, tilting her head to one side and flicking her hair back over a shoulder.

"What they don't know won't hurt them," the second voice replied.

Anya felt a strong sense of déjà vu, but was sure she'd never been in this place before.

She tried to say something herself, but another flash of light obscured her vision and when it cleared a much sadder version of the girl appeared. She was sitting on the end of the bed and not looking at her this time. The music was gone too.

"I'm not going," she said quietly.

"What? Why not?" the voice from earlier asked, sounding angry. "Don't be a prude."

"I'm not a prude," the girl snapped, turning to glare at her. "We're going to get in trouble."

"So what?" the voice retorted.

"So I don't want to get in trouble," the girl said, her voice rising to match the first.

"I knew it! You're just a prude," the voice accused her. "I'm going to tell Dozer you don't like him anymore."

"Don't you dare!" the girl said, looking shocked in a way that made Anya feel extremely satisfied.

"I will," the voice said, the anger now replaced with intent. "But you can tell him whatever you want if you come with me."

The girl looked at her hard for a moment, but somehow Anya knew she was going to give in.

"You can be a real bitch sometimes, Anya."

"*What did she say?*" Anya thought, her mind reeling in shock. "*Did she just use my name?*"

But before she could think anything else, the light obscured her vision again and something new swam into focus that blurred and glistened as if seen through water.

"I'm sorry, Anya," an indistinct figure said from somewhere above her. "They were killed instantly. There was no pain."

"*What?*" Anya screamed in her mind. "*Who was killed? Who are you?*"

She heard a sobbing moan that wrenched at her heart and the image blurred even more.

"You're lucky you weren't with them," the voice said calmly. "You would have died too."

At this, the figure snapped into sudden focus and she saw a man wearing a policeman's uniform.

"No!" the girl's voice screamed. "I should have been with them! Don't you see? I lied! I lied to them all! They're dead because of me!"

The voice broke off with a sob and the image blurred once more and turned toward the ground.

"It's not your fault, Anya," the policeman said quietly. "These things just... happen."

"They're gone," the girl's voice sobbed. "They're gone because of me."

She felt a hand on her shoulder and the policeman's voice spoke once more.

"They'll always be with you, Anya. All of them will live on in your memories."

At this, Anya felt a sudden pain in her chest, as if a ghostly hand had reached in and sunk its fingernails into her heart. At the same time, the policeman's words echoed through her mind.

They'll always be with you... They'll always be with you...

It was her. She'd known it from the beginning, but didn't want to admit it. What she was seeing were memories from her past. Memories of her sister. Her *twin* sister.

"*Fayina,*" she thought with a chill.

"*No!*" Fayina's voice screamed in her mind. "*That's not me! You stupid, fucking, lying slut!*"

The fingernails piercing Anya's heart suddenly stabbed deeper and Anya recoiled from Fayina's rage.

"*Do you see?*" Ianka's shrill voice added. "*You shouldn't have come here!*"

"*You dirty fucking whore!*" Fayina screamed. "*You deserve to die!*"

"*No, I don't,*" Celia replied, her voice trembling with emotion. "*No, I don't. No, I don't!*"

"*They waited for you,*" Dr. Haig said quietly. "*Fayina was being honoured with an award in astrophysics. They wanted you to come.*"

"*Please,*" Celia sobbed. "*I didn't mean for them to die.*"

"*You were more interested in seeing Kevin,*" Dr. Haig continued. "*Feeling his touch. His warm body.*"

"*Stupid slut!*" Fayina screamed.

"*He was so hot,*" Celia sobbed, "*and the ceremony was going to be so boring.*"

"*They waited for you,*" Dr. Haig repeated, "*and when they eventually decided you weren't coming home, they left without you.*"

"*Do you see?*" Ianka broke in, her voice pleading now. "*Do you see why you created us? We protected you, Anya. We kept them with you.*"

"*They never made it to the graduation ceremony,*" Dr. Haig continued in his calm, droning voice. "*An unregistered street racer lost control on the corner they were crossing and ploughed into them at over one-hundred kilometres an hour.*"

"*Aaargh!*" Fayina screamed, as if she were in terrible agony. "*Aaargh!*"

"*I'm sorry,*" Celia pleaded. "*So, so sorry. I thought I was in love. I didn't know. I didn't know!*"

"*They died instantly,*" Dr. Haig finished solemnly, "*but you didn't kill them, Anya. It wasn't your fault.*"

At his words, Anya felt her heart tearing beneath the grip that held it and the pain, grief, and guilt she'd been holding within her seemed to gush out of the wound.

She heard Ianka, Fayina, Celia, and Dr. Haig all speaking at once and, for the first time ever, saw that they had no real life of their own. She was creating all of them. It was something she'd known for as long as she remembered, but now she could *feel* it too.

Unwittingly, Isaac's accusation had led her to a truth that she'd buried long ago. A truth that had fractured her mind and allowed her lost family to remain a part of the life Anya didn't think she deserved.

Her mother, depicted by Ianka – intelligent, firm and demanding. Her father, Dr. Haig – wise, patient and respected. Her twin sister, Fayina – angry. Forever angry at what Anya had done and yet driven by the guilt she felt for letting her twin die. And Celia, made of all the parts Anya didn't think she deserved to enjoy and had thus abandoned to be experienced by someone else.

It was all her. Creations fuelled by the memories she'd locked away. Memories stained with guilt and despair.

Anya knew it was better for her to know all this, but at the same time it had torn open an emotional wound that never had a chance to heal. Right now it felt as if she'd only lost her family yesterday.

She could feel her personalities calling to her, willing her to pass the pain onto them as she'd done for so long, but Anya refused to let denial rule her life any longer. This tragedy was a part of her life, part of who she was, and it had to be dealt with.

Opening her eyes once more, Anya looked up and saw the world from a whole new perspective. She could feel her personalities, still talking at the back of her mind, but there was a difference now. The balance she'd been holding inside of her was no longer required. She was now in complete control and for the first time in a long time, Anya was alone like she'd never been before.

It was then that she realised why Isaac refused to let go of his brother.

"I know, because I've felt it too," she said quietly.

Rising to her feet, Anya looked around at the people streaming past her and wondered if she should be thanking Isaac, or cursing him.

Not surprisingly, her now strangely muted personalities happily provided some answers, but Anya quickly decided this was one decision she had to make on her own.

"I'll help you find the truth, Isaac," she promised firmly as she re-joined the crowds, "whatever it takes."

MIANA NERVOUSLY SCANNED THE TUNNEL AHEAD OF them for obstacles. Despite her protests, Kurt was completely ignoring the path she'd programmed into the nav-system and she found herself wishing he would either slow down or at least engage the automatic drive.

"Do we have to take every possible detour?" she asked as he pulled the truck round another tight corner.

"Of course we do," Kurt assured her with a grin. "It might not get us there faster, but it'll confuse anyone following us. You did say we were in danger, didn't you?"

"Yes," Miana conceded. "I did."

"Well, there you go then."

Miana gave him a wry look. It was a fair point, but she was fairly certain Kurt's reckless behaviour had more to do with having fun than it was about safety.

She gripped her harness reflexively as he forced them around another turn and wondered, not for the first time, if she would end up regretting his involvement. He was a handsome, friendly guy and she was glad she was no longer alone, but he was also clearly addicted to risk and she wasn't sure she could afford to take much more of it.

"If we die before I even reach the caves," she thought to herself, *"Loc will laugh his evil head off."*

"So," Kurt said as they trundled down another long stretch of tunnel. "Where are we headed, exactly?"

Miana looked at him and pondered how much to tell him. She knew it would only cause her problems later on if she lied to him now and since he'd chosen to accompany her whilst knowing there was danger involved, it only seemed fair to give him the real story.

"An ancient volcanic cave system," she said after a moment, "where… a scientist called Doctor Naseem Indari was researching a sub-surface ocean."

"Really? That sounds amazing," Kurt said with enthusiasm. "But where's the danger in that?"

"Doctor Indari's dead," Miana told him bluntly. "He was… killed about six months ago. I investigated his death."

"Oh yeah. You were a forensic detective, right?"

"Not anymore," Miana replied, feeling a little sick as she said it.

"Oh," Kurt said quietly. "Okay, I'm feelin' the vibe. You're not happy about it. Do you want to tell me what happened? You don't have to."

Miana looked at him again and was surprised to find that she did. Quite badly, in fact. It was as if now that she had an opportunity to share the burden, she was finally realising how heavy it actually was.

"Alright," she said with a sigh. "I guess I better start at the beginning. I was assigned to Doctor Indari's case earlier this week. It sounded interesting at first and I was looking forward to the challenge, but I had no idea how strange it would become."

As they travelled through the tunnels, pausing briefly each time Kurt decided to confuse any possible pursuers by taking them in an entirely new direction, Miana gradually explained what had happened. She left nothing out and included everything that had happened since her arrival at Dr. Indari's research station up until her encounter with Loc and subsequent dismissal from the LCPD.

A little surprisingly, Kurt was a great listener. He might have been a bit too enthusiastic in sharing his opinion of events as she explained them, but not once did he act as if he didn't believe her.

"I was ready to give up," she admitted at the end. "I didn't know what to do and so I wandered aimlessly until you spoke to me. I saw the advertisement outside your apartment and... well, here we are."

"It's a wicked showcase, hey?" Kurt said with a grin. "I had one of my diving buddies put it together. He's a Davinci-level designer and a Cameron-level director."

"It's pretty good," Miana conceded with a smile. "It certainly inspired me. Made me realise I could go get the answers for myself if I was desperate enough. You see now why I had to go it alone, but... I'm glad you followed me."

"That makes two of us," Kurt said with a wink. "And I've gotta say, all that talk of psychic manipulation has really blown my world view right out of orbit. I mean, it's scary and all, but fascinating too. How does he do it? Who else can do it? And what did he kill the Doc for in the first place? What's he hiding? The questions just keep piling up. Funny how it feels like the more you learn the less you know sometimes, hey?"

"Huh," Miana replied, amazed at his reaction. "It really is, isn't it?"

"So, when we reach the surface, do we need to stay off the beaten track to avoid notice?"

"I don't think it will matter," Miana said, her frown returning. "If they know I'm out here, they'll easily track us from orbit. I'm just hoping we managed to slip out of Lynt City unnoticed."

"Well, you did a decent enough job staying out of sight," Kurt offered as they bounced over a rocky section of tunnel. "I only kept up with you 'cause I'm stubborn when I get an idea in my head. And lucky, of course."

Reaching into a pocket at his chest, Kurt pulled out what looked like a mangled metal hook.

"Saved my life," he said, as if in explanation. "You see, being in the adventure business on a place like Mars, you experience plenty of… let's call them incidents. And what you don't experience, you hear about. Collecting a few good luck charms along the way is inevitable."

"That's… good to know," Miana said with a raised eyebrow.

"Hey, after all you've told me, surely you can't poo-poo a little superstition," he said with a laugh.

"I guess not," Miana replied, letting the frown go.

She turned to look down the tunnel ahead of them and saw the glimmer of stars in the distance. She squinted for a moment, wondering if it was simply the glow of some strange underground flora, then Kurt rocketed out through a tunnel entrance and the sky exploded with points of light.

"*We made it,*" she thought, staring up at the Milky Way's impressive expanse.

"So, where's the entrance to your cave system?" Kurt asked.

Pulling out her data pad again, Miana brought up the map linked to the one displayed on the truck's windscreen and dragged a finger down the interface. The map zoomed out, showing more of the terrain surrounding Dr. Indari's research station, and she tapped in the latitude and longitude she remembered from her investigation notes. The location appeared as a blinking marker on the map and Kurt studied it for a moment.

"Right," he said with a nod. "Should be easy enough to get to. I'd say it'll take us a few hours at most. In the meantime, I think you should try and get some rest. You look pretty beat, Miana."

Miana looked at him and then turned to glance at herself in the truck's side mirror. Kurt was right. Her skin was pallid and her eyes had the hint of dark rings beneath them. It also felt like the tension that had been propelling her forward was starting to fade now that she'd shared everything with Kurt.

"I think you're right," she agreed. "But if I do fall asleep, make sure you wake me when we're close, okay?"

"You got it," Kurt promised with a smile.

Miana returned it as she settled back in her seat and felt a pleasant little buzz when she noticed Kurt decreasing the intensity of the cabin's lights. Behind his boyish demeanour, he was actually quite a gentleman. She still wasn't sure if his involvement would turn out to be a mistake, but it certainly felt good knowing someone else was aware of her situation.

"*Hope where there was none before,*" she thought as the gentle rocking of the cabin and the constant hum of the engine began to drag her into sleep.

2.34am

"What?" Miana snorted, flinching at the feel of a hand on her arm.

"We're here," someone said in a strangely familiar voice.

Sitting up quickly, Miana looked toward the voice and saw Kurt smiling back at her.

"Oh," she said, rubbing the sleep from her eyes as her memories flooded back.

She turned to look out through the windscreen and saw that Kurt had parked them on a small rise that looked down on the entrance to the volcanic cave system. The windscreen was automatically enhancing the low light and so everything looked just a touch greener than it should have, but the familiar sight lifted another weight from Miana's shoulders.

It was just as she remembered it, nestled at the bottom of a gentle fold in the landscape. The surrounding rock had been scoured smooth by the elements and as Miana ran her eyes across the undulating terrain, a light wind whisked some dust up in a sinuous wave that scattered across the nearby sand dunes.

"That's it," she said with a nod of satisfaction. "We made it."

"Nice," Kurt replied. "I'll just take us down next to the-"

But before he could finish the sentence, the tunnel entrance lit up in a blinding flash and a resounding *BOOM* shook the truck's cabin. Miana screamed and shielded her eyes, but could barely hear herself over the thunder that rolled over them.

The glare only lasted a few moments, but it seared a white after-image into Miana's vision and kept her blind for the better half of a minute. In that time, her mind roiled with fear and she couldn't help wondering if the next explosion she heard would be much, much closer.

"Are you okay?" Kurt asked loudly.

"They found us," Miana said, her voice trembling. "We're dead! Both of us!"

"Calm down, Miana," Kurt told her, his voice firm. "Just think about your body. What do you feel? Are you injured?"

"No… no, I don't think so," Miana replied, shaking her head.

"Good, that's good," Kurt continued calmly. "Then we're no worse off than we were a moment ago. If they wanted us dead, they could have easily waited until we were inside that cave before they blew the entrance."

"How can you say we're no worse off?" Miana asked, sitting up so she could glare at him. "Loc did this. He's playing with me! That bastard is playing *games* with me. He knew I was coming here and wanted me to lose hope all over again."

"Well, are you planning on giving him that satisfaction?" Kurt asked, a little aggressively. "Are you going to let him win, Miana? Or are you going to keep playing so you at least have a chance of beating him at his own dirty game?"

"Are you insane? It's already over," Miana said, pointing at the destroyed entrance. "Can you not see that smoking pile of rubble? There's no way we're getting down there now."

"Is that all you're worried about?" Kurt asked with a sudden laugh. "Miana, I've explored hundreds of volcanic cave systems and there's always another way in. Do you have a map of the tunnels you investigated?"

"Well… nothing physically accurate," Miana replied irritably. "I lost access to the real maps when I was fired, but I've got a good memory. It helped me mock up a basic layout of the tunnels leading down to Doctor Indari's research station. Just basic information on the number of junctions, their depth, and whether we went left or right."

"That's all I need," Kurt assured her. "Look, I know this is asking a lot, especially after what just happened, but I'm going to ask you to trust me. I won't be able to explain myself if I'm going to try what I'm planning."

"What are you talking about?" she asked in confusion.

"What do we know?" Kurt asked in reply. "Loc knew you were coming here. Hence the explosive welcome. And for the moment at least we can assume he wants to keep you alive. But that could change at any moment. I don't know about you, but I don't particularly like the idea of some company assassin breathing down our necks. We've got to get clear of whoever's following us if we're going to have any chance of reaching the Doc's research station."

"O… kay," Miana said slowly, "but how are we going to do that?"

"I told you, I have a plan," Kurt assured her, "but if we do have an unseen escort then they could be monitoring our every word."

As the words sunk in, Miana looked out the windscreen at the billowing dust cloud that now obscured the rocky landscape and a chill rolled through her.

"Do you trust me?" Kurt asked, interrupting her morbid thoughts.

Miana turned to look at him and took a moment to consider it.

"*I do*," she thought with a little surprise, before answering him. "Yes."

"Okay then," Kurt said with a smile. "Let's see what we can do about our little problem."

And with that, he pulled a data pad from his survival suit's chest pocket and quickly linked it with Miana's. As far as she could follow, he seemed to download her rough map of the cave system before spending the next few minutes playing with some kind of three-dimensional mapping software. He hummed an unfamiliar tune as he worked, which made the whole thing feel a little surreal, then he grunted in satisfaction and put the data pad back in his pocket.

"Right. Are you ready?" he asked, looking at her again with his trademark grin in place.

"As I'll ever be," Miana replied, trying to ignore the sick feeling in her stomach.

"Then let's get moving."

At this, Kurt pressed the accelerator to the floor and Miana was once more thrown back in her seat. The truck lurched around in a tight circle and they were soon travelling back the way they'd come.

While Miana held onto the hope that trusting Kurt was the right call, they travelled about a kilometre or so before he made an abrupt ninety degree turn. Miana had to clench her jaws to keep from screaming as the truck thundered up the side of a jagged hill, shaking the cabin mercilessly, and when it eventually reached the top, a yawning chasm appeared just beyond the rise.

"What are you doing?" Miana screamed, this time letting all her fear and anxiety be heard. "Aaaargh!"

Her scream got momentarily louder as the truck's bonnet dipped over the edge of the chasm then it faltered when their tires suddenly lost traction. For a sickening moment the truck dropped like a stone and Miana could only watch with her stomach in her throat as they arced toward the chasm bottom several hundred metres below.

She had just enough time to silently curse herself for trusting a complete stranger before the truck slammed into a rocky ledge that seemed to appear out of nowhere.

The impact was incredible, but Miana's restraints held her firmly in place and so she simply acted on her lungs' insistent demand to refill them. She vaguely noticed Kurt pulling the steering wheel hard to the right and felt the truck bounce and slide dangerously close to the ledge's jagged edge. Then the thick tires finally caught on the rock and the truck's powerful engine pulled them away from danger at the last moment.

For several seconds, Miana could only gulp air back into her lungs then she heard Kurt laughing and turned to glare at him.

"That was *not* a good plan," she shouted.

"Hang on," Kurt replied, still laughing as he wrestled with the steering wheel. "We're not done yet."

Miana turned to look out the windscreen again and her stomach churned in horrified anticipation when she saw the ledge that had just saved them ended not far ahead.

"*Oh no,*" she thought, tightening her grip on the harness that cradled her.

The edge rushed toward them faster than it had any right to and Miana screamed even louder as the same weightless feeling grabbed at her stomach.

"Aaaaargh!"

Another ledge appeared beneath them, not quite as wide as the first, but halfway along there was a large cave opening that disappeared into the cliff face. As soon as their tyres hit rock, Kurt wrenched the steering wheel sideways and they skidded toward it. Miana ran out of breath at this point and had to heave in a new lungful so she could scream at Kurt, but her voice trailed off when the truck's headlights illuminated an enormous column of stone, right in front of them.

"Hold onto your hats!" Kurt yelled with a whoop of delight.

"You can't–" Miana screamed, but before she could finish, the truck smashed into rock with a resounding *CRUNCH!*

The whole cabin shuddered as the crash's echo grew louder and Miana looked back to see the entrance behind them disappear in a shower of dust and large rocks.

Kurt gunned the truck's engine one last time and they shot forward for a few dozen metres before pulling to a halt barely a metre in front of another sheer wall of rock.

For a long moment, Miana could only suck in air as her quaking mind tried to process what had just happened.

271

"That…" Kurt said, sounding a little breathless himself, "went perfectly."

"I can't believe you just did that!" Miana screamed, finally finding her voice. "Are you insane?"

"The jury is still out," Kurt replied with a grin.

"We're trapped," Miana continued indignantly. "You caused a rock slide at the entrance and trapped us in here!"

"Damn right I did," Kurt said with a raised eyebrow. "We're trapped in here and Loc Breeden's company assassin is trapped out there."

Miana opened her mouth to shout something else, but then shut it again when no rational argument presented itself.

"As I said, my plan worked perfectly," Kurt said with a grin.

"You…" Miana said slowly, her mind roiling. "You're incredible."

"Why thank you," Kurt replied, bowing his head and waving a hand.

"That wasn't a compliment," Miana said, still glaring at him. "Just tell me what we're meant to do now."

"Of course," Kurt said with a placating gesture. "You deserve to know the full extent of my brilliance. First of all, as I mentioned earlier, I've explored dozens of volcanic cave systems and in my experience there's always another way in. Secondly, your memory is quite good. I cross-referenced the map you made with some global scans I already had for this area. They've covered the entire surface of Mars from orbit hundreds of times since settlement. Even some of the publicly available maps go a few hundred metres deep. All I had to do was align your map with what I already had and then look for a surface entrance nearby that eventually meets up with your cave system. There were a few, but this one just happened to be fragile enough to demolish in a hurry. And voila! We're back on track with a serious head start on the competition."

Miana looked at him with a fresh, grudging respect.

"Where there's a will, there's a way," Kurt added, before crossing his arms with a grin. "That's what my Nan always used to say."

Miana had to admit, it was a brilliant, if simple plan. Risky, yes, given the entrance he'd just demolished could have buried them instead of blocked off the outside, or he could have misjudged the ledge and they could have plummeted to their death, but now that it had worked, could she really complain?

"I'm... sorry," she said after a moment. "I shouldn't have doubted you. That was a good plan and I... I lost control there for a second."

"Hey, you didn't know what I was doing. It must have been terrifying," Kurt said with a shrug. "And to be honest, you did great. I've seen a lot of people tested like this and you'd be surprised at how some people react to a little danger."

For a moment, Miana was reminded of Lance and she felt an urge to smile. This was the second time she'd admitted to losing control and although this time her admission was honest, Kurt had brushed her concerns aside with a confidence that was hard to doubt.

"*I really like this man,*" she thought, before adding, "Alright, Mister adventurist. Let's get this tour moving. I don't want to waste any more time."

"You got it, ma'am," Kurt said with another grin.

SABIAN KNELT BEFORE HIS COMPUTER HUB, CLUTCHING his cross in trembling hands and praying earnestly. Every screen in front of him buzzed with solar static and it felt like a scene out of his worst nightmare.

As the Holy Messenger predicted, the second sign had arrived, but for some reason he had not been told how drastically it would affect his psychic control.

"My God," he whispered in a trembling voice, "I failed you again."

He knew it this time for sure. He had lost his psychic link with the Security Chief Levine and his soldier, Greer, and had no idea what was happening to the Messiah. It was almost as if the solar flare was interrupting his psychic abilities in the same way it did the live feeds coming from the satellites.

Sabian had tried to leave his command station, to go to Isaac's location and re-establish control in person... but his anxiety was too great. He just couldn't face all those people that would be between here and there. Not without the information he would require to organise in advance.

The thought of unplanned interactions created a fear in Sabian so intense that even his love of God could not motivate him to move.

"I'm useless," he sobbed. "Worse than useless. I'm weak. Sinful. Unworthy of Your love."

Each accusation drove a burning nail deep into his heart and yet Sabian knew it wasn't enough. He had to be punished. He must pay penance so he could be forgiven.

Lifting the cross he was holding up to his face, Sabian twisted the clasp that attached it to the chain and watched as the silvery metal that held the rubies in place began to darken. A tiny battery was heating the metal to several hundred degrees Celsius and soon the air held the distinct tang of ozone as it shimmered around the cross.

"Forgive me, Lord God," Sabian whispered, before laying the cross against his palm and firmly closing his fingers.

As soon as it touched his flesh, a sizzling *hisss* split the air and the stench of roasted flesh replaced the ozone in Sabian's nostrils. Bright sparks of pain began to obscure his vision and Sabian had to bite his tongue to avoid screaming.

He didn't let go until the pain finally began to ease then he opened his fist and brought it back up to his face. The cross left a bright red impression in the flesh of his palm and strings of melted skin stretched between his fingers in a gruesome black web.

With a sharp gesture, Sabian pulled the cross free and gasped as the metal gradually heated back up.

"I am a sinner," he said, a tear trickling down his cheek, "and I must pay for my sins."

He glared at the wavering air that framed his cross, willing himself to endure another round of punishment, but before he could follow through the screens before him flickered back to life.

"The second sign has passed," he whispered. "My God has forgiven me."

Twisting the cross's clasp once more so it would cool down, Sabian allowed it to fall back against his chest and scrambled back to his chair. He immediately re-established the satellite connections that had linked him with Hadrian and Greer, and saw that Greer was dead with a broken neck. Hadrian, on the other hand, was alive but no longer following Isaac. Instead, he was shadowing Anya Polovski who appeared to be talking to herself in a corner alcove within Lynt City's night entertainment district.

"*What is he doing?*" Sabian thought in outrage.

He'd already set up an algorithm that funnelled any information associated with Laura Gideon directly to his station, and so the next thing he noticed was a police report in the process of being drafted.

Quickly reading through it, Sabian felt his heart skip a beat when he saw evidence of an explosion at Laura Gideon's residence.

"*Did something happen to the Messiah?*" he thought in horror.

But his faith quickly assured him Isaac could not have been harmed. The prophecies included no such event. And yet, it wasn't until he saw the picture of the unidentified man who'd been taken into custody at the scene that his anxiety eased.

"The Messiah," he breathed with a surge of emotion. "He's alive."

Laura Gideon, however, had died at the scene and it looked as if Isaac had been arrested on suspicion of having something to do with the explosion that killed her.

Quickly returning to his security Chief, Hadrian Levine, Sabian realised that he no longer felt the psychic connection that had been severed by the solar flare. Unlike his satellite feeds, it could not be re-established so easily. If he wanted to retake control, he would have to make contact again.

The thought immediately brought back the fear that had held him paralysed, but Sabian refused to let it control him this time. He didn't necessarily have to leave this location. After being freed of his psychic control, the Security Chief could have run. He could have dumped everything that linked him to Sabian and gone into hiding. But he hadn't. That meant he was either smart enough to realise he would easily be hunted down, or scared enough not to risk it.

Either way, his loyalty may remain suspect, but he was still a useful resource.

"*We'll see where his loyalties lie,*" Sabian thought, before opening an audio connection. "Security Chief Levine."

277

"Sir," Hadrian replied promptly.

"*A good sign,*" Sabian thought, before replying, "What happened at Laura Gideon's residence."

Hadrian paused before answering and Sabian had to supress a surge of frustration. He couldn't afford to lose his temper now.

"Solar activity disrupted our communications link," Hadrian began, clearly choosing his words carefully. "And… your psychic connection."

"So it did," Sabian agreed. "Tell me what happened to the Messiah?"

"Greer was… agitated," Hadrian continued. "I ordered him to stay in position, but he disobeyed and fired on the primary target before I could stop him."

Sabian's outrage flared at the words. Greer had fired on the Messiah! His actions were unforgivable, *sacrilegious*, but Sabian already knew the attack had not been successful. The Messiah was alive and Greer was dead for his transgression, so he contained his anger for now and remained silent.

"Both the primary and secondary targets survived the blast," Hadrian continued. "The owner of the residence, Laura Gideon, sustained serious injuries and died at the scene. Following the attack, I immediately subdued Greer and was forced to kill him. I then returned to the mission."

"And the Messiah?" Sabian asked.

"The primary target was pulled out of the wreckage by the secondary target, but they began arguing and the second target fled the scene. When the primary target returned he was placed into police custody."

"And you chose to follow Anya Polovski," Sabian finished for him.

"Yes, sir. While I awaited renewed contact."

Sabian glanced at Hadrian's location and used it to pull up an image of Anya Polovski from one of the nearby traffic cameras.

He glared at her for a long moment, certain she was to blame for everything.

"*What were you fighting about?*" he wondered. "*And why did you leave him?*"

Reluctantly returning his focus to Hadrian, Sabian decided there was only one way to test the man's loyalty and see if he'd been compromised by his brush with God's power.

"I will maintain contact with the secondary target," he said firmly. "Return to Greer and get rid of his body. Ensure there is no trace for anyone to find. He shall be judged by God and God alone. When you are done, proceed to the secondary target's location, apprehend her, and deliver her to the location I am sending you now."

Hadrian remained silent for a moment.

"Is there a problem?" Sabian asked.

"No, sir," Hadrian replied smartly. "I'll do as you ask, but… I need a guarantee."

"A guarantee?"

"I'd like you to guarantee I will not be killed when you're done with me. I've honoured every stipulation in our contract. I have not deviated from your commands and I believe I deserve the opportunity to prove I can be trusted with life."

Sabian thought about it for a moment. Hadrian was wise to make the request without adding any threats or ultimatums, but he had no idea that continued life would mean nothing given what was coming.

"Agreed," he said eventually. "I personally guarantee you will be allowed to live if you continue to honour your contract and do as I command."

"Very well, sir."

At the Security Chief's words, Sabian felt his anxiety slowly leave him. Perhaps things were not as bad as he imagined.

"Get moving," he finished curtly.

"Yes, sir."

As he cut the transmission, Sabian realised he felt much better. No longer would he need to venture out into the crowded masses again. And although he still wasn't entirely sure he could trust Hadrian Levine, he was certain the man's survival instincts would provide another chance for him to retake control with God's gift.

Returning his attention to the image of Anya Polovski, Sabian frowned in agitation. He may not need to immerse himself in the sinful population again, but he still didn't understand why his God had blessed such a pathetic soul with the opportunity to be close to the Messiah.

"But I will find out soon enough," he promised himself. "And when I know the truth of God's Will, nothing will keep me from the Messiah again."

LOC CASUALLY PICKED AT THE PLATE OF FOOD IN FRONT of him, feeling pleased with himself. It had been a long day of negotiations and despite the solar storm that had interrupted things around midnight, everything was developing just as the Triumvirate predicted.

So far he'd managed to secure the rights and titles to significant tracts of Marsian land in the northern hemisphere. They were considered useless now, but once the terraforming process had begun their elevation and equatorial proximity would make them priceless. Cosmotech would very soon be in a position to either sell the land at an outrageous profit, or simply develop it into farms, factories, or even cities of their own design.

The prospect made Loc salivate with anticipation. He'd known for some time that his subservience to the Triumvirate would one day allow him to join them, but it was the knowledge that their power was still growing that excited him the most.

"The future is bright," he said with a grin, before biting into a particularly good pastry.

A short tone interrupted his chewing and Loc glanced down to activate the internal call with a brush of his finger.

"Sir, you have a call on secure line Delta."

"Thank you," Loc said, swallowing quickly and using a hot napkin to wipe his lips.

He quickly activated the desk's mirror and grinned at his reflection for a moment to ensure his countenance was, as his clients would expect, flawless. Then he spoke again.

"Put the call through."

The mirror image hovering above his desk dissolved into the face of someone who certainly wasn't one of Loc's clients, but it was one he'd been hoping to see all day.

"Mister Drevit," he said warmly. "I trust you have good news for me."

"There's been a development, Mister Breeden," Drevit replied, his expression grim.

Loc allowed his winning smile to fall away. Despite all the successful negotiations he'd facilitated in the past twelve hours, this was the one thing he could not afford to go wrong.

"Continue," he said calmly.

"The target picked up a companion on her way out of Lynt City."

Loc frowned in irritation. Miana Raiken was meant to endure her punishment alone.

"Who?" he asked.

"Kurt Jones," Drevit replied as an information packet appeared on the screen next to him.

Loc quickly surveyed the profile and recognised the adventurist Miana had bought her equipment from. Kurt was accredited in nearly every adventure sport allowed on Mars and a few more that weren't.

"You should have killed him," Loc said coldly.

"I planned to," Mr. Drevit replied calmly. "I was simply waiting for the right moment to maximise the distress his death would cause."

"Hmmm," Loc mused, liking the sound of that. "I would have preferred him dead at the outset, but I understand your restraint."

"Your preference would seem to have been the prudent course of action, Mister Breeden."

"What happened?"

"As requested, I destroyed the location you gave me," Drevit explained. "The target's reaction was as expected."

Two images took the place of Mr. Drevit on the screen. One showed the cave entrance leading to Dr. Indari's research station while the other showed the truck Miana and her companion had used to reach the caves. There was a faint cross hair at the centre of the second image, as if Drevit had been recording through the scope of a rifle.

Loc watched carefully as the image wavered slightly and then zoomed in on the cabin. Miana was immediately recognisable and she actually looked happy. Then the first image flared suddenly – the destruction of the cave entrance captured beautifully – and Loc smiled as he watched Miana's reaction. She was clearly devastated. Mr. Drevit had constructed the perfect ambush and it should have driven her all the way to despair, but Kurt Jones began talking soon after the explosion and she visibly calmed down.

Loc scowled. He was starting to dislike Kurt very much.

"What did they do?" he asked coldly.

"The target spoke with Kurt for several minutes then they turned the vehicle around and headed back the way they'd come. I decided it was time to remove Miana's final source of hope and was preparing to shoot Kurt Jones in the driver seat when he unexpectedly veered up an embankment and drove off a cliff. By the time I reached the chasm myself, the truck had already crashed through into another cave system and I was unable to follow because the entrance was destroyed behind them."

"You fool!" Loc swore, his anger flaring. "Is there any chance the new cave system is connected with the one you destroyed?"

"Almost certainly, yes," Mr. Drevit replied calmly.

Loc's jaws clenched in frustration.

"What is the likelihood you can reach their destination before they do?" he asked, keeping his tone carefully neutral.

"Nil," Mr. Drevit replied. "There are other cave systems that will allow me access, but they have several hours advantage and Mr. Jones' caving skills are considerable."

"Argh!" Loc grunted, slapping the desk before sitting back to absorb the implications.

This wasn't good. Miana would definitely need to be killed now and probably in the quickest and most boring way possible. The Triumvirate would never accept her walking around with knowledge of whatever was down there.

"*Have I taken this too far?*" he thought with an icy chill.

Whatever he did now, the Triumvirate would not be pleased. And yet, as Loc contemplated how he would contain the problem, a dangerous idea sprang to life in his mind.

"Follow them," he told Mr. Drevit firmly. "Get to them as fast as you can and re-engage the target. Kill Kurt Jones and even Miana if you have to, but make sure you bring her body back to Lynt City. She must be found dead in her apartment by her own hand, so make sure it looks convincing."

"I understand, Mr. Breeden."

"Once you're safe, destroy the cave system completely. No one can be allowed to return to that location after today."

"Very well."

"And Mister Drevit," Loc added.

"Yes, Mister Breeden?"

"Before you kill Miana, find out everything she knows. If they discover anything down there, I want to know about it. Every detail they can give."

"Understood," Drevit said with a nod.

Cutting the connection with a jab of his finger, Loc sat back in his chair and pondered his decision. The Triumvirate clearly had reason to keep him in the dark on this matter, but what if he found out something on his own?

Loc knew it was a dangerous game to play. He might be difficult to replace, but the Triumvirate's psychic abilities far exceeded his own. If they were unhappy with him, for whatever reason, they could make him a puppet just as easily as Loc had done to so many others. Or even worse, they could lock him in a mental prison and make him suffer torments beyond even the most ridiculous notions of torture that existed in the real world.

And yet... Loc also knew that one day it would be him in their position. Despite their incredible power, the Triumvirate would not live forever. And if he wanted to ensure he would be next in line, he needed an edge. There was no success without risk, after all, and ultimate success clearly demanded ultimate risk.

"*We'll see,*" he thought to himself.

Turning his attention to the next delicate negotiation, Loc jumped slightly when another short tone sounded.

"You have another call, sir," his assistant said. "Secure line Alpha."

"Alpha?" Loc said with a frown, before adding, "put it through."

At his command, a hunched old man with long, greasy hair and eyes that flickered constantly around the room appeared on his screen.

"Doctor Grayson," Loc said warmly, forcing a smile he would never truly feel for this man. "What can I do for you?"

"Isaac Taylor," Dr. Grayson replied, as if Loc should know the name.

"Yes?" Loc said patiently.

"He's here," Dr. Grayson added, his gaze resting on Loc for a moment before darting away again. "I know, I know."

Again, Loc waited for some kind of context. It was always frustrating talking with Dr. Grayson. His particular eccentricity seemed to be hearing imaginary voices and he would occasionally talk back to them as he conversed with others.

"You're aware of the recent solar activity?" Dr. Grayson said after a moment's pause.

"Of course," Loc replied, hoping the question was meant for him. "It disrupted some very important negotiations. Is there a problem with-"

"You know nothing," Dr. Grayson snapped.

Loc's jaw firmed, but he carefully held his tongue. He was about as high up in Cosmotech's chain of command as it was possible to go, but Dr. Grayson was the most senior scientist they employed. He was considered a genius and the architect of so many Cosmotech successes that he'd become indispensable to both Cosmotech and the Triumvirate. Which, unfortunately, meant he was one of a very limited number of people who was able to give Loc orders.

"And?" he said after a moment, carefully holding on to his temper.

"The brother is revealed in the spectrographic disturbance," Dr. Grayson continued, frowning hard for a moment and closing his eyes as if in pain. "Yes, yes. Isaac has made contact with a reality outside our own."

Loc's eyes widened in surprise. He didn't know what a spectrographic disturbance was, but the last sentence was clear enough.

"Another reality?" he said.

Dr. Grayson's roving eyes locked onto him for a moment and he glared with an uncomfortable intensity before looking away and pulling at his hair.

"Isaac must be persuaded to let us help him."

"Help him?" Loc replied, confused and a little annoyed. "Help him do what?"

"Return home, of course," Dr. Grayson said irritably.

"And what would you like me to do about it?" Loc asked.

"Go get him. Persuade him. That's what you're paid to do, isn't it?"

Loc carefully ignored that last comment and silently promised that he would one day make this man pay for his disrespect.

"Where is Isaac Taylor?" he asked calmly.

"Being held at the Lynt City Central Police Station," Dr. Grayson said, waving his hand as if the details were inconsequential. "Arrange for his release and negotiate our assistance. I have work to finish, but I'll arrive in Lynt City shortly thereafter. Make sure he's treated well."

Loc held back a grimace when he heard Dr. Grayson was coming to Lynt city. The irritating savant spent most of his time working aboard Cosmotech's largest orbital space station and very rarely came to the surface.

"This Isaac Taylor better be important if I have to put up with Grayson," he thought to himself.

The man was hard to deal with at the best of times, but what Loc disliked the most was his tendency to take over all operations around him. He was the worst kind of control freak and if it wasn't for the Triumvirate, Loc would have had him demoted, or even better, assassinated, a long time ago.

"Of course," he said out loud. "I'll make the arrangements immediately."

"Relevant information will be sent," Dr. Grayson finished with another dismissive wave. "Use it."

He didn't look up before terminating the call and Loc was glad. Despite his ability to deal with all types of personalities, the disturbed look in Dr. Grayson's eyes always unnerved him. He looked haunted, tortured even, as if he wasn't one of the most powerful people on Mars and instead a slave to whatever madness filled his waking thoughts.

Shaking his head in dismissal, Loc brought up the profile Dr. Grayson had sent him. It was a little light, to say the least. Apparently there was no information about this 'Isaac Taylor' beyond a day ago and according to every database Loc had access to, he literally didn't exist.

"He's really from another reality?" Loc mumbled in disbelief.

It was a hard pill to swallow, but ignoring Dr. Grayson was harder. He was known for operating on the very fringes of science and if he said something was true, no matter how crazy it sounded, it probably was.

"I'm sure I can find a way to turn this to our advantage," Loc said quietly as he studied an image of the young man in question. "Well, welcome to Lynt City, Isaac Taylor. I think it's time you made a few friends."

ISAAC SAT ALONE IN A SMALL, WINDOWLESS ROOM
behind a grey metal table. The police officers that brought him there
had already confiscated everything he had on him and, after putting
him through an intensive scanning process, cuffed him to the table
and left him there.

He'd been treated reasonably well after being arrested, but the
way the police officers looked at him made Isaac feel sick. He knew
the first thing they would have done was try to confirm his identity,
which meant they either knew his passport was fraudulent or they'd
discovered he didn't exist on any official database. Either way, he
was certain to be in serious trouble.

He looked around the featureless room for the hundredth time
and sighed. It felt like he'd been here for hours, but it was impossible
to tell with only his thoughts for reference. And they weren't being
helpful. All he could think about was what Jason had told him before
they'd been cut off.

"*Parallel universes.*"

It sounded insane, but he couldn't think of anything else that
might explain what he'd experienced. Not yet, anyway.

Sighing again, Isaac wished he'd been allowed just a little more
time with his brother. Jason was so much better at thinking about

289

theoretical stuff. Isaac always got it once Jason explained things, but he rarely made the intellectual connections on his own.

"I never realised how useless I am without him," he thought with a grimace.

As an unpleasant wave of self-pity washed through him, the only door to the room suddenly opened and Isaac looked up. His heart skipped a beat when a large, angry-looking police officer appeared and strode purposefully toward him, but the man simply grasped Isaac's cuffs, opened them with a deft movement and then turned to walk out again.

"Um, what…?" Isaac said in confusion, then he stopped when he saw another man standing in the doorway.

This one was wearing a brilliant, reassuring smile.

"Hello, Isaac," he said warmly. "It's a pleasure to finally meet you."

Isaac smiled warily back at him and rubbed his tender wrists. The guy was tall, handsome in a movie-star kind of way, and dressed in a gleaming, expensive looking suit. He turned for a moment to give the large officer a similar smile and then stepped inside and closed the door behind him.

"Uh… who are you?" Isaac asked as the man strode confidently forward and took the seat opposite him.

"My name is Loc Breeden," he replied with a small bow from his chair, "and hopefully, you will come to think of me as a valued friend."

"Are you… meant to be my lawyer?" Isaac asked, even more confused now.

"Hah! No, I'm not your lawyer, Isaac," Loc said with a smile, "but neither am I connected to the Lynt City Police Department and I can assure you, I'm not here to try and trick you into incriminating yourself. In fact, you don't have to worry about any of that anymore."

"I don't… but–" Isaac said uncertainly.

"Forget about the death of Laura Gideon," Loc interrupted with a wave of his hand, "or any involvement you might have had. Forget about the fraudulent identification you were carrying. None of that matters, Isaac, truly. The only thing I'm interested in is the fact you don't exist in any official capacity. Anywhere. And believe me, I have access to every database there is."

Isaac was thrown by the man's bluntness. Just when he thought he'd clawed his way onto the firm ground of understanding, it turned into the quicksand of confusion.

"But I'm sure you have as many questions as I do," Loc added smoothly, clasping his hands on the table. "And I'm committed to answering everything I can. I can't understate how important you are, Isaac."

"*Me?*" Isaac thought with a sinking feeling. "Oh no, you're not going to start calling me the Messiah or something, are you?"

"What?" Loc said with a laugh. "No, I didn't plan to. Why do you ask?"

"Oh," Isaac said. "It's just… I've had an… interesting day, that's all."

"I assume you're referring to your kidnap in the Valles Dome and subsequent rescue by Anya Polovski?" Loc asked innocently.

"I… yes," Isaac replied, completely dumbfounded now. "How did you know about that?"

"I know because I work for a corporation who specialises in knowing things," Loc replied with another brilliant smile. "Have you ever heard of Cosmotech Defence, Isaac?"

"No," he replied. "Should I have?"

"Not if you weren't born in this reality," Loc said with a knowing look.

"What?" Isaac spluttered. "Are you saying…? How did you…? Who *are* you?"

"I told you, Isaac, my name is Loc Breeden and I work for Cosmotech Defence. I know about your predicament because one of our scientists heard you talking with your brother earlier today."

Isaac stared at him in disbelief.

"How could you have possibly heard that?"

Loc gave him a small shrug.

"That, I honestly can't tell you," he said. "Not because I won't, but because I simply don't know. All I can say is we have people working on very strange things at Cosmotech Defence. Apparently we had some sophisticated instruments set up to study a recent and extremely powerful solar storm. Some of those instruments picked up your conversation and, I have to tell you, it's caused quite a stir amongst our scientists."

"So you really believe I'm from another reality?" Isaac asked, not sure he believed it himself.

"Our top scientist does," Loc replied simply, "and that's good enough for me and many others, I can assure you. His name is Doctor William Grayson and he believes your conversation with your brother... Jason, is it?

"That's right," Isaac confirmed.

"Well, he believes it proves you've found a way to move between realities."

Isaac was momentarily speechless. Could it really be true? Had their psychic experiment opened a door to another reality and somehow pulled him through it?

"I can see you're finding it as hard to believe as I did," Loc said lightly, "but don't worry, Isaac. You'll get a chance to see all the information our scientists used to reach that conclusion."

"That would be… good," Isaac said uncertainly. "But what is it, exactly, that you want from me?"

"We just want to help you, Isaac," Loc said, sitting back and raising his hands for a moment. "We want to reunite you with your brother and help you return to your own reality."

Isaac frowned in suspicion. This sounded way too good to be true.

"But why?" he asked. "What's in it for you?"

"Are you kidding?" Loc said with a raised eyebrow. "The technology you and your brother have developed is priceless. The way I see it there are, at the very *least*, two realities that will benefit from this discovery. Yours and ours. We clearly hold no claim over anything that exists or is produced in your reality, but the knowledge you could share with us – that we would gain through helping you – is worth far more than any resources we might expend in doing so. There is also the matter of public good, Isaac. Cosmotech Defence is one of very few publicly funded organisations with the resources and intellectual capacity required to make this happen. If you agree to let us help you, we would be in a position to ensure any benefits to this reality are shared by everyone. Not just some soulless corporation."

"That's very... altruistic," Isaac said, a little uncertainly.

"Oh, don't worry, Isaac," Loc said good-naturedly, "Cosmotech will benefit greatly from the extra funding that will be awarded to us once we get you home, believe me. Not to mention the prestige and historical credit we'll gain in becoming the first to contact an alternate reality. On the flip side, however, we also have an obligation to monitor any attempt that might be made to replicate your work. This is brand new science, Isaac, and I'm sure you of all people will appreciate any mistakes could have dire consequences."

"Understatement of the year," Isaac mumbled.

"Hah!" Loc laughed in appreciation. "Don't worry, Isaac, we'll help you fix that mistake. If you'll let us, of course."

Isaac thought it through for a moment. He had no reason to believe any of what Loc was saying was true, or a lie for that matter. He instinctively wanted to say yes and get started on whatever they had in mind, but the cynic inside him held back. If something appeared too good to be true...

"What about the people who kidnapped me back in the Valles Dome?" he asked.

"Yes, I'm afraid they could try to take you again," Loc said, his expression becoming concerned. "Whether you agree to let us help you or not, we'll need to keep you under tight security until they're apprehended."

"I guess I don't really have much of a choice then, do I?" Isaac said sourly.

"Of course you do," Loc said, looking a little hurt.

"You say that," Isaac said, "but what happens if I say no?"

"That is entirely your right," Loc replied firmly. "There is absolutely no threat you'll be put on trial for Laura Gideon's death, or face any charges of fraud whatsoever. I certainly don't want you to think there are any ultimatums attached to this offer. However, it would be remiss of me to say… well, since you don't come from our reality, if this situation moves beyond Cosmotech's influence then others will be given an opportunity to act. There are some who believe you have no rights at all, Isaac. That is, in fact, why Cosmotech Defence has presented you with this offer so soon after becoming aware of your unique circumstances. We have a vested interest in keeping you free and safe."

Isaac felt a chill run down his spine. The thought of having no rights at all was too easy to imagine.

"What will they do to me?" he asked quietly

"Well, my guess is if you refuse our help, you'll be held in LCPD custody while they debate the extent of your rights. I honestly can't tell you how long that might take and I really don't want to speculate as to what they might eventually decide. Cosmotech would spend considerable effort to ensure you're treated fairly, but again, I can't guarantee anything."

Isaac felt the sour feeling in his stomach turn rancid. He knew enough of Earth's history, and Mars', to know that governments could only ever be trusted to act in their own best interests. If they decided he was some kind of threat then this opportunity to actually get help returning to Jason might disappear, along with him, for a very long time.

"I know this isn't an easy decision, Isaac," Loc said after a moment, "but as I'm sure you can appreciate, your situation is the very definition of unique. All I can say is that I personally believe you're a valuable asset to both Cosmotech Defence and every man, woman, and child in this reality. You're essentially the first ambassador from a nation we never dreamed of being able to contact. For the sake of civilisation and taking the right first step in forging a peaceful relationship between our worlds, I'd like to see you treated with the respect a fellow human deserves."

Isaac looked into Loc's eyes and saw only conviction and integrity. This man truly believed what he was saying. The cynic inside him still refused to believe there wasn't some ulterior motive he hadn't been told, or worked out for himself, but it was becoming pretty clear he'd be stupid to pass up this offer.

"Is there anything you'd like us to do for you?" Loc asked when he didn't answer right away. "To help you make this decision easier?"

"Well… there is something, actually," Isaac said.

"Please, tell me."

"Anya Polovski, the woman who saved me in the Valles Dome," he said slowly, "she came to Lynt City with me. After the explosion at Laura Gideon's she ran away and… I need you to find her. I have to explain all this to her, if possible. And I also owe her some money, which I obviously won't be able to repay. Do you think you can find her?"

"Of course, Isaac. I'll have someone begin the search as soon as we're done here. We'll make sure you get to see and talk to her as soon as possible and any debt you owe will be settled immediately."

"Oh," Isaac said, thinking back with a little guilt. "I also stole a data pad in the Valles Dome that I'd like you to pay for and there was an old woman – Miriam was her name – who I took some tools from. Could you take them back and make sure her plumbing is fixed?"

"On my honour as a gentlemen," Loc said with a smile, "I promise it will all be done within the next twenty four hours."

"Then… I guess I'll gladly take your help," Isaac said with a shrug.

"Excellent," Loc said, reaching across the table to shake Isaac's hand. "You won't regret this, Isaac. I promise you, we're going to get you back to your brother and make sure this momentous occasion is handled properly."

Isaac smiled back and realised he was starting to believe what Loc was saying almost as much as Loc seemed to. And, for the first time since he'd arrived in this alternate reality, he felt like things were going to be okay.

"*Hold tight, Jason,*" he thought to himself. "*I'll be home soon.*"

LYNT CITY PRECINCT STATION - June 6, 2147 - 3.35am

ANYA STOOD ACROSS THE STREET FROM THE LCPD precinct station. She knew he would have gone back to the apartment Fayina had pulled him out of. The bond with his brother Jason, dead or not, made sure of that. And from there, it wasn't a difficult feat of logic to determine that he'd been arrested.

"*Not very smart,*" Ianka commented quietly.

Ignoring her, Anya wondered how she was going to get to Isaac. She could simply walk in and demand to see him, but that might not be a good idea given the fraudulent identity she'd provided him with. Lynt City police might be generally corrupt, but they weren't stupid. Another option was to pose as Isaac's lawyer, but even that was dangerous. When it came to the justice system in Lynt City, money and influence spoke much, much louder than any concept of civil rights.

But how else would she get past security? In a building like this it would be heavier than usual and, without a good reason, Anya knew she was unlikely to get anywhere near Isaac.

As she puzzled over the dilemma, Anya felt her intuition flare and sensed something sinister at the building's entrance.

She instinctively moved back around the corner so she wouldn't be seen and then carefully searched for what had caught her attention.

"Isaac," she said with a gasp.

She recognised his distinctive aura immediately and his face only a moment later. But it wasn't Isaac that had caught her attention. It was the man beside him in a dark, well-made suit that wasn't quite as black as his boiling aura.

As soon as she saw him, Anya felt an urge to look away and hide so this monster wouldn't see her.

"*He's with Isaac,*" Dr. Haig said thoughtfully. "*We must find out more about him.*"

For an uncomfortably long moment, Anya fought the urge to step back behind the corner and focussed on studying the darkness that swirled through the mysterious man's aura. There were several negative energies contributing to the shadows, but the easiest to recognise were greed, arrogance, and fear. Anya had never witnessed them in such potent amounts before and a sudden concern for Isaac made Fayina rise to take control.

"*Not now,*" Anya thought and she pushed Fayina away with an ease that left her momentarily stunned. "*I'm... sorry, Fayina,*" she added, feeling guilty. "*I'll need your strength before this is over, I promise, but not yet.*"

She sensed a grudging capitulation as Fayina receded to the back of her mind, but knew her darkest personality wasn't happy.

By now, Isaac and his frightening escort had reached the bottom of the precinct stairs and were about to get into a sleek, official-looking vehicle.

"*Don't lose him,*" Dr. Haig warned in her mind.

"*He isn't worth the danger,*" Ianka added.

Deciding to take Dr. Haig's advice over Ianka's, Anya stepped out from behind the corner and flagged down one of the public vehicles on her side of the street. They were quite different to the ones in the Valles Dome – all white and shining as if they'd just been polished – and Celia didn't hesitate to push forward so she could take control.

"I'm sorry," Anya said quietly, easily pushing her back. "It's illegal to manually control vehicles in Lynt City."

This time, she clearly felt Celia pouting as she reluctantly backed away in her mind and Anya knew cutting her personalities off like that wasn't going to be healthy in the long run. At some point, she was going to have to decide how she would handle her condition now that she knew what the underlying cause was.

As the small car approached her, it automatically opened its canopy and Anya quickly got inside. The control screen was already lit up, waiting for a speech-activated location, but she had no idea where Isaac was being taken and so she activated the vehicle's semi-automatic pilot function. Now she would have to indicate a direction each time she wanted to turn at an intersection.

She then strapped herself in and the vehicle closed its canopy and pulled away from the curb. Isaac's car had only just got underway itself, but from the look of its acceleration, there was a powerful engine under the hood.

"*I hope I can keep up,*" Anya thought grimly.

As she followed them through the gleaming city streets, past a kaleidoscope of attention-grabbing shop fronts and faces of all colour and description, Anya felt as if she was seeing the world in a whole new light. Something inside of her was different, she could feel it, and it made her eager to catch up with Isaac so she could discuss it with someone.

Luckily, the car he was in wasn't travelling too fast to follow and so Anya just had to indicate turns when necessary and ignore Celia who was complaining about not being allowed to drive. As they moved deeper into the city, she gradually grew more confident that she'd be able to follow Isaac to wherever he was going, right up until a tone sounded from the vehicle's console and a sign appeared on the windscreen.

Approaching restricted area

Beyond the windscreen, about four hundred metres in the distance, a blinking red barrier appeared across the road that indicated in no uncertain terms that Anya was not allowed past it.

"Fudge," she said quietly.

It was the Cenovian district, where only the richest and most powerful people lived. Here, vehicle access was strictly controlled and Anya certainly didn't have permission to enter. She could only watch as Isaac's vehicle continued smoothly on through the blinking red barrier before reluctantly instructing her own to pull to the side of the road.

"*Shit,*" Celia swore in her mind.

"Don't worry," Anya said out loud. "We'll just have to go in on foot."

"*If pedestrian access isn't blocked as well,*" Ianka added.

"*I'll get us inside,*" Fayina growled.

"*Isaac can't be left alone with that man,*" Dr. Haig warned.

Ignoring them all, Anya unbuckled herself and waited for the canopy to open, but the vehicle surprised her by pulling away from the curb instead. She frowned in alarm and reached out to make it pull over again, but the vehicle didn't respond.

"*We're being remotely controlled,*" Dr. Haig said, his concern clear.

"*Smash the controls!*" Fayina snarled.

"*I told you this was a mistake,*" Ianka chimed in.

"But who's controlling us?" Anya asked.

"*The same fucks who nearly blew us up earlier,*" Fayina said, as if it were obvious.

"*Where are they taking us?*" Celia wailed.

"*Somewhere we don't want to go,*" Dr. Haig offered in a grim tone.

Anya was about to say something else when she heard a sudden *chink* from above her. She glanced up in alarm and saw something protruding through the glass windscreen. It looked like the head of a tiny arrow with a fat body and a strange looking nozzle in its pointed head.

"Oh, shit!" Fayina swore loudly. "*Give me control!*"

But before Anya could do anything, a thin stream of gas shot from the nozzle with a loud *HSSSsss*. The gas hit her square in her face and Anya choked back a gasp of surprise as she held her breath and brought a hand up to her mouth and nose.

"*It's too late!*" Celia whined.

And Anya knew she was right. Her vision was already blurring and her senses whirled as if the vehicle were suddenly skidding in a circle. She felt Fayina and Ianka struggling against the effects of the gas and battling each other to take control of her body, but even their formidable wills couldn't hold out against this kind of physical attack. Anya was falling under someone else's control, just as she'd regained some of her own, and there was nothing she or any of her personalities could do about it.

The irony of it hit her just as the last of her consciousness faded and Anya's lips stretched in a bitter smile.

"*Not fair...*"

DOCTOR GRAYSON AMBLED THROUGH THE LYNT CITY space port, escorted by eight serious-looking bodyguards. Security was always tight for Cosmotech's most valuable mind, but that wasn't the only reason he needed them.

Dr. Grayson didn't function well on his own. His demons wouldn't let him. When he wasn't doing specifically what they demanded of him, Dr. Grayson was hounded and harangued incessantly. It was only when he was lost deep in scientific work that they seemed to recede into the background, and even then it was only if his work was designed to further their wicked desires.

Dr. Grayson shivered. Those desires were so terribly wicked that sometimes he wasn't sure if he was simply imagining the voices to avoid facing the reality of his own evil. And yet, as disturbing as that thought might be, it wasn't nearly as disturbing as the possibility that his demons were real.

Focussing on the task ahead of him, Dr. Grayson kept his head down as they moved through the space port. The voices were whispering again, telling him things he already knew, and he didn't want to see their glowing red eyes peering at him from the shadows.

"I know," he hissed in irritation.

How he hated them. How he wanted them gone more than anything in the world. But he knew they would never leave him alone. Not until it was done. Not until Isaac helped him finish it.

Dr. Grayson felt an unfamiliar sense of hope at the thought of Isaac. Everything his demons had predicted was finally coming true and soon the entire fabric of this reality, one he so rarely got the opportunity to experience, would be altered forever.

"I'll finally be free," he murmured longingly.

The voices in his head grew suddenly quiet at his words, as if honouring some kind of twisted promise, and Dr. Grayson looked up to find they'd reached the space port's entrance. His bodyguards wasted no time steering him toward one of several black vehicles waiting at the curb and once he was inside they quickly piled in around him.

As they got underway the city glided silently past them and the voices began whispering again. They were never quiet for long. And in response, Dr. Grayson slumped in his seat and turned his thoughts inward.

As usual, he'd planned ahead. The laboratory at Cosmotech's giant office block was now stocked with everything they would need to begin the next stage of development. There would be no mistakes. Isaac would be given every resource Cosmotech had to offer and it would be enough. Dr. Grayson's demons assured him of it.

A firm grip on his arm brought him back from his thoughts and he looked up to find himself being gently pulled out of the vehicle. They had reached their destination.

The knowledge made his demons grow quiet once more and Dr. Grayson took the opportunity to stare up at the magnificent building before him. It was an impressive structure to say the least. They'd ascended nearly a dozen city levels to reach this entrance, but there were still a dozen more before Cosmotech's enormous office block brushed Lynt City's impressive dome ceiling.

Dr. Grayson stared at it in silence. He was rarely afforded this clarity of mind and he used it to admire the skill and artistry on display before him. It was such a shame. Humans were capable of so much.

Not surprisingly, his demons did not approve of this momentary lapse in resolve and their barks of anger forced him back into himself like a dog on an electrified tether.

"I'm sorry," he whimpered, swiping at the air in front of him. "It won't happen again."

A large hand closed around his arm and Dr. Grayson felt himself being moved through the large rotating doors at the front of the building and into a bright, opulent foyer. The next thing he knew, he was standing before a group of high ranking Cosmotech executives and security staff.

"Welcome to Lynt City, Doctor Grayson," one of them began with a welcoming gesture. "It is a pleasure to have you with us."

"Take me to Isaac," Dr. Grayson said, waving them away.

"Mr. Taylor has been taken to his-"

"Yes," Dr. Grayson interrupted him, "and he is waiting."

The flustered executive disappeared as Dr. Grayson's bodyguards expertly swept him aside and then some gleaming elevator doors were gliding open in front of him. His demons were still promising obscene things when the elevator whirred into motion and Dr. Grayson felt nauseous, hoping desperately that reaching Isaac would placate them.

The elevator was thankfully fast and when its doors opened again, Dr. Grayson looked up to find a familiar young man standing not far down the corridor beside Loc Breeden.

Suddenly, every voice inside of him fell silent.

Dr. Grayson blinked in surprise.

"Isaac," he whispered, certain it was the presence of this boy that had quieted his demons.

Ignoring the bodyguards that were exiting the elevator in front of him, Dr. Grayson stepped forward eagerly.

"Ah," Loc said, noticing his presence and turning with a grand gesture. "Isaac, let me introduce you to the man who discovered your predicament. Doctor William Grayson, Cosmotech's – and arguably the solar system's – most brilliant scientist."

"Isaac Taylor," Dr. Grayson said, grasping the hand Isaac offered and letting his eyes roam the boy's face hungrily.

He appeared no different to any terrestrial human. He looked relaxed, but definitely tired, and Dr. Grayson could see a familiar yearning in his eyes.

"*Oh, how I feel your pain,*" he thought within the blessed silence that filled his mind.

"Hello," Isaac said, a little uncertainly.

Dr. Grayson smiled, staring into Isaac's eyes for a long moment, then he reluctantly turned to Loc Breeden.

"You may go," he said curtly, before ushering Isaac into the room beyond the door.

"I'll speak to you tomorrow, Isaac," Loc said before one of the bodyguards firmly closed the door in his face.

Dr. Grayson was well aware Loc was a gifted manipulator and master of his emotions and he hated him for it. It was a talent he would never possess because his demons rarely allowed him any interactions with other humans. Beyond commanding others, he was as socially illiterate as a toddler and so whenever his work required the finesse provided by such skills, he was forced to rely on men like Loc Breeden.

"We have much to discuss," he said, guiding Isaac to a couch and sitting opposite him.

"Uh, yeah, sure," Isaac replied as he sat down.

Once he'd taken a seat himself, Dr. Grayson stared at the young man in front of him and revelled in the silence in his mind. He'd never felt so lucid, so *alive.*

"Uh... what would you like to discuss?" Isaac asked hesitantly.

Realising his silence could be construed as socially inappropriate, Dr. Grayson quickly smiled. It was amazing how easy it was to notice such things when voices weren't interrupting his thoughts every few seconds.

"I'm sorry," he said. "I'm just more than a little excited to meet you, Isaac. It's not every day we receive visitors from another reality."

"It's pretty crazy," Isaac agreed with a smile.

"Not crazy," Dr. Grayson said, holding up a finger. He didn't like that word. It was lazy, ill-defined and as good as profanity in his opinion. "Merely unprecedented."

"Sure," Isaac said, his smile giving way to a frown.

"Now," Dr. Grayson continued, "I'm told you brought some of your experimental equipment with you."

"Uh... yeah," Isaac replied. "It's a kind of skull cap set with electrophoretic samplers. It's what linked my brain with P.A.T.R.I.C."

"Patrick?"

"It's an acronym. Psychic Amplification Through Resonant Interface Crystals."

"Ah ha!" Dr. Grayson laughed, his mind filling with images of the forces and energies that Isaac's words implied. "Of course! Excellent. Excellent! And do you believe you can reproduce the rest of your device?"

"I can certainly give it a try," Isaac said.

"I am so glad, Isaac. So glad!"

Dr. Grayson wanted to know more, wanted to plumb the very depths of Isaac's knowledge and glean what he needed to bring an end his suffering, but the voices had started again. They were telling him to leave. They were insisting Isaac was tired and it was easy to see that they were right. The boy's face was pale and the shadows under his eyes were dark. Not surprisingly, he was struggling with the reality of his situation. *This* reality. And even without demons urging him to get out of there, Dr. Grayson felt a sense of fear deep inside him.

What if he pushed too hard, too soon? What if it all went away and his nightmare never ended?

"But you are tired!" he said loudly, trying to drown out the voices. "When was the last time you slept?"

"Uh... not for a while," Isaac replied, eyeing him warily.

"Then you must eat, shower, and sleep," Dr. Grayson said, getting to his feet and slowly backing toward the doorway. "There will be more than enough time to create another P.A.T.R.I.C. over the coming days and I will need you rested if we are to accomplish the impossible for a second time."

"Yeah, okay," Isaac said, standing up himself. "Thanks... Doctor Grayson."

"Oh, there's no need for that," Dr. Grayson said, waving the thanks away and glancing up at the bodyguard that had opened the door for him. "You just rest and I'll see you afterwards."

As soon as he was outside, Dr. Grayson motioned for the bodyguard to close the doors and his demons immediately became louder, telling him what to do next. They sounded almost as excited as he was and several of them talked over one another in their insistence to be heard.

Dr. Grayson turned away from the door, ready to do as they commanded, but was pulled up short when he was confronted by Loc Breeden. He frowned, irritated that this was one man he could not so easily brush aside.

"Why are you here?" he asked curtly.

"I'd like to know what you have planned for Isaac," Loc said calmly.

The voices in Dr. Grayson's head fell to a whisper, just as they always did when he spoke to Loc Breeden.

"Many things," he replied, his mind filling with the schematics and mathematical equations that more accurately answered Loc's question.

"Any specifics you can provide will be greatly appreciated," Loc added diplomatically.

Dr. Grayson looked at him for a long moment and contemplated just how much this manipulator might know of his demon's ultimate plans.

"Experiments, analysis, testing," he blurted, disliking the need to explain himself, "technological reproduction, nothing you'd understand."

"Do you plan to open a doorway back to his reality?"

At this, Dr. Grayson barked a laugh. It was such a simplistic description for the complex matter of trans-dimensional resonance. A doorway suggested free passage; the possibility of re-use; movement from one reality to another without cost. What Isaac and his brother had achieved was nothing like a doorway. And it would allow him to do so much more.

"No," he replied after a moment. "Now get out of my way."

Loc did as he was asked, but not with any haste and it made Dr. Grayson's jaw clench. He deplored such displays of disobedience and wished he had the authority to have this man punished. But the voices wouldn't let him. They whispered many things about Loc Breeden, assuring him that the insufferable man was an integral part of their final goal. But it didn't stop Dr. Grayson from hating him. In fact, it only made his dislike for the man worse.

"I look forward to working with you," Loc called after him as he stalked down the corridor.

"I'm sure you don't," Dr. Grayson mumbled as his demons surged forward, forcing him back to his deeper thoughts and closing him off from reality once more. "And I'm even more certain that you won't."

MIANA STARED DOWN THE CRAGGY ROCK FACE, FEELING
a little faint. The lights Kurt had set up illuminated the rock wall all
the way to the bottom, but being able to see what was below wasn't
as reassuring as he assumed.

Miana was determined to do what was necessary, but she'd never
rappelled before and certainly not down a hundred metre rock face,
deep in an underground cave, whilst possibly being hunted by a
deadly corporate assassin.

As the events of the last few hours swirled through her mind, a
wave of vertigo sent a prickling chill down her spine and she had to
step back for a moment.

"There's nothing to worry about," Kurt chatted calmly beside her.
"The guide lines can hold several tonnes if they need to and I'm
going to be right there beside you the whole time. Just keep listening
to my voice and look at me if you want to copy what I'm doing."

"Okay," Miana said, taking a deep breath. "I'll be alright. I've just
never done this before."

"That's cool," Kurt said with a reassuring touch on her arm. "I've
seen hundreds of people tackling their first time and believe me,
nerves are a good sign. Just make sure you take all the time you need

and trust that your muscles are capable of doing what's needed. The nerves might be unpleasant, but they can't hurt you. They're just your brain's way of preparing you for a new experience. If you let them, they'll keep you more alert than you're used to being. Trust me, in a moment you'll be wondering why you never tried this before."

Miana gave him a doubtful look, but reserved any judgement for later. First, she had to get this done.

"Alright," she said, taking in a deep breath. "I'm ready."

"Right, let's move to the edge and turn around," Kurt told her calmly. "Just follow my lead. Like I said, we're going to take this slow so I can explain each step and then give you a chance to try it for yourself. Remember, gravity is much lighter on Mars than it is on Earth. You'll be fine."

As Kurt chatted continuously, Miana did everything she was told and found that his soothing voice was exactly what she needed to keep her mind off the lethal drop below.

He was certainly a good teacher. Patient, encouraging, and clearly knowledgeable. It made Miana want to master the techniques he was explaining just so he would be proud of her.

"*I can see how he's managed to make a living out of this,*" she thought to herself.

The progress was slow and steady, just as he advised, and by the time they'd reached the bottom, Miana's nerves were replaced with exhilaration.

"That was amazing," she said, unable to stop grinning.

"You did great," Kurt said with a laugh. "And I'm glad you enjoyed it. There'll be more of this before we reach our destination."

Miana felt a little anxious at the thought, but with Kurt helping her, she felt like she could accomplish anything.

As they travelled deeper into the cave system, Miana found her respect for him growing. Their progress was slow, even with Kurt's unique talents, but Miana didn't mind. She was enjoying the challenge and it was nice to be distracted from the real reason they were here.

She also thought he'd been bragging when he'd escaped from her clumsy knots earlier, but the longer she was with him, the more obvious it was that he really did have a special relationship with ropes. Each time they needed to rappel down a wall, or climb one, he would set up anchor points and attach ropes with a speed that clearly came from experience. But it was his knowledge of knots that was incredible. Everything they did seemed to come with a different knot that was perfect for the job. And whenever their ropes weren't needed, Kurt deftly tied them into beautiful braided creations that attached neatly to their survival suits and never got in the way.

Watching him unravel them with a few swift movements was a delight and it made Miana think of the magicians she'd enjoyed watching as a child.

Eventually, after nearly three hours of trekking through the darkness, they reached a tunnel that looked familiar and Miana's heart skipped a beat. She moved forward and ran her hands over two distinctive volcanic bulges that protruded into the tunnel from one side.

"This is it!" she almost squealed, spinning toward Kurt. "We made it!"

And before she realised what she was doing, she flung her arms around him and hugged him tight. He laughed in surprise and picked her up in a bear hug of his own, swinging her round in a circle.

Miana felt a flush of exhilaration and surrendered to it willingly, but when Kurt put her down and didn't let go, the moment sidled away and left her feeling awkward.

"I told you we'd make it," he said with a grin.

"We'd... better get moving," Miana replied, gently pushing him away.

Kurt let her go, still grinning, and Miana tried to ignore the sudden empty feeling in her chest.

She focussed instead on the map they'd created and noticed that they weren't far from the cavern where Loc Breeden had forced Dr. Indari to kill himself.

"We're not far," she said, even though she knew Kurt could see for himself. "Let's get moving."

"Sure thing," he replied, as if nothing important had just happened.

Once they were moving again, it took them another ten minutes to reach the cavern and when they turned the final corner, Miana recognised it immediately. The pool of water that glistened at one end was almost indistinguishable from the chilled air, but it lit up brightly in her helmet.

She walked to the edge of the pool and crouched down to run her fingers through it.

"How's the temperature?" Kurt said behind her. "Good enough for a swim?"

"A few degrees above freezing," she said with a wry smile. "Not ideal if you ask me."

"What are you talking about?" Kurt said in mock puzzlement. "That's perfect!"

Miana turned to look back at him and was just in time to see him bound past, splash a few steps into the pool and then leap head first into deeper water.

Taken completely by surprise, Miana stepped back from the edge and stared down at the rippling glow of Kurt's head lamps. She expected him to come back up straight away, but his light got dimmer and dimmer until his indistinct form disappeared completely beneath a submerged overhang of rock.

"What are you doing?" she asked, feeling a little worried. "Kurt? Where are you going?"

But she got no answer and soon began to wonder if she should dive in after him. The idea wasn't at all appealing, but before she could convince herself it was necessary, a dim light finally reappeared in the pool's depths.

With a rush of relief, Miana watched Kurt stroking powerfully toward the surface and had to force a disapproving expression when he eventually burst out of the water.

"That…" he said, breathing hard from the exertion of swimming, "was wicked. And it sure is… deep. Do you know how… deep it goes?"

"No idea," Miana replied, a little annoyed her look had elicited no response whatsoever. "We recovered nothing from Dr. Indari's equipment."

"Doesn't matter," Kurt said with a shrug. "Let's set up base camp, have a feed, and then get a few hours' sleep. After that, we can go down and find out for ourselves."

With mention of food and sleep, Miana realised just how hungry and tired she was. The excitement of caving for the first time had fuelled her for longer than she'd expected and finding their way down after watching the entrance being destroyed had boosted her energy even further. She was still itching to see what Dr. Indari had found and had no idea if the assassin was still behind them, but she could certainly do with some rest.

"Good idea," she said with a sigh.

Just as he'd been with the caving equipment, Kurt was quick to set up camp. In less than ten minutes, he'd unpacked and set up a small habitat with three compartments. One had just enough room for two chairs and a small table, another held two generous cots, while the last and smallest contained a traveller's shower and toilet.

When it was ready, Kurt quickly checked the seals and then began flooding the compartments with heat and breathable air. In the meantime, Miana searched through the tightly packed rations they'd brought with them and chose a few containers of chicken soup, a three-bean salad, and some chocolate protein bars.

While Kurt finished up, she pulled the heating strips off the soup cans and, as they gradually warmed, opened the bean salad and placed a few utensils neatly beside the food.

"The air's breathable," Kurt said, stepping into her compartment and sitting opposite her. "Let's eat."

Together, they took off their survival suit helmets and Miana took in several deep breaths of the warm air before opening her soup.

"My God, this smells good," she said breathing in the steam that came from her container.

"You're not wrong," Kurt agreed as he munched on a protein bar.

Miana was ravenous and it didn't take her long to finish the meal. When she was done, she sprayed her utensils with a bacterial spray that would eat away any remaining food and then packed them away and sat back with a sigh.

Now that she'd begun to cool down from the exertion of climbing through the cave system, her muscles were beginning to ache. It was an LCPD requirement that all staff maintain a minimum level of fitness, but it wasn't enough to keep pace with Kurt. Miana was pleased she'd been able to do so without complaining, but she wasn't so sure it had been a good idea now.

She reached over her neck to massage the tight muscles in her upper back and closed her eyes. It felt good, but wouldn't make much of a difference. She was going to be sore after her nap. She began to stretch her neck muscles by tilting her head from side to side and jumped in surprise when she felt hands on her shoulders.

"You're muscles are full of lactic acid," Kurt said gently. "Let me help."

Miana's first instinct was to decline, but something stopped her. She wasn't used to being touched. She'd been in plenty of relationships, but they'd always been brief and touching hadn't been a big part of them. But she trusted Kurt. If he was offering help, it was probably because he knew her muscles needed it rather than any sexual desire.

A pleasant shiver passed through her at the thought of Kurt wanting her body, but she pushed the reaction to the back of her mind and tried to tell herself this had nothing to do with intimacy.

"Okay," she murmured. "Thanks."

Not surprisingly, Kurt's strong hands kneaded her muscles with an expertise that suggested he'd had some kind of training and Miana found that relaxation came without trying. It felt amazing. And after a moment, she was surprised a second time when a gentle vibration joined the kneading.

"Vibe-sense gloves," Kurt explained gently. "You'll feel heat in a moment too."

And he was right. Soon, a gentle, pulsing heat joined the kneading and vibration, and Miana's social reluctance quickly melted beneath the healing strokes of Kurt's hands.

"Come and lie down," he said eventually.

Again, something inside Miana resisted, not willing to relinquish control so easily and a little afraid of where it might lead, but her aching muscles demanded satisfaction.

"Okay," she said in a husky voice.

They moved into the second compartment and Kurt told her to lie face down on her cot. His hands began to move down her body and he gradually massaged her back, buttocks, and legs with the same expertise he'd used on her neck.

Time seemed to lose all meaning as the healing sensations washed over her and Miana was so immersed that she didn't think twice when Kurt asked her to roll over. His hands slowly began to work their way up from her feet and Miana felt an embarrassing flush of heat when his hands approached her groin.

Her pelvic muscles tensed of their own volition, protesting this pleasurable indulgence for the first time, but Kurt smoothly moved past without touching anything inappropriately and they soon relaxed again.

Feeling a little disappointed, Miana's drowsy mind contemplated the growing attraction she was feeling for Kurt. She studied it like a piece of evidence, factoring in their current situation and imagining where it could lead. She enjoyed the speculation, but couldn't escape the question that her investigative process led to.

"Should I be letting this feeling grow?"

It was a hard question to answer, harder than most of the questions she dealt with as a forensic investigator, and for a brief moment she tried to come to an objective conclusion. But the feel of his hands moving through her hair kept grabbing at her attention.

She couldn't help but surrender to his touch once again and before she knew what was happening, she was drawn into a deep, healing sleep.

ISAAC TAYLOR'S MIND - June 6, 2147 - 11.18am

ISAAC DREAMED. HE KNEW HE WAS DREAMING BECAUSE
he was surrounded by the glittering expanse of space and yet he was
still breathing steadily.

It felt good. The distant stars were warm and their radiant heat
washed over him with a sure, steady hand. He could feel himself
floating slowly through space and as he gradually turned, his eye
caught the edge of something waiting behind him.

It was white, almost blindingly so, but as he turned to face it,
the glare gradually receded to reveal something breathtakingly
beautiful. A comet, more immense than anything he'd ever seen. It
glittered like the stars that surrounded it and Isaac realised it was
made of ice. Enormous, crystalline mountains of ice. It also turned
ponderously as it went and Isaac saw flashes of brilliant blue, green,
pink and red as impurities in the ice stole part of the sun's visible
spectrum.

As the comet slowly passed him, Isaac's gaze turned to its
immense tail. It was much larger than it should have been and as
his ponderous flight took him toward it, he noticed something else
looming within the fog-like swirls of gas that streamed from the
comet.

It was dark. Human made. A space craft of some kind that would have looked enormous if it wasn't being dwarfed by the colossal comet it was following.

As Isaac moved closer he marvelled at the craft's design and noticed a string of tiny satellites were exiting from its rear. They glistened in the sunlight as they arced toward the tail of the comet and then, in syncopated rhythm, tiny puffs of white gas bloomed on the side of each one and sent bright tracers spearing in toward the comet. When the tracers eventually hit the comet's surface, a small flash of light accompanied each impact and a steady stream of broken ice streamed out as a result.

Isaac watched it all in amazement. He had no idea what the satellites were doing, but before his dreaming mind could speculate on an answer, he was swept into the glittering stream of icy debris that trailed behind the comet.

Beyond the comet that loomed large before him, he saw the sun burning bright, glimmering and pulsing in a chaotic rhythm that didn't look natural.

An unknown dread crept over Isaac and he tried to turn away, but his gaze was riveted. He could only watch as the sun pulsed brighter and brighter, growing so intense that even his dreaming eyes couldn't handle the glare. He instinctively shied away and this time managed to turn and see that the comet's icy tail was now glittering with a strange new light.

He understood now that it was a solar flare that had almost blinded him and he watched as it travelled down the comet's tail, ionizing the particles of ice with solar radiation. As it went, the tail began to glow in the darkness of space and Isaac saw just how far it actually went. Then he gasped when the distant light suddenly flashed red.

Now, the light that had moved away from him was suddenly moving toward him again. Only this time it was a brilliant crimson – the same red light that Isaac had seen in his visions.

It traced the comet's tail in red fire, twisting through the expanse of space like a great, angry snake, and as it moved ever closer, Isaac felt a terrible new fear wash over him.

He was directly in its path with no way to run. And it was coming for him.

He opened his mouth to scream, to set free the terror that pounded inside of him, but before he could make a sound the red fire slammed into his body with a violence that defied explanation. Red fire obliterated his delicate, human limbs in an instant and as his body was smashed into a cloud of its constituent atoms, Isaac was finally able to scream.

"Aaargh!" Isaac yelled, waking with a start.

He sat up with a jolt and grabbed at his arms as if they'd actually been blown to ashes. But they were still there, solid and reassuring.

For a long moment the terror from his dream clung to him and Isaac could only gasp for breath as his conscious mind woke and gradually calmed him.

"Shit," he swore softly. "That was intense."

Rubbing his eyes in the hopes it would help the images he'd just witnessed fade away, Isaac slowly got out of bed and padded into the adjacent bathroom.

It had been a long time since he'd had a nightmare so vivid and disturbing.

"*Where did it come from?*" he thought as he aimed for the toilet and let fly. "*I've never seen anything like that before.*"

When his bladder was empty, he quickly pulled off his clothes and stepped into the bathroom's enormous shower, eager to wash away the last of his nightmare.

Just like the rest of the suite, everything in here looked amazing and the modern-looking tiles and chrome fixtures gleamed as if they'd been buffed especially for his arrival.

It took Isaac a good ten minutes before he was ready to leave the relative safety of the shower then he towelled himself down with a huge, fluffy blue towel and stepped into the connecting ensuite. Inside, there were three large mirrors that reflected him from every angle and a neat rack against one wall which displayed a white T-shirt, a pair of white pants, and some white sneakers. The way they were arranged made it look as if they were being worn by an invisible man and Isaac frowned for a moment, not sure what he was meant to do.

He eventually found a screen recessed into the wall and when he touched it, the screen lit up with images of many more styles and colours of clothing. He absently brushed his finger past one of them and the rack holding the plain white outfit suddenly whirred and the clothes were replaced with a combination that matched what he'd touched on the screen.

"Cool," Isaac said with a smile.

He scrolled through the clothing options, enjoying the way his choices appeared and then disappeared into the wall behind the rack, and eventually chose a pair of dark grey jeans made out of a slightly shiny fabric, along with a plain black T-shirt and a trendy, expensive-looking jacket that he doubted he'd ever be able to afford.

"They really do think I'm important," he said with a smile.

When he'd put on the surprisingly comfortable pants, T-shirt and jacket, he chose some expensive sneakers to go with the outfit and then walked back into the bedroom.

"Woah," he said in surprise.

The lounge was full of people.

"Good morning, Isaac," Dr. Grayson said from his place on the giant couch.

He was surrounded by bodyguards, just as he'd been the night before, and the enormous apartment suddenly didn't look so large with six burly men in expensive suits standing inside it.

"Uh… good morning," he said uncertainly.

"You're hungry," Dr. Grayson said, gesturing toward a large platter of fruits, pastries and other breakfast foods that had been arranged on the coffee table in front of him. "Sit, eat."

Isaac felt a little uncomfortable being watched so intently as he ate, but he was famished and so his awkwardness fell away quickly. It certainly helped that the food was delicious.

"He will be rested, fed, and ready to engineer," Dr. Grayson mumbled as though talking to someone else, before looking up at Isaac again. "You'll enjoy working in our laboratories. They have everything you'll need. Absolutely everything. I look forward to hearing about the work that led you here."

Isaac noticed that Dr. Grayson seemed to speak in a strange mix of factual statements and future predications. It was a little disconcerting and made him wonder if the man absorbed what he was saying.

"I'll… do my best," he said.

"You will," Dr. Grayson agreed.

As Isaac ate, Dr. Grayson continued mumbling to himself. His eyes were closed most of the time and his expression moved through a range of emotions as if his internal conversation was taking many turns. Occasionally he opened his eyes and glanced at Isaac with a look of alarm, as if checking to make sure he was still there, then he closed them again and lost himself in whatever was going on in his head.

Eventually, when Isaac had eaten as much as he could manage, he reached out to take a sip of coffee and nearly inhaled it when Dr. Grayson abruptly stood up and started toward the door.

"Yes, yes. I'll show him the laboratory," he said, waving a hand absently.

Isaac quickly got to his feet and one of the bodyguards placed a hand on his back and gestured for him to follow Dr. Grayson. He did so quickly, not entirely sure what the bodyguard would do if he hesitated.

Outside the apartment, Dr. Grayson's bodyguards quickly surrounded them and Isaac couldn't help feeling intimidated. He knew Loc Breeden had talked about the need for security given the fanatics that had kidnapped him in the Valles Dome, but he got the distinct impression these men were here for Dr. Grayson's benefit alone.

As they set off down the corridor, the bodyguards began a well-rehearsed dance that Isaac found hard to ignore. The leading men would stop at any doorways or side corridors, placing themselves between any possible threat and Dr. Grayson, while another two would take the lead in their place. Then, when they passed the supposed threat, the waiting bodyguards re-joined the pack while the two now at the front began the same procedure all over again.

Anyone they came across didn't just step aside either, they quickly came to a halt and walked the other way. One unfortunate young lady came round a corner at just the wrong moment and found herself face-to-chest with one of the looming bodyguards. She wasn't touched, but Isaac could see the terror in her eyes as they passed her by.

"I'm fascinated with the technique you used to amplify the psychic signal," Dr. Grayson said as they left her behind. "How is this done?"

"Well," Isaac replied slowly, "in our search for other psychics, my brother and I researched several psychic phenomena, two of which turned out to be integral to our work."

"And they are...?" Dr. Grayson enquired thoughtfully.

"Psychic imprinting and psychic resonance within certain crystals," Isaac answered.

"Imprinting and crystals," Dr. Grayson said quietly.

"That's right," Isaac continued. "We theorised that many ghost sightings and psychic readings or impressions were actually caused by these two phenomena. But I should probably add that most of our theories rely on the existence of an emotional spectrum that permeates the universe, much like the electromagnetic spectrum, but operating on a different level."

"Hmmm…" Dr. Grayson mused for a moment. "And how does this relate to psychic imprinting?"

"Well, when there's a significant change in the emotional spectrum, like what would occur during a violent death for example, a psychic memory of the event may be imprinted within the physical world. Of course, it requires certain materials to be present during the event."

"Such as the crystals you mentioned."

"That's right," Isaac replied with a smile.

He didn't expect to find something he actually liked about Dr. Grayson, but it was nice talking to someone who clearly already believed his work had merit. Most professional scientists he and Jason had talked to in the past found it simply too difficult to look beyond the education that had imposed so many limitations on their thinking.

"Please go on," Dr. Grayson said with a wave of his hand.

"Well," Isaac said, warming to the topic, "not surprisingly, it turned out that not all of what is claimed about psychic crystals was true. Like the idea they contain psychic energy in their own right. Completely untrue. To a non-psychic, crystals are just pretty lumps of rock. But they do seem to resonate with the emotional spectrum and so people with real psychic abilities can use them to amplify the psychic energy they produce. They can even focus or transform it in ways we don't fully understand. Well, not yet, anyway."

"Transformation," Dr. Grayson snapped, looking away from Isaac as if he were speaking to one of the bodyguards.

Isaac frowned, waiting for something more to help explain the outburst, but after a few moments, it was clear he wasn't going to get anything.

"Uh… yeah," he continued warily. "But the, uh, process also seems to suck energy from the surrounding area. People who see ghosts often talk about the temperature falling, the lights flickering on and off, that kind of thing. Well, we think that's because nearby sources of energy, like heat or electricity, are consumed via whatever the imprinted medium happens to be. This energy is then channelled into a psychic event, which is usually a ghost-like image of the person or animal that was involved in the imprinting process."

"You confirmed this?" Dr. Grayson asked.

"We tried," Isaac answered, "but we found the phenomenon to be quite erratic and not easily repeatable. Jason believed it had something to do with ripples created in the emotional spectrum. But whatever the reason, it's kept scepticism alive for centuries."

"There's no other way," Dr. Grayson snapped, again as if speaking to someone else, and Isaac paused.

Dr. Grayson turned to him with a pained smile on his face and rubbed his arm as if embarrassed.

"And what type of imprinting medium worked best?" he asked.

"Right," Isaac said, wondering just how sane his conversation partner really was. Maybe this type of behaviour was normal in this reality? "Well, the type of material doesn't seem as important as a psychic event's ability to change its internal structure, which is why crystal is usually the best. When a significant emotional event occurs and the crystal is keyed into the same psychic frequency, its atomic structure aligns in a tertiary lattice that then resonates with similar emotional frequencies, creating a kind of psychic trap that triggers ghost sightings and other supernatural phenomena."

"Fascinating. And what kind of crystal did you use for P.A.T.R.I.C.?"

"Funnily enough, we eventually settled on a piece of quartz that was found in a meteorite."

"And you used this as a kind of transformer, yes?" Dr. Grayson asked.

"That's right," Isaac confirmed. "It wasn't particularly difficult once we isolated the structures within the crystal that resonated with psychic energy. The tricky part was finding enough of it to make the thing work. Boosting a psychic link so it's strong enough to measure in the physical world was harder than we imagined."

"But possible," Dr. Grayson said excitedly. "Inevitable!"

Isaac looked at him warily again.

"That's right," he said carefully.

"How long will it take to recreate P.A.T.R.I.C.?" Dr. Grayson asked eagerly.

"I'm... not sure," Isaac replied. "It'll be difficult without Jason."

"And that is where I come in," Dr. Grayson said forcefully. "I assure you, Isaac, you will be given all the assistance you need."

"Great," Isaac said, a little reluctantly. "But we'll need another psychic to establish the connection. That's something we really can't do without."

"It will all be arranged," Dr. Grayson said, smiling now in a rather disturbing way. "You will have fun, Isaac. You will make us your machine and I will ensure that it works."

"Sure," Isaac agreed with a frown.

At this point, Dr. Grayson and his hulking dance crew reached a more serious looking doorway and it slid open to reveal what Isaac assumed was the laboratory.

"Wow," he said in amazement.

It wasn't the largest lab Isaac could imagine, but it was much bigger than he expected and full of the shiniest, most expensive apparatus he'd ever seen.

Dr. Grayson led him inside and to the centre, where a large tilted desk waited. It was see-through, touch-sensitive, and had several drafting tools aligned neatly along one edge.

"Your work space," he said with a gesture, as if it wasn't the coolest desk Isaac had ever seen.

He touched the surface to see what it felt like and got a strange vibration in his fingers as the desk suddenly chimed to life. A wash of colours rippled out from the point he'd touched and it painted the entire surface white. A series of icons appeared down one side of the screen and some menus appeared requesting what function Isaac wanted to initiate.

He grinned widely. It looked a little different to the operating system he was used to working with, but there was a familiarity there that he knew would be useful.

"So cool," he said quietly, before turning to the machines that filled the rest of the laboratory.

For a long moment he ran a professional eye over them and felt an urge to start pulling the beautifully designed hardware apart just to see how it worked. He could tell most were for rapid prototyping, but some seemed capable of more intricate engineering tasks.

"This is incredible," he said, turning to Dr. Grayson with his mouth open.

"Not particularly," Dr. Grayson replied, looking around the laboratory as if seeing it for the first time. "But adequate. Now, you will concentrate on recreating all the components required to build your machine, P.A.T.R.I.C. I will study what you produce and focus on explaining the science behind the device in the hopes of explaining how you moved between realities."

"Sounds good to me," Isaac said, keen to get started.

"Isaac," Dr. Grayson said quietly, an unexpected sincerity in his voice, "I can't thank you enough for this opportunity."

Isaac looked at him, not sure where the sudden emotion had come from, and was surprised to find a tear tracking down Dr. Grayson's cheek.

"Uh... are you okay?" he asked hesitantly.

"Nothing is out of scope!" Dr. Grayson said abruptly, as if yelling at someone behind him. Then he turned on his heel and stalked away, muttering to himself. "If resonance is achieved, the entire emotional spectrum is compromised to a degree that..."

His voice quickly faded to a level Isaac couldn't make out and it left him shaking his head. Clearly his conversation with the good doctor was over for the moment.

"*Strangest lab partner I've ever worked with,*" he thought to himself. "*Although he certainly seems to know what he's doing when he's not off with the fairies. Let's hope he can actually do what he says.*"

And with that, Isaac stretched his fingers and focussed on the interactive drafting desk in front of him.

"*Time to get to work,*" he thought with a smile. "*I don't want to keep Jason waiting.*"

BLACK SITE BETA, LYNT CITY - June 6, 2147 - 4.43am

HADRIAN LEVINE'S HEART RACED AS HIS VEHICLE approached the black site location Sabian had given him. He couldn't remember a mission when he'd felt this afraid. He'd faced the threat of serious injury, torture, even death countless times, but it had never bothered him like this.

"*There's no other way,*" he reminded himself. "*Sabian has to die.*"

He'd long since decided not to trust the religious zealot. The man may have given his personal guarantee, but Hadrian didn't believe it for a second. He knew Sabian was operating on the belief that Isaac Taylor was some kind of Messiah and that he answered only to whatever God it was he believed in. And if that God should decide Hadrian was no longer useful and perhaps even better off dead, Sabian would not hesitate to make it so.

No. If Hadrian wanted to live long enough to fight for his continued existence then he had no choice but to eliminate Sabian.

It was a risky proposition. If he failed he would very likely end up Sabian's psychic slave again and this time, there may be no escape. And even if he succeeded, Hadrian had no doubt he would be hunted down by whoever was ultimately bankrolling this mission.

But there was more than mere survival motivating Hadrian this time. He also wanted revenge. Sabian was responsible for the death of every member of his team, either directly or indirectly, and despite his usual professional detachment, Hadrian couldn't let that go.

He held no emotional attachment to his fellow soldiers of fortune. His profession didn't allow for such weakness. But he did respect them and his safety had been in their hands on so many occasions that their eventual deaths at his own hands cut deep.

For both his survival and his mental wellbeing, he needed to see Sabian die.

Glancing to his left, Hadrian looked at the body currently slumped on the seat beside him. He had no idea what Sabian wanted with Anya Polovski, but she was deeply sedated and would remain that way for some time. Given her ability to overcome the tranquilizer they'd used in the Valles Dome, he'd decided to use a more powerful concoction this time. There was a chance she'd never even come out of it, but it was a risk he was willing to take. He couldn't afford her waking at the wrong time and getting in the way of his plan.

Returning his focus to the world outside the vehicle, Hadrian stared out at the slowly waking city with its well-lit streets and walkways, gleaming buildings and oblivious early morning citizens. They had no idea of the seething underworld that fought for control of their lives.

"*Huh,*" Hadrian thought with a smile.

This was the first time he could remember wishing he was one of them. He'd seen far too much in his long and bloody career and would gladly return all the riches he'd accumulated if it meant he could become ignorant of the evil in the world once again.

A short tone interrupted his thoughts and Hadrian turned to the map being displayed on the windscreen to find they'd reached their destination. In response, the vehicle smoothly pulled out of the sparse morning traffic and slid into a cramped garage space that opened ahead of them.

Hadrian waited patiently for the vehicle's canopy to open fully then he got out, turned, and lifted Anya easily onto one shoulder.

He knew very little about how Sabian's psychic powers worked, but he was certain they were linked to visual contact. He vividly remembered the moment he'd become a psychic hostage back in the Valles Dome and had no doubt making contact with Sabian's gaze had triggered it.

He would have happily blindfolded himself for safe measure, but he knew he was being monitored closely and couldn't afford to give Sabian any reason to think he was trying to hide his eyes. He needed to get close to him or his plan would never work.

The solution turned out to be simple. He would use his glasses as a sort of visual shield by projecting a virtual image of the world into his HUD. They were already configured to do this when he encountered a smoke screen or there wasn't enough visible light to see by. And, as a bonus, they were programmed to identify human targets automatically, so he would have all the information he needed without making himself vulnerable to psychic attack.

At least... that's what he hoped. All he had to do now was activate the setting at the right time.

Exiting the garage space, Hadrian walked down a short corridor and approached the door at the far end. It opened automatically as he grew close and Hadrian quickly averted his gaze to the floor.

"*At least I don't have to bluff my way inside,*" he thought.

The room beyond was small and bare, apart from a few pipes running down one wall, and it had the faint smell of a maintenance shaft. There was another doorway on the far side of the room and Hadrian could see Sabian standing next to it in his peripheral vision.

"Lay her on the floor," Sabian commanded in his usual tone and Hadrian did so quickly and stepped back, careful not to look at him directly.

Sabian didn't move from his position for a long moment and Hadrian felt the tension in him rising.

"How long will she remain sedated?" Sabian asked eventually.

As soon as the question began, Hadrian reached up to his glasses and flicked the smoke screen on. The room immediately went dark and flickered once before a new view was overlaid on his glasses.

When he was certain his direct view was now blocked, he whipped out his pistol in a smooth motion and fired two rounds toward Sabian's position without looking at him. He then finally lifted his gaze toward the target outlined in his HUD and unloaded the rest of his clip, just to be certain.

The weapon's barely audible report sliced through the tail end of Sabian's question with a silken *ssft, ssft, ssft,* but the sound of projectile hitting flesh never came and the target outline did not fall to the ground as it should have.

"*Why am I hitting nothing?*" Hadrian thought in confusion.

As the sound of ricochets echoed around him, the virtual view in his glasses suddenly disappeared and Hadrian saw Sabian step out from behind the corner.

Immediately recognising his mistake, Hadrian tried to look away, but it was too late. The room was already receding into blurred shadows and only Sabian's eyes remained, growing ever larger. His eyes and his voice.

"Did you really think you could trick me so easily? I understand the sinful mind well, Hadrian Levine, and I control far more than you think. Your glasses were easily hacked, for example. The image and voice you clearly thought was me was as virtual as the rest of the room you were seeing. I'm afraid your plan was doomed from the moment it was conceived. So tell me, why did you feel the need to kill me?"

In reply, Hadrian felt his lips moving and his lungs expelling air, but he couldn't hear what he was saying. He had no doubt, however, that he was explaining every detail of the deception he had planned.

"So disappointing," Sabian added after a moment. "I'd hoped you'd come to understand the importance of our mission. You were privileged to be a part of seeing God's will done on Mars. You met the Messiah and knew him for what he truly is and yet... your sinful ways could not be changed. Just another example of why this world needs to end."

At Sabian's words, Hadrian felt the fear inside him become desperate. This was the first time he'd heard Sabian speak of ending the world.

"Tell me," Sabian's voice continued after a moment, "how long will Anya Polovski remain sedated?"

Again, Hadrian felt himself answer, but could not hear it. He assumed he was telling Sabian that the powerful sedative he'd used would not wear off for at least 12 hours, and may take longer depending on Anya's physical condition.

"Not ideal," Sabian said after a moment. "Very well then. You shall stay here and wait. Do not leave this room or move from a standing position. When Anya Polovski awakens you will notify me immediately and wait for me to join you. I must return to my surveillance of the Messiah."

For the last time, Hadrian felt himself say something short and sharp, then Sabian's eyes turned away.

As soon as they were gone, the room returned around Hadrian, but control of his body didn't come with it. He could see Anya from the corner of his eye and knew it was enough to know when she awakened. And so he remained still. Locked with his rifle in hand and his fears screaming inside his mind.

VOLCANIC CAVE SYSTEM - June 6, 2147 - 11.23am

MIANA AWOKE FEELING STIFF AND TIRED. HER EYELIDS were heavier than usual and as she groggily looked around the space she'd woken into, her thoughts took a moment to organise themselves.

"Oh," she said as her memories lined up.

The reality of her situation came with an unpleasant mental weight and Miana did her best to ignore it as she pushed herself into a seated position and looked for Kurt.

He was nowhere to be seen. For a moment, Miana's mind flashed back to what he'd been doing when she fell asleep and her cheeks flushed.

"*Oh God,*" she thought. "*I can't believe I fell asleep.*"

Turning to the side of the tent, she reached up a finger and traced a diagonal line down the fabric. The touch of her finger activated the smart fabric and a rectangle of cloth became transparent. Miana could now see Kurt over by the water, crouched beside one of the underwater propulsion units she'd purchased from him earlier.

"*I wonder if he even slept?*" she thought to herself.

For a long moment, Miana watched him work. He was ruggedly handsome, despite his age, and the confidence with which he dealt with things made him even more attractive.

It was years since Miana had any kind of romantic involvement. Her job didn't exactly allow her the time, or appropriate conversation material for that matter. But Kurt was nothing like the men she usually interacted with. He was far more active, for one thing, and he seemed to view the world with a kind of optimism that Miana found infectious.

She touched the communicate icon glowing in the corner of her makeshift window and a close-up image of Kurt's face appeared in an extra window.

"Morning sunshine," he said, turning toward her with a smile.

Miana glanced around the well-lit, but otherwise dank and ominous cavern.

"Not much of that down here," she replied.

"You got that right," Kurt agreed. "I'll have our equipment ready in a few minutes. You should eat something before we head off again. You really pushed yourself getting here and we'll need plenty of energy for the dive."

"Okay," Miana replied, hesitating when her memories once again returned to the night before. "Uh… sorry for falling asleep while you… during the massage."

"Hey, no worries at all," Kurt said with a wink. "Shows it worked."

"It was good," Miana agreed, stretching her arms over her head. "I really appreciated it."

"Stretching's a good idea too," Kurt added as he returned to his task. "Getting the blood flowing through your muscles will take away some of the stiffness and prepare them for the strain of diving."

"Right," Miana said. "I think I'll have a shower too."

"See you shortly then."

Miana touched the transparent panel once more and when it disappeared, slowly got up and headed for the tent's modest toilet and shower. Nature and vanity were calling and despite knowing she could satisfy both urges while still in her survival suit, if there was one thing the suit couldn't do, it was effectively mimic the feeling of being naked.

After stripping down to nothing, Miana stepped under a stream of hot water and stood there for a long moment. The water felt amazing. Its gentle, massaging touch washed away the lingering effects of her more unpleasant memories and she felt much better when she eventually climbed out again.

After drying down and pulling her survival suit back on, she got a satchel of coffee from their luggage, set it to brew, and breathed in the steaming mixture with a sigh. It smelt divine.

She took a long sip and then decided to eat a protein bar as well, partly because Kurt had suggested eating something, but mostly for the taste of chocolate. When she was finished, she spent a few minutes stretching her muscles as Kurt had suggested. The survival suit seemed to sense what she was doing and it heated the muscle being stretched while releasing or applying tension on either side of her limb to make the stretch easier.

Once she got used to it, Miana found that the whole process to be quite pleasant and by the time she'd put her helmet back on, she felt ready to tackle anything.

When she headed out the double-layered entrance, Kurt had finished checking the propulsion units and was now wearing a thick vest that Miana recognised from his explanation the day before. Apparently it helped regulate buoyancy under the water and soaked up oxygen to feed their survival suits.

"Feeling better?" he asked when she appeared.

"Much," Miana replied with a smile. "It feels like I got a lot more sleep than I did."

"Great," Kurt said, before waving her over. "Now, let's get you into one of these vests."

Miana joined him next to the water and once more let Kurt take the role of teacher. As usual, he was both easy to follow and encouraging at the same time. It wasn't long before Miana was kitted out and ready to dive.

"Alright," Kurt said when they were done. "You can pop your flippers on now. Probably best if you actually sit in the water before you do, though. It'll make it easier to launch."

Miana splashed into the water as he suggested and then sat down to pull on her flippers. As she did so, her gaze kept being pulled toward the deeper water and a sense of trepidation slowly took hold of her.

She was fully committed to finding out why Loc had killed Dr. Indari, but it didn't mean she couldn't be afraid. They had no idea how deep Dr. Indari might have gone in his search and the underwater tunnels were likely to be as labyrinthine as the ones they'd used to get here. She knew it was stupid, but Miana couldn't help imagining herself lost and alone within the watery darkness.

"Right," Kurt said with a serious tone. "I really appreciate the amount of trust you've shown me so far, Miana, but I need to ask you for a little more before we get going."

"Go on," Miana said, turning to him hesitantly.

"I know time isn't exactly on our side, but there's plenty that can go wrong under the water. I've thought this through as much as I can in the time we've had and, even with the possibility of pursuit, I honestly think it would be best if we took this slowly."

Miana didn't like the idea of spending more time under water than was necessary, but she knew it was a fair request and so she just nodded.

"You had a lot of beginner success on our way in," Kurt continued, "and in my experience that usually leads to something I like to call 'eager complacency' or Ee-See. A little success makes you eager for more, which can make you complacent."

"Okay, I get it," Miana said, feeling a little patronised for the first time since she'd been with him. "What do you need from me?"

"Just let me pace you," Kurt replied. "I've got enough experience working with beginners to know how far to push before taking a break. All I really need from you is an agreement that you'll stop when I ask."

"Sounds fair to me," Miana said with another nod. "You've given me no reason to doubt your expertise, Kurt, and plenty of reasons to trust you. I'm in your hands."

"Great," Kurt said, rubbing his hands together. "Then let's get started."

Glad his little safety talk was done, Miana shuffled into the deeper water and carefully slid beneath the surface. The water closed over her without any change in temperature and it was so clear that the cave walls below didn't look any different from the ones above. The only change seemed to be that she was now floating well above the cavern floor.

As Kurt suggested, they began slowly, first on controlling their buoyancy and then on the easiest way to move through the water. It took a while for Miana to get comfortable thinking about moving in three dimensions, but she eventually got the hang of it and was soon impatient to dive deeper, her initial trepidation gone.

"Remember our agreement," Kurt told her when she suggested it. "We still have to learn how to monitor our vital signs."

"Of course," Miana agreed reluctantly.

Time seemed to drag as Kurt showed her how to check that her vest was drawing enough oxygen from the water and Miana had to focus hard to remain engaged while he explained how it regulated the nitrogen levels in her blood so they could dive to incredible depths without creating nitrogen bubbles when they resurfaced. Apparently there were ways to treat the condition, but Kurt assured her it was a painful experience that was best avoided.

"Okay, good," he said at last. "I think we can start moving deeper."

Feeling a little thrill alongside a traitorous urge to sigh theatrically, Miana gratefully followed Kurt down into the underwater cave system.

As with rappelling, she grew comfortable with the mechanics of diving quickly and was soon marvelling at the natural formations that glistened under their lights. Curious patterns in the igneous rock; the illusion of life that was created by the shadows from their lights; the way her movements felt a little more sluggish the further down they descended. All of it delighted and fascinated her and, despite the extenuating circumstances, it was an amazing experience.

"*I just hope it won't be my last,*" Miana thought to herself.

As they travelled deeper, Kurt carefully mapped their progress and shared it on the survival network their suits were creating. Miana could easily view it on her helmet's head-up display and it soon became clear that these tunnels were far more extensive than she'd imagined.

They travelled from tunnel to cavern to tunnel for what felt like hours and Miana was beginning to wonder if they would even recognise what Dr. Indari had discovered when she finally noticed something strange inside one of the smaller side-caverns.

"*This is it,*" she thought in excitement.

There was a circular shaft in the floor, too perfect to be natural, and as soon as she saw it, Miana knew it had been drilled through the rock.

"What have you found?" Kurt asked, moving in beside her.

"There's a shaft drilled in the floor," Miana replied, struggling to keep her breathing steady. "Dr. Indari must have been here."

Kurt floated down to inspect it for a moment and then turned to offer a thumbs-up.

"Okay," he said. "Let's send down a drone and make sure it's safe."

Miana's spirits took a dive as she realised they would have to wait. Again.

"Can't we just go down ourselves?" she asked. "It looks big enough."

"It is," Kurt replied, giving her a firm look, "but this is one of those times when I need you to trust me, Miana. We don't know what's down there. I'm sure Dr. Indari knew what he was doing, but who knows what's been done to this shaft since he was murdered? If there's any chance it might be unstable, I need to know. Remember, there's no rescue for us down here. All we have is each other."

"Okay, I get it," Miana said with a sigh, feeling foolish. It was usually her job to douse the enthusiasm of inexperienced detectives. "I'm just… this is important to me, that's all. I'm trying to be patient, Kurt, really, but I've got to know what's down there. And it's so close!"

"I get it too," Kurt assured her. "But let's do it right, okay? Whatever happens, we need to document whatever we find properly. You don't want to give Loc any chance of covering it up again, do you?"

Miana knew he was right, but she didn't particularly feel like acknowledging it. Perhaps it was the small amount of sleep she'd had or the stress of being hunted by an assassin, but she wasn't in the right frame of mind for prudent decision making.

As Kurt remotely guided one of the propulsion units down the shaft, Miana tried to occupy herself with the rest of the naturally formed cavern. It looked like all the others she'd been through, apart from the perfectly drilled shaft at its bottom, and so her thoughts quickly returned to what they might find below.

She assumed it was some kind of rare mineral deposit, valuable enough that Cosmotech Defence was willing to kill rather than share it with anyone. Or perhaps Dr. Indari had inadvertently drilled into one of their secret installations, hidden deep underground and far from the prying eyes of government. Maybe they were running illegal human experiments? Could this be where Loc Breeden had acquired his incredible psychic abilities?

But none of it sounded plausible and Miana knew it was pointless speculation at this point. They wouldn't know for sure what was down there until they saw it for themselves.

Thankfully, Kurt's scouting foray didn't take long.

"Alright," he said eventually. "It looks like there's another cavern down there. No different to any we've already been through apart from the fact it has no other exits."

"Is it stable enough?" Miana asked hopefully.

"Sure," Kurt answered. "Enough for us to take a closer look ourselves."

At his words Miana felt another thrill of excitement, but this time it came with a touch of fear and it took a surprising amount of courage to enter the smoothly bored tunnel.

Their lights were bright enough to illuminate about twenty metres ahead of them and as the hole continued deeper and deeper, Miana began to wonder if they would ever get out again. She knew it was an irrational fear and was glad when Kurt reminded her that their diving vests would adjust the mixture of oxygen and nitrogen to compensate for the mounting pressure. It was just the distraction she needed to keep moving forward.

When the smooth walls eventually became jagged again, Miana's eyes widened when her lights suddenly glinted off something red in the darkness below. She had to resist a sudden urge to turn around and head back the way they'd come, and was glad her weighted vest was dragging her down at a steady pace. Otherwise she might have frozen in place.

She tried not to hold her breath as more reflections of red light glistened across the walls and instead focused on them, certain that studying something real would steal the sting from her anxiety.

"*Wow,*" she thought as the red light's origin swam into focus.

There were symbols, just like the ones Dr. Indari had carved into himself, but made of a red gem stone, or crystal, and somehow imbedded in the walls.

With a chill, Miana drifted closer to them and noticed that the crystal glistened softly as she approached. She knew the glimmer had to be caused by her lights, but the reflections didn't match her movements properly and Miana frowned in thought.

"Hey, Kurt," she said quietly. "Can you turn your lights off for a moment?"

"Sure," he replied, sounding as distracted as she was.

When the lights blinked off, Miana was surprised when the strange reflections she'd seen in the crystalline symbols remained.

"They're reacting to our presence," she said in amazement.

"Could be the turbulence we're creating in the water," Kurt offered, swimming up beside her, "or our heat maybe."

Kurt was almost whispering, as if the site they'd entered was sacred, and Miana didn't blame him. She got a very real sense that this chamber was ancient beyond any history humans had come to understand.

"Could be," she conceded slowly. "Doctor Indari must have thought this would make his career."

"It still might," Kurt said.

Miana turned to look at him and was surprised she hadn't thought of it herself.

"Of course," she said with a smile. "If anyone deserves the credit for this discovery, it's him. Let's photograph what we can."

With a nod, Kurt headed for the other side of the chamber and for several minutes the two of them documented what they found in silence. The symbols covered almost every available surface and the only other thing in the chamber seemed to be a thin film of mud that had settled in a perfectly flat plane on the bottom of the cavern.

Eventually, Miana found herself studying a small alcove near the spot she'd come to think of as the chamber's centre. There was a pedestal nestled in the alcove and imbedded in the top of it was a much larger, much more intricate crystal symbol.

As all the other symbols had done, this one gleamed brighter at her approach, but Miana felt something strange brush against her consciousness as well. She turned, expecting to find Kurt coming up behind her, but he was still studying the cavern's far wall.

Not sure if she'd simply imagined the sensation or not, Miana turned back to the pedestal and carefully began to photograph the area around it. When she was done, she aimed her camera directly at the pedestal and let it focus in on the glowing red crystal.

As if in direct response to her actions, the strange sensation brushed past her mind again and Miana turned around, certain that Kurt had come to join her this time.

But he was still on the other side of the cavern. There was nothing, or no one, there.

Feeling a little unnerved now, Miana turned back to the pedestal and stared at the symbol imbedded in its centre. It was beautiful – much more complex than the ones that covered the walls – and as Miana stared at it, a deep sense of calm settled over her.

The light that glimmered through it changed in a subtle, yet noticeable way, and Miana felt an urge to reach out and touch it. She lifted her hand, marvelling at the way the symbol's inner light shone through her fingers, and was surprised to feel a soft heat through the insulated lining of her gloves.

Smiling in amazement, she brushed her fingertips over the symbol's hard surface and felt a tingling sensation prickle through them.

"Wow," she whispered in awe.

Lost in the calm that had washed over her, Miana barely noticed the tingling sensation had become stronger and was taken completely by surprise when it suddenly shot up her arm. She gasped in alarm and tried to pull her hand away, but before she could move something exploded in her mind.

Suddenly she was enveloped in darkness.

It wasn't the darkness of unconsciousness, because she could tell she was still definitely awake. And the longer she looked around, the more she realised it wasn't complete darkness either. She could see the faint gleam of light reflecting off rocky surfaces, as if she were standing within another cave. And she was moving. She could feel herself shuffling forward. But there was something incredibly wrong with the sensation. It wasn't the shuffle of two legs that she was used to. There were many more than two. And they were heavier. Larger.

As Miana puzzled over the strange sensation, the rock she could barely make out gradually began to lighten and she realised she was moving toward a light source. Her strange shuffling gradually took her round a corner and she saw a sharp beam of daylight in the distance.

The shuffling continued until she was standing at the very edge of the sunlight and she realised she was now looking out of a cave recessed deep in the shadow of an enormous mountain.

On either side of her, towering mountains of rock rose beyond the edge of her vision. And in the distance, past the chasm that flanked her, were unfamiliar plains of green and brown.

For the first time, Miana's viewpoint began to move independently and she realised she was seeing all this through someone else's eyes.

"*Or some*thing," she thought, remembering the sensation of having too many legs.

Her unknown host's gaze wandered across the landscape and systematically focussed on the varied geographical features within her field of vision. It was spectacular. Miana saw thick forests teeming with bird life; winding rivers that glistened in the morning sun; rocky outcrops that appeared to have been carved into intricate sculptures of unknown purpose.

It was such an incredible sight that it was several seconds before she realised there were hundreds of unfamiliar buildings scattered throughout the landscape. They weren't easy to see because they were constructed as if in imitation of the area they inhabited. Many could also just as easily have been part of the forest canopy they inhabited, or hills they'd been carved from.

Miana couldn't see the inhabitants from this distance, but as the question of who the architects might be formed in her mind, her host's viewpoint moved up to the mountain peaks high above her. There were structures here as well, like nests, but larger and more intricate than anything Miana had ever seen.

Although the closest nests were quite a distance away, she saw a figure rise above the edge of one and, without warning, Miana's viewpoint suddenly rippled and changed.

Now, rather than looking up at the nests, she was peering down at a shadowy cleft in the mountain far below her.

She could barely make out a figure standing at the entrance, but could clearly see two gleaming points of red light that must have been its eyes.

At the bottom edge of her vision there was an intricately woven blanket of twigs and moss and it took Miana a moment to realise that she'd somehow jumped into the creature that had moments ago appeared from the nest.

She felt her panic rising, but before she had a chance to freak out, the creature's gaze moved to the horizon and it leapt from its perch. In a rush of vertigo, Miana felt her new body falling into the chasm, then a thermal current seemed to flow in around her and she rose into the sky.

Suddenly... she was flying!

It was far more bizarre than the sensation of having many legs and exhilarating barely described it. She could feel the thermal currents bending individual feathers on her wings. She could sense the converging streams of air and the tickle of turbulence they created. She could feel every nuance in the air around her and knew her host was using it to bank, roll, and glide in perfect harmony with the winds.

After several minutes of almost overwhelming physical exhilaration, Miana's bird-like host descended toward the sweeping forest below and began to skim across the canopy. Unfamiliar species of bird more colourful than Miana thought possible streamed forth from the greenery and formed up behind her, hitching a ride on or just playing within her powerful wake.

Her host's eyes began to scan the canopy on either side of her and she saw shadows moving through the branches. They were hard to make out because the creatures who owned them were camouflaged and swinging through the trees with incredible speed, but her host was clearly practiced at finding them.

It focussed on one that wasn't moving like the others and when the creature glanced up at the shadow whipping toward it, Miana's viewpoint suddenly shimmered and changed again.

For a moment, she saw an enormous bird through the branches, its wings wide, head sleek, and its eyes large and intelligent. Then it flicked a wing and was gone.

Her new host moved its gaze back to the forest around it and she saw it was sitting on a vast network of platforms and artificial branches that spanned the immense space between the trees. Around her, dozens more agile, monkey-like creatures swung through the trees with long tails and grasping fingers on all four limbs. Their fur was a blotchy green and white and many of them seemed to move in pairs. She could hear them chattering to each other in a pleasant, almost singing language and wondered what it was they were saying.

Then her host caught the eye of one that was swinging past and her viewpoint changed again. Now she was swinging through the leaves, looking back at the monkey-like creature she'd just inhabited.

Her new host made rapid progress through the breathtaking forest and Miana quickly became captivated by its many strange plants and creatures. She was carried past trees hundreds of metres high and above dense, luscious undergrowth that teemed with life. Other animals moved along with her, smaller monkeys, rainbow coloured birds, insects that glistened every time the sunlight touched them, until eventually she broke through the foliage and alighted on a branch that stretched out across a mighty river.

Her host's gaze moved across the water and settled on a group of lizard-like creatures that sat atop almost invisible, transparent structures that protruded from the water like rocks. They seemed to be set in a network that funnelled the river into small, swirling eddies and the lizards gathered at each of these points, scooping fish and other creatures into a large pouch at their crotch. Miana saw the water spill through, along with nearly all of the creatures, and she wondered if something nutritious was being sieved from the water or they were simply fishing for the right prey.

One of the lizard creatures eventually looked up at her and, just as before, Miana's viewpoint changed.

This time, her new host stared up at the forest with eyes that weren't very good and Miana was taken by surprise when its vision blurred and she felt her new body hitting the water.

Beneath the surface, her host's vision became suddenly better and as it wound through the translucent structures it had been sitting on, Miana was once more amazed at the amount of plant and animal life she could see all around her.

Smooth rocks littered the river floor, mottled with ever-changing shadows as the sunlight filtered through the water. Glistening bubbles of air traced dancing currents that seemed to collect in deliberate pockets beneath some of the transparent structures. Fish of all sizes darted in and out of the funnelling system, as if aware they would be scooped up and then released again, and Miana wondered if she was witnessing some kind of symbiotic relationship.

But her window for understanding was brief, for her new host seemed eager to pass her on to another creature and it soon resurfaced near an entirely new kind of structure.

This one was carved into the rocky cliffs on one side of the river and the creatures Miana assumed had created them were hairless, grey, and powerfully built. Their massive shoulders dominated their thick, rugged figures and hard, bone-like protrusions extended well past their hands. Miana saw some using them to gouge and smash the rock and the violent process didn't seem capable of creating the amazing complexity in the hive-like architecture around them.

She felt her host splashing its webbed feet in the water and saw one of the behemoths turn toward the sound. Again, her viewpoint changed, this time to something completely unfamiliar.

She heard a splash as the lizard creature she'd come from plunged back into the river, but her new eyes didn't seem capable of seeing it. All she could see was a blurry outline of the river with strange, coloured sparks that seemed to be coming from the rocks at its bottom. She felt her host turn back to the rock face it had been working on and was given the sensation of very heavy, very powerful limbs.

At the same time, the world was suddenly lit with sinuous curves of blue light and Miana didn't know what she was looking at. Her groping mind began to recognise metal fixtures that had been sunk deep into the carved walls, but they weren't illuminated by the light, they were surrounded by it. She could also see something in the rock itself, flecks and veins of different colours, and her aching mind decided she was somehow seeing magnetic shapes in the air.

For whatever evolutionary reason, her latest host seemed able to perceive what the rocks were made of – the metals, salts, and other impurities. The knowledge came to Miana in an instant, but the concept was so strange and overwhelming that, for the second time since her strange vision had begun, she began to panic.

She tried to speak, but no words came. She tried to scream, but had absolutely no control over the hulking body she seemed to inhabit. It made her think back to Loc's psychic violation and her panic increased. She struggled mentally against whatever it was that was holding her and the strange magnetic lights gradually faded to black.

Miana's eyes opened. She was back on the cliff edge where she had begun her bizarre journey.

Not sure what had just happened, but thankful it was over for the moment, Miana began to calm as her original host turned away from the spectacular view. As before, it began shuffling forward on its many legs and continued deeper into darkness until a new, red light began to colour the rock.

Her host paused at a ledge that looked down on a larger cavern and she saw half a dozen shadowy shapes in the gloom below. The strange red glow that lit the cavern seemed to be coming from their eyes and she assumed this was another alien species that lived within the depths of the mountain, perhaps similar to the 'being' she now inhabited.

The figures were arrayed in a rough circle and their shadows swayed to the rumbling pulse of a rhythmic growl. As Miana watched, the growls grew louder and she felt a strange sensation of power building inside her. It was like nothing she'd ever experienced and although her host didn't move forward to join the others, it was soon swaying along with them.

Again, Miana's vision began to blur and she found herself standing at the side of the mountain again, only this time, the sky glowed a fiery red. She felt fear from her host as it looked up at clouds stained with crimson light and wasn't at all prepared for the immensity of what came next.

Without warning, a colossal column of red energy broke through the clouds, speared down through the atmosphere, and slammed into the ground with the force of a moon-sized asteroid. Time seemed to slow as the atmosphere boiled away from the sizzling column of energy and Miana watched as the ground was torn apart in an awesome display of destruction. Enormous chasms thundered out from the point of impact in a destructive web and as the searing bolt of red began to move across the landscape, it was whipped into a twisting tornado that roared with indescribable power.

Massive pieces of charred rock were whipped up and thrown into the atmosphere and Miana saw one of them careening toward her. It moved so slowly that at first it didn't seem real, until she realised it was the size of an entire city block. Unable to look away, Miana watched in horror as it made a final, ponderous turn before the devastating red light was blocked out as it smashed into the side of the mountain and rebounded straight toward her!

Suddenly Miana's view changed.

The devastation was done. The aftermath of the event was arrayed before her in all its terrible glory and Miana stared at it with a mix of shock and awe. The sky roiled with dirty storm clouds and ash rained down in shifting, grey streaks. Immense canyon-like cracks stretched from one horizon to the other and could only be seen through the ash because they glowed red-hot as they cooled from the red energy's assault.

Everywhere was utter devastation. The forests were gone. The intricately carved hills had been replaced by ugly chasms and violent outcrops of tortured rock. The mighty rivers were now bare, muddy trails that twisted through charred mountains of ash. Miana recognised none of the amazing landscape she'd marvelled at only moments before.

A crippling sadness washed through her as she looked out across the ruined landscape and Miana knew it wasn't coming from her.

She wished there was a way to communicate with her host, to console it somehow, but a moment later the view faded and was replaced with a Mars that was much more familiar – rocky, sandy, desolate mountains and canyons.

The only exception to the rusty expanse glittered within the canyon that had been torn into the landscape perhaps millions of years earlier. It was the Valles Dome – its immense, transparent rooftop spanning only one small section of the Valles Marineris Canyon, but home to millions of humans.

Then the sky began to glow red once again.

"*Oh no,*" Miana thought in desperation. "*Please no, not again!*"

But her plea went unanswered and the red glow intensified until she could feel the impending disaster prickling against her skin. She wanted to cry out, to warn the people in the city of what was coming, but it was already too late. The immense column of red energy speared through the atmosphere once more and Miana watched it slam into the dusty landscape with terror screaming through her mind.

This time the shock wave travelled across the surface of the planet like a hydrogen bomb and it shattered the Valles Dome like it was made of delicate sugar crystals. The ground was once more opened in a web of tortured rock and the column of red light began tearing across the landscape in another immense tornado of destructive energy.

Miana knew the crumbling remains of the Valles Dome were doomed and held onto the fact that it had to be a quick end as she watched the debris glisten in the harsh red light moments before it was swallowed by the fiery tornado.

She felt like crying herself now and it was at this point that the image faded along with the terrible noise of an entire world under attack.

Miana's view changed. Suddenly she was back in the chamber where the swaying figures had shared the terrible vision.

"*They saw it coming*," she thought in realisation.

The gathered creatures continued swaying, but they were no longer in unison. The growling had also changed and Miana got the impression they were now discussing what they'd just seen.

She felt a new growl, this one coming from the chest of her host, and the creatures below turned toward her. Their glowing red eyes flared with a frightening intensity, as if enraged at her presence, then everything went dark.

Miana blinked. It was over. She was back in the present, in her own body, which was floating within a water-filled cavern deep below the Marsian surface. As her mind puzzled over what she'd just seen, she felt something touch her hand and looked down to see Kurt grasping it firmly. He was floating beside her, also touching the pedestal and his expression was as disturbed as Miana assumed hers must be.

"Did you... did you see that?" he asked, blinking slowly.

Miana nodded, the movement dislodging a tear that had collected in her eyes.

"What was it?" Kurt asked hesitantly.

"I think it was Mars," she said, her voice a little hoarse, "a very long time ago."

"Well, whatever it was, it was way too intense," Kurt said, shaking his head. "Are you okay?"

Miana wished she could wipe the tears from her face, but she made do with blinking several times to get rid of the moisture.

"I'm fine," she said after a moment.

Kurt squeezed her hand and then let it go.

"So..." he said slowly, "do you think that was some kind of alien documentary?"

"A history lesson," Miana agreed after a moment.

"Did you... did you jump into the bodies of all those... animals?" Kurt asked hesitantly.

"I did," Miana said, looking at him again. "I saw the world through their eyes and... felt what they felt."

"It was pretty wild," Kurt added. "They all seemed smart, too. Did you notice that?"

Miana's mind returned to the beautiful structures that each species had created within their chosen habitats. It was incredible to think of so many sentient beings evolving in one place and living in what appeared to be peace.

"Yeah," she replied. "But the creatures I'm interested in are the ones who lived in the mountain. Did you see them?"

"Not clearly," Kurt replied. "I only saw glowing red eyes. They didn't seem to like being interrupted at the end there. Do you think it was them who built this cavern?"

"I don't know," Miana said, looking around at the glowing walls.

"You saw the Valles Dome, didn't you?" Kurt asked, his tone suddenly grim.

"Yes," Miana replied, closing her eyes for a moment as the image replayed itself in her head. "I think they saw it too."

They both remained silent as the reality of what they'd seen sunk in.

"Do you think it's actually going to happen?" Kurt asked eventually.

Miana looked at him with an uncomfortable new tension in her chest.

"I hope not," she said quietly, "but we have to assume it will."

"But... what can we do? No one will believe what we've seen."

Miana knew he was right. Trying to communicate something of this magnitude was going to upset a lot of people and many would simply choose not to believe. And to make matters worse, there was no point in time attached to the warning. They didn't know if they had days, months, or even years before this was going to happen.

"What would you do if you saw the end of human civilisation approaching?" she asked Kurt.

"Base jump Olympus Mons with a beautiful woman," he replied simply.

Miana gave him a wry look.

"And if you were responsible for the safety of the human race?" she asked pointedly.

"Okay, that's a different question," Kurt replied thoughtfully. "I mean, I'd like to tell everyone to get the hell off Mars, but it wouldn't happen quickly and you can guarantee people would die in the rush to be first off the planet. In the end, if it was my responsibility, and it's not, I couldn't lie to them. I guess I'd just tell them the truth and let them work it out for themselves."

Miana knew that would never happen. For some reason, people didn't seem to react rationally when confronted with a frightening truth. And she had no doubt some would go to great lengths to convince themselves, and others, of a more convenient lie.

"What I'd like to know," she said with a frown, "is why Loc Breeden wanted to keep this secret. What does he gain by keeping it to himself?"

"You got me," Kurt said with a shrug. "I've got no interest in political or financial manipulation. But I bet Loc is just the kind of bastard who'd know how to squeeze an advantage out of the end of a planet."

"You're probably right," Miana said with a grimace. "I think we need to get back to the surface and regroup. We've seen enough for now."

"Yeah," Kurt replied distractedly. "I think we've seen more than enough."

And with that, Miana and Kurt began their ascent, with the end of the world echoing unpleasantly in their minds.

VOLCANIC CAVE SYSTEM - June 6, 2147 - 12.51pm

MR. DREVIT STALKED THROUGH THE DARKNESS WITH
a calm he only ever felt when hunting humans. He wasn't sure
exactly what it was, but there was something about tracking sentient
prey that seemed to re-wire his brain. It focused him. Made him
more competitive than he was in others part of his life.

It was the reason he'd been drawn to this kind of work in the
first place. As an analytically-minded youngster, his life had
quite naturally gravitated toward investigation. Forensic science,
psychology, and statistics. The skills he acquired led him to a short,
successful career as a forensic detective, but the work left him
unsatisfied. Even his most successful investigations had required
endless politics and it became clear, early on, that Mars wasn't ruled
by law. It was manipulated by big business solely for the benefit of
profit margins.

And so, rather than fighting it, Mr. Drevit had decided to leave
the politics to those who knew the game best and became a hunter,
pure and simple.

As he expected, work was plentiful. It took only a few difficult
contracts to establish his credentials as a professional and, after that,
his plentiful work became lucrative as well.

There was always the possibility of being targeted himself, of course, but Mr. Drevit wasn't overly concerned. As long as he continued to deliver what others could not, he was a resource too valuable to sacrifice.

His current contract was turning out to be quite satisfying indeed. Although it started as a simple job of surveillance and intimidation, the unpredictable nature of his prey had led him quite quickly into a hunt worthy of his skills.

It was exhilarating. His primary target, Miana Raiken, would have surely provided poor entertainment had she been alone, but her adventurist companion, Kurt Jones, was proving to be a cunning opponent.

Mr. Drevit smiled as he remembered the risky manoeuvre Kurt had used to elude him earlier. It was clear his prey's addiction to danger was equal to his own relationship with the hunt.

The fact it was a deliberate move and not some unfortunate accident was simple deduction. He already knew their ultimate destination and so it was no surprise that the cave system Kurt had chosen was connected to their original route. It had taken Mr. Drevit several hours to locate a similarly connected cave system and several more before he was able to converge with his prey's path, but after a delay of almost ten hours, the hunt was close to being over.

Moving silently through the caves with his rifle at the ready, Mr. Drevit kept a careful eye on the readings being relayed to his goggles. He'd switched to passive scanning as soon as he'd reacquired Miana and Kurt's tracks – the last thing he wanted to do was alert his prey – and in his goggles, the cave was lit up as bright as if it were open to sunlight.

When he came within visual range of the cavern Loc Breeden had identified in the original contract, Mr. Drevit squatted behind a rocky outcrop and waited for any sign his prey were present. Beyond the entrance there was plenty of light, but no sound, and he wanted to make sure there were no surprises waiting for him.

After nearly five minutes of remaining silent and motionless, he decided it was safe to run a quick, active scan of the cavern and soon had a detailed representation of the space lit up in his goggles.

As the absence of light and sound suggested, his prey were absent. There were two luggage containers packed neatly inside an unoccupied habitat and some diving equipment that had been left by the edge of the pool. More interestingly, however, was an intricate trap set at the cavern's entrance.

It was an amazing construction made almost entirely of rope and Mr. Drevit studied it with honest admiration. He'd never seen anything like it. The ropes were secured around the entrance in an intricate series of knots that followed the natural formation of the rock and anyone without Mr. Drevit's active scanning capabilities would have easily missed it.

The entire thing was anchored to two powerful mechanical winches imbedded either side of the entrance and despite his detailed scan, Mr, Drevit wasn't sure what the unfamiliar knots would actually do when tension was applied. He assumed they would act like snares, dozens of snares, and that they would snag an intruder from every angle.

"*Ingenious*," he thought with a smile.

It would have been easy enough to disable the trap, or avoid it altogether, but Mr. Drevit enjoyed finding opportunities in threats and so he slung his rifle over his back, allowed it to attach securely to his backpack, and then moved out of cover and walked deliberately toward the entrance.

As soon as he passed the cavern's threshold, he heard a faint *snick* and the wonderful trap sprang into motion.

The first knot unfurled with a silky *hiss* and threw up a snare from the cavern floor. Mr. Drevit's finely tuned reflexes allowed him to leap aside and avoid the closing loop, but even as it slid closed without touching him, a second snare snapped down from above, caught his neck and cinched tight.

Mr. Drevit would have been impressed if there'd been enough time to think, but as fast as the second snare followed the first, a third came up from the floor again and snagged one of his legs. Another snapped at him from the side, then another, and another, and soon he was snared by more than a dozen loops. Half a dozen more didn't quite manage to take hold, but Mr. Drevit was, nevertheless, left standing in a web of rope that held his entire body immobile.

"Brilliant," he said with a grin.

With the sheer amount of rope that was now holding him, Mr. Drevit didn't think it was possible for any normal person to escape. He was familiar with the brand of rope Kurt had used and knew it was strong enough to withstand significant cutting forces. That didn't mean he couldn't escape, of course, but even with the tools he had within reach, it would take several minutes to work his way out of the trap that now secured him. But that wasn't part of his plan. He wanted to be caught, just as they hoped he would be, and now he was in a position to spring a little trap of his own.

"I look forward to meeting you, Kurt," he thought with a smile. *"It's only a shame it will be our last."*

VOLCANIC CAVE SYSTEM - June 6, 2147 - 1.22pm

KURT COULDN'T BELIEVE HOW MUCH FUN HE WAS having. As a veteran adventurer, he craved new experiences like a master chef craved recipes, and Miana was providing more than he could have hoped for.

He liked her too. She wasn't like the clients he usually took into the Marsian wilderness or the thrill-seeking friends he spent the rest of his time with. She had an admirable strength of character and a determination he envied. He honestly believed she would have found her way here without him, one way or another. It may have taken her longer and the assassin might have killed her in the process, but Miana wouldn't have given up. That clearly wasn't her style.

Kurt wasn't sure what he would have done in her place. He certainly doubted he would have been this courageous. In fact, he probably would have gone off the rails and killed himself doing something stupid. But Miana? She just picked herself up off the floor and did what she obviously did best – investigate the crime and search for evidence that would eventually lead to justice.

"*What a woman,*" Kurt thought with a smile, wondering how far he was going to fall for her.

He'd already seen and felt the signs of a romance blossoming and could have pushed for a physical encounter already, but he held off for a few reasons. The most obvious was that their lives were in serious danger and he wasn't the kind of person to invite disaster. But there was also something about her that both fascinated him and demanded his respect. She was worth more than just another mid-adventure hook up.

"*Maybe closer to the end,*" he thought wistfully.

But the pleasant thought didn't last after what they'd just witnessed. Despite his feelings for Miana, Kurt was still rattled by the vision they'd shared. He fervently hoped it wasn't real, but something told him it was. Even the part that hadn't happened yet.

The image of an exploding Valles Dome was hard to get out of his head. So many people dead. So many lives lost to something Kurt didn't understand. It hurt just to think about it.

Shaking the unpleasant feeling off, Kurt saw that they'd thankfully reached the curving tunnel that lead out of the underwater caves. He swam toward the guide rope that he'd left anchored beneath the water and felt a surge of adrenalin when he saw that it was pulled taught. His trap had been sprung.

"Miana," he said, turning toward her, "we've got company."

"What do you mean?" she replied, coming to a stop beside him.

"I set a trap at the cavern entrance while you slept. Someone's caught in it."

Miana's eye widened noticeably.

"The assassin," she said, her voice as grim as her expression.

"Okay. What do you think we should do?"

"You've still got that tazer, haven't you?" Kurt asked. Miana nodded. "Well whoever's up there will probably want you dead now that we've found… whatever that was down there. So you wait here while I take the tazer and–"

"That's a bad idea," Miana interrupted him firmly. "You're not trained for this kind of thing, Kurt. And even if you were, you'd need backup. Whatever we decide to do, I'm coming with you."

Kurt frowned, ready to argue his point, but Miana's expression made it clear there was nothing more to be said.

"Alright," he capitulated after a moment, "but we need to do this carefully."

"I agree," Miana replied, "which is why I need to ask you to do something for me."

"O...kay," Kurt said slowly, not liking where this was headed.

"We don't know if he has the same ability to control people as Loc Breeden does, so we can't look him in the eyes."

"Oh, of course," Kurt replied with a nod. "We can just keep our sun-blinders down and re-route our helmet cams into our head-up displays. We could even use add our wrist cameras as an inset."

"I guess that will have to do," Miana said with a nod. "We'll need to look at the assassin at some point and I don't see any other way."

"Done," Kurt said, ready to get started.

"And one more thing," Miana added, making him pause. "I'd like to ask the assassin some questions and..."

Miana paused, as if reluctant to continue.

"Yes?" Kurt prompted.

"I need you to remain silent during the interrogation."

Kurt frowned again, feeling a little insulted.

"Hey, I know I talk a lot, but you can trust me to shut up when it's important."

"I'm serious, Kurt," Miana replied, giving him a look to prove it. "I don't want you to say a single word. No matter what this person says to you, or me. Can I trust you to hold your tongue?"

Kurt held her gaze for a moment. It wasn't an unreasonable request, but for some reason he found it hard to agree with. He didn't like that they'd been followed. He didn't like what Loc Breeden had done to Miana. He felt an overwhelming urge to protect her and was looking forward to giving whoever they'd captured a serious piece of his mind. But at the same time, he wasn't stupid. Miana was a forensic detective, or at least used to be. She knew better than he ever would how to interrogate a prisoner.

"Okay, sure," he said eventually. "You can trust me, Miana. I won't say a word, I promise."

"Good," she replied with a nod.

"Just…" Kurt said, before pausing for a moment. "Just promise me you'll give this assassin some serious attitude, okay?"

Miana looked at him again, this time with a smile.

"He'll get what's coming to him, don't worry," she replied. "Now let's go, tough guy."

With a final smile, Kurt activated his sun blinder and the hardened polycarbonate screen of his helmet quickly grew cloudy, blocking all light from the outside. The camera feed from his helmet blinked on, filling his vision with a view that looked almost exactly like what he would otherwise be seeing, then he led Miana under the low rock ceiling and up toward their base camp.

It was a little disorienting using the camera to guide their passage. Although it was perfectly aligned, the depth of field just didn't quite match reality and it was only Kurt's experience that allowed him to compensate and move confidently.

When they eventually reached the surface, he extended his wrist camera on a short mounting rod and slowly lifted it out of the water.

Just as he expected, there was someone caught in his trap. It was a man, dressed in an XT-5 survival suit that sported large goggles instead of a helmet and faceplate. Kurt had reviewed that model only a few months ago and knew it wasn't cheap. He didn't use it himself because he disliked the amount of physical augmentation it gave the owner. Increased strength was a real benefit in some situations, but it tended to slow your movements and decrease the thrill of using your own muscles.

The prisoner was securely tied up with one of his hands in view and the other behind his back.

"Do you see him?" he asked Miana.

"I see him," she replied quietly. "I want you to go out first and move to the left of the entrance. Watch that hand that's not in view."

"On it," Kurt said simply, glad she'd noticed it too.

As she suggested, he quickly removed his flippers and then slid out of the water so he could stalk across the cavern. His helmet cam worked well, but he kept his wrist cam fixed on the pool so he could keep Miana in view as well.

As he approached the assassin, the familiar thrill of danger electrified Kurt's senses. He knew smiling was inappropriate, but despite the serious nature of what they were doing, he couldn't deny that he was enjoying himself.

He tried to get an angle on the assassin that allowed him to see the hand tied behind his back, but without squeezing between the ropes that were holding him, it wasn't going to happen.

"Welcome back," the assassin said when Kurt stopped not far away from him. "I've been looking forward to meeting you."

A sharp reply rose in Kurt's mind, but he reluctantly let it go.

"*Don't screw up,*" he thought to himself.

Glancing at his wrist camera feed, he watched as Miana slid out of the water behind him and strode toward their prisoner.

"And we're all here," the assassin said with a grin. "The party can finally start."

"Who are you?" Miana asked, stopping a few metres in front of him.

"Just a messenger," he replied with a shrug that pulled at the ropes holding him.

"Who do you work for?" Miana asked when he didn't say more.

"I think you know, *ex*-detective Raiken," he said with a smirk.

"Loc Breeden," Miana said slowly.

"Well done," the man replied, his arrogant tone making Kurt's fists itch.

"And the message?" Miana asked, much calmer than Kurt felt.

"Did you find what you were looking for?"

"You're in no position to be asking questions." Miana said firmly.

"There's no need to be rude," the assassin replied, turning to smile at Kurt before returning his gaze to Miana. "I just wanted to know if you'd found anything worth your life?"

"You're risking your own life by not answering my questions," Miana replied.

"Am I?" the man said with mock concern. "Well, thank you for pointing that out to me. I didn't realise you'd turned violent, *ex-detective*."

Kurt didn't like the way he kept emphasising the ex in ex-detective, but again, he held onto his temper. Miana didn't need him to defend her honour.

"Desperate times call for desperate measures," she replied calmly. "And if you've been following me then you know just how desperate I am."

"True," the man said casually, "but I honestly never expected to find you this paranoid. Why are you hiding your face from me, ex-detective?"

"How much do you know about your employer?" Miana countered, ignoring his question.

"Enough to know he has a soft spot for you. You don't have to die here if you don't want to."

"Does he control you?" Miana asked, once more ignoring his response. "Has he used his psychic powers on you?"

At this, the assassin gave her an incredulous look.

"Really?" he said with a raised eyebrow. "I thought you'd last a little longer before snapping under the mental pressure. What a disappointment. I very rarely over-estimate my prey."

"Then you have no idea," Miana said, shaking her head.

"Oh, I've seen it many times before. The stress of being hunted just gets to people sometimes, believe me."

"No, I mean you have no idea what this is all about," Miana snapped. "You're just following orders like a faithful dog. Slavering after the scent your master waved in front of your snout without wondering why. You don't even know what you're meant to stop us from finding."

The assassin's mocking smile remained in place, but Kurt saw the muscles round his eyes squeeze in irritation.

"*Nice work, Miana,*" he thought with a smile.

"I know all I need to, *ex*-detective," the assassin replied.

"No, I don't think so," Miana continued calmly. "You're just a killer for hire. Good at hunting people down, but too stupid to understand the bigger picture."

"The bigger picture?" the assassin said with a laugh. "Motivations? Politics? I'm afraid you have your dog analogy the wrong way round. You're the naïve bitch here and I'm afraid you're barking up the wrong tree."

"So it's the details you're not aware of then," Miana added. "I should have guessed. You're just an obsessive compulsive coward without a shred of moral fibre. I bet you take every opportunity you're offered. Too addicted to murder to control yourself. No wonder Loc didn't waste his time trying to force you."

This time the assassin's smile lost its lustre and he had no witty rejoinder. Kurt felt a rush of satisfaction and he looked at Miana with a new found respect.

"*You're good,*" he thought with a grin. "*I'm glad you made me keep my big mouth shut.*"

"Tell me, *ex*-detective," the assassin said after a moment, his smile a simple baring of teeth now. "Will anyone notice when you're dead?"

Miana paused for a moment then her sun-blinder abruptly disappeared and she looked the assassin directly in the eye.

"Not for a few weeks at least," she answered calmly.

The assassin seemed as surprised at her actions as Kurt was and he shifted slightly in his ropes before answering.

"A few weeks?" he said, attempting a nonchalant tone. "Not at all. You see, I don't plan to leave you here, *ex*-detective. They'll find your broken body much sooner than that."

"So, you're planning to fake my suicide," Miana said casually. "How ironic. I was investigating a suicide faked by Loc Breeden when this whole episode began. I wonder if your methods are anywhere near as effective as his."

"My methods are flawless," the assassin snapped.

"Flawless?" Miana replied, gesturing toward the ropes that held him. "From where I'm standing, your methods look about as flawed as your understanding."

The assassin's eyes flashed with anger and he strained forward in his ropes. Kurt crouched down, ready to pounce, but the assassin suddenly relaxed and cocked his head to one side with a sly expression.

"Methods and motivations," he said slowly. "You know, you're quite good, ex-detective. I may not have over-estimated you after all. But I'm truly glad we had a moment to talk before concluding our business."

"I never underestimated you," Miana replied coldly. "Not for a moment."

"Oh, I don't know," the assassin replied, his smile firmly back in place. "Would you like to tell me what you found before I finish this?"

"You could always go and see for yourself," Miana offered. "Although I doubt your employer would want you to see what's down there."

"My employer will know only what I tell him."

"Then I guess he'll learn nothing," Miana said, abruptly lifting the tazer.

Kurt wasn't expecting it to end this quickly, but before he could even blink, half his muscles seemed to contract at the same time and the floor suddenly lurched beneath him. He fell roughly to the ground, confused at his body's betrayal, and quickly tried to get back up, but his randomly contracting muscles wouldn't cooperate and every time he managed to stiffen a limb and push against the floor, it jerked beneath him as if the volcano that created it had suddenly reawakened.

"Feeling unstable?" the assassin asked, before laughing loudly.

Through his shuddering camera feed, Kurt saw the assassin calmly cutting himself free with a blazing blowtorch.

"Miana!" he tried to yell, but his lips and tongue didn't cooperate. "*The assassin did something to us,*" he thought, sure that what he was feeling wasn't real.

The heaving ground had to be a fault with his inner ear, but his randomly contracting muscles were another matter. They seemed to be firing on the command of someone else and Kurt couldn't even grit his teeth as he tried to take back control.

As he fell flat against the rock once again, he noticed the assassin was no longer in view and tried to turn off his sun-blinder so he could get a better view. But even that simple task was too much for him.

He ground his chattering teeth in frustration and slowly forced his convulsing arms to aim his wrist-mounted camera around the cavern. After a few blurred jerks, he saw Miana lying not far away. She too seemed to have lost control of her body and it made Kurt feel even more vulnerable.

His shuddering muscles involuntarily moved the camera again and he saw the assassin striding across the cavern with something that looked like a small shoulder-mounted rocket launcher.

"*Oh God, what the hell is he doing? He'll collapse the whole place around us!*"

He desperately tried to stand again, but another random contraction sent him back to the heaving floor and he found himself facing the cavern's pool. The assassin was standing next to it, his weapon aimed directly into the water, and Kurt was just in time to see a streak of vapour erupt from the barrel before something disappeared beneath the surface. A moment later, something detonated in the water-filled tunnels below and the cavern was momentarily lit by a flood of rippling reflections.

"*He's sealing off the alien cave,*" Kurt thought in realisation.

But it didn't happen the way he expected. The rocket the assassin had fired wasn't explosive, it was chemical. Whatever reagent had been released upon detonation was now reacting violently with the water and causing thick white foam to boil up from the pool.

Great bulbous mounds climbed over one another in their haste to escape the underground ocean and they changed rapidly from bright white to a dirty orange colour.

When the rising orange mounds eventually slowed and became still, the assassin stepped forward and gave the foam plug a kick. It was hard as stone. Then, clearly satisfied that his first job was done, the assassin turned and walked out of Kurt's view again.

"*Shit!*" he swore in his mind.

By flailing his uncooperative arms he eventually managed to find the assassin again and this time saw him standing over Miana with a rifle in place of his rocket launcher.

"So," he heard the assassin say, before kicking her hard in the stomach, "an obsessive compulsive coward, was it?"

A surge of anger heated Kurt's face, but he couldn't even keep his wrist camera pointed in the right direction, let alone leap to Miana's aid. As she disappeared from view, he tried to shout again, but his vocal chords simply mocked him with the pathetic mewl of a sick puppy.

Wishing he could scream in frustration, Kurt was surprised when his sun-blinder suddenly disappeared and the assassin appeared above him.

"And you," the assassin said, kneeling next him. "I'm honestly impressed with you, Kurt. That trap was ingenious, if a little juvenile. I would have added a lethal element myself."

Kurt tried his best to swear, but the foul word came out as a barely audible gurgle.

"You have my respect as a hunter," the assassin said, standing above him now, "but I'm afraid that doesn't give you a pass."

He levelled his rifle at Kurt's face and said one final word.

"Goodbye."

Kurt stared into the assassin's eyes, certain he was about to die. It was a desperate realisation, different to any of the dangerous situations he'd experienced in his life, and he was surprised he wasn't more afraid.

But he didn't want to die. He didn't want to let this man win. He didn't want to leave Miana alone or allow the secret they'd discovered to die along with them.

His frustration and desperation exploded inside him like an emergency flare and his eyes burned as he forced out one, final protest.

"Stop..."

The assassin didn't react, of course. He simply held his faint smile and didn't move the barrel a millimetre.

Kurt waited for the flash of the muzzle that would signal his death, his mind roaring with the injustice of what was about to happen, but after several seconds, it was clear that something wasn't right.

"*What are you waiting for?*" he thought angrily.

But the assassin wasn't moving. It was almost as if he'd been frozen in place.

As Kurt began to wonder what kind of game he was playing, he gradually became aware of a strange sensation at the back of his mind.

"*What is that?*"

There were so many emotions boiling inside him that he couldn't pick it out of the chaos, but as the seconds stretched out and his desperation ebbed away, he began to realise that not all the shock and fear was his own.

He puzzled over the revelation for a moment and an incredible possibility occurred to him. Could these emotions belong to someone else? Could they be... the *assassin's?*

Staring up at the frozen assassin, Kurt eventually decided it was the only explanation that worked. Somehow, he was in the assassin's head. It felt like a ludicrous conclusion, but now that he'd worked it out, Kurt could feel it. And to prove it to himself, one way or the other, he forced his trembling vocal chords to speak once more.

"Let... us... go..." he said slowly.

At his words, the assassin lowered his rifle immediately and then twisted the fingers of his right hand into a strange orientation. Suddenly the convulsions that tore at Kurt's muscles stopped.

Gasping for breath, he rolled over and struggled to his feet, ready to fight. But the assassin hadn't moved. He just stood where he'd been a moment earlier staring blankly at the ground.

Not sure what to do next, Kurt was surprised when Miana took the decision out of his hands by pushing past him and firing the tazer straight at the assassin.

The man slumped to the floor.

"What did you do?" Miana said, turning on him.

"I don't know," Kurt said honestly.

Whatever the assassin had done to them was over, but he still felt weak and the cavern was still spinning.

"He was going to kill you!" Miana nearly shouted.

"Yeah… he was," Kurt agreed, taking a step back from her intensity. "I didn't want to die. I was desperate. I… looked him in the eye as he was about to pull the trigger and… he just stopped."

"No," Miana said, her voice quieter now. "You *told* him to stop."

"What?"

"You told him to stop," Miana said, louder this time. "You controlled him, like Loc controlled me."

"Oh… fuck!" Kurt swore, the truth of it hitting him like a hammer to the sternum. "I think… I think you're right."

For a moment, Kurt could only stare at the slumped assassin and contemplate the implications of what he'd just heard.

"Help me," Miana said, interrupting his thoughts.

Kurt looked up to find her bending over the assassin and was about to ask her what she was doing when she picked up the assassin's feet and gave him a meaningful look.

"Right," he said, quickly joining her.

At Miana's urging, they carried him into the habitat and carefully stripped the XT-5 suit off him. They did it slowly, not wanting to set off any weapons like the one that had paralysed them earlier, and eventually ended with a small pile of knives, caving tools, and a few other unfamiliar devices that Kurt didn't like the look of.

Miana made them take the time to redress him in an emergency survival suit and then Kurt tied him up again, this time with knots that locked his fingers in place as well.

"He won't get out of it this time," he said when they were done.

He looked over at Miana and wasn't surprised to find her frowning in thought. Time seemed to have eased the side effects of whatever had been done to them, but he still felt a bit sick and was looking forward to getting some sleep now that they knew there was no assassin on their trail.

"So," he said casually, "what do we do now?"

"Well, we obviously can't go back down to the alien cave," she said, turning to look at the orange mound and then slamming a fist into her palm. "Damn!"

"Hey," Kurt said putting a hand on her shoulder, "at least you got what you came for."

Miana gave him a look that suggested his comment wasn't helpful and he quickly removed his hand.

"I still have plenty of questions," she said, glaring at the assassin.

"Easy," Kurt said, looking at the man himself. "I can make him–"

"No!" Miana snapped.

"What do you mean?' Kurt asked, confused. "If I can really make him do whatever we want–"

"We can't abuse that power, Kurt," Miana cut him off with a righteous wave of her finger. "Corruption always starts with honourable intentions and this… I can't see how it couldn't corrupt you."

Kurt frowned himself.

"I think the circumstances might be a little more than extenuating in this case," he argued.

"And when will it stop?" Miana countered. "Power without accountability is never a good thing, Kurt."

"I'm accountable," he said defensively.

"To who?"

"To myself," Kurt replied loudly. "And that's been plenty good enough up until now."

Miana stared at him for a moment and then seemed to deflate a little.

"Look, Kurt, I don't mean to insult you, or your morality, but I've seen this so many times it's not funny. People given power very quickly begin to think that the rules don't apply to them. They become hypocrites so fast it's hard to believe they ever believed in anything honourable. And what could be more powerful than the ability to control others?"

Kurt stared at her for a moment, wondering where all this was coming from, but it was clear Miana was seriously worried.

"Okay, look, I get what you're saying," he replied, trying not to be offended, "but what are our options here? Do you really plan to take him back to Lynt City and hand him over to the authorities?"

"I… don't know yet," Miana replied, turning away from him. "We don't have enough evidence to convict him of anything. And even if we did, someone with connections like Loc Breeden wouldn't stay in custody for long."

"So, what else can we do?" Kurt said, allowing a hint of frustration to enter his voice.

"I don't know yet," Miana snapped, clearly irritated as well.

Kurt could see a pointless argument looming and carefully swallowed his objections. As far as he was concerned, this arsehole deserved whatever he got. Kurt certainly wasn't going to let him get away with what he'd tried to do here. For that, and for all the atrocities this man had likely committed in the past, he would find a way to make him pay.

"Why don't we just tell people?" he asked. "Blow the lid off this thing so loud there's no way they can keep it a secret any longer."

"I wish it were that simple," Miana said, sitting down.

"It is," Kurt said, gratefully sitting beside her. "You don't have to shoulder this responsibility any longer, Miana."

She turned to look at him for a moment then her concern melted into a smile.

"So what, tough guy?" she said in a way that made Kurt's irritation fade as if it had never been. "We're just going to hand this incredible power over to whoever gets here first?"

Kurt paused. He hadn't thought of that. The assassin may have sealed off the alien cave for the near future, but if the right people found out about it, they'd just drill their way back in. And what would they do with the ability to control others?

"Well, Loc's already tried the alternative," he said. "Locate and kill everyone who knows anything about this and make sure no one ever finds it. We're obviously not going to do that. So as far as I'm concerned, it's either tell everyone, or tell no one."

"I'm just..." Miana began, then she stopped, sighed, and looked at the floor. "I'm just afraid of the consequences, no matter what we do."

Kurt looked at the floor as well. He wasn't used to this type of dilemma. He just wanted to hand this problem over to someone else so he could get lost in the wilderness for a while.

"Look, don't worry," he said, putting a hand on her leg. "You'll find the right approach, Miana. You just need a little time to think about it."

"I wish that were true," Miana said, shaking her head, "but there's so much more to this than we know. Loc Breeden might be powerful, but he's only one man and I get the feeling he was as ignorant of what we found down here as the assassin was."

"Really?" Kurt said with a frown. "How could he not know?"

"Doctor Indari was murdered six months ago," Miana explained, closing her eyes and pinching the bridge of her nose. "Do you really think Loc would have left this cave system intact if he knew how easy it was to gain psychic powers?"

"Maybe he was planning to come back himself?"

Miana opened her eyes and looked at him again.

"Maybe," she conceded, "but it doesn't feel right. I think there's another hand at play here."

"Another hand?" Kurt said. "You mean someone else is pulling Loc's strings?"

"That would be my guess," Miana replied.

"Well… that sucks," Kurt said in frustration. "Just when I felt like we'd made some progress."

"We have," Miana replied. "We've made more progress than I ever thought possible. We just need to be careful we don't ruin it with hasty decisions. Eager complacency, remember?"

"Hey, that's my line," Kurt said, putting on an affronted expression.

"It's a good one," Miana said with a laugh. "You should be flattered I'm using it."

"I guess so," Kurt said with a grin.

They smiled at each other for a moment and once again Kurt felt the tension in him fading away.

"Okay," he said, reluctantly breaking the spell. "Well, I don't know about you, but after whatever that assassin did to us, I'm wrecked. And our trip back to the surface will take a lot longer than the one that got us here. It must have taken the assassin anywhere from eight to ten hours to reach us and we'll both need sleep before we attempt to retrace his tracks."

Miana glanced at the assassin with a grim expression.

"I don't know if I could sleep with him here," she said softly. "Can we even afford to let our guard down?"

"We can and we will," Kurt replied firmly. "Sleep is important, Miana. I'll take the first watch while you-"

"No," Miana interrupted him, even more firmly. "You need it more than I do, Kurt. I'll take the first watch."

"Alright," Kurt conceded after a moment, the ache in his limbs quickly overwhelming his reluctance, "but I want you to wake me if I'm out more than five hours."

"Agreed," Miana said with a nod, before placing her hand on his leg. "And thanks, Kurt. I really didn't expect to get this far. I was... well, I was desperate when I made the choice to come down here and would have tried to find the answers with everything I had, but... now that I'm here, it's pretty clear I couldn't have done it without you."

"Oh, you would have," Kurt assured her. "It just wouldn't have been half as fun."

At this, Miana smiled in a way that made Kurt feel a little lighter then she took her hand away and stood up.

"Right," she said, her determined expression in place again. "Off to bed with you. The sooner we both get some rest, the sooner we can get out of here and find a way to make this right."

"Sounds good to me," Kurt replied with a grin.

STAGE 4: SOLAR FLARE APPROACHES JUPITER

June 7, 2147 - 1.45 pm

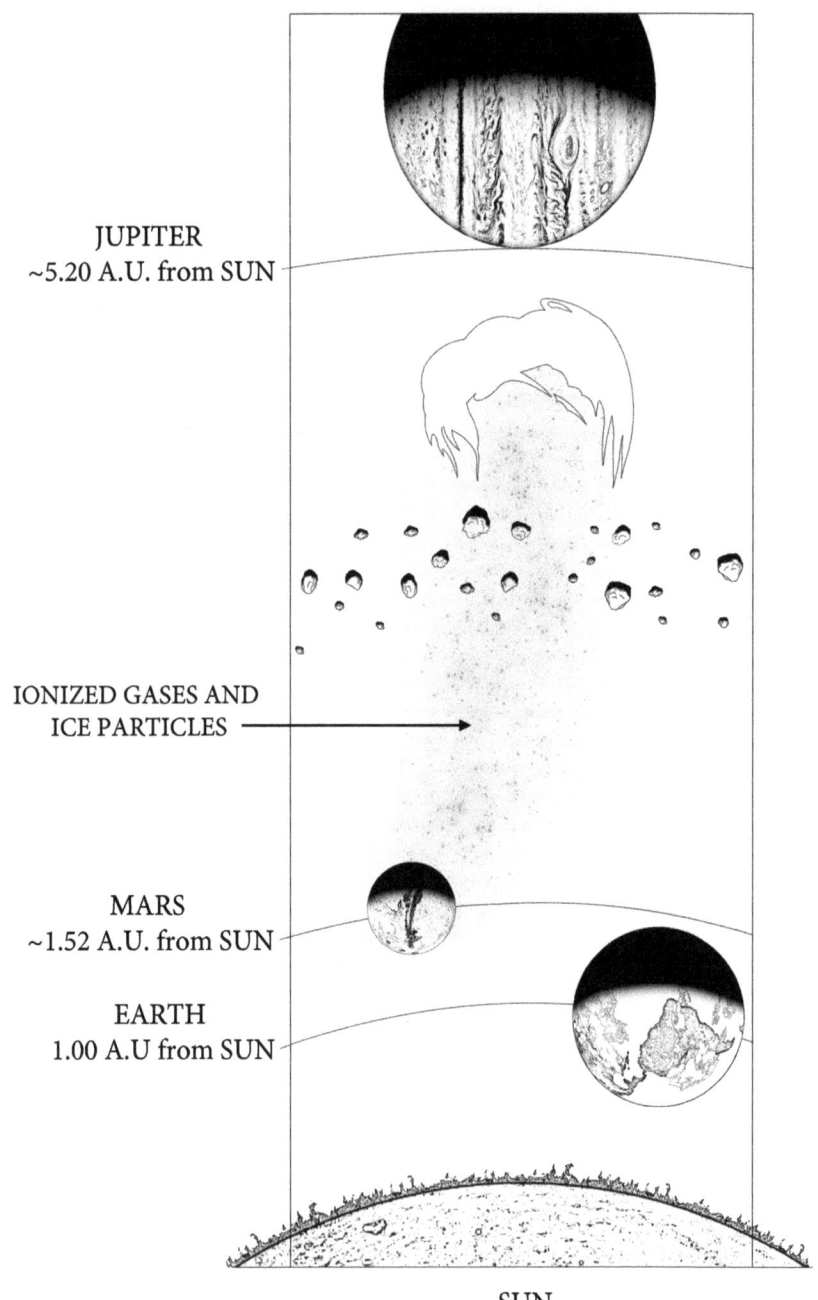

JUPITER
~5.20 A.U. from SUN

IONIZED GASES AND
ICE PARTICLES

MARS
~1.52 A.U. from SUN

EARTH
1.00 A.U from SUN

SUN

1 Astronomical Unit (A.U.) = ~149.6 x 10^6 km

ISAAC FELT ROTTEN WITH GUILT. WITH SO MUCH AT stake he knew he shouldn't be enjoying himself, but the Cosmotech laboratories were just so *cool*.

Their rapid prototyping machine alone was capable of moderate, if not mass, production and its range of robotic tools was insane. He could whip up anything from the smallest transistor to room-sized structures in no time at all and assemble the most intricate circuits and mechanical couplings in the process. He also had a list of raw materials and pre-made components to choose from that, frankly, made him feel a little weak at the knees.

Given their budget limitations, he and Jason usually had to salvage parts from other mass-produced products. It was why Isaac was so good at pulling things apart. But as much as he enjoyed deconstructing things, he'd give all that up for the chance to continue working with the equipment they had here.

He knew Jason wouldn't have been distracted by all the flashy machines and endless resources, but for Isaac this was about as close to heaven as he was likely to get.

Of course, that wasn't the only reason he felt guilty. He never thought he'd meet someone as smart as Jason, but Dr. Grayson had blown that assumption right out of the water. He had a little trouble communicating and talked to himself more often than seemed sane, but the speed with which he picked up concepts was amazing.

After barely a day and a half of hard work they'd already managed to recreate P.A.T.R.I.C. to the standard he and Jason had reached and were now working on improving its design so the process could be measured and monitored at all stages. The only thing missing now was someone else with psychic abilities.

"*Where are you, Anya?*" Isaac thought with a frown.

Despite Cosmotech's obvious wealth, they still hadn't managed to find her and Isaac was beginning to worry that she'd gone back to the Valles Dome. He wouldn't blame her if she had, not after the way he'd treated her, but if there was anyone able to help him make this work, surely it was Anya.

And besides that, even if she didn't want to help, Isaac needed to apologise for his behaviour. He still felt like a complete asshole for yelling at her.

Taking a deep breath, he rubbed his eyes for a moment and then pulled his thoughts back to the task at hand.

"*She'll turn up,*" he thought. "*I just need to be patient.*"

"I have a theory," Dr. Grayson said, appearing at his side.

Isaac jumped in surprise.

"Uh... sure, Doc," he said, attempting a smile. "Go ahead."

"Based on your description of the initial incident, I've been working on several hypotheses that might explain the occurrence."

"Great," Isaac said, leaning forward with interest.

"You said the initial incident caused a localised blackout in your version of Lynt City."

"I did."

"Well, I believe your device – which was designed to measure changes in the emotional spectrum via a link with the electromagnetic spectrum – created a potentiality cliff between the two."

"You mean, like a pressure difference?" Isaac said slowly.

"Exactly like a pressure difference," Dr. Grayson replied, "just with vastly different energies. Now, the blackout you caused suggests the potentiality cliff pulled a massive amount of electrical energy from your Lynt City's grid and converted it into emotional energy."

"Through the psychic link," Isaac said quietly, remembering the overwhelming sensation he'd felt during the experiment.

"I believe the rift between our realities was created by focussing that surge of emotional energy within the limited space-time that existed between you and your brother. Until we can test our own version of P.A.T.R.I.C. we have no way of estimating the effect a sudden, focussed increase in the emotional spectrum will have, but it is reasonable to assume it may be comparable to focussing electromagnetic energy."

"But... focussing that much electricity into a single point would release an electromagnetic pulse that would take out Lynt City."

"It would have a considerable impact, yes," Dr. Grayson agreed.

Isaac thought about it for a moment. Given what they already knew it was an entirely plausible hypothesis and Isaac had to admit it also made a strange kind of sense. He and Jason had never even contemplated what effect such an accumulation of emotional energy might have on their immediate environment. It didn't seem to be an issue since they'd been tapping into it their entire lives.

But what happened when a city's worth of electricity was converted into emotional energy?

"It makes sense," he said quietly.

"And it gives our research focus," Dr. Grayson added with a forceful gesture. "When we find you a suitable partner, we will control the amount of electrical energy being fed into the psychic connection and measure any localised impacts in the space-time continuum. Once we have that data, we will concentrate on recreating the conditions that caused the initial rift."

"And I can return to my own reality," Isaac said with a grin.

"Yes, precisely," Dr. Grayson said distractedly. "For now, however, another candidate awaits."

Isaac felt a sinking feeling and took a deep breath before turning toward the door.

"*Another psychic candidate*," he thought with a shudder.

They'd been bringing him a string of so-called 'psychics' all day, but none of them had given Isaac any indication they had real psychic abilities. It was frustrating seeing so many frauds in such a short period of time and knowing how important it was to find a real one only made it worse.

Feeling less than confident, Isaac watched as a lab assistant walked in with a chubby, middle-aged woman with a far-off look in her eyes. She wore a long silken dress that shimmered purple and green in the room's light and a thick silver sash at her waist that dripped with hundreds of glittering charms.

"Hi," Isaac said, holding out his hand. "I'm Isaac."

"And I am Madam Soza," she said, squinting into his eyes and stepping forward to grasp his hand in both of hers. "You are troubled, Isaac. Grieving for something lost."

"Right, very good," Isaac said as he tactfully extricated his hand and stood back. "Please, have a seat on the other side of the desk."

"I sense a great sadness in you, Isaac," the woman continued, holding his gaze as the assistant gently led her round the table. "Have you lost someone close to you?"

"Hasn't everyone?" Isaac replied, feeling a little annoyed.

Nearly every psychic they'd brought had started with this and he was beginning to wonder just how transparent his emotions were.

"Hostility," the woman said, nodding slowly, "an understandable response. I see you are struggling to understand something of great importance."

"Remarkable," Isaac replied, unable to resist the temptation. "How did you know?"

"I can sense it," the woman answered with a knowing smile. "My spirit is attuned to the energies of the universe."

"So it wasn't the fact you were paid to come into a scientific laboratory?"

The muscles around the woman's eyes pulled tight for a second and Isaac was certain they'd brought him another fraud.

"Doc," he said, turning to Dr. Grayson with a meaningful look. But the doctor was already on the far side of the lab, deep in conversation with himself and working on something new.

"Fine," Isaac said, turning back to the woman. "I'm sorry, Madam Soza. You're right. I'm just feeling a bit hostile. Please, take a seat and the lab assistant will help you with the skull cap."

The woman sat down with an indignant swirl of her dress and Isaac was engulfed in a cloud of floral perfume. He lifted a fist to his mouth and coughed as quietly as he could, resisting the temptation to wave his hand through the air.

There was an awkward scuffle as the lab assistant attempted to place the skull cap over Madam Soza's beautifully sculpted hair, but eventually the assistant won and Isaac's latest psychic partner was hooked into P.A.T.R.I.C.

"May I hold your hand?" Madam Soza asked, her brow furrowed in a slightly concerned, slightly constipated expression.

"If that's how you… read minds," Isaac said slowly, "but you're not here to do a reading, okay? These skull caps have been designed to facilitate a psychic link between us."

"Very well," she replied with a dramatically raised eyebrow.

Isaac was distracted by the mysterious look for a moment then he shook it off and continued.

"I'm going to initiate the psychic link," he explained, "then I'm going use it to share a mental image with you. Once you see it in your mind, I'd like you to try and change that image and send it back to me. Does that make sense?"

"Of course," the woman said with a smile. "Let us commence."

"Right," Isaac said, trying not to sound sceptical. "Phase one."

He touched a small icon on the desk in front of him and watched the information that scrolled across the screen beside it. It was immediately clear there was nothing more than the usual psychic background registering within the emotional spectrum.

"Phase two," Isaac said, preparing himself for the mental jolt to come.

When it came, he saw the woman opposite him twitch and for the first time realised there might actually be some small psychic talent there after all.

Then he leaned forward and spoke again.

"Phase three."

This time, he felt nothing at all, but it didn't mean Madam Soza was another failure. Not yet anyway.

"Alright," he said, noticing that her eyes were now as wide as they could go. "I'm going to create the image in my mind and send it to you."

Madam Soza nodded distractedly and so Isaac did as he'd promised, creating a small white terrier in his mind and then psychically offering it to her.

"What do you see?" he asked.

"I see... a Maltese terrier," the woman responded slowly. "Is... is that right?"

"It is," Isaac replied, honestly impressed. "Now I'd like you to try and copy the image in your mind if you can, and make the dog walk."

The woman nodded slowly then her mysterious look became constipated again.

The image in Isaac's mind shimmered slightly as Madam Soza tried to do as he asked. The little dog's legs became cloudy and faded in and out of focus for a moment, but they didn't move.

Isaac was certain now that she did have some ability, but the more she tried to use it, the more he realised she was too weak and inexperienced to be of any help. He let her continue trying for several minutes, just to be sure, but eventually let the image disappear himself.

The woman noticed his reaction immediately and leant forward with a desperate look.

"I can do it," she said, sounding genuine for the first time. "I just need more time."

"Thank you," Isaac said kindly, "but I'm afraid you don't have the psychic strength we require."

The woman looked truly forlorn at the news and Isaac found himself feeling sorry for her.

"At least you now know your psychic abilities are real," he said, hoping it would make her feel better.

But his well-meaning words had entirely the opposite effect. The woman's expression skipped from pleading to outrage in an instant and she tore the skull cap from her head in indignation.

"I don't need *you* to tell me that," she snapped, slamming it down on the table.

"I'm... sorry," Isaac spluttered, "I didn't mean-"

"I've never been so insulted," the woman cut him off sharply. "Who do you think you are, young man?"

Isaac leaned away from the searing heat of her glare and opened and closed his mouth in astonishment.

"Your fee will be transferred when you sign out," Dr. Grayson said, appearing smoothly at her side. "The assistant will escort you out."

"Please, Madam?" the assistant spoke up quickly, placing a hand on her arm and gesturing toward the exit.

"How indescribably rude," Madam Soza snapped, pulling away from her. "There is no way you will find what you're looking for with such a disregard for the effect of such negative energies."

"This way, please," the assistant said with a strained smile.

For a moment Isaac felt as if Madam Soza was going to reach across the table and slap him, but instead she lifted her chin with an offended "hurrumph" and stalked out of the room.

"Wow," he said when she was gone. "That... could have gone better."

"It will," Dr. Grayson said, studying the data he'd gathered during the exchange. "However, she did have some psychic talent."

385

"Did you get anything useful?" Isaac asked hopefully.

"Not enough to recreate the rift," Dr. Grayson replied, "but enough to confirm my hypothesis."

"Really?" Isaac said. "What did you find?"

"It has to be controlled," Dr. Grayson snapped, turning away from him suddenly. "Don't tell me that!"

And Isaac knew he was gone again. He still wasn't entirely sure if the Doc was talking to someone on a hidden communications device, or if he was just talking to himself, but he was becoming grudgingly accustomed to these half-finished conversations.

Isaac sighed. At least he had some good news. Whatever they'd done to get him here, it looked like they were on track to get him back.

"*I'm on my way, bro,*" he promised in his mind. "*One way or another, I'll be home soon.*"

COSMOTECH OFFICES, LYNT CITY - June 6, 2147 - 2.30pm

LOC WATCHED ISAAC WORKING ON THE SCREEN THAT hovered above his desk with a frown. He still didn't fully understand what this boy meant to Dr. Grayson, or Cosmotech Defence for that matter, but he didn't believe for a minute they were actually going to help him get back to his own reality.

He wasn't even sure he believed what he'd been told. He knew better than to reject any scientific claim that came from Grayson, but Loc lived and breathed the world of lies and half-truths and he could sense something was being concealed from him.

He would have liked more time to investigate, but the Lynt City officials he'd met with two days ago had been keeping him busy. It helped that they were falling into line like dogs begging for treats, but the contracts being negotiated were intricate and their legal ramifications far reaching. And after so many years of experience, Loc knew this was a process that couldn't be rushed.

Steepling his hands beneath his chin, Loc glanced at the status bar near the bottom of his working screen.

"*Where's my update, Mr Drevit?*" he thought with a frown.

387

Mr. Drevit had remained out of contact for nearly a day and a half now and if Loc had been an anxious man, he would have been worried. He knew it had been a gamble letting Miana live in the first place, but the potential satisfaction had seemed worth it at the time. *"Have I overstepped the Triumvirate's strict professional boundaries?"* he wondered.

They were unforgiving masters at the best of times, but this was clearly important to them and their disapproval might go beyond a rebuke on this occasion. Loc may have done well with the Vita Nova negotiations, but he had a feeling Miana was becoming a risk to his eventual ascension into the Triumvirate's ranks.

"Hmmm," he mused, twisting the red-stoned ring on his finger in irritation.

His overconfidence was to blame, of course. But when so much came so easily, and for so long, it was hard to accept your own fallibility, particularly when you had the power to control others.

And yet, deep down, Loc still resented the fact he needed to worry at all. If the Triumvirate had trusted him with the knowledge of whatever it was Miana might discover in those caves, he wouldn't be in this position.

Grimacing in anger, Loc pushed himself to his feet and was about to stalk out of his office when he felt a warning pain at the back of his neck.

"The Triumvirate," he thought, sitting down again. *"Damn."*

The room soon began to shudder around him and he placed his hands on the desk, preparing himself for the pain to come. It was a little sharper than usual and when the Triumvirate appeared on the other side of his desk, all of them wore disapproving expressions.

"Triumvirate," he said, bowing his head in greeting.

"Your assassin has failed," the Third began coldly, his cruel eyes ablaze with anger. "Miana Raiken and Kurt Jones have made contact with the Heretic."

Loc felt a sudden chill in his stomach. It was worse than he'd feared.

"Who is the Heretic?" he asked, keeping his tone calm.

"That is of no importance," the Second replied firmly, flicking his long black hair over his shoulder and crossing his thickly muscled arms, "but technology has changed hands. You will no longer be able to control Miana or her companion."

"What?" Loc said, startled. "How is that possible?"

"You have become complacent," the Third added with a sneer, ignoring his question. "Your arrogance has put our plans in jeopardy."

Loc felt his jaw muscles tighten.

"I… apologise," he replied slowly, "but I had no information to judge the importance of this matter."

"You had your orders," the Third growled.

"But no context," Loc shot back. "I've never failed you before. The only difference this time is the amount of information you provided me."

"Your actions were guided by hubris alone," the Second said sharply, his voice cutting right through Loc's anger. "You cannot lie to the Triumvirate, Loc Breeden."

"You are right, of course," Loc replied carefully, "but my arrogance would have been balanced with caution had I known the risks."

The Triumvirate glared at him for a long moment then the First finally spoke into the silence.

"You know all that is necessary," she said firmly.

"Of course," Loc said, deciding he could not to push any further. "Please forgive my impertinence. I only seek to serve you better."

The Triumvirate remained silent again then the Second spoke, his dark eyebrows low over his glowering eyes.

"Miana Raiken and Kurt Jones must be killed," he said deliberately. "They cannot be allowed to interfere with our plans."

Loc met his gaze in surprise. The Triumvirate very rarely ordered executions. They almost always arranged it so that others would do it for them.

"Their deaths… will cause controversy," he said slowly.

"Then ensure the relevant authorities are provided with a reasonable explanation," the Third snapped, raising a finger. "We cannot afford extra scrutiny at this time."

"I… understand," Loc replied.

"Consider this your second priority," the First added, the poison unusually absent from her eyes.

"My second?" Loc said. "What could be more important than this?"

"Another threat," the First replied. "A woman named Anya Polovski is on her way to your Cosmotech offices. She must not be allowed to interact with Isaac Taylor."

"Isaac is working with Doctor Grayson," Loc replied.

"His work will not be completed here," the First told him. "You will take them both to the Bas Quirat."

"The Bas Quirat?" Loc said, genuinely surprised this time. "But we have no relationship with the Quirations. They won't–"

"They are already aware of your impending arrival."

Loc stared at the Triumvirate in disbelief. He knew that their influence was almost God-like within the realms of Lynt City and their connections in the Valles Dome were almost as powerful, but the Bas Quirat was foreign territory – an Islamic democracy that inhabited a single, giant mega-scraper on the other side of Mars. Cosmotech had never been able to influence anyone within its walls. Or not in any way that Loc was aware of, at least.

It was a double-edged revelation. Realising the Triumvirate was even more powerful than he suspected was good news given he was destined to become one of them. But was his ignorance also evidence that his eventual ascension was not as likely as he'd been led to believe?

"As you say," he said after a moment. "I will make arrangements to move Isaac immediately."

"Our plans have reached a fragile stage, Loc," the Second added coldly. "There is much that could occur counter to our desires. The future is far from immutable."

"Do not fail us again," the Third growled.

At this, a sharp tingle swiped the back of Loc's neck and the Triumvirate disappeared.

Loc waited a moment until he was sure they were gone then he slammed his fist into the desk with a roar of frustration.

"What the fuck is going on?" he snarled.

With heat still prickling unpleasantly at the back of his neck, he activated the Security icon and an officer appeared on the screen above his desk.

"Yes, sir?"

"Have a transport prepared immediately," he said, allowing a little of the anger into his voice, "and scramble my Alpha Security team. I want them ready to depart in twenty minutes."

"Right away, sir," the officer said with a nod.

After ending the communication, Loc slammed his fist on the desk again. He could tell this wasn't going to go well. Everything that had gone wrong up until now was due to a lack of information and he was about to intentionally enter a situation where it would only get worse.

"The Bas Quirat," he said incredulously, shaking his head.

He knew the situation with Miana was partly his own fault, but how could the Triumvirate have kept their connection to the Bas Quirat from him for so long? And what did it have to do with Isaac's work? His world revolved around access to information and it was professional torture knowing he was missing such important pieces.

"*Well, I don't intend to remain in the dark for long,*" he thought grimly. "*If I'm going to the Bas Quirat then I'm bringing the best I have with me.*"

Pushing himself to his feet, Loc strode to the door and headed for Dr. Grayson's lab. He knew it was unwise to confront Grayson in the mood he was in, but for the moment at least, he didn't care. The pompous old bastard could deal with the Triumvirate's orders, just as he had to.

As he approached the laboratory, two of Dr. Grayson's bodyguards moved from their easy stances into a more ready position and Loc glared at them with a hatred he kept solely for their insubordination. *"One day I'll make them all kill each other in the slowest ways I know,"* he promised himself.

He headed straight for the laboratory entrance, daring them to prevent him access, but was pre-empted by the sudden appearance of Dr. Grayson.

"Ah, Loc Breeden," he said distractedly, his eyes flickering around the corridor. "We will now be moving our research to the Bas Quirat."

Loc felt a surge of surprise at this and had to pause for a moment before answering.

"The preparations are already underway," he said, hoping to make it clear Grayson was not the one giving orders this time.

"Yes, yes," Dr. Grayson replied with a wave of his hand. "I've been looking forward to this for some time."

"What is at the Bas Quirat?" Loc asked, trying to keep the exasperation from his tone.

"Success, power, revelation," Dr. Grayson replied in a mumble, as if it were obvious. "The end approaches."

"What are you talking about?" Loc said with a frown.

Dr. Grayson looked up, as if seeing him for the first time. Then he frowned in distaste.

"Time doesn't wait," he snapped, before turning and striding down the corridor with his bodyguards in tow.

Loc gritted his teeth as he watched the man go. He knew Grayson had some kind of connection with the Triumvirate and he burned to know how much this eccentric fool really knew. It certainly seemed to be more than he did. But there had to be as much that the scientist was unaware of. Loc had always believed his political and financial manipulations were far more important than the technology Dr. Grayson traded in, but what did the Triumvirate value more?

All he could hope now was that he would rise to take his place among the Triumvirate before Grayson did. Then he would ensure that such confusion and ambiguity never occurred again.

As he finished his musing, Isaac appeared in the doorway and Loc slipped on his best smile.

"Isaac," he said, gesturing him down the corridor. "Has Doctor Grayson told you we're moving your research to the Bas Quirat?"

Isaac frowned.

"Kind of. But… well, I wasn't sure he was talking to me."

"Hah! I understand completely," Loc laughed heartily. "The good doctor can be a little strange at times, but his scientific mind is without equal, believe me."

"Oh, I do," Isaac said with feeling. "He reminds me of my brother Jason, sometimes."

"Don't worry, we'll get you back to him," Loc said with confidence.

"I hope so," Isaac replied absently. "So, what is the Bas Quirat?"

"Ah," Loc said, putting his arm around Isaac and leading him down the corridor. "You're in for a treat, my boy. The Bas Quirat is the largest mega-scraper in the solar system. It towers so high into the Marsian atmosphere that near the top you can see the curvature of the planet."

"Woah. Really?" Isaac said, looking up at him. "And… why are we going there?"

Loc hesitated for a moment as his frustration once more rose to the surface. He wanted to know that just as much as Isaac did.

"To finish your research," he said dismissively, sure that at least that much was true, "but there'll be time for more explanations later. My duties as an ambassador conveniently coincide with your change of scenery, but they require that we depart immediately. If you'd like to change your clothes, you'd better be quick. We only have about twenty minutes before we have to leave."

"Twenty minutes?" Isaac protested as they stopped in front of his quarters. "But what about all the stuff we've been working on?"

"What needs to come will come, don't worry," Loc assured him. "And if there's anything you want to work on during the journey, just let me know when I come and get you. We'll organise everything then."

"What about Anya? Have you found her yet? We really shouldn't leave without her."

"Of course," Loc said, sucking a breath in between his teeth. "In the rush I almost forgot to tell you. I'm afraid Anya left Lynt City on the mag-lev not long ago. She's headed back to the Valles Dome."

"Oh," Isaac said, looking disappointed and a little guilty.

"Not to worry," Loc said with another winning smile, "once she returns home, I'll make sure there's time for you to call her."

"I'd better," Isaac replied. "Apart from… saying goodbye, she might be the only one who can help us recreate the psychic link."

"Well, we'll see what the Bas Quirat can provide first, shall we?" Loc finished, ushering Isaac into his suite. "Now, please excuse me while I make a few arrangements of my own. I'll be back for you in twenty minutes, Isaac. Make sure you're ready."

"Sure thing," Isaac replied, looking a little sad.

Loc watched him go until the door closed and then dropped his smile instantly.

This wasn't good. Things were rapidly moving out of his control and that was never a good thing. He couldn't afford for anything more to go wrong if he wanted his ascension to the Triumvirate to occur any time soon.

"*No one will stop my ascension,*" he promised, stalking back the way he'd come with a fiery resolve. "*Not Miana Raiken, not Doctor Grayson, not anyone.*"

And as his mind transitioned to what he needed to do to ensure that promise, Loc knew that he would triumph in the end. He was better than anyone and everyone, and not even Isaac Taylor, a boy from a parallel universe would get in his way.

BLACK SITE BETA, LYNT CITY - June 7, 2147 - 9.01am

ANYA WOKE GRADUALLY TO A SHARP PAIN IN HER wrists and a deep ache in her back. She tried to move her wrists, but they were stuck behind her. Tied behind her.

"*What happened?*" she thought groggily.

Her whole body ached as if she'd been lying here for days and her head felt heavier than it had any right to.

She blinked in the gloomy light and saw that she was on a cold, dirty floor. There were pipes running along the wall she could see and her nostrils caught whiffs of damp and corrosion alongside the more pungent smell of ammonia and faeces.

She strained her stiff neck to see more of the tiny room and flinched when she saw someone standing beside a cramped doorway.

"God," she swore quietly. "Who... who are you?"

The figure didn't answer.

"What do you want with me?"

Again, she got no reply.

"Why did you bring me here? Where am I?"

Once more, the figure said nothing and Anya frowned. She wriggled around in a circle, grimacing as the movement brought fresh pain to her joints, until she could see the person properly.

It was one of the soldiers Fayina had disabled while rescuing Isaac in the Valles Dome. But there was something terribly wrong. For one thing, there was a large wet patch on the front of his uniform, as if he'd gone to the toilet where he stood. And his expression was blank, catatonic even. And then there was his aura.

"My God," Anya whispered in horror.

It was like nothing she'd ever seen, streaked with the same darkness she'd seen in the man who'd left the police station with Isaac and flickering like a guttering flame, as if about to go out.

"*His spirit has been violated,*" Dr. Haig's voice spoke solemnly in her mind.

"*More like raped,*" Fayina growled.

"*I don't understand,*" Celia whined. "*What happened to him?*"

"*You don't need to know,*" Ianka replied firmly. "*Don't look at him, sweetie.*"

Anya let them talk and focussed instead on freeing her wrists. She couldn't see what held her, but it felt coarse and had rubbed her skin raw. Every move she made hurt and her struggles didn't seem to accomplish anything and so she quickly gave up. Even with Fayina's help, she wasn't strong enough to break free.

Glancing back at the man standing by the door, she decided to try talking to him again.

"Who are you?" she asked loudly. "My name's Anya. I can… I can help you. Tell me who did this to you."

Again, the man remained silent and Anya felt a sudden resolve harden in her heart.

"I'm going to try and help you," she said firmly. "Stay there."

She heard Celia laughing at her request, but ignored it and focussed instead on shuffling forward. Any movement hurt and it took several minutes to work out how to move across the floor, but soon she was close enough to the soldier to touch her face to his boot.

"I'm going to make contact with your aura," she said, staring up at him, "and see if I can work out what's wrong with you… okay?"

MARS - TWIN PROPHECIES

Once again, the man ignored her.

"*This is not a good idea,*" Ianka warned.

"*Compassion is always a good idea,*" Dr. Haig replied quietly.

"*Fuck him!*" Fayina snarled. "*He put us here.*"

"*Well...*" Celia added, "*we don't really know that for sure.*"

"Be quiet," Anya told them all firmly. "I need to concentrate."

And to her surprise, they did as she asked.

"Thank you," she said quietly, before turning her attention back to the man by the door.

Shuffling a little closer, Anya gently laid her cheek against the man's ankle, ignoring the stench of urine. There was no immediate sense of what was wrong with him, but as her aura mixed with his, a creeping sense of fear and hysteria began leaking into her mind. She reached out with her spirit, searching for the man's identity, but every time she thought she was close, one of the black shadows polluting his aura swooped in and pulled it from her grasp. The terror that was invading her mind grew stronger with each attempt, but Anya refused to let it win.

"I won't give up," she promised him firmly.

Battling on, Anya found and lost the man's identity again and again, until the darkness stopped pulling it away from her and gathered around it instead, as if trying to protect it from her touch. She pushed her spirit through the darkness, moving ever closer to whatever lay within, and finally felt the man stir beneath her cheek.

"*He senses me,*" she thought, looking up at him.

And she was right. He was staring down at her now with wide, frightened eyes.

"Please," he said in a trembling whisper, "help... me."

Anya wanted to recoil from the fear and desperation in his gaze. It awakened her primal instinct to flee, to run as fast as she could and escape the terrible danger she could sense but didn't understand. But she refused to abandon this man. No matter what he may have done to her, in this moment he was simply a fellow human being, asking her for help.

"I'll try," she promised him.

Reaching into her own aura this time, Anya brought forth all the healing energy she could muster and prepared to flood his spirit with everything good that was inside of her. She had no idea if it would free him of the negative energy that held him captive, but it was all she could think to do.

She locked gazes with him, taking in all the fear and desperation she'd instinctively wanted to run from, and sent back all the positive energy she had.

"Please…" he whimpered, his entire body trembling now.

She could feel it working. His aura was growing brighter before her eyes and the shadows surrounding his identity were clearly agitated. They flitted from side to side, as if trying to escape the positive energy that flowed in around them, but Anya wasn't going to let them escape. She was determined to purge this darkness from his aura once and for all and nothing was going to stop her.

The battle raged on for several minutes, good energy against evil, and Anya was just beginning to think she might win when the man suddenly broke eye contact and looked up.

"No…" she hissed in desperation, but it was too late.

All the healing energy she'd poured into the man disappeared in an instant. His face spasmed as if he was trying to look back at her, but as soon as his eyes focussed on something behind Anya, his trembling ceased and the piece of him she'd found was once more pulled beyond her grasp.

"Impressive," a voice said behind her.

Quickly rolling over, Anya grimaced as the movement crushed her hands and stared at the one who'd spoken. It was a man of medium height wearing an immaculately clean, wrinkle-free uniform that Anya expected was a perfect indication of his personality.

This was a neat, organised man with a neat, organised mind. He was also absently fingering a ruby-encrusted cross at his chest – possibly Christian – and looked at her through sleek, transparent glasses, but his focus never seemed to settle on her directly.

"What have you done to him?" she asked coldly.

"Your concern is misplaced," he said, not moving from his position, "but as you have asked, I'll show you. Hadrian, unsheathe your combat knife and push the blade through your forearm."

Anya was shocked at the demand, but when she turned to the man standing above her, she was just in time to see him draw a knife from his belt and hold it above his forearm.

"No!" she said sharply, turning back toward the man at the door. "I understand! I don't need to be shown."

"I think you do," he replied calmly.

Anya heard a wet, gristly *shunk* from behind her and winced in horror.

"Why?" she asked, refusing to look back. "Why are you torturing him?"

"Again, your concern is misplaced," the man at the door said, shaking his head. "This soldier means nothing to you. I suggest you concentrate on your own predicament."

"He is a fellow human being, suffering for no reason. That means plenty to me."

"Then perhaps I should remove this distraction," the man replied. "Hadrian, take your combat knife and-"

"Alright!" Anya said loudly. "I'll ignore him. He's got nothing to do with me. I get it. Just don't hurt him again. Please."

The man looked at her for a long moment and then nodded once.

"Very well. I have questions for you, Anya Polovski. You will answer them honestly."

Anya felt a wave of relief, but knew her troubles were far from over.

"I'll try," she said quietly.

"It was not a request," the man said, his eyes locking onto hers.

Anya felt something brush against her aura as their eyes met and everything around her suddenly went silent. There hadn't been much noise to begin with, only the whisper of ventilation and distant hum of machinery, but now there was nothing.

The small room began to blur, as if the loss of noise was affecting her vision as well, and yet at the same time the man's eyes grew sharper, larger, and more menacing.

Anya tried to look away, but something held her frozen. She could feel her aura being drawn out of her, surrendering to this stranger's will, but there was nothing she could do about it. She was as helpless as the poor man, Hadrian, standing behind her.

"*What's happening?*" she thought as the primal fear that had attacked her earlier returned with a vengeance.

But no one answered. Not any of her personalities. And as Anya descended into the helpless unknown, she could only focus on the man's eyes. Those cold, glowering eyes.

Sabian stared at Anya Polovski with a mix of satisfaction and disgust. He'd been looking forward to breaking her, but being in such close proximity to this unholy beast was making him anxious. Not to mention the stink of Hadrian Levine.

He longed to tell her how he felt, to explain how unworthy she was to have spent time in the presence of the Messiah. But first he wanted to know what she was capable of.

"What were you doing to Hadrian?" he asked.

"I was helping him," she replied in a familiar monotone.

"How were you helping him?"

"I was…"

Anya's voice trailed off for a moment and Sabian felt a touch of unease.

"*How is she resisting me?*" he thought to himself.

It shouldn't be possible. No one should have the ability to counter the gift his God had bestowed upon him, but this woman clearly was.

"Tell me how you were helping him," he demanded again.

"I was searching his aura," she answered, without hesitation this time.

Sabian felt another jolt of uncertainty. Nothing in his Lord's teachings explained the existence of auras. This woman was clearly delusional. Another reason why she should have had nothing to do with the Messiah.

"What were you searching for?" he demanded with a frown.

"His identity," she replied immediately.

Sabian's frown rose into a peak of confusion.

"Did you find it?" he asked.

"Yes."

"And what did you do when you found it?"

"I… I tried to free it."

There it was again, another hesitation that should not have been possible. But at least she'd finally made reference to something that made sense. She was trying to free Hadrian. Clearly this woman had some real psychic power, but didn't understand its true nature. Auras were clearly her misguided attempt to rationalise her abilities. She was confused, plain and simple, and so Sabian decided it was time for other, more important, questions.

"How did you meet Isaac Taylor?" he demanded, trying to ignore the envy that gnawed at his stomach.

"He procured my services as a psychiatrist," Anya explained. "He'd recently been separated from his twin brother, Jason, and was experiencing psychic side effects."

"Psychic side effects?" Sabian said, his interest piqued. "Explain them to me."

"Heightened psychic awareness. Irrational anxiety. His aura was turning dark purple."

Sabian frowned at the mention of the Messiah's aura. As with her powers, Anya clearly knew nothing of Isaac's true nature. Sabian was willing to humour her talk of auras to find out what she knew, but he promised himself that her blasphemy would not go unpunished.

"How did you treat him?" he asked firmly.

"I used my own psychic influence to calm his aura."

"So you believe you're psychic?"

"I am psychic, yes."

Sabian noted the confidence in her response and wondered if it were true. It would certainly explain her resistance, but what else had it allowed her to do?

"Did you use your psychic ability to anticipate our arrival at the planetarium?"

"No, that was... Isaac," she replied, hesitating again. "He... had a premonition."

"*A premonition?*" Sabian thought in surprise. "*The Holy Messenger told me the Messiah would have powers, but...*"

He had never doubted the divinity of Isaac Taylor, but hearing evidence of his power from this woman left him with a conundrum. He wanted to accept it, knew in his heart that Isaac was capable of such things, but the more Anya talked, the more Sabian felt like she was finding a way to lie to him.

"Do you know that Isaac Taylor is the Messiah?" he asked her.

"Isaac Taylor is not a Messiah," Anya replied.

Sabian felt a surge of anger.

"Hadrian," he snapped, "slap her across the face."

At his command, Hadrian stepped forward immediately and slapped Anya firmly across the face.

Sabian felt an almost sensual rush of pleasure at the sound. He wasn't sure why the Holy Messenger hadn't appeared to him since his failure in the Valles Dome, but for the first time, he was certain he was doing God's work again.

"That was for blasphemy," he said coldly, "and it was far less than you deserve. Now, before I exact a more appropriate penance for your sins, tell me where you learned to work with... auras."

"My... my..." she stammered, her brow furrowing.

Sabian's irritation grew. Anya shouldn't be capable of any expression at all and he wondered for a moment if Hadrian had broken her jaw.

"Where did you learn how to manipulate auras?" he repeated firmly.

"My…"

"Tell me!" Sabian commanded, putting all the force he could muster into his voice.

Anya's brow furrowed deeper in response and her eyes showed clear lines of tension. Then she did something impossible.

She blinked.

"Her sister you fuck!" she snarled.

"What?" Sabian gasped, recoiling in surprise.

He fell back and tried to re-establish psychic control, but for some reason it wasn't working. Anya managed to sit up, her eyes locked on him the whole time, then with a snarl of defiance she rolled backward and brought her legs up over her head.

Before Sabian could react, she crashed into Hadrian, the knife still protruding from his forearm, and the two of them fell to the floor in a heap.

"Restrain her!" Sabian barked.

Hadrian followed his command immediately and the two began to struggle, but it was clear the security Chief was having trouble. As Sabian watched in mounting horror, Anya managed to position her feet near the knife in Hadrian's arm, and with a savage twist, a faint *snick* split the air.

"*She cut the cable,*" Sabian thought in amazement, before shouting at Hadrian again. "Stop her! Hold her down!"

The security Chief tried his best to do just that, but Anya smashed her head into his face with a sickening *crunch!* He fell back, blood streaming from a broken nose and barely managed to hold onto Anya's leg, although it didn't stop her from reaching her feet.

"Stop!" Sabian yelled, trying to compel her again.

"Fuck you!" she replied, before kicking Levine hard in the temple.

Sabian knew he would have no chance against someone who'd taken out his entire security team and so he turned to run. But before he reached the door, something slammed into his back.

As he crashed to the ground, he twisted and fought with all his strength, but after a brief struggle, Anya had him pinned to the floor with her knees pressed against his upper arms and a hand on his throat.

"Your turn, *fucker*," she snarled into his face.

"Get off me," he commanded, trying his best to ignore the fetid stench of her body.

"Not going to work," she said, tapping her temple with an evil grin. "Owner's not at home right now, just us psychological coping mechanisms. My name's Fayina. I'm the nasty one."

"How are you doing this?" he demanded.

"We're asking the questions," she replied in a completely different voice. "Tell us who you are?"

Sabian looked up at her in confusion. It wasn't just her voice that had changed. Moments before Anya's face had been twisted with anger, now it was stern and disapproving in a way that made her look like another person entirely.

"*Multiple personalities?*" he wondered. "*Is this how she threw off my control?*"

"Tell us!" the angry personality called Fayina demanded.

"I'm... one of the chosen," Sabian replied, turning away from her.

"Your name, fucker," Fayina snarled, before slapping him hard across the face.

The pain slashed through Sabian's jaw like fire and he was shocked at its intensity. He'd experienced a lot of pain in his life, but not like this. Not caused by another's hand and not since he'd been a very small boy.

"My... my name is Sabian," he replied, working his jaw to help with the pain.

At this, Fayina's wild eyes lost their blood-lust and this time Sabian clearly saw her expression change. It softened into a look that could have been pity and the flesh on her face seemed to relax and sag, making her look older. Much older.

"Why do you believe Isaac is the Messiah?" she asked in a more rational voice that matched the age of her face.

"Because that's what he is," Sabian said, gritting his teeth. "We must protect him."

"Tell me everything you know about him," she said in her raspy older voice.

"No," he replied with as much conviction as he could muster.

In response, the muscles and skin of Anya's face pulled taught again and fire exploded in her eyes. Suddenly, the wild, unflinching rage had returned.

"Oh really?" she growled, before turning away from him.

Sabian felt her weight shift off him for a moment, but before he could take advantage, Fayina was back, holding something dark in front of his eyes. It filled his nostrils with a sharp, metallic odour and when Sabian focused on it, he recognised the knife he'd made Hadrian push through his own arm.

He felt his gorge rise, but couldn't look away as a drop of sticky blood stretched down from the blade's edge and landed gently against his cheek.

"Get that away from me," he snapped, straining to move out of range.

"I don't think so," Fayina replied, although she did thankfully remove the knife from his vision.

For a moment, all Sabian could focus on was the sensation of blood slowly tracking down his cheek. He flicked his head to the side, hoping to dislodge as much of it as he could, but his concerns were soon replaced by a sharp pain in his left thigh.

"*She stabbed me!*" he thought as he screamed in agony. "Aaaargh!"

It was like nothing he'd ever experienced. He'd hurt himself many times in the past, but it didn't mean he was immune to pain's bite. He needed it. He *deserved* to feel pain for his sins, as did all humans. But for the first time in his life, Sabian wished he couldn't feel it so keenly.

He wanted to resist, wanted to spit in Anya's face and tell her he'd rather die than betray his God, but the pain was all he could focus on. And, despite the shame that screamed as loud as his vocal chords, Sabian knew he couldn't endure it for long.

"Stop!" he screamed, feeling wretched and yet at the same time desperately hoping she would listen. "I'll tell you anything you want. Please! Just stop! Please!"

"You snivelling little coward," she hissed in his face. "You just ordered a man to push this knife through his own arm and he couldn't plead for you to stop. You deserve far worse!"

Sabian felt the knife twist in his leg and screamed again. The pain tore at his body in thundering waves of fire and just when he thought he couldn't take any more, the knife became still and his scream gurgled into a sob.

"Please…" he begged, tears streaming down his face. "Please take it out."

With a scowl, Anya's raging personality finally did as he asked and a wave of indescribable relief swept through him.

"Tell me where Isaac is," she demanded, holding the knife in front of his face again.

"He's… at a Cosmotech research facility," he gasped weakly. "In the Cenovian district. Grevin lane, fourth quadrant, level twelve."

"Very good," she replied, her face and voice stern again. Another personality. "Now tell us why you call him the Messiah?"

"He… was sent by God to save us all," Sabian stammered.

"Save us from what?"

"Eternal damnation," Sabian said, sobbing again.

"You believe the world is ending," Anya said in a different voice, her face old again.

"The signs have come. The end… is near," Sabian whispered.

For a moment, Anya's face changed into a much younger looking version and she recoiled with a frightened expression. Then it was replaced by a snarl and the wild personality was back.

"Fuck that!" she spat in defiance. "Tell me how Isaac is going to save us?"

"I don't know," Sabian replied honestly.

"Bullshit!" she swore at him. "Tell me how you expect him to save us!"

"Only God knows," Sabian said desperately, the thought of enduring more pain adding a manic edge to his voice. "Please, I'm telling you the truth!"

But the knife disappeared again and Sabian barely had time to protest before pain exploded in his leg again.

He didn't know how it could feel worse than the first attack, but it did. The blade seemed to burn his leg from the inside out and when she twisted it, the agony was so great it nearly drowned out his screams.

Eventually, Fayina wrenched the knife from his leg again and the room began to spin as the pain gradually dulled.

"Who else are you working with?" the stern personality demanded, peering down her nose at him.

As his mind processed the demand, Sabian felt something he could only assume was courage rise within him. He was going to die here. He was certain of it. And he refused to betray his God again.

But even as he thought it, he couldn't bring himself to vocalise the conviction. He knew it would only bring back the pain and despite the fearsome loyalty that had risen within him, he just couldn't invite it in.

He began to cry harder, for shame now as well as pain.

"Tell me," she growled, tapping the blood-soaked blade on his chin, "or I'll stick this in your other leg."

Sabian's mind staggered under the weight of indecision. He wanted to beg her not to hurt him again, to tell her he didn't know anything, that he wouldn't tell her anything, but he could only whimper meaningless sounds in reply.

"I... ks... grt... pfff... carg..."

Anya gave him a disgusted look then her face became old again and she sat back.

"I think it's time for you to release Anya."

Sabian frowned in confusion, but before he could blubber another consonant, she spoke again, as if answering the demand for him.

"No! We don't need her. I should just slit his throat."

At this, she placed the knife against his throat and Sabian willed her to use it, to finish him while he hadn't completely betrayed his God. But her expression softened and the younger personality spoke.

"I miss her," she said.

"And we do not kill," the stern voice added firmly. "We are not murderers!"

"What makes you so sure, Ianka?" Fayina snarled. "We killed everyone we cared about, didn't we?"

"We weren't responsible for their deaths," the stern voice – Ianka – replied.

"Fuck that!" Fayina snarled. "They died because of us."

"I don't want to kill him," she added in a trembling voice, her face young again.

"Shut up, Celia," Fayina snapped.

"This is unwise," the older personality pointed out soberly.

"And fuck your wisdom too, Haig." Fayina snarled. "I don't need any of you."

Sabian flinched. That made four personalities in all. Fayina, the rage filled psychopath. Ianka, stern and disapproving. Celia, young and innocent. And Haig, the older, more rational personality.

"One personality is not enough," Ianka said firmly. "You won't be able to function properly, Fayina."

"You're assuming I want to," Fayina snapped back.

"We have to share," Celia sobbed.

"No! I'm sick of being forced to sit at the back of this shattered mind. She locks me away for weeks at a time! The last time she freed me outside of training was so I could save that pathetic boy's life! I want to *live*."

"Do you have any idea how psychologically dangerous that could be?" Ianka demanded.

"We can't let her do it," Haig added, her face becoming slack and wrinkled again. "We have to stop her."

"Stop me? You can't stop me!"

"You're out of control, Fayina."

"Are you honestly that stupid? I'm finally *in* control, you disapproving old hag! And I'm not just going to give that up!"

"We must work together," Haig added quickly.

"Come on then! Give me your best shot!"

Sabian wasn't sure what was going on, but he assumed Anya was waging some kind of psychological war with herself. Whatever mental instability had allowed her to break free of his control was now causing the personalities inside her to fight with one another.

"It's not working," Ianka said after a long pause.

"Not so easy, is it?" Fayina replied with a laugh. "Come on you weaklings, try harder!"

"I'm scared," Celia said.

"Concentrate," Haig added, "we must…"

As the argument continued, Sabian watched on in horrified fascination. He knew his life could depend on the outcome of this internal struggle and he really didn't want to see what would happen if Fayina triumphed.

"*What if I release Anya from my control?*" he thought to himself. "*She could retake control of her personalities and I might have a chance of getting out of this alive.*"

"*No,*" an angelic voice spoke suddenly in his mind. "*You must not interfere.*"

Sabian flinched in surprise and looked up to find the Holy Messenger standing over Anya's shoulder.

"*I don't understand,*" he replied in his mind.

"*She must be allowed to fight this battle,*" the Holy Messenger replied.

"*She'll kill me,*" Sabian thought weakly.

"*Have faith, Sabian,*" the Holy Messenger assured him. "*Your God has seen this and it is His plan.*"

At the mention of God, Sabian felt the warmth of conviction flow through him. He *did* have faith. He *knew* his God would protect him and whatever happened next was for the good.

And with this new resolve in his heart, he returned his gaze to Anya and watched her raise the knife high above her head, as if preparing to plunge it into his heart.

A traitorous urge to beg for his life rose within him, but when he tried to make a sound, nothing came out. He looked back at the Holy Messenger and realised that the angel was holding him still. And Sabian was glad. He knew he was weak. He knew that even here in the Holy Messenger's presence his humanity made him capable of betraying his God.

But there was still hope. Anya's violent personality had not yet won the battle. Her face continued to flicker between different personalities, even though the knife didn't waver above him.

Sabian's eyes came to rest on the blade, its bloody tip looking sharp and cruel, and he could almost feel its bite already.

"Time to die," Fayina growled, teeth bared.

Then the knife came down and Sabian wished he had enough control to vocalise the emotion that crashed through his mind. But he could do nothing as the blade hit home with a sudden *thunk*.

"Fuck!" Fayina swore savagely.

She'd missed him completely. The knife had hit nothing but concrete and was now somewhere beyond the edge of Sabian's field of vision.

"Fine, you simpering weaklings!" Fayina snarled. "He'll probably bleed out anyway."

She then moved her face close to his and bared her teeth one last time.

"Come after me again," she said, as if she wanted him to. "Give me a reason to end you once and for all."

She held his gaze for a moment, her hate pouring into him, then she abruptly ducked to one side and was gone, along with the pressure on Sabian's chest.

He lay silent for several seconds, studying the Holy Messenger as his mind raced to make sense of what had just happened. Then a scraping sound caught his attention and the angelic voice spoke once more in his mind.

"*You have served your God well, Sabian. Now you will serve Him one last time.*"

Sabian felt a flood of relief at the angel's words and knew he was safe. His God would protect him. His God would *save* him.

"*Tell me what I must do,*" he thought.

"*You must die.*"

At this, Sabian's eyes went wide.

"*What? No. My Lord, please. I don't want to die.*"

But the Holy Messenger simply faded away and, in its place, a figure was revealed. It was the Security Chief, Hadrian Levine, awake and holding his weapon so that Sabian could see straight down the barrel.

Sabian moved his gaze to Hadrian's eyes and instinctively tried to take control, but there were no eyes to see. Only two bloody holes where the soldier must have gouged them out.

"*My God,*" Sabian thought with a perverse rush of pious satisfaction, "*why have you abandoned me?*"

Then the world flashed white. There was no pain. Only light. And somehow Sabian knew that everything was going to be alright. He felt a sensation of movement, toward the light, and distantly wondered why he'd never seen anything like this before.

But it didn't matter. Nothing did anymore.

Sabian was finally home.

END OF BOOK ONE

AVAILABLE NOW

More stand alone novels in the
System Series.

AVAILABLE NOW

More stand alone novels in the
System Series.

Pluto - Secrets Within is available as an e-book on Amazon.com
and paperback from www.kynanwaterford.com.au

A note from the author.

I know, I know. So many questions left unanswered. But I can assure you, the next book, *Mars - End of Days*, will provide all the answers you crave, including some you may not have thought to ask for... yet.

However, I feel I must apologise for making you wait. As you know from my previous novels, I'm not in the habit of extending my stories over several books. But allowing my characters the freedom to be themselves as the story progresses can be a double-edged sword. It makes for a more unpredictable and, in my opinion at least, more satisfying story, but I clearly didn't kill enough of them off soon enough this time. In fact, at times it was a struggle to even herd them toward the epic climax to come.

Of course, I would never dream of removing any of the characters that have insinuated their way into this tale. The story would be irreparably damaged if I attempted such foolishness. But I do sometimes wonder how much sooner Mars would have been done if I'd resisted their siren call in the first place.

So please, indulge me this brief intermission between novels. I promise you it will be worth it.

And as you may have also noticed, I've experimented with some visual aids this time to help illustrate the timeline and perhaps provide a little clarity around the creation of a Jupiter flare. I'd love to hear what you thought of this little detail and whether it aided in your understanding of what on Mars was going on.

If you'd like to contact me with your thoughts, please fire off a quick email to kynanwaterford@gmail.com or visit my webpage at www.kynanwaterford.com.au

And if you happen to have an Amazon account, please take a moment to leave a quick star review for *Mars - Twin Prophecies*. It's a tough world out there for authors and any artist will tell you there are times when they wonder if all the hard work is worth it. But I can personally attest that the occasional glowing review really makes a difference. So many thanks to all those who've either taken the time to write a review, clicked on a star rating, or simply contacted me personally to let me know you enjoyed my earlier novels. It really made a difference.

Thanks also to those who provided feedback whilst developing this book, in particular my wife, Cassandra, father, Colin, brother, Galen, and good friend Andrew. As always, your insights were invaluable.

And finally, special thanks to Walter Myers. I really, REALLY enjoyed working on the cover art for *Mars - Twin Prophecies* and I have Walter's amazing rendering of the Valles Marineris canyon to thank for that. His work is beautiful and inspiring and this one was perfect for depicting the cosmic ferocity of a Jupiter flare. If you'd like to see more of Walter's work, check out his website at www.arcadiastreet.com

Wishing you and your imagination all the best,

Kynan Waterford

Printed in Australia
AUOW01n1535220218
295019AU00004B/4